Home to Khorvaire's most ...

a land only newly reunited as a nation.

Darguun's fragile unity rests in the fist of Lhesh Haruuc, the greatest leader to rule his people in a thousand years. But the Lhesh is growing old. The sun will soon set on his reign. Whether his nation will survive him or shatter into a hundred factions rests in the hands of an unlikely hero.

The shifter met Haruuc's gaze. "There are people in Khorvaire who don't like Darguun. They'd like to see Darguun fall apart into squabbling clans again. They're afraid you're just waiting for another chance to come over the Seawall Mountains and attack."

"All of the human kings and queens watch each other because they're afraid of the same thing," Haruuc said. "When will Breland invade Thrane or Aundair attack Karrnath? Those people who don't like Darguun don't see it the way I do. United, Darguuls can find pride again and climb back to the heights of culture we once knew, but if Darguun falls, the chances that my people will attack are even greater. Ekhaas has told me you're a veteran of the Last War. You know the chaos of country fighting country, clan fighting clan." The lhesh sat forward. "Give my nation the chance to win its place in Khorvaire."

Geth was silent, and Ekhaas felt as if a hundred needles were being pushed into her scalp and back—then the shifter took a deep breath and nodded.

"I'll do it," he said.

EBERRON

The Legacy of Dhakaan

By Don Bassingthwaite

The Doom of Kings

The Word of Traitors

The Tyranny of Ghosts

EBERRON®

THE DOOM OF KINGS

LEGACY OF DHAKAAN | BOOK 1

DON BASSINGTHWAITE

Wizards of the Coast®

The Legacy of Dhakaan Book 1

THE DOOM OF KINGS

Published by Wizards of the Coast, Inc. EBERRON, WIZARDS OF THE COAST, and their respective logos are trademarks of Wizards of the Coast, Inc., in the U.S.A. and other countries.

Printed in the U.S.A.

Cover art by Michael Komarck
Map by Rob Lazzaretti
First Printing: August 2008

9 8 7 6 5 4 3 2 1

ISBN: 978-0-7869-4918-2
620-21822740-001-EN

U.S., CANADA,
ASIA, PACIFIC, & LATIN AMERICA
Wizards of the Coast, Inc.
P.O. Box 707
Renton, WA 98057-0707
+1-800-324-6496

EUROPEAN HEADQUARTERS
Hasbro UK Ltd
Caswell Way
Newport, Gwent NP9 0YH
GREAT BRITAIN
Save this address for your records.

Visit our web site at www.wizards.com

Lake Brey
BRELAND
THE MOURNLAND
The Lightning Rail
Skullreave
Sterngate
Matshuc Zaal
Trade Road
Lyrenton
Ghaal River
The Gathering Stone
Rhukaan Draal
Zarrthec
ZILARGO
Ghaal'tash
DARGUUN
Rheklor
Seawall Mountains
Zalanberg
Grellreach
Arthuun
Torlaac River
The Khraal
Torlaac Moor
Korranberg
THUNDER SEA
N
W
E
S
0
400
miles

Raat shi anaa.

"The story continues."

— Traditional opening to hobgoblin legends.

PROLOGUE

In the beginning, there had been some agitation to abandon the human dating of years and declare an era of sovereignty for the triple race of hobgoblins, goblins, and bugbears, but Haruuc had crushed such posturing before it got out of hand. Even as the dry summer of 969 YK drew out and Haruuc's triumphant campaigns carved a new nation out of Cyre and Breland, there were already voices rising against his growing power. Someone had resurrected the ancient title of *lhesh,* meaning "high warlord"—and this Haruuc had accepted without question, since it had, in fact, been his idea—but there were also tongues wagging among the united Ghaal'dar clans, reminding everyone that when the title of lhesh had last been used in the dying days of the Empire of Dhakaan, it had been a temporary title. A warlord had been proclaimed lhesh for a short period, then had stepped down. It was clear, the wagging tongues said, that Haruuc was gathering too much power and that his clan, the Rhukaan Taash, would hold all the power in the new nation that was being born.

Haruuc had waited, with the patience that his enemies had always underestimated, until the loudest of those tongues had wagged themselves into undeniable treason, then personally cut them out of their owners' mouths. The remaining tongues had stopped wagging of their own accord, but Haruuc knew the silence wouldn't last. The Rhukaan Taash *was* gathering power that would lead to unrest among the other clans—and unrest from within was as much of a threat to his vision of a new nation as enemies without.

Fortunately, Haruuc thought as he looked across the ordered ranks of the warlords assembled before his field command tent, there had been a way around the problem that fought two battles with one army.

A burly hobgoblin of advancing years, his age frosting the wolflike ears that poked out from a helmet decorated with curling horns, rose from a bench and met Haruuc's gaze with silent intent. Haruuc nodded and said, "Munta the Gray of Gantii Vus wishes to speak."

Young warriors given the honor of acting as attendants rapidly raised the banner of the Gantii Vus, a fanged maw wreathed in flames, on the Pole of Order. The assembly fell quiet as the banner rose against the evening sky. Many of the chiefs still saw Munta as someone who might have been able to challenge Haruuc if he chose, even though the wily old chief had been one of the warlord's first and strongest allies when Haruuc was still just an upstart warrior. Munta spoke as soon as the banner reached its height, choosing his words with the deliberate care of someone who knows he walks a narrow path.

"Lhesh Haruuc and exalted chiefs, no one of honor can turn his back on his clan. Do you agree?" There was a general murmur of assent to which Haruuc added a slow nod. Munta continued, his sharp teeth flashing as he spoke. "If no one of honor can abandon his clan, Lhesh, we must accept that the Rhukaan Taash will have power as long as you have power. I put it to you: For our nation to rise above clan wars, there must be a place where all clans are equal. I urge you to establish a seat for your power in neutral territory, where the might of the people comes before the might of any one clan, and the chief of one clan can speak for all."

He sat down to the approving sound of hands slapping against chests. The banner of the Gantii Vus was lowered from the Pole of Order. Haruuc made a show of sitting and pondering the idea before gesturing to the warriors attending the pole. As lhesh, he didn't need to wait for the banner of the Rhukaan Taash to rise before speaking, but he did it this time. It showed his humility. The assembly whispered in surprise as the razor crown of the Rhukaan Taash rose. When it was at its height, Harucc said, "This suggestion is worthy. The humans of the Five Nations consider such places to be their capitals, and they are great cities. Why should we not have one? I accept the suggestion of Munta. There will be a city where the nation comes before the clan."

More applause greeted the statement, even from some of those who had wanted to replace the human calendar and who wouldn't normally have had anything to do with something inspired by the customs of the Five Nations. Haruuc caught a gleam in the eyes of Munta and held back an answering smile. The plan they'd hatched together had worked. He raised his hand, gesturing for silence.

"Where should this city be?" he asked. "Where will we find neutral territory?"

Munta spoke up again—strictly speaking, he was out of order, but they needed to keep the excitement of the assembly high and not give any of the chiefs a chance to think too deeply. "Claim one of the cities we've taken from Cyre!"

There was a buzz of acclaim for the idea, but Haruuc shook his head as Munta sat down. "The Cyran cities are razed. What is there to claim? And why should we claim them? They stood on the fringes of our conquered territory. If I must build a new city, it should be central."

"Lhesh, I know a place," said a bold, crisp voice. "May I speak?"

All eyes turned to the three *shava,* Haruuc's sword brothers, who stood close behind the lhesh. Specifically, they turned to Fenic of the Mur Talaan. Haruuc's ears flicked, and he nodded to the attendants of the pole. It took them a moment to find the banner of the minor clan, but Fenic waited. When the banner of three tribex horns was raised, he continued. "On the edge of Mur Talaan territory, there is a Cyran town. It's not much, but it's well-located. It sits on the Ghaal River just below the first cataract, and the dragonmarked humans of House Orien have recently built a trade road to service it. To the Cyrans it was a frontier town, but their frontier is now the heartland of our new territory."

"I know the place," said Haruuc, his ears flicking thoughtfully. He fell silent, letting the assembly wait again. He was certain that most of the chiefs and warlords had some idea of the place, too. Even if they didn't, they knew of the first cataract on the Ghaal and they knew that it was a respectable distance from the lands of the Rhukaan Taash. When it seemed that they'd waited long enough, he looked up and nodded again to Fenic. "It is a good place. The new city of our nation will be there."

The assembly burst into applause for a third time, the loudest and longest yet, and the gleam in Fenic's eyes was the same as that in Munta's. Haruuc looked out over the assembly and this time allowed himself a smile.

Two weeks later, Lhesh Haruuc wasn't smiling. He swung his sword and the magnificent weapon—more than an armslength of heavy battle-scarred steel, sharp as death on one side, jagged as a dragon's teeth on the other—split a human warrior almost in two. It wedged against a rib and he had to kick at the corpse to free the weapon. "You didn't say these people were so stubborn!" he said.

Fenic's shield swept past him, blocking a blow from another human. His *shava's* sword cut the legs out from under the man. "This place was your idea," Fenic answered. He grunted as he slammed the edge of his shield down to crush the injured man's skull and end his life. "They're not usually stubborn. The conquest has filled the town with refugees. They're fighting because they don't have anywhere else to go."

Haluun, Haruuc's brother by both the sword and birth, laughed. "They can go to the fields and the mines! My wife has the chains ready!"

"That's what they're afraid of," said Fenic.

Haruuc paused to shake the blood from his sword and look around the square of the Cyran frontier town. There were nearly as many banners showing in the fight for this one town as there might be in a far larger battle—a deliberate choice. When his new city rose, there would be warriors in almost every clan who would be able to say they'd fought with the lhesh to make it happen. What should have been a swift strike, however, had turned into a long day's battle. Fenic was right. Refugees had packed the town, and desperation had given the humans courage. They'd made an effort to fortify the town, throwing up barricades in the streets and setting traps and ambushes. They'd seldom stood to fight but had retreated to alleys and rooftops to harry their attackers with arrows and stones.

Haruuc had the foresight, though, to buy the services of the goblins of the *sharaat'khesh.* The Silent Blades wouldn't normally have waded into an active battle, but he'd promised them and their cousin clan, the Silent Wolves, a place in his new city if they wanted it, and that had earned him their favor. A handful of the slippery goblins had easily cleared the rooftops in places where the town's defenders had trapped his regular troops.

The barricades in the streets, cunningly placed to keep the attackers away from the town's center, had been more of a problem—at least until Haruuc had called on the brute strength of the bugbears among his troops. Hobgoblins were broader and more powerful than humans, but bugbears, largest of the goblin races, were broader, taller, and more powerful still, standing shoulders and shaggy head above most hobgoblins. Arming his bugbears with battering rams fashioned from logs and beams, Haruuc had broken right through the walls of the town's houses to make his own streets. The bugbears' big ears—stiffer and less expressive than a hobgoblin's—had quivered at the simple joy of wanton destruction.

The closer Haruuc's troops got to the center of the town, though, the fiercer the resistance had become. Anyone among the townspeople who could hold a weapon had fought, with just enough experienced fighters and battle-trained mages among them to inflict some damage. When the attackers finally reached the town square, they found townspeople and refugees crowded into ranks, and the fighting had begun in earnest.

What puzzled Haruuc was why they were fighting instead of fleeing. Masses of them could have escaped—the Ghaal River protected the north side of the town from direct attack, but it hardly prevented flight. Then for a moment the battle parted before him and he saw the reason.

The human who strode across the far side of the battlefield, here and there plunging his sword into the fighting, must have been the lord of the town. His shield was painted with an elaborate crest, and the armor that he wore was good. What captured Haruuc's attention, however, was his helmet. It looked old, but the plume of feathers that crowned it rippled and shone like fire. Wherever the lord went, swinging his sword alongside his people and urging them to fight harder, the efforts of the defenders seemed renewed.

The tide of battle closed the gap, but Haruuc had seen enough. "Vanii, open the way to that man!" he ordered.

"Mazo!" His third *shava,* Vanii of the Ja'aram, surged ahead, his twin axes whirling like a storm. Fighters fell back from them or died. The lord of the town turned to find Haruuc before him. He tried to get his sword up but failed. With a roar that stopped the fighting around them, Haruuc raised his blade and cut down. His sword slammed through plumes, metal, hair, bone, and brains. He ripped it free as the corpse fell, then bent and severed the corpse's neck.

Hoisting the head by the fading plumes of the ruined helmet, still tied under the chin by a cord, he raised it in one hand and his bloody sword in the other. "Your lord is dead!" he howled in the human language. "The battle is done! By my sword, I claim this place and name it Rhukaan Draal, the crown city of Darguun, the land of the people!"

All of the energy seemed to fade from the defenders closest to them. Defeat pulled on their faces and dragged down their weapons. A few fought on in pockets, but they died quickly. A great cheer washed over the town as goblin, hobgoblin, and bugbear troops rushed to secure the spoils of war.

Haruuc let his grisly trophy drop. The impact finally dislodged head from helmet and the split and startled face of the last human lord of the town rolled into the yellow dust. Vanii poked at the shattered helmet. "Powerful magic," he grunted. "Too bad it's broken—it would have been a fine thing to keep."

"There was no great magic in it," Fenic said. "My people knew the lords of this place for generations. The only magic was in the feathers. The helmet was a show piece, passed from lord to lord as a symbol of the right to rule. It connected the lord who wore it to all of the lords who came before. The town didn't stand by the man. It stood by its history."

Haruuc laughed. *"Ban,"* he said. "But beginning now, the history of this place and this land"—he brought his boot down on the helmet, crushing the last of the plumes and cracking the metal—"is what we make it!"

Haruuc opened his eyes to sunlight on the roofs of Rhukaan Draal thirty years from the memory of that triumphant day. The yellow dust of the city rose in a drifting haze, thicker over the bustle of the Bloody Market. From the window where he stood, Haruuc could hear the sounds of combat that rose with it, different from the normal sounds of the late-morning market. The clash of steel on steel, the screams of defiance, the shouts of command, the wails of the fatally injured. Violence in the market wasn't uncommon, but no merchant ever defended his stall with such vigor or mourned the loss of his goods with such deep agony.

A party from the Gan'duur clan, outspoken opponents to his rule, had entered the city the day before to trade in the market, or so they had claimed. The Gan'duur weren't a subtle clan. Presented with a spear, they'd throw themselves onto it. And from the signs of the fight in the Bloody Market, they'd found the spears Haruuc had sent to them in the hands of his own disguised warriors. The corpses of the Gan'duur would be left where they fell, victims of the market violence. Haruuc had crafted the strategy with care. By tradition, the corpses of the Gan'duur should be hung in gibbets before the gates of his fortress, a warning to anyone who might consider crossing him. Public display, however, would show his involvement in the deaths and enflame the remaining Gan'duur. Worse, it would be proof to the other clans of the growing unrest, another hint that Haruuc's grasp on power was slipping. Left in the street, the corpses would be as anonymous as their killers. The chief and elders of the Gan'duur would surely guess what had happened, but there would be no proof of Haruuc's hand in the matter. The doubts of the chiefs and lesser warlords would be staved off—until the next time the Gan'duur rose.

The Gan'duur or some other ambitious clan scratching for fleeting power. Fenic, he thought, I should have listened more closely to you. He looked down at the hands that gripped the windowsill—deep yellow skin slowly growing thin and increasingly stained with dark spots.

There were voices beyond the door, and Haruuc turned away from the window. A moment later, the door opened and Tariic entered. "We depart, uncle."

It came to Haruuc that Haluun had always insisted that Tariic had been conceived the very day that they had captured that Cyran frontier town. He had never believed in omens that he didn't make himself, but if he had, surely that was a good one. His ears rose. "Swift travel and great glory," he said in blessing. "Bring back our history, Tariic."

CHAPTER ONE

15 Lharvion, 999 YK (midsummer)

A shout of rage was the only warning Geth had before a fist that smelled of onions and dirt smashed into the side of his face. Caught by surprise—his own fists were already twisted in the loose fabric of another man's shirt—Geth rolled with the blow. Pain spread across his cheek, but it was dull and distant. The odor that trailed the punch was stronger. A growl tore out of Geth's throat. He pitched away the man who lolled in his grasp and bared his teeth at the farmer who had hit him.

The sight of a shifter's mouthful of sharp teeth didn't even give the man pause. He lunged at Geth, wrapping thick arms around him and bearing him backward off his feet. The smell of onions and dirt, topped off with ale, surrounded Geth as they both stumbled backward. The hard edge of a table bit into Geth's lower back. *That* hurt. Geth ground his teeth together and slammed his forehead into the other man's face. There was another burst of pain, but the farmer's grasp weakened. Geth butted him again. The man let go and staggered back, cursing. Geth shoved himself away from the table and twisted to drive his knee up into the man's gut. Breath whooshed out of him. Geth grabbed his shoulder and brought up his knee a second time for good measure. The farmer went down, and Geth whirled, fists raised, looking for the next attacker.

There wasn't one. The man he had tossed aside was hobbling away, supporting a friend whose smashed nose bore the imprint of Geth's knuckles. The other patrons of the tavern had pulled back from the fight and stood in an uneasy circle around Geth, each of them looking nervously at the others, none of them willing to make the first move.

"Get out," said a voice behind Geth. He turned around. The tavernkeeper stood at his bar, one hand below the top of its well-scrubbed surface. The bend of an arm tattooed with the dragonhawk crest of Aundair hinted that his hidden hand grasped a club or a knife—maybe even a wand. The thick hair that covered Geth's forearms and the back of his neck bristled and lifted slightly. The nation of Aundair had more than its share of mage-trained veterans of the Last War.

Keeping an eye on the tavernkeeper's hidden hand, Geth stood straight and opened his fists. "Easy there," he said. "I was defending myself. They started this. Did you hear what they said to me? Boar's snout, they accused me of stealing sheep and raiding vineyards!"

The tavernkeeper's face was hard. "I'd believe them before I believe you. They come from Lathleer. They belong here. Where do you belong, shifter? We've seen enough of your kind since the end of the war. Just another war-torn wanderer. Get out of my tavern and get out of Lathleer!"

Geth stiffened. "I'm not a wanderer. I'm on my way back to Fairhaven. I just want a—"

"Get out," the tavernkeeper said again, and this time he raised his hand from below the bar. Geth had been right. It was a wand, an unpleasant-looking black stick bound with dull rings of lead and capped with something that might have been rune-inscribed ivory but was more likely bone. A wizard or an artificer might have been able to guess what magic was contained within such an ugly device. Geth couldn't, but he had a strong feeling that it was nothing gentle.

The crowd of patrons must have known. A murmur of eagerness swept through the room, and from the corner of his eye, Geth saw the circle around him tighten slightly. His hands clenched. Armed with a sword to keep them back, he might have been able to face the crowd, but not unarmed. They wouldn't make the same mistake as the first three men. They'd rush him all at once and bring him down through the sheer weight of their numbers. Assuming the tavernkeeper's wand didn't bring him down first.

"I'm going," he said. Keeping his eyes on the tavernkeeper, he backed toward the door. The man gave a quick jerk of his head and Geth heard murmurs of disappointment and the shuffling of feet as the circle opened to let him out.

Beside the door was a niche lined with cubbyholes where patrons left bags and packs—and, more importantly, weapons—while they were in the tavern. Crouched on a stool inside the niche was a wizened little goblin in a shabby dress. The creatures weren't as common in Aundair as they were in the cities of the south, where they formed a menial underclass, but even in a town like Lathleer they were far from unknown. Standing, the top of the goblin's head would have been below Geth's waist, but the commotion in the tavern had left her curled up into a tight ball, as if she could fold herself up and disappear. Small dark eyes stared at him in fear from a face that looked like it had been pressed flat, lips squeezed so tight her wide mouth was barely a crease in the wrinkled yellow parchment of her skin.

"Give me my pack!" Geth snapped at her, not wanting the distraction of groping among the cubbyholes himself. The circle of tavern patrons had closed again, folding in on itself to follow him to the door.

The goblin didn't move. Geth's breath hissed between his teeth and he repeated himself—this time in the Goblin language. *"Roo! Piiroto kaana!"*

He was still learning Goblin, and he knew that he spoke the language like a child, but at least the goblin woman blinked and uncurled a bit, her large pointed ears twitching. *"Piiroto!"* said Geth again. He dug in a pouch, groping blindly for a coin, and flicked what he found at her. *"Kaana kaana!"*

A thin copper crown flashed on the air. Uncertainty crossed the goblin's face, but it lasted only as long as it took for her to stick out an arm and snatch the coin. The rest of her body uncoiled as well, and she hopped to one of the cubbies. Pulling out a pack that was almost as big as she was, she shoved it at Geth.

Geth grabbed the pack so quickly he almost pulled her off her feet. As she jumped away from him again, he raised the pack, putting it between himself and the small mob of tavern patrons. The men he had actually fought had made their way to the front of the crowd now, and if the other patrons looked unfriendly, these three looked outright hostile. Geth took three steps back and felt the wood of the door against his shoulders. He pulled the door open with one hand, keeping his eyes on the mob. Warm night air blew inside, a breeze that ruffled his hair and made the lanterns that lit the tavern dance slightly. Geth slid a foot over the threshold, then deliberately caught the gaze of the most aggressive of his attackers, the one who had started it all.

"If you want to keep this going," he told him in a growl, "you come after me. I'll be ready for you."

He stepped back through the door, pulled it shut after him, and darted down the night-empty street, running not for the outskirts of Lathleer, but deeper into the town. The instant a hiding place presented itself, Geth dove into it. The hiding place happened to be a narrow, wet shadow between a public fountain and a wall, but he was in no position to be particular. Indeed, no sooner was he under cover than he heard the shouts of men spilling out of the tavern. He froze.

"Nowhere in sight!" Geth recognized the voice of the man who had first picked the fight with him. "Bloody full of wind, shifters are! Cowards, just like I told you. Won't stand up to a fight."

"He stood up pretty good inside, Urik," said someone else. "Let him go."

"When did you turn into your wife, Saal? He asked me if I wanted to keep this going and I do. He can't have much of a head start. Follow me!"

A chorus of cheers met the command, and boots hit the packed surface of the street in a heavy rhythm—heading the other way. Geth released his breath and risked a slow glance up over the rim of the fountain. The men from the tavern had done just what he'd hoped they would and assumed that a stranger and a fugitive would try to escape the town by the shortest possible route.

Geth had some experience in running, though. At one point in his life, he'd lived on the run for the better part of two years and he still remembered most of the tricks he'd learned back then. Lathleer was no village, but it wasn't exactly a metropolis, either.

He ought to be able to find his way out of town as easily one way as another. Although it would have been nice if that hadn't been necessary. "Rat," Geth cursed and let his head sag back against the fountain.

The movement almost brought another curse from him. The stones were cold, slick, and slimy. Clenching his teeth, Geth rose, shouldered his pack, and hurried through the shadows of the street. Outside and away from the mob, he could have taken Urik and his friends, but brawling in a tavern was one thing and fighting in the street was another.

If Singe and Dandra had been with him, things wouldn't have gotten out of hand. Either the swordsman-wizard or the kalashtar psion would have had the words to ease the situation. And if they didn't at least there would have been three of them to stand together. But no, his friends were still several days' travel away in the city of Fairhaven. The pair's recently kindled relationship reflected the fiery magical energies that fascinated them both: burning with passion, occasionally flaring in anger, always uncomfortable for those around them. All three of them had been quietly happy when he suggested that he'd enjoy exploring the Aundairian countryside for a few months—by himself.

Singe's last words as they parted had been, "Stay out of trouble."

Geth turned down the first corner he came to, getting out of sight of Urik and his cronies in case one of them chanced to look back, then slowed his pace and exhaled. He couldn't say that he regretted the weeks spent traveling around Aundair on his own. The transition from spring to summer was a pleasant time to be outdoors—although he would have preferred the countryside even in winter to staying in Fairhaven. It took a certain kind of shifter to enjoy life in a city, and Geth wasn't that kind. The crowded, noisy conditions kept him constantly on edge, his instincts reacting to nonexistent threats. The countryside and small villages were better, and most of them had been far more welcoming than Lathleer. He'd traveled south, following the line of the lightning rail across Aundair to Lake Galifar, then wandering around the shores of the lake into the south of the country before turning back north again. In most places, he'd been welcomed, if not with open arms then at least with an open palm and hospitality. In a few places, he'd even found a couple of days' work doing odd jobs. On the whole, it had been much better than lingering in Fairhaven.

Just about the time he began his journey back north, though, Geth had realized that he did miss his companions. Not just Singe and Dandra, but all of his friends: Natrac, the half-orc merchant who had once been a crime lord; Ashi, the scion of House Deneith who had once been a marsh hunter; Orshok, the young orc druid; Ekhaas, the hobgoblin storyteller; even Benti Morren, agent of the King's Citadel of Breland. He'd gotten used to their presence. It had been almost a year since they'd come together, a year of massive change and adventure for all of them. For Geth, it had been the end of seven years of hiding from his past and an enforced confrontation with an ignominy he had taken on himself. The events of the year had shown him that he didn't have to be the grim, solitary warrior he had been for so long—that he could, if he chose, take on the role of a hero. And that felt good.

Of course, it also felt good to know that he had killed a dragon—with help—and stopped the rise of an ancient force of dark madness. That in the distant swamps of the Shadow Marches, orc tribes were already telling stories about him, Singe, Dandra, and the others who had stood with them.

He missed having people around who believed him about the dragon. It wasn't the kind of story that was easily brought up in casual bragging over ale. Or anywhere, really.

It was going to be good, he thought, to see Singe and Dandra again. Maybe he could convince them to go looking for some of the others. Ashi was lost to the clutches of House Deneith—for a time at least. But the city of Zarash'ak wasn't so far away that they couldn't visit Natrac—

Something moved ahead of him.

Geth's pace faltered for an instant, but only for an instant. He forced himself to keep walking. Several of Eberron's twelve moons had risen, and their combined light cast a confusion of shadows onto the streets. A shifter needed very little light to see, and the moons gave more than enough of it for Geth to see clearly that the street ahead was empty.

He had seen something move, but it hadn't been ahead of him. The movement had been a shadow, as something broke the moonlight over the peak of a roof. The movement had actually been *behind* him.

A bird? A cat? A bat? He kept walking, eyes on the shadows, ears alert. Not likely a bird—they would all be roosting for the night. A bat would still have been visible as it flapped its wings. A cat—possibly, but surely he would have seen its shadow again, yet there was nothing.

Could it be Urik and his friends, back on his trail? Geth couldn't believe they could be so stealthy.

He walked a little farther, taking the measure of the street ahead and the town around him. He'd wandered into an area of Lathleer that seemed a little more down on its luck than other areas. The streets were narrow and twisting, the windows on the buildings tightly shuttered. He had a strong feeling that if a fight broke out here, no one would be rushing to see what was happening.

A short distance ahead, the street split into two lanes that passed on each side of a closed-up shop before meandering on through the town. Geth made a rough guess at how long it would take him to reach the intersection—then took a firm hold on his pack and broke into a sprint.

The slapping of his steps echoed from the walls and wrapped him in noise. If there were any sounds of surprise from whatever—or whoever—was behind him, he couldn't hear them. Maybe his own footsteps were too loud. Maybe his pursuers were even more subtle than he thought. He put his head down and ran fast, veering slightly toward the lane that looked most likely to lead out of Lathleer.

Did something move against the moonlight? More shadows, breaking concealment to give chase? At his running pace, it was difficult to tell. Still no sound of pursuit. The intersection and the closed shop drew closer, and the lane opened before him.

At the last instant, Geth turned aside and whirled. His shoulders and pack slammed against the wooden shutters of the storefront with a loud crack, and Geth stared back along the street.

His pursuers—still racing after him—stared back, caught by surprise at the move. Geth caught a glimpse of black-clad figures moving like shadows along the street and the rooftops. A glimpse was all he caught, however. As soon as they saw that he had stopped, the figures froze and vanished. Their disappearance was so sudden and complete that Geth could almost believe what he had just seen had been his imagination.

He knew better though. Caught, the figures weren't quite so subtle now as they had been before. If he looked closely, Geth could see the bulge of a shadow where one sought to hide. A roof tile clicked as another, unseen, shifted its weight.

Alarm rose in his throat. Grandmother Wolf, he thought, who were they?

In one way, at least, it didn't matter who they were. Fists might have been fine against brawlers like Urik, but he'd be damned if he was going to face these mysterious figures with empty hands. Geth shrugged and his pack slid from his shoulder. In one swift movement, he freed the long, wrapped object that had been loosely lashed to the side of the pack. A twist and a shake sent the wrappings slithering to the ground. Holding the hilt of his sword in one hand and the wide scabbard in the other, Geth stepped clear of the discarded pack and wrappings. Then he drew a deep breath, reached down inside himself—and shifted.

Long, long ago, the gift—some said curse—of lycanthropy had risen among humans. By day men and women might have been as normal as their neighbors, but by night, when any one of Eberron's twelve moons shone full, they became beasts. Werewolves. Werebears. Rats. Tigers. Boars. Sometimes they had managed to escape the anger and fear of their neighbors and live out their lives hidden in the wilderness. And as they lived, they had children, sometimes with others like them, sometimes with those who did not carry their gift. The children born of such unions weren't fully human, but neither were they lycanthropes. Over time a new race was born, neither human nor lycanthrope nor animal, but something of each. Shifters were strong, they were fast, and they were marked by the blood of beasts. Thick hair, sharp teeth, eyes that could see as well by night as by day—and a touch of their ancestors' shapechanging abilities. Each shifter's connection to his or her ancient heritage was different. Some, when they shifted, gained a bear's claws or a wolf's fanged bite. Others gained speed or heightened senses.

Geth's gift was sheer toughness.

The breath he had drawn hissed out between his teeth as the shifting passed through his body. His skin became tougher, his hair even thicker than it normally was. A sense of invincibility burned like hot steel in his veins and muscles, lending a sharp clarity to the night. With a grim smile, he sank back into a defensive posture, ready for the attack.

His black-clad pursuers must have recognized that their quarry was through running. They reappeared, the first dropping like a spider from high on a wall into the street below. The others followed until there were eight of them, silently watching Geth, every one crouched and as ready to fight as he was.

And not one of them stood any taller than his waist. Tiny dark eyes watched him from parchment-skinned faces that had been stained as black as their clothes.

His pursuers were goblins.

Another warrior might have forgotten his fear and fallen on the goblins with a foolhardy bravado, but Geth had seen what groups of the little creatures working together were capable of. Numbers always gave an advantage. Some of the goblins also had daggers drawn, the short blades smeared with something dark. Poison. Another advantage. The first goblin to reappear gestured, and all of the goblins began to creep forward.

But Geth had an advantage, too. His grim smile tightened. He raised his sword above his head so the goblins could see it, then snapped his arms wide, drawing the blade in a sharp, fluid motion. "Behold!" he shouted. *"Aram!"*

The word meant "wrath" in Goblin, and it was the name of the sword. Geth had carried the weapon out of the ghostly fortress of Jhegesh Dol where it had been lost for thousands of years. It was broader and heavier than any human sword, with one edge sharp and the other notched with deep serrations, the end not pointed but instead forked like a serpent's tongue. The blade, forged from the rare metal byeshk, carried a deep purple sheen that almost seemed to consume the moonlight rather than reflect it. Wrath was a hobgoblin sword, created in the time of the ancient Empire of Dhakaan by one of the empire's greatest wizard-smiths. It was the sword with which Geth had slain Dah'mir, the mad dragon who had given his soul to the terrible Master of Silence.

And it was a *lhesh shaarat,* a warlord's blade, a weapon of kings and heroes. He'd been told that any descendant of Dhakaan—goblin, hobgoblin, or bugbear—recognized such a sword, and that anyone who dared to draw a *lhesh shaarat* proclaimed his power. Geth had drawn Wrath once to fight off a gang of goblins. The mere sight of the twilight blade had sent the whole lot of them fleeing in startled terror.

The black-clad goblins stopped their advance and stared at the ancient weapon—then looked back to Geth without any change in their harsh expressions. They continued their slow advance, four moving to flank the shifter on one side, three on another. Their leader, still facing him, wore daggers in sheaths on the inside of each forearm. He slid one arm across the other and, from the left sheath, drew an ugly curved blade that looked very nearly as nasty as Wrath.

An unpleasant feeling knotted in Geth's gut, and he lowered Wrath, ready to defend himself.

"Rat," he said.

CHAPTER TWO

The door steward of Sentinel Tower was a man of middle years, solemn and unflappable, an ideal man for a role that was mostly about showing up to ceremonies and reciting a few ritual phrases. Ashi—once a hunter, now a scion of House Deneith—had been in the city of Karrlakton and a resident of Sentinel Tower for only eight months. She'd seen the door steward no more than four times, though it felt like she heard about him every day. Elders and instructors held him up as a model of dignity and loyalty to Deneith. He was moderate in all things, knew when to speak and when to remain silent. Through thirty-one years of service in his position, it was said that he'd never betrayed any trace of what thoughts or emotions might lurk behind the ritual phrases.

As he stepped into the expanse of the great Hall of Shields, however, the door steward was flushed and trembling. Ashi felt a prick of anticipation. She wasn't the only one to notice. A soft murmur swept through the other men and women who stood in ranks on the dais at one end of the hall. The woman who stood—strong and stiff in spite of the fifty or so years that lined her face and streaked her black hair with iron-gray—at the front of the dais, beside and just forward of Ashi, turned her head slightly and glanced over her shoulder. The murmur died.

The door steward cleared his throat. "Lady Seneschal Vounn, my lords and my ladies of Deneith," he said, his voice echoing like a shout in a canyon. "Sentinel Tower admits Tariic of Rhukaan Taash, son of Haluun, nephew and personal emissary of Lhesh Haruuc Shaarat'kor of Darguun!"

The words were hardly out of his mouth before the great age-blackened doors of the hall were thrown wide, seemingly blasted open by a noise that wailed in Ashi's ears and punched into her belly. The door steward broke and ran for the side of the hall.

Through the doors passed the source of the staggering sound: two rows of musicians marching three abreast. The punch of the music came from big drums beaten with short rods nearly as thick as Ashi's wrist. The wail of it came from strange pipes with two brass stems sticking up from an inflated sack of bright leopard skin held under the musician's arm and a third, pointing down, with wind holes for the musician to play—three powerful tones from a single instrument. It was war music, meant to inspire troops and terrify enemies. Ashi's heart raced to the sound of it. She leaned forward, as if the weight of the music was enough to support her.

Lady Seneschal Vounn d'Deneith glanced back a second time, this time directly at her. Behind the veil that hid her face and covered her thick, dark gold hair, Ashi clenched her teeth and stood straight again.

The musicians seemed to see nothing of the grandeur around them or of the delegation waiting at the far end of the hall. They marched and played with perfect discipline. All six were hobgoblins, tall as humans but broader in chest and arms, with dark skin that varied from deep orange-red to rich brown-yellow. When one of the pipers opened his mouth to gulp air and reinflate his pipe-sack, sharp teeth flashed behind thin lips. Like the small eyes above his flat nose, the hobgoblin's ears—long and tall like a wolf's—were fixed straight ahead.

Ashi knew a hobgoblin, though she had seen no more of her in the last eight months than she had any of the other friends she'd left behind in giving herself to Deneith. Ekhaas of the Kech Volaar clan was a fine fighter, a sword-wielding storyteller—a *duur'kala* or "dirge-singer" in her own language. The last time Ashi had seen her, Ekhaas had been on her way to Darguun to carry to her clan elders the story of the adventures that they and their other friends had shared. Ashi had learned first-hand from Ekhaas what kind of focus and discipline hobgoblins were capable of. To see that focus from a friend and ally was one thing. To see it in advancing troops, even a ceremonial guard, was awe-inspiring. Maybe not so ceremonial, Ashi thought. All of the musicians wore light armor of leather studded with polished brass, as if ready to drop their instruments on command and throw themselves into battle. She wouldn't have been surprised if that was exactly the case.

Behind the musicians walked half a dozen banner-bearers, not hobgoblins but short and lithe goblins. They might have been only half the size of the hobgoblins, but side by side, the relation of the two races was emphasized. They had similar colors and shared the same flat, thin-lipped faces, though the goblin noses were larger and their ears wider and more stiff. They marched with the same stern discipline as their larger cousins, holding up tall, narrow banners with strange symbols: the crests of the major clans of Darguun. A crown of sharp blades. A fanged maw wreathed in flames. A beast in chains, a brutal spiked flail, and others. The banner with the crown of blades was at the center of the display and was carried slightly higher than the others. Of all the clan crests, it was the only one Ashi recognized because it was the sign of Rhukaan Taash, the "Razor Crown," the clan to which the emissary Tariic—and Lhesh Haruuc—belonged.

As the banner-bearers passed through the door, they parted, and for a moment the musicians' savage music paused. In the unexpected quiet, the gasp that rose from the humans on the dais was clearly audible. Following the banner-bearers were two more hobgoblins, this time mounted, but not on horses. The hobgoblins that guided their mounts through the doors of the Hall of Shields rode on tigers.

"Rond betch!" Ashi murmured in awe. In Azhani, the language of the Shadow Marches clan she'd been born into, it meant "fierce darkness." She seldom spoke Azhani anymore, but when it came to cursing, she fell back on it instinctively.

The woman at the front of the dais didn't even turn her head, but in the music's lull Ashi still heard her disapproving warning. "Ashi! Language!"

The pipes and drums rose again. Unseen behind her veil, Ashi closed her mouth and tried to hold back her frustration and her excitement. Her part in this spectacle was coming soon. Her hand tightened on the hilt of the sword that hung beneath her robes. The robes concealed both the weapon and the fitted trousers and sleeveless shirt that she wore, as well as the sheen of oil on her lean, muscled arms. It wasn't typical attire for a formal reception ceremony, but her role was going to be a bit more active than that of most of those gathered on the dais.

For the past month, almost since the moment it was announced that Lhesh Haruuc would be sending an emissary to Sentinel Tower, she had been training in the demanding moves of the sword dance, one of the great traditions of House Deneith. The idea had been Vounn's, of course, but Ashi had found that she enjoyed the training more than most that the lady seneschal had forced on her. The time to show off the results of her hard work was almost upon her. Ashi put Vounn's rebuke out of her mind and focused on breathing, pushing an easy calm through her limbs. It wasn't all that different from the anticipation before a battle.

The musicians, banner-bearers, and riders had moved to the sides of the hall, making way for soldiers dressed in full armor. Goblins in light armor with round shields on one arm and maces in the opposite hand, thin javelins strapped across their backs. Hobgoblins in heavier armor, with tall shields and polished swords. Bugbears—the largest of the three goblin races, a head taller than the largest hobgoblin and heavily muscled—with only partial armor to protect their massive frames, carrying huge spiked morningstars that Ashi thought she might have been able to lift but doubted she could have wielded.

And walking behind them, the emissary from Darguun, Tariic of Rhukaan Taash. A handful of other goblins and hobgoblins, a mix of functionaries and councilors, followed in his wake, but Ashi's eyes—and she felt certain the eyes of everyone else at the front of the hall—were on Tariic. He walked alone, proud as a prince. He wore armor, too, though his was far finer and more ornate. His gauntlets had been fashioned into claws. Spikes protruded from knees and elbows. A skull had been worked in brass along the overlapping plates that protected his chest, and thick tongues of razor-edged steel crossed over his shoulders. Lhesh Haruuc's emissary could have walked from the halls of Deneith right onto a battlefield and not been out of place.

The last of the marchers parted and took places along the sides of the hall. The plain-garbed functionaries who followed Tariic stopped just inside the doors. Tariic himself strode forward to stand at the heard of his delegation. The music of the pipes and drums swelled, then fell silent. For a moment, all was quiet in the hall. No one and nothing moved, not even the great tigers. Tariic swept the dais with eyes that were a brown so bright they verged on red.

Ashi's mouth went dry. Her fingers shifted on her sword. Her time was close. The calm in her limbs tightened.

A single gesture broke the stillness in the hall, a single sound the silence. Throughout the Darguuls' entry, four ranks of black-clad Deneith guards had stood before the dais without moving or reacting. Now, at their head, a guard wearing the plumed helmet of a captain lifted the spear he held and rapped the butt against the stone-tiled floor.

In perfect unison, the ranks stepped apart, splitting and reforming into four tight squares. The movement was so precise that forty-eight pairs of boots made only one sound. The captain's spear rapped twice on the floor. Two squares advanced. The other two moved in behind. Spears rose—from the back ranks first—and fell forward, then rose again, like wheat bending and standing before gusting wind. The squares broke apart once more, leaving each man standing alone as the guards moved into a series of stamping, thrusting spear forms.

The display was similar to the Darguuls' only in its incredible discipline. Where the goblins had moved to the din of drum and pipe, the Deneith guards moved only to the cadence of their own boots, the rap of spear butts, and sometimes a sharp shout punctuating the rhythm. Where the Darguuls had been bright and flashing in polished armor, the guards were dark. Even the heads of their spears had been blackened. Where the Darguuls awed with their presence and natural intensity, Deneith awed with consummate skill that came from long hours of training. If any one of the guards had fallen out of rhythm with the others, he would have been skewered.

Ashi saw Tariic's ears rise in interest and his head nod in appreciation. She drew a deep breath. Now. The guards moved into the last pattern of their drill. Ashi stepped forward.

Vounn put out an arm, blocking her way. Ashi froze, her carefully rehearsed timing broken. "Vounn?" she whispered.

Vounn's mouth pursed, and her eyes narrowed. Her head twitched in a nearly imperceptible shake as the guards split for the final time to form two lines on each side of the hall and the butts of their spears hit the ground in unison.

The cadence of the drill was replaced by a rippling cry as a figure wearing a robe much like Ashi's leaped from the other side of the dais. One of the tigers growled and crouched at the sudden movement. Many of the Darguuls flinched, instinctively going on guard.

The figure shrugged as it landed and the enveloping robe fell away. A somewhat older man, a sword in his hand and his chest bare beneath a close-fitting vest, stood revealed. High on his right shoulder, a small pattern of blue and green lines stood out against gleaming, oiled skin. It resembled a tattoo, but no tattoo could have been so bright and alive, and no artist had etched the pattern on the man's skin. It was a dragonmark, the Mark of Sentinel, a sign of the power that the man carried in his blood as a true-born scion of House Deneith.

Ashi's gut dropped. Baerer. Her instructor. She twisted and glared at Vounn. "What's going on?" she asked, her voice low. "What's Baerer doing out there?"

Vounn's face tightened. "Keep your place, Ashi. We'll discuss this after the reception."

"But—"

"Keep your place!" Vounn pushed her back and turned away.

Around them, the other members of House Deneith who stood on the dais shifted in silent witness of the exchange. Ashi clenched her teeth and stepped back. The Darguuls noticed nothing—all their attention was on Baerer as he swept into the sword dance.

Blade up, body rigid as the fine metal. Somewhere in the back of the hall, a bow scraped unseen against the strings of a viol in a long pure note. On the draw of the bow, the blade dropped and Baerer made a slow, stalking circle around the lowered point. There was a soft intake of breath from those on the dais. The point of the sword, suspended in the air, had wavered no more than if it had been fixed in a pivot. A difficult movement, but Baerer had pulled it off.

Anger seethed in Ashi.

The pulse of the music quickened, the viol joined by the soft percussion of a drum. Baerer stepped forward, slashing right and left in time with the music, then stepped again—and again, crossing the empty floor between Deneith and Darguuls. His footsteps were as light and precise as the movements of his blade. He paused, then dove into a series of acrobatic thrusts and lunges as the music blazed up. Thrusts and lunges became a whirl of motion. Even the Darguuls were caught up in the dance now. Tariic followed Baerer's movement with undisguised fascination, but even a few of the honor guard were watching, their heads turned as much as discipline allowed.

Ashi's body twitched with every spin, every thrust. She knew the movements. It should have been her dancing for Lhesh Haruuc's emissary. Breathe, she told herself. Be calm. Lose yourself in the dance. Baerer had taught her that. The bastard. She pressed her lips tight together. The two rings that pierced her lower lip—rings that had once been bone but had been replaced by gold at Vounn's insistence—made two spots of pain against her upper lip.

The music slowed. The second part of the dance began. Baerer's strikes became wide and sweeping, as slow as the music but with a deliberate intensity. He began to use his body more. The dance remained focused on the sword, but now Baerer also incorporated sharp jabs from his empty hand, elbow strikes, and elegant yet powerful kicks. He might just have been working sword forms on a training floor, but the grace of his movements elevated them beyond mechanical posing. Many of the Darguuls stared openly. On the dais, most of the gathered lords and functionaries of Deneith were murmuring to each other and twisting for a better view.

Vounn didn't move, though satisfaction radiated from her. Ashi glared at the back of her head and, underneath her robe, gripped her sword, imagining it stuck through Vounn's gray-streaked hair.

Viol and drum rose once more. The murmuring on the dais fell silent as everyone watched Baerer. In spite of herself, Ashi glanced away from Vounn and down at the swordsman—and couldn't look away.

It was the third part of the dance, the climax. Baerer's movements became tighter, closer, as if being pressed on all sides. The fight had turned against the warrior. What had been sweeping blows became desperate parries, though no less graceful for it. If anything, Ashi knew, there was even more art in the third part of the sword dance. It was far easier to simulate a believable blow than a believable block. But Baerer did it, and did it well. In her imagination, Ashi could almost see the enemies that surrounded him, unleashing a rain of lethal blows. Faced with the unrelenting assault, Baerer retreated, every step as light as his first passage across the floor, yet at the same time slow and weary.

When he reached the spot where he had begun, Baerer stopped as if unable to retreat any farther. His parries became even more rapid, even tighter and closer to his body. Enemies were all around him, close enough for their hot breath to stir his hair. The drum fell silent and only the viol played on. A long note—the same note that had begun the dance—soared on the air. Baerer's movements became tighter. Tighter. His sword rose before his stiff, quivering body—

And the note faded away, leaving man and sword once more in silent rigidity. Baerer held the pose for a moment longer, then lowered his sword and bowed low before Tariic.

Vounn spoke into the silence that gripped the hall. "Tariic of Rhukaan Taash, emissary of Lhesh Haruuc Shaarat'kor, in the name of Baron Breven d'Deneith, patriarch of this House, be welcome in the halls of Sentinel Tower."

Tariic pulled his eyes away from Baerer. "Lady Seneschal d'Deneith," he said, "Lhesh Haruuc Shaarat'kor sends his greetings." His voice was deep and rough but pleasant and assured, with no trace of a Goblin accent. He nodded back at Baerer. "Deneith honors us with a performance like nothing I have seen before." He stood straight and shouted, *"Paatcha!"*

The goblins, hobgoblins, and bugbears of Tariic's guard burst out in a deafening roar of admiration, made even more deafening by the slapping of gauntleted fists on armored chests and by the screams of one unnerved tiger. Vounn, wearing a barely concealed expression of triumph, turned and made a small gesture to the members of Deneith gathered on the dais. Released from the bonds of ceremony, they added their applause to the din. Baerer bowed and bowed again, his face restrained but his eyes bright with pleasure.

Ashi focused on breathing and not killing anyone before she could get out of the hall.

The chambers she had been assigned were down the hall from Vounn's suite. Even in private, she couldn't be away from the lady seneschal. Ashi thrust open the door to the chambers, then slammed it behind herself. Dust that had probably been lodged in the frame for decades or more drifted down over the old wood. Ashi passed through the sitting room and into the bed chamber, tearing off the dancing garments as she went. The veil fell, crumpled, across a chair in the sitting room. The enveloping robe dropped to the floor of the bed chamber. The sword, a light piece of metal intended mostly for show, clattered alongside it. Ashi started to rip at the fitted shirt—a seamstress had all but sewn her into it that morning—then stopped.

There was a gown laid out on her bed. It was deep crimson silk, with full Fairhaven sleeves and a stiff collar of fine gnomish lace. Something inside her stirred and she knew that the cut and color of the dress had been chosen to flatter her height and features—

With a wordless cry of fury, she snatched up the sword and plunged it through the gown, stabbing deep into the mattress beneath. The blade pierced silk, bed-clothes, ticking, and stuffing to jam hard into the wood frame beneath. Ashi released the hilt and staggered away, her lips drawn back. "It's not supposed to be like this!" she snarled through her teeth.

A year ago she hadn't known about the cut of gowns or the origins of lace. She'd barely known anything of the world outside of the Shadow Marches. She'd been content as a hunter of the savage Bonetree, one of the most feared of the Marcher clans. She'd dimly been aware of the thirteen dragonmarked houses, knowing them only as distant clans rumored to carry magic in their blood.

Then she'd discovered that she carried that magic, too.

She raised her arms in front of her. Bright blue-green lines traced her skin from the backs of her hands to her shoulders, disappearing under her shirt. The Mark of Sentinel wrapped her in a pattern that covered almost her entire body, from feet to face. Only her fingers and palms and a strip from her cheekbones to just above her eyebrows were unmarked by the power within her. The dragonmark was far larger than the one on Baerer's shoulder. Larger even than the mark that Vounn carried on the inside of her right arm and that curled over her wrist. The scholars of the civilized world called it a Siberys Mark, rare and powerful.

Sometimes Ashi couldn't call it anything except a curse. It was the reason she was here, wasn't it? When the wizard-swordsman Singe had first opened her eyes to the corruption of the Bonetree and the possibility that another clan waited for her beyond the Shadow Marches, she'd actually been afraid that House Deneith might not accept her. All she'd had to prove kinship had been a sword inherited from her grandfather, an outclanner captured and brought into the Bonetree to sire new children. Then she, Singe, Ekhaas, and her other new friends had faced Dah'mir the dragon, and she had, without thinking, reached out with all the force of her will to deny Dah'mir a hold over the kalashtar Dandra's mind—and succeeded. Dandra had been shielded from Dah'mir's influence. In the same moment, the dragonmark had drawn itself across Ashi's skin in a flash of color, undeniable proof that she belonged to Deneith.

But was the mark really a curse? Her anger ebbing, Ashi let her arms fall. The power that the mark granted her to shield a mind from magical influence had not only protected Dandra, it had made the defeat of Dah'mir possible. Even indirectly the mark was a blessing: Deneith's desire to bring her within its fold had been so strong that she'd been able to barter her willing surrender in return for the use of mercenaries from Deneith's Blademarks Guild to stop one of Dah'mir's mad schemes. The fighting men bought by her freedom had saved lives.

And if she had to admit it, there was a lot about House Deneith that fascinated her. The House was like nothing—no clan, no home, no life—she'd ever known. In the eight months since she'd left her friends and been taken away to Karrlakton, she'd discovered so many new things. Strange customs. New people and sights. A sense of history that was sometimes frightening—Sentinel Tower was, at its core, many centuries old, and the lore of Deneith contained even older tales of those who had borne the Mark of Sentinel. She'd had the chance to train with the masters of a martial house. She'd witnessed the awe-inspiring advance of the Darguuls and very nearly performed for them. Who among the Bonetree or even among her friends could claim the same?

Ashi turned around. A tall mirror hung on the wall of her bedchamber, and she looked at herself—at the reflection of a strong woman marked by a rare power. She drew herself up straight. The dragonmark was no curse. In fact, if any curse had been visited on her, it was—

The outer door of her chambers creaked open. "Ashi!" called Vounn. Footsteps in the sitting room said that the lady seneschal had not waited for a response or an invitation.

Ashi's jaw tightened again. Most members of Deneith were brought up within the House, surrounded by its traditions and by the trappings of civilization. To have a savage of the Shadow Marches wielding the greatest power of the House had been too much for many of them. The lords of Deneith had welcomed her to Sentinel Tower, then had given her into the care of a mentor. Someone who could shape a rough savage into a proper lady of Deneith, a true asset to the House.

To the world, Vounn d'Deneith was a consummate diplomat, gently guiding the relationships between Deneith and the nobles of the nations of Khorvaire, maintaining good relations at the highest levels. In private there was nothing gentle about her. Charm and grace became an unyielding, single-minded focus on her goals with no mercy for anyone who got in her way.

One of those goals was shaping Ashi.

The lady seneschal appeared in the doorway of the bedchamber. Her lined face was hard. "Ashi, you left the reception before—" Her voice stopped as she took in the discarded robe, the impaled gown, and Ashi's face. Her lips pressed together until they were thin lines. "You were supposed to wear that gown to the feast for Tariic tonight," she said, her voice cold.

The anger she had felt earlier surged back through Ashi's gut. "I was *supposed* to perform the sword dance for him!"

Vounn folded her hands, unmoved by her rage. "That doesn't justify storming out of the Hall of Shields before proper introductions were made." She went over to the bed and began working the sword free with practiced ease. Deneith was a martial house. Even the diplomats knew how to handle a weapon. She kept talking as she pulled at the sword. "You know how significant Tariic's visit is for Deneith."

For you, you mean, Ashi thought. She didn't say it, though. Instead she repeated what her history tutor—hired by Vounn, of course—had drummed into her. "When Haruuc led the clans of the goblin races in the rebellion that carved Darguun out of southern Cyre thirty years ago, he did it on the back of a betrayal to Deneith, leading tens of thousands of hobgoblin mercenaries in turning against the House and the nations that employed them. Baron Jannes d'Deneith saved the honor of the House by entering Darguun and making peace with Haruuc, who personally guaranteed the future loyalty of mercenary troops supplied to Deneith. The ties between Deneith and Darguun have been strained, though. Tariic's visit is the first to Sentinel Tower by an emissary of Haruuc since the founding of Darguun."

The message that had arrived only a little more than a month before from Lhesh Haruuc, delivered by a uniformed gnome of House Sivis, had been unexpected but had set off waves of excitement. Vounn had brought it to a classroom where a tutor was conducting one of Ashi's excruciating reading lessons—there had been little need for reading and writing among the Bonetree—and stood over her as she puzzled out the words.

Lhesh Haruuc accepts your invitation and will send his personal emissary to meet with House Deneith to discuss matters of concern to us both.

Such a short message for all the chaos that had followed it.

"I've been working on persuading the Darguuls to make a diplomatic visit since I was raised to my rank," said Vounn without looking up. Her voice warmed with ambition. "It will be the first step to equalizing the relationship between Deneith and Darguun. We hire Darguuls, but they want nothing from us. That's going to change. Too much depends on this visit to leave anything to chance." The sword came free and Vounn set it aside, then added, "I saw you practicing the sword dance before the reception. Your steps were too raw. I had Baerer dress and slip into the ceremony to take your place. Based on the Darguuls' reaction, I think it was the right decision."

Ashi's face burned. "Why didn't you just use Baerer from the beginning, then? Why put me through the training?"

Vounn raised an eyebrow. "Having the sword dance performed for you is a statement of honor. To have the sword dance performed by the bearer of a Siberys Mark is a statement of strength."

For a moment, Ashi could only stare at her. Blood thundered in her ears and her vision dimmed as the urge to strike the older woman burned through her. She held back, though. Sometimes the ways of the Bonetree came too easily. Instead, she just clenched her fists and said, "You only wanted me to dance because of my mark?"

"It's your duty to serve Deneith," Vounn said without hesitation. "I did think you might have a talent for it, but I see I should have given you more time." She lifted the gown from the bed and inspected the holes in it. "The cuts are clean. Call for a seamstress, someone with magewright training. A mending spell will close these, and you can still wear the gown to dinner."

Anger shifted inside of Ashi. "I'm not going to dinner." The words sounded childish, but they came from deep inside her. Vounn blinked, astonishment at this rebellion leaping into her face. Ashi cut her off before she could say anything. "You heard me. I'm not going."

Vounn's astonishment vanished into a cold neutrality. "You have a place of honor two seats from Tariic. You must go."

"Baerer can go in my place." Ashi put her back to Vounn and went to her wardrobe. Her fingers fumbled with the seams of her fitted dancing shirt, then she simply grabbed the fabric and tore the stitching apart. A sleeveless shirt—the better to show off her dragonmark. Her mouth twisted in disgust. Flinging the rags away, she reached into the wardrobe. "Or better yet," she said, "let my mark sit in the chair. Ah, but you can't, since it's coming with me."

The shirt she pulled from the wardrobe had long sleeves. She tugged it over her head, then grabbed the fingerless gloves and scarf she habitually wore, when away from the enclave of Sentinel Tower, to hide the magical pattern on her skin.

"You can't do this," said Vounn.

Ashi glanced over her shoulder at the lady seneschal. There were two spots of color high on her cheeks. "Why not?" she asked her. "Because it will spoil your plans? Because it will mean trouble for the relationship between Deneith and Darguun? I don't think my being there or not will make that much of a difference."

She reached back into the wardrobe and took out one thing more: her sword. Her real sword, not the lightweight piece of metal from the dance but a proper blade, the one thing she'd carried away from the Bonetree clan and her old life. Singe had identified it as an honor blade of the Sentinel Marshals of House Deneith, a weapon presented only in recognition of the most heroic acts. It had belonged to her grandfather, a legacy along with the blood of Deneith. Ashi buckled the sword belt around her waist, then turned to go.

"You're not leaving Sentinel Tower," said Vounn. She hadn't moved, as if frozen with disbelief that her charge would disobey her. "You *will* be at that dinner."

Ashi stopped and met her gaze. "How will it look to the Darguuls," she asked, "if they see House guards dragging the bearer of the Siberys Mark of Sentinel through the halls and up to the dining table?"

Vounn closed her mouth, but her eyes remained hard. Ashi could guess what was going on in her mind. There was more than one way to get an unwilling person to do something, and she didn't doubt that Vounn would use any means at her disposal. Fortunately, Ashi had the ultimate defense against any sort of mental manipulation. She narrowed her eyes and concentrated. For a moment, the lines of her dragonmark seemed to brighten. Heat flared across her skin, wrapping her in a flash of warmth that, when it faded, left a kind of hard-edged clarity behind it.

The power of her mark had stood against Dah'mir and against his lord, the terrible, alien daelkyr known as the Master of Silence. It would stand against anything Vounn could throw at her. What was more, its power would conceal her from any divination magic the lady seneschal might order used to try to locate her.

"Give my regards to Tariic," said Ashi, and she walked out of the room.

CHAPTER THREE

The passages of Sentinel Tower were generally bustling at any hour, but as Ashi stalked from the living quarters of the great tower into the more public areas, it seemed to her that even more people than usual were rushing about. Most were talking about the Darguuls, about Tariic and the evening's feast, about Baerer and his performance of the sword dance. Ashi did her best to avoid the thickest knots of gossip—a goal made easier once people got a look at the fury on her face and quickly moved out of her way. She'd never been good at concealing her emotions, and while Vounn had managed to teach her some control, the last thing Ashi felt like doing was following Vounn's lessons.

No, she realized as she turned a corner and stopped sharply, following Vounn's lessons was the second to last thing she felt like doing.

Around the corner, as startled and frozen as she, was Baerer. Her one-time instructor was dressed in fine clothes, clearly ready for dinner. His face still glowed with the joy of his dance, though that glow vanished even as she watched, replaced by a kind of haunted shame. "Ashi—"

"Lord Baerer," she said formally, some vestige of eight months of Vounn's training fighting to the surface. By ancient tradition, any bearer of a dragonmark could claim the title of lord or lady, no matter what their actual station. Even after eight months, Ashi still found the tradition ridiculous and fortunately the members of the houses seldom used the titles among themselves in casual conversation or with friends. There were times, however, when even she had to admit they were useful. Baerer winced at the harshness in her voice.

"I'm sorry," he said. "Vounn took me aside just before the reception and said there'd been a change in plans. She offered me the chance to dance for the Darguuls. Who could say no to that?"

"Not you, I see. I thought you were my friend, not just my teacher, Baerer." Hot anger scorched away formality. "You know how hard I worked. Did you think I would just give up?"

"Vounn didn't tell me anything about why you weren't dancing."

Ashi scowled. "Because *she* didn't think I was good enough. She thought my dance was too raw."

"Raw?" Baerer looked her in the eyes for the first time. "I would have said that was the most attractive thing about your dancing." He shook his head. "I'm sorry I took your place, Ashi. I think you would have been good. Vounn should have let you dance."

"Tell her that," said Ashi. "You're probably going to be sitting beside her at dinner."

Confusion crossed Baerer's face, but she'd had enough of talking and she wasn't in the mood to explain herself. She pushed past him and strode on down the passage.

"Ashi, wait—" He caught her arm.

She turned on reflex, twisting her arm around his and swinging him around. The dancing master kept his balance and turned with her, but still ended up thrust face-first against the nearest wall.

"Leave me alone, Baerer," she said in his ear, then let him loose.

He looked back at her with alarm and a little fright on his face. "I just wanted to warn you," he said. He twitched his head down the hall. "If you're going that way and through the Venture Court, you're going to run into the Darguuls. Tariic's honor guard is camped out in the court. The atmosphere is . . . uneasy."

Ashi smiled, baring her teeth. "Good." She turned again and continued on her way.

Sentinel Tower had been built upon and expanded many times during its centuries of existence. In many ways, it had become more of a sprawling complex than a tower. Its inner reaches were forbidden to all but the members of House Deneith while the outer areas were filled with workshops and supply yards, all as busy as any market. A middle ring was where business with major clients took place and where important guests like Tariic were lodged. The entire tower was riddled with ancient passages that no longer went anywhere, abandoned chambers waiting for a new use, and old courtyards that had once been open to the sky but were now closed in by more recent construction.

The Venture Court was one such courtyard. It hadn't yet been covered over entirely, but the rooms above it had been built progressively out into open space, leaving only a small gap to the open air. Ashi had always thought the court resembled nothing so much as one of the long houses built by the orc tribes of the Shadow Marches, complete with a smoke hole in the roof.

That night, the gap to the sky really was a smoke hole. Ashi paused at the edge of the court and stared in spite of her anger.

Baerer hadn't been exaggerating when he'd described the Darguuls as "camped out" in the court. A big fire built in a great copper bowl cast a flickering light that reflected in streaks and sparks from the weapons and armor of Tariic's musicians, banner-bearers, and guards. While some of the goblins dozed near the fire, others stood in a watchful perimeter as if they expected an attack at any time—defensive measures more suited to soldiers on the move than guests at Sentinel Tower. And the goblin races, she knew, didn't need the fire. They could see perfectly well in the dark. The fire was there so that others could see them and be intimidated into keeping their distance. It set the warrior in Ashi on edge.

Apparently she wasn't the only one to react that way. At every entrance to the court and from the windows overlooking it, House guards stood in silent response to the Darguuls' presence. One of them stepped into her path to block her from entering the court, then saw the mark on her face and stepped back again.

"Lady Ashi," he said with a nod. "You might want to go around Venture Court tonight. It may not be safe to cross."

One irritation after another. Going around the court would just slow her. The nearest gate out of Sentinel Tower was just beyond the court. Going around would all but force her to another gate. "Thank you," she said, "I'll be fine."

She saw the guard's throat move as he swallowed. "Lady Seneschal Vounn won't be—" His words faded as he watched her expression darken at Vounn's name, and he swallowed again. "May we at least escort you across the court, lady?"

Ashi fought the temptation to punch him in his whining mouth. "No," she said and walked out into the courtyard.

She could feel every gaze inside and around the court, human and goblin, turn to follow her. It only fuelled her anger. Was she some delicate flower in need of protection? Clenching her teeth, she marched straight across the court, heading directly for the passage that would take her to the gate and out of Sentinel Tower.

Straight across the court was also straight through the massed Darguuls. One of them, a hobgoblin, came to meet her as she approached. "I am Aruget," he said. Unlike Tariic, he had a heavy Goblin accent that drew out the middle of his words and bit off the end. "I serve Tariic, who serves Lhesh Haruuc. Go around our lines."

Ashi stopped and glared at him. "I am Ashi d'Deneith. I am angry. Get out of my way."

Aruget's eyes were deep brown flecked with orange, and he had the ritual scars across his forehead that Ashi had learned were a sign of the Rhukaan Taash clan. He stared at her and she stared back, neither of them blinking. For a very long moment, the only sound and movement in Venture Court came from the jumping, snapping flames in the big fire bowl.

The hobgoblin was the first to look away, his gaze lifting and going over Ashi's head. "You may pass," he growled softly and moved out of her way.

"Ta muut," Ashi said as she passed. It was a Goblin phrase she had learned from Ekhaas. Roughly translated, it meant "you have honor," but Ekhaas had explained that it was the proper way to say thank you without implying weakness or debt. She didn't look back to see Aruget's reaction to being spoken to in his own

language. She kept her eyes on the Darguuls ahead, walking without hesitation. Hobgoblins, bugbears, and goblins stepped aside to let her by. As she passed one knot of goblins, she heard a thin murmuring break out in her wake. She looked over her shoulder, her hand hovering near her sword briefly before falling away. One of the goblins was trying to suppress laughter—not at her, but to judge from the nervous glances of those with him, at Aruget. The hobgoblin's face darkened, and he bore down on the laughing goblin like a storm, snarling rapid words that made the goblin stop snickering very quickly.

It felt good to see someone else on the receiving end of trouble for a change, Ashi decided. It felt good to have her way in an argument, too. A little of her anger lifted from her, and her step was lighter as she passed into the shadows of the passage on the other side of the court.

No one in the outer zone of Sentinel Tower stopped her or even bothered to give her a second glance. The gate she had chosen was a grubby thing, used mostly for the movement of supplies and mercenary troops into and out of the tower. The higher ranking members of House Deneith almost never came this way. She paused for a moment before approaching the gate and covered up her dragonmark as best she could. Gloves hid the backs of her hands, and a carefully folded and tied scarf masked her forehead and the lower part of her face. Within Sentinel Tower, her Siberys Mark gained her respect. Beyond, it just as often aroused suspicion and superstition. It also identified her. Even covered, she felt a knot in her belly as she walked under the stone arch, half-expecting that word from Vounn might have reached the guards ahead of her and that at any moment they would call out for her to stop.

They didn't. She left Sentinel Tower and walked out into the city of Karrlakton.

There was little to reveal at first that she had left the tower, aside from open sky and crooked streets instead of straight passages. The area outside the gate was all but an extension of the area inside, bustling with evening trade. There was a sense of greater freedom out of the tower, though, a more relaxed tone in the voices of traders and carters who dealt with the great house but didn't serve it. The farther she went from the tower and the more evening slid into night, the lighter the traffic in the streets became. The tension between Ashi's shoulders eased a bit more.

It was impossible to escape Deneith entirely, however. The House didn't rule in Karrlakton, but it certainly dominated every aspect of the city. As vast as Sentinel Tower was, Deneith's activities spilled out of it. Training grounds and barracks, workshops and warehouses, even ordinary houses—every third building that Ashi passed bore the crest of Deneith. The roots of Deneith went even deeper, Ashi knew. Warlords who carried the Mark of Sentinel had ruled the area of what would become Karrlakton before the founding of the ancient kingdom of Karrnath, even before the creation of House Deneith proper. The city had grown under the gaze of the House. Parts of it were as old as parts of Sentinel Tower. For many centuries, Deneith money had built roads, walls, and shrines.

Ashi turned toward one of the oldest sections of the city. The sense of history appealed to her. It was soothing to be among things that had stood for centuries, unchanged and unaffected by the small frustrations of everyday life. When she was gone—when Vounn was gone—they would still be there. As old as Sentinel Tower was, she couldn't feel the same thing there. Everything was too busy, too imprinted with the ordinary. The oldest areas of the tower were forbidden to all but the most senior members of the House, as if the stones held some dreadful secret. The only peace she had found was in the archives, where books replaced stone, and if they weren't quite as permanent and unchanging, they had even more fascinating stories to tell as her ability to read grew.

She had found her grandfather in the archives. All she'd known of him before she met Singe was that his name had been Kagan and that the hunters of the Bonetree had found him in the Shadow Marches, badly injured and clutching his fine sword. Too deeply wounded ever to fight again, he had been brought into the clan and had fathered many children for the Bonetree over several years—until he'd gone mad and murdered all of them save one, who had become Ashi's father, before taking his own life.

In the archives of Sentinel Tower, she'd discovered a different man, a hero of the Sentinel Marshals. He had been awarded an honor blade, the same bright sword that rode her hip, for bringing to justice a pair of notorious murderers. The archive's record ended with his final assignment: the pursuit of one of the pair after her escape. To the best knowledge of House Deneith, neither he nor his quarry had ever been seen again.

After reading the record of Kagan, Ashi had promised herself that she would become a Sentinel Marshal. She'd mentioned the idea to Vounn. The lady seneschal had answered her with a silence that spoke louder than words. Ashi carried the Siberys Mark of Sentinel. She was too valuable to be allowed to roam far from the reach of the House.

She clenched her teeth as she reached Karrlakton's old quarter. Anger rose in her again, replacing the calm she should have felt in the shadow of the ancient buildings. She was more than her dragonmark, no matter what people might think, whether they were people like Vounn who expected her to use the mark for the profit of Deneith, or people like the anonymous House guard who saw her only as a scion of the house, or people in the street who reacted to a Siberys Mark with superstitious unease, or people like Aruget and the other Darguuls who—

Ashi paused in midstride, breaking her pace as she broke her silent rant. How had Aruget reacted to her? The Darguuls had to know what dragonmarks were—they were dealing with House Deneith—and they must have known that the larger the mark, the more powerful it was. Aruget had recognized her as a lady of Deneith, but it had been her hard stare that had forced him to back down, not the sight of her mark. Maybe her mark *didn't* matter to them. No dragonmarks manifested among the goblin races, a mystery that had always puzzled sages who cared about such things. Maybe to goblin eyes, the mark on her face was no more unusual than the piercings in her lip or the scars across Aruget's forehead.

"Rond betch!" Ashi muttered, for the first time keenly disappointed that she was missing the opportunity to meet Tariic. If he'd

reacted as Aruget had, she would have enjoyed watching Vounn's dismay. Ashi smiled to herself.

If she hadn't been standing still and her mind hadn't been, for the moment, clear, she might have missed the quiet, muffled sound of breaking glass. And if she hadn't immediately and instinctively turned to look for the source of the sound, she would have missed seeing the figure that slipped through a narrow window high on one of the ancient buildings nearby.

A thief. There could be no other explanation for someone climbing up and breaking a window to gain access to a building. Ashi glanced around her. Only a few of the ancient structures that lined the lanes of this area were residences, and all of the windows in them were dark. The only light came from the moons that peered down into the narrow old streets. The folk of the neighborhood were in their beds, dreaming of another day's work to come. There was no sign of the night watch. Ashi and the thief were the only ones abroad.

Ashi knew the building the thief had entered. She'd visited it during a rare and closely supervised excursion into the city. It was a shrine of sorts, erected by some long ago lord of Deneith in remembrance of a great campaign in the distant south long before even the beginning of the Last War. The importance of battle and lord were almost forgotten, but the memorial remained, seldom visited but maintained by the House, like dozens of others in Karrlakton, out of a sense of duty. A Deneith memorial, a Deneith responsibility.

With no one else, no night watch, around, that made it her responsibility. Ashi felt her blood stir at the idea. A fight. A real fight, not sparring in the training ground, not rehearsed steps on the dance floor, but a real, dangerous fight—that's what she had been missing for the last eight months. She smiled again, this time out of pure, fierce joy, and ran for the memorial.

Ashi had been one of the most accomplished stalkers and trackers among the Bonetree. Whatever new skills and knowledge Vounn tried to force on her, those old skills remained. Moving like a ghost, she raced from shadow to shadow, staying out of the moonlight in case her prey happened to glance out of one of the memorial's windows—or in case the thief wasn't alone.

The moons' light fell full on the doors of the memorial, revealing heavy locks. There would be no entry that way, but Ashi had anticipated it. Her back against the stone wall, she slid around the building until she stood beneath the window through which the thief had entered. It was on the more shadowed side of the building, but up close, she could see the faint line of the rope that the thief had used to climb. Ashi adjusted and tightened the scarf around her head, took hold of the rope, and scaled the building as silently as she could. Just below the broken window, she stopped and listened. There was no sound from inside. She shimmied a little farther up the rope. The window had been made of small panes of glass held in place with lead strips. The thief had broken some of the panes and ripped back the leading to make a hole big enough to pass through. The hole was easily big enough for Ashi as well—the thief was at least her size. That was big, Ashi thought, for someone doing this kind of thing regularly. She shifted from the rope to the window sill and ducked in through the hole.

The window was well above the nearest level surface. She had to twist around and lower herself down, then drop the last couple of feet. She tried to do it as silently as possible, but she still landed with a soft thump. She froze in a crouch, not even breathing, and listened again. Everything was quiet. Too quiet. Ashi scowled. Her drop had alerted the thief. He was listening now, too. She waited.

Her patience was rewarded. Somewhere in the memorial, not too close, leather creaked as thief moved again. Ashi let out her breath. She hadn't been discovered. She rose from her crouch, remembering everything she could of the memorial layout from her previous visit.

The interior of the memorial was open, with two galleries rising above the ground floor. She stood on the second gallery. A shrine dedicated to Dol Arrah and Dol Dorn, the martial gods of honor and strength, stood in the very center of the ground floor, the focal point of the memorial. Spread out around the ground floor and lining the walls of both galleries, however, were the real reason the memorial's few visitors might come: cabinet upon glass-fronted display cabinet of trophies taken during the campaign and of relics commemorating the fallen. Arching over the whole was a vaulted ceiling painted with an age-darkened image of what might have been the greatest battle of the campaign but to Ashi had looked like any other chaotic battlefield.

By night, however, the painted ceiling was completely lost in shadow, along with most of the cabinets. The only light in the memorial came from four candles lit with magical cold fire on the shrine far below, supplemented by dim shafts of silver moonlight penetrating the windows on two walls of the building. Ashi had hunted by night before, however. It was enough light for her. She scanned the gallery for any signs of movement, but there were none. The creak of leather had come from below. Ashi walked to the edge of the gallery and peered down.

CHAPTER FOUR

Moonlight fell across the stairs leading from the lower gallery down to the main floor. As Ashi watched, a figure moved through the patch of brightness. The pale light drained color and detail, but she could make out that the thief was tall and lean, wearing dark leathers and with a hood pulled up over his head. Down the stairs and onto the ground floor, he skirted the shrine and vanished again into the shadows. Ashi stepped back and made her way to the stairs as well, moving slowly and carefully to avoid stumbling over anything in the darkness. On the lower gallery, she paused again, assessing her options. She could just make out the thief as an indistinct figure moving from cabinet to cabinet as if looking for something inside one of them.

The thief had no light—if he was examining the contents of the cabinets, he must have had some magic or natural ability allowing him to see in the dark. She would be at a disadvantage in the deeper shadows. She needed to get the thief into better light. Approaching across the ground floor would put her in danger of being spotted, either as she crept around the dim perimeter or as she crossed the open center through the candlelight of the shrine.

But there was another way. She left the stairs and crossed along the gallery in the direction of the thief, taking care to stay well back from the gallery's edge. She was partway around the gallery, almost above the place where she had seen the thief, when she heard a soft murmur of satisfaction from below. The thief had found whatever he was looking for. Ashi paused and heard the scratching of metal on metal. He was trying to open the lock on a cabinet. She moved back to the rail of the gallery, then oriented herself on the thin sound. When she judged she was nearly directly over the thief, she glanced down. The floor below was empty. Ashi swung herself silently over the rail and, gripping tight, lowered herself hand over hand down its stout spindles until she dangled in the air. The thief was a few paces in front of her, hunched over his work.

She took a quiet breath and dropped. The floor met her, but she rolled as she landed, coming up in a crouch and drawing her sword in one smooth movement. She caught a brief glimpse of the thief whirling in surprise. The cabinet behind him stood open.

"Hold!" Ashi shouted. "Hold in the name of—"

The words weren't out of her mouth before the thief reached back into the cabinet, grabbed something, and hurled it at Ashi. She didn't see what it was, but she jumped to the side to avoid it. Whatever the thief had thrown whistled past her to shatter on the floor. Even as she jumped, though, Ashi recognized it as a distraction. In the moment that she was off-balance, the thief's hands shaped an arcane gesture and a husky, almost musical whisper rippled from his lips. A spell. The thief was more than he seemed! Ashi didn't have any chance to dodge. The magical energy formed around her—

Then slid away like beads of water on a hot iron as it met the shield of her dragonmark. A tingle passed across Ashi's scalp, but nothing more. Gritted teeth turned into a grin and she flung herself at the thief with a shout. The only way to deal with a spellcaster was to stay too close to give him time to cast.

The thief recovered quickly, though, drawing a heavy dagger and falling back into the shadows. Ashi aimed her first blow not at the thief—she wanted him alive—but at the dagger. If he faded too far into the darkness, the last thing she wanted was an unseen blade plunging between her ribs. Her honor blade flashed, reflecting what little light there was, as it struck hard against the dagger, and the shorter weapon jumped out of the thief's grasp. Ashi stepped in behind the blow to grab the thief's shoulder. With a twist and a shove, she sent him staggering back toward the center of the memorial and the light that shone from the shrine.

Except that he grabbed her arm as well, pulling her with him. He staggered into the light, but Ashi crashed into another display cabinet. Wood cracked, glass smashed, and artifacts from the cabinet rained to the floor in a metallic cascade. Ashi cursed and pulled herself free, turning to face the thief as he regained his balance. The light silhouetted him, obscuring his features further, but Ashi could see that he was, like her, wearing a scarf under his hood. Her glimpse was brief, however. Drawing himself up, he spat another musical word of magic.

Like ink on wet paper, the outline of the thief's body seemed to run and blur. Every movement left a confusing streak on the air. Ashi hissed under her breath and leaped at him, but what should have been a clean blow passed through empty air. A smudged leg lashed out and she skipped aside to avoid it. The thief whirled and dashed across the memorial—straight for a rack of old weapons, rusted polearms standing like aged soldiers in drill formation.

"Betch." Ashi ran after the thief, snatching up a wide-mouthed bronze vessel resting atop a low cabinet as she ran. She'd thought to hurl the vessel at her opponent or maybe hit him with it, but it was heavier than she expected, and it rattled when she grabbed it. Ashi glanced inside, then, instead of throwing it, grasped one side of the rim and scattered the contents across the floor.

Hundreds of small knucklebones—soldiers' dice—bounced on the stone, spreading out in a dry rattling wave that swept around and under the thief's feet as he tried to stop and grab one of the polearms. Some of the old bones crunched into powder, but others held their strength and rolled. The thief's momentum on the unsteady footing kept him moving forward and right into a cabinet with a very solid smack. Thief and cabinet slammed to the ground, dragging down half the rack of polearms as well. Ashi went around the treacherous field of bones and tangled staves with long strides. "In the name of Deneith," she said hoarsely, "surrender!"

The thief answered with a savage growl. He twisted and came to his feet with one of the polearms in his hand—or rather a length of one of the polearms. The ancient wood had splintered like a twig. The thief flung it at Ashi, but the throw was neither hard nor accurate and Ashi grabbed the spinning wood out of the air and flung it back at him. Magic still blurring his form, the thief ducked.

The stick whirled over his head and swept across the shrine in the center of the memorial. Candles, ritual objects, and the accumulated offerings left behind by visitors to the memorial went flying everywhere in a tinkling, crashing cascade. Ashi winced. She wasn't particularly religious, but the thought of disturbing the shrine, even accidentally, crawled across her skin. If it was possible, the gods of the shrine were already taking petty revenge—only one of the candles remained upright in its holder. The others tumbled and rolled around the memorial. Their magic kept them burning, but their dim light was spread even more thinly, and the shadows they made jumped and wavered crazily.

The thief dove through one of the shadows and emerged with something else that had been knocked off the shrine: a short sword, its design old but the edge of its blade still gleaming. This time his grip on the weapon was sure and his stance solid. Ashi clenched her jaw and closed in warily. For a moment, she and the thief faced each other, blades wavering, balance shifting.

Ashi struck first and struck hard. She had to—if the thief took control of the fight, she had a bad feeling that she'd quickly find herself forced back into the darkness. If she took control, she had a better chance of keeping the fight where she could see.

The thief twisted and caught her sword on his, parrying the blow. Ashi let him bear her blade down for a moment, then whipped it up again and thrust hard. Only the blurring effect of the thief's spell kept him from ending up on the blade. Instead, Ashi's bright blade sliced through leather and nicked flesh. She heard the thief hiss in pain. He tried to push back with a lunge, but Ashi slid aside easily. The thief was a good fighter, but she was better. Eight months with House Deneith might not have made her much of a lady, but it had honed her fighting skills like a whetstone honed a fine blade. She let her opponent try another strike, then she unleashed a flurry of blows that kept him on the defensive and forced him to yield ground. Step by step, Ashi bullied him across the memorial. The clash and shriek of their blades filled the darkness, ringing and reverberating inside the hollow tower.

Beneath her scarf, Ashi grinned in satisfaction at the fight. A thrust from the thief slipped past her attack. She swayed away beyond the point of his sword and answered with a sharp kick that sent the thief hopping back. They were past the shrine now. Ashi lunged, then lunged again, not giving the thief a chance to recover his balance, always driving him backward. She slashed at him and he hopped back one more time—slamming into the doors of the memorial hard enough to make them shake.

Ashi checked her next blow, holding her sword back. "Surrender!" she said. "You have no right to be here!"

Eyes flashed deep in the hooded shadows of the thief's face. "You have no right to what is kept here!"

The voice, like smoke from burning cedar wood, was a woman's. Ashi blinked in surprise—then blinked again at the sound of another voice, this one on the other side of the door.

"Get it open! By Dol Dorn's mighty fist, get it open! Swords ready!"

Keys scratched at the locks on the doors. Karrlakton's night watch had finally arrived. Ashi raised her voice. "Easy! I have everything—"

The thief moved. Bracing herself against the doors that trapped her, she reared back and kicked out. A boot caught Ashi in the gut and she hunched over, her sword dropping. The thief darted past her. Ashi turned after her, struggling to catch her breath, but the thief paused just beyond her reach and spoke the word of another spell.

A sound like a massed chorus of voices mixed with the roll of thunder erupted around Ashi, pummeling her with its force. On the other side of the door, the men of the night watch cried out, some of them in alarm, at least one of them in command—the sergeant, urging his men to action. Ashi shook her head and forced herself upright.

The thief was back on the other side of the memorial, back at the cabinet she had initially opened. One of the candles from the shrine had rolled in that direction and Ashi finally saw what the thief had come to steal. Gloved hands reached into the cabinet and lifted out—almost reverently it seemed—a small casket only a handspan long and wide, made of age-darkened iron bound in bright gold. Cradling the casket, the thief turned to the stairs and her escape.

Ashi pushed herself into motion. She had only moments or the thief would be gone. No time to go around the shrine. A jump put her on top of it, scattering anything still left there. A leap and the wild fluting battle cry of the Bonetree hunters set her into the air.

The thief half-turned in response to the cry. Ashi saw her stiffen, her arms wrapping protectively around the cask, then she slammed into her and both of them went down. They tumbled across the floor in a tangle of arms and legs, the thief struggling to protect her prize, Ashi fighting to stay on top—which was how she landed when they finally came to a stop. Her hands were on the thief's shoulders and her weight over the other woman's hips, pinning her down. Ashi's scarf had finally come loose and it hung around her face, puckering and billowing with each panting breath that she took. "Surrender!" she gasped.

The thief's eyes, however, had gone wide. "Ashi?" she said.

The blurring effect vanished. Ashi stared down at amber eyes in a lean yellow face. The thief's hood had fallen back to reveal orange-brown hair pulled back in a knot and a hobgoblin's wolf-like ears. Ashi lifted one hand and tugged down the scarf that had covered the thief's face.

"Ekhaas?' she asked.

Then the doors of the memorial slammed open and the intense light of everbright lanterns flooded over them. The slap of boots and the hiss of drawn swords filled the ruined space. "Don't move!" roared the voice of the sergeant. "Under the authority of Karrlakton, you're both under arrest!"

CHAPTER FIVE

The watchmen of Karrlakton gave Ashi and Ekhaas no chance to speak until they'd marched them to the nearest watch station and deposited the pair in a cell. They recognized Ashi's dragonmark and handled her with a certain amount of deference, but Ekhaas didn't receive the same favor. The men left both of them with their hands tied behind their backs—they knew at least one of their two prisoners was a spellcaster and they thought they were being cautious. Ekhaas saw no reason to tell them that she knew several spells that could be cast with song alone. Apparently the Karrlakton watch had little experience dealing with a Kech Volaar *duur'kala.* She held her tongue as the cell door swung shut behind them, instead watching through the bars to see what the watch did with the weapons—and other items—they had confiscated.

Ashi did enough talking for both of them. "It's a Deneith memorial!" she said to the station commander. "I was protecting it on behalf of the House. But it was all a mistake. This woman is my friend. There's no reason to keep us."

The argument worked no better on the commander than it had on the sergeant who had arrested them. "House Deneith is ruled by the law just like everyone else in Karrlakton—a dragonmark is no protection. You broke into a public building in the middle of the night and caused serious damage. You desecrated a shrine of the Sovereign Host. You may or may not have stolen from the memorial." The commander looked at Ekhaas. She ignored him, flicking her ears in disdain. He looked back to Ashi. "Your House will be contacted.

We'll see what they have to say. In the meantime, I'd suggest that you sit down and behave yourself."

He walked away, closing the door of the the cell behind him. Ashi watched him go with what Ekhaas thought looked like a curious mix of frustration and horror.

"What do you mean the House will be contacted?" Ashi called after the commander. "Who did you contact? Who—"

"Sit down, Ashi," said Ekhaas. She settled herself on the bare plank bench that was the only thing in the cell and tried to think of a way out of the situation. Ashi leaned her head against the bars of the door and cursed.

"Khyberit gentis." She turned around and glared at Ekhaas. "Well?"

"Well what?"

"Are you going to tell me what you were doing breaking into that memorial? What's so special about that casket? What are you doing in Karrlakton at all?" She dropped onto the bench beside Ekhaas. "You could have at least told me you were here."

Ekhaas's ears rose. "I didn't know you were in Karrlakton. I could ask you what you were doing at the memorial, too."

"*I* was trying to stop a thief." Ashi grimaced. "This is my fault. If I hadn't tried to stop you, neither of us would have been arrested and you would have gotten away with your little casket."

"Je'shaarat mi paa kotanaa," said Ekhaas. Ashi looked at her, and she translated the expression: "A sharp sword hurts less when you fall on it."

Ashi wrinkled her nose. "What did you want with the casket?" she asked again. "I saw one of the watchmen trying to open it, but he couldn't."

"It's sealed. It's not meant to be opened."

"Then what's inside? Why would you steal it if . . . ?" Ashi's question trailed off and she twisted around to face Ekhaas directly. Anger rose in her voice. "You said Deneith had no right to what was in the memorial. Is the casket an artifact of Dhakaan? Are you still trying to protect things from us *shaat'aar?"*

Anger crept into Ekhaas as well, though she kept it out of her voice. Her ears, however, bent back. *"Chaat'oor,"* she corrected. It was a harsh word, usually translated as "defilers." The word was old, as ancient as the dying of the great empire, and it referred to any race not native to the continent of Khorvaire. Usually that meant humans, but it could refer equally to the changelings or shifters who had joined the migration to the land that had once belonged to her people. When she'd first met Ashi, Geth, Singe, and Dandra in the south of the country of Droaam, she'd called them *chaat'oor,* assuming they'd come to loot the Dhakaani ruins in the area. She'd discovered a greater respect for them, but the reverence for the past that was the duty and right of every descendant of Dhakaan was not something to be dismissed.

"Yes," she said, glaring back at Ashi, "it's an artifact of Dhakaan. And yes, I was taking it back. It belongs in a shrine, not in a dingy cabinet. It's a reliquary. It holds the tongue and brain of Duural Rhuvet, the last great strategist of the empire. For untold generations, it was kept by our greatest leaders and carried onto the battlefield as a source of inspiration—until it was lost at the Battle of Starkhan." A little of her seething anger broke through her control. "An important part of our history, carried away as a looted curiosity!"

Ashi twitched. "Couldn't you have just asked for it back?"

"If your House had known what it had in its possession, what treasure it had seized at Starkhan, would it have given it back?"

"Probably not." Ashi shifted as if uncomfortable, then asked, "Ekhaas, what's the Battle of Starkhan?"

Ekhaas stared at her. "Starkhan was the key battle in the Torlaac Conquest."

Ashi shook her head.

Ekhaas's ears drooped in disbelief. "The campaign that memorial was dedicated to! *Khaavolaar,* what has Deneith been teaching you?"

"How to be a lady." Ashi scowled when Ekhaas raised her eyebrows. "Don't ask," she said. "I don't want to think about it. Have you heard from any of the others? I haven't had any news. Have you heard from Dandra or Singe?" Her face brightened. "What about Geth?"

Geth. Ekhaas held her expression, voice, and ears absolutely neutral. "I haven't heard from him—or anyone," she said.

"Oh." Ashi looked disappointed. "I would have thought you might have kept in touch with Geth because of his sword."

"Aram," said Ekhaas, giving Geth's Dhakaani sword its proper name. She flicked her ears casually. "I'd like to know how he is, but both he and I are wanderers. Either of us could be anywhere."

"Too bad. I feel so cut off." Ashi left the door and sat on the bench beside Ekhaas. The hobgoblin felt sorry for her. She was a wanderer and a loner by nature, but Ashi had left first the clan that had raised her, then the newfound friends who had introduced her to the wider world to become part of House Deneith. She put her hand on Ashi's in a human gesture of empathy.

"If I'd known you were here in Karrlakton, I would have come looking for you," she said.

Ashi snorted. "What? You would have stolen the casket, then carried it along to Sentinel Tower to see me?"

"I would have gone to see you first. I would have come as soon as I arrived today."

Ashi pushed Ekhaas's hand away with a grin. "You only arrived today? You didn't waste any time before you tried to steal—" She paused abruptly and gave Ekhaas a narrow look. "You arrived today? The same day an emissary from Darguun arrived to meet with House Deneith?"

"Coincidence," Ekhaas said, but Ashi's probing expression didn't change. Ekhaas sighed, leaned her head back on the cold stone of the cell's wall, and gave her some of the truth. "I'm here with Tariic," she confessed. "Haruuc is courting the favor of my clan, the Kech Volaar. I'm part of Tariic's delegation as a representative of my clan."

"They didn't have anyone more senior to send?" asked Ashi.

Ekhaas raised her ears in angry pride. "I am senior now," she said. "The name of my clan means 'Wordbearers' in our tongue. The Kech Volaar gather history. The history of Dhakaan is the most important, but the *duur'kala* of the Kech Volaar gather tales of all kinds. When I returned from the Shadow Marches with the story of the discovery of Aram and the defeat of Dah'mir, I gained a certain amount of recognition in the clan."

She stopped herself short of claiming that being sent to accompany Tariic was a reward, but she let Ashi assume what she would. There was still disbelief in her friend's face. "Does Tariic know you were out stealing the casket?" Ashi asked.

"Ah." Ekhaas's ears dipped along with her pride. "Tariic is almost as much human as he is hobgoblin. He wouldn't have understood . . . what needed to be done." She bared sharp teeth. "Tonight was the best chance I had. I was supposed to be at a banquet given in Tariic's honor, but I knew no one would miss me." A harsh laugh from Ashi brought her head up. "What?" she asked.

"I was supposed to be at that banquet, too," said Ashi. She stretched out her legs and tried to settle herself more comfortably on the hard bench. "Were you at the reception ceremony?"

"Yes, at the back of the delegation. It was astounding. The rhythm was perfect." Her training as a *duur'kala* brought the music back into her memory and she clapped out the desperate rhythm of the climax. "Were you there?"

"I was supposed to be the one performing the sword dance." Ashi's mouth twisted. "My mentor decided I wasn't good enough and sent my instructor out instead. We had an argument about it afterward."

Ekhaas frowned. "That's too bad. Tariic would have been even more impressed at having the bearer of the Mark of Siberys dance for him."

Ashi flung up her hands. "That was the idea!"

"Who's your mentor?"

"The person Tariic has come to Karrlakton to see." Ashi sat back again. "Lady Seneschal Vounn d'Deneith."

Once again, Ekhaas could only stare at Ashi, but this time she had no words. Ashi must have mistaken her silence for incredulity. Her mouth twisted even farther. "Tariic is lucky he only has to deal with her as a diplomat. Since I got here, she's been hammering on me like a smith on a sword—and there's nothing I can do about it." She squeezed her hands into tight fists. *"Rond betch,* if I could stick a knife in her . . ."

She kept talking, pouring out a litany of restrictions and punishments that Ekhaas had to admit were more appropriate to the training of a child than a grown woman, but the *duur'kala* was only half-listening. Ideas and possibilities began rearranging themselves in her head. Her ears twitched. Blood of Six Kings, she thought, was it possible they could be so lucky?

There was scarcely a break in Ashi's rambling tales of Vounn's heavy-handed mentoring. Ekhaas had to speak over her to get a word in. "Ashi, how bad was the argument you had tonight with Vounn? Will she take you back?"

"Take me back?" Sitting forward, Ashi groaned. "Ekhaas, she's never going to let me go. I don't think I'm even a person to her. I'm just an asset of Deneith—or I will be once I'm trained to her satisfaction. Even then she'll probably still want me under her thumb." She lifted her head and looked around the cell, then laughed. "You know, I was almost frightened of what she'd do when the watch contacted Deneith and she found out I'd been arrested. Now I wish I could have been there to see the look on her face. I wonder how she reacted."

Muffled voices from an outer room of the watch station reached Ekhaas's ears. "I don't think you'll have to wait long to find out," she said. One of the voices was the watch station commander, and it sounded as if the proud man was actually being subservient. The voices were getting closer. Ekhaas turned to Ashi. "Listen to me," she said. "You need to smooth things over with Vounn. Ease the tension between you. Apologize to her."

"What? Why—?" Ashi said, then she heard the voices as well. For all her talk of anger and confidence, the color drained from her face and she stood up. *"Betch."*

"Apologize," Ekhaas hissed, standing with her, then the door of the room beyond the cell opened—and Ekhaas felt the heat fade from her cheeks, too.

The station commander was the first one through the door, followed by four humans armed with spears and wearing the crest of House Deneith on polished breatsplates. After them came Vounn d'Deneith. The lady seneschal wore a fine gown, too fine to be marching through a watch station. She'd probably come straight from the banquet.

After Vounn, and dressed just as magnificently, came Tariic. He'd put aside the spiked armor he'd worn for the reception ceremony, replacing it with a high-collared doublet of black leather stitched so heavily with bronze it could have turned a blow. Heavy bracers and high greaves on his boots were likewise Darguul in style, but Tariic had added a long, full-sleeved Karrnathi coat that swirled behind him.

Four hobgoblins, members of his honor guard, followed Darguun's emissary, but Ekhaas hardly noticed them. Vounn's face was a dispassionate mask. Ekhaas could read no emotion in it at all. Tariic also aspired to present an emotionless mask, but he didn't succeed nearly as well as Vounn. His skin, naturally a rich red-brown, was tinted an even brighter red by suppressed anger. His jaw was clenched so tight the muscles stood out and his dark eyes focused on empty air rather than look at her. His ears were most telling, however, standing straight and stiff.

Vounn glanced at the station commander. "Thank you. I'll call when we're ready." The man nodded and left the room. One of the Deneith guards followed and took up a position outside the door, presumably to be certain no one tried to eavesdrop, before closing it. Tariic, however, was the first to speak to the prisoners.

"Ekhaas of Kech Volaar," he said, "you dishonor our hosts by stealing from them. You dishonor me, and you dishonor my uncle. You dishonor your clan, and you dishonor Darguun." He spoke with admirable restraint—and in the human language, obviously for the benefit of Ashi and Vounn. Heat returned to Ekhaas's face, and she surprised herself by feeling vaguely ashamed. In her mind, she knew she actually had very little to fear—Tariic couldn't afford to mistreat her—but in her gut she still felt guilt. Stealing the reliquary while in Karrlakton as a guest of House Deneith, even if she was only part of a larger group, broke ancient laws of hospitality. It reflected badly on Tariic as the leader of the delegation and, through him, badly on Lhesh Haruuc.

On the other hand, he probably had no idea what was inside the small casket. She wanted to argue with him and point out that the reliquary of Duural Rhuvet was an important part of their heritage. At the very least, she should correct his galling statement that she had dishonored her clan. She'd done no such thing. If she'd brought the reliquary back to Volaar Draal, the stronghold of the Kech Volaar, she would have been honored as a hero and a protector of Dhakaan's glory. Shame turned to anger—and she swallowed both emotions. There were larger and more important things she needed to tell Tariic.

She looked down and away, her ears bent in contrition. *"Sit gath'muut chib-rhu,"* she said. *I am without honor in this, high one.* Formality demanded that the apology be spoken in Goblin, but Ekhaas was fairly certain that Ashi and Vounn would understand the spirit of her words.

Tariic gave a little grunt of approval—approval that turned to a flicker of surprise when Ekhaas raised her gaze just enough to meet his again and twitched her ears twice sharply. A simple signal, *be alert.* Tariic's eyes widened, but there was no change in the tone of his voice. "I'm not the only one you should apologize to," he said.

Ekhaas, her head down once more, turned to Vounn. "I'm sorry for any trouble or embarrassment I've caused you, Lady Seneschal. Please don't think less of Tariic or Lhesh Haruuc because of my actions."

"I welcome your apology," said Vounn coolly. Ekhaas noticed that nothing in her voice or her stance implied that she actually accepted the apology, though.

Clever, the *duur'kala* thought, she leaves the incident open. She could still come back at us with demands for something more than an apology. In spite of Ashi's complaints about her mentor, Ekhaas felt a grudging respect for the older woman's guile.

Vounn's attention had turned to Ashi, who met her gaze with unbowed sullenness. "I didn't do anything wrong," she said. "I tried to stop a thief."

Ekhaas held back a wince. Just apologize, Ashi, she thought.

Vounn looked at Ashi with the cold but focused expression of a snake about to strike. "And in the process devastated a respected memorial, desecrated an altar of the Sovereign Host, and were arrested. You should have summoned the watch and let them deal with it. You haven't just embarrassed Deneith in front of our guests from Darguun, you've embarrassed yourself and Deneith in front of Karrlakton and the other dragonmarked houses. Do you realize that stories about this are already circulating in taverns?"

She looked to Tariic and added, "I'm sorry you have to see this. Discipline in Deneith is usually conducted in private."

Tariic nodded graciously, but Ekhaas's ears flicked in something between outrage and appreciation: outrage at Vounn for dragging Ashi through briars, appreciation for her expert manipulation of the situation. She very much doubted that stories of Ashi's misadventure had actually found their way into taverns just yet—or even if they would. Likewise, she would have been surprised if details of the night's events would reach other dragonmarked houses without being significantly altered. She had no doubt, however, that Vounn was not in the least sorry to have Tariic witness the confrontation. It showed him that she both understood the importance of honor and was willing to deal swiftly with disobedience from those in her command—both valued traits in the culture of Darguun. The lady seneschal's reputation as a master diplomat was, it seemed, well-earned.

Ashi looked as if she was ready to burst. Her face had turned red except for a thin white line where she pressed her lips together. For a long moment, she just glared at Vounn, then, with a sharp glance sideways at Ekhaas, her lips parted and she said, "I'm sorry."

Vounn raised her eyebrows, less in surprise, Ekhaas suspected, than as a prompt, and Ashi expanded on her apology. "I'm sorry I didn't call the watch. I'm sorry I've embarrassed you and Deneith. I'm sorry I didn't go to the banquet tonight and that I left Sentinel Tower." There was no grace in the apology, but Ashi managed to make it sound at least partly sincere. She even turned to Tariic and mimicked Ekhaas's words to Vounn. "I'm sorry for any trouble I've caused you. Please don't think less of Vounn or House—"

"Thank you, Ashi," said Vounn. "That's enough. I don't think you've caused any trouble to Tariic." She nodded to Haruuc's emissary and for the first time, Ekhaas saw some of her charm slip through the dispassionate mask. Once again, she was amazed by Vounn. She'd backed Tariic into a corner. If he protested, Vounn could point out that it had been Ekhaas who really committed the crime of breaking into the memorial. All he could do was . . .

"It has been no trouble," Tariic said. "I apologize to you, Vounn. Allow me to pay for the repairs to the memorial."

"That isn't necessary, Tariic. The repairs are likely to be expensive. House Deneith can cover them."

Tariic's ears twitched back. "Darguun will pay," he insisted.

Vounn smiled. "The honor of the Darguuls speaks for itself."

Khaavolaar, Ekhaas thought. She wondered if Tariic realized that Vounn had just had him agree to restore a memorial commemorating a Deneith victory over the ancestors of Darguun. The lady seneschal was already gesturing for one of her men. "Fetch the station commander," she said. "Have him bring the keys to cell. We're ready to leave."

Their release was accomplished quickly. For all of the station commander's bluster that House Deneith was treated the same as anyone else under the law, it took only a few words from Vounn to get them out of the cell and any mention of the night's incident removed from the station's log books. Ashi's sword was returned to her, but there was no sign of the dagger Ekhaas had carried into the memorial. She supposed it was still there, lost in the shadows and indistinguishable from the much older weapons scattered during their fight.

Nor was there any sign of the reliquary. Ekhaas felt its loss more keenly. She was fairly certain that the station commander must have given it to Vounn, but the lady seneschal betrayed nothing. If it was in her possession, at least it was safe. Ekhaas kept her mouth closed. They were too close to getting away to worry about the reliquary for the moment. She and Ashi walked out of the watch station side by side behind Tariic and Vounn. Ekhaas managed to sneak a reassuring glance at her friend—though Ashi looked more bad-tempered than reassured—then they were separated as Tariic and Vounn bid each other good night. Two carriages waited outside the watch station. Vounn and Ashi got into one, Tariic and Ekhaas into the other. Their various guards fell in behind.

The interior of the carriage was dark, but the lack of light only drained color from hobgoblin vision. As the carriage jerked into motion, Tariic fell back into the seat and let the tight control slip from his face. *"Maabet!"* he spat, lapsing into Goblin. "What are you playing at, Ekhaas? This isn't going to help our mission. What were you thinking?"

Ekhaas stayed sitting upright. "I thought that I was rescuing a part of our people's heritage," she said. "I wouldn't have been caught. If it had been anyone else, I could have stopped them and got away, but Ashi's Siberys Mark of Sentinel resists most of my magic—"

"A Siberys Mark?" Tariic sat up. "Is that what you were trying to warn me about? Vounn didn't mention her charge carried a Siberys Mark." He frowned. "I remember your tale of the Shadow Marches and the mad dragon. If she carries the Siberys Mark, then isn't she . . . ?"

"She's my friend." Ekhaas met Tariic's gaze. "And Geth's friend, too—and now she's become Vounn's charge. That's why I signaled you. I didn't want you to insult her or get her into more trouble."

Tariic looked at her for a moment, then sat back. "Vounn's charge and Geth's friend. This . . . could be useful."

Ekhaas nodded. "That's what I thought."

CHAPTER SIX

The arrival of a maid in her bed-chamber broke Ashi's restless sleep. She raised her head and glared at the woman who stood, frozen, in the doorway. "What is it?"

The maid swallowed. "Lady Seneschal Vounn wants to see you, Lady Ashi. She says for you to wash, dress, and come to her immediately." She moved to put down the tray she was carrying.

The anger that had kept Ashi tossing since she and Vounn had returned to Sentinel Tower and Vounn had ordered her to her rooms—with a guard posted outside the door to be sure she stayed there—came back with fresh heat. She sat up and growled, "Take a message back. Tell Vounn I'm not going anywhere on her say so."

The maid frozen once again, tray hovering a handspan above a chest. "Lady Ashi—?"

"You heard what I said." Ashi flung back the bed clothes and stood. Her hands clenched into fists. "Now get out!"

The tray dropped with a clatter and the maid dashed from the chamber. A moment later, the outer door of Ashi's sitting room opened, then slammed shut. Ashi straightened her shift and stomped over to the tray. Hot water from a tall pitcher had splashed out, soaking towels and leaving a basket of breakfast rolls sitting in a puddle. Ashi plucked out one of the rolls and tore into it with her teeth.

She'd followed Ekhaas's advice, apologized to Vounn, and what had it gained her? Maybe a shorter lecture at the watch station. The carriage ride back to Sentinel Tower had been utterly silent. Not a word had passed between her and her mentor. If Vounn wanted to cut into her now over the previous night's misadventure, Ashi wasn't going to give her the satisfaction of going meekly before her. Vounn's apartments were close. She could come deliver her lectures in person. Soon enough, she heard the outer door open and close again. Ashi turned to face Vounn as the lady seneschal advanced across the sitting room, her face like a storm cloud.

"What are you doing?" she demanded. "Get dressed!"

"I don't think I will." Ashi ripped a chunk from another roll. "Come out with it, Vounn. Tell me what you want to say about last night. I know there's something."

Vounn's cheeks turned red. "Oh, there is," she said, "but this isn't the time for it. Tariic has asked for an early meeting. We can only keep him waiting so long." She went to Ashi's wardrobe and flung it open.

Ashi whirled and slammed it shut again. "Get out of there! I don't care if Tariic wants an early meeting. Stop treating me like a child."

"I'll stop treating you like a child when you stop acting like one!" Vounn glared, so close that Ashi could feel the hot breath of her words. "You're not a savage living in a swamp anymore. You have responsibilities now, and you are going to have to accept them."

"I had responsibilities in the Bonetree," Ashi growled back at her. "I was a hunter. I brought food to the clan. I defended my people."

"And now you're an heir of Deneith. You'll bring wealth to the House and defend our honor with your behavior. Get dressed or I'll call the House guards and drag you with me in your shift." Vounn stepped back, crossing her arms. "You wouldn't be leaving this room for a fortnight if Tariic hadn't asked that you come with me this morning."

Ashi had almost been ready to tackle Vounn and drag her down to the floor for a beating that would have earned cheers among the Bonetree, but the other woman's final words made her stop. "He what?" she asked, a faint hint of curiosity filtering through the red haze that clouded her mind.

Vounn raised an eyebrow. "When I said *we* can only keep Tariic waiting so long, I meant it. Tariic requested a meeting with both me and you." She looked down her nose. "Trust me, I wouldn't be taking you if I didn't think I had to."

"Why would he want to see both of us?"

"I don't know, but I imagine it has something to do with last night. Are you going to get dressed, or do you want to try strangling me first?"

Ashi looked down at her hands. Her fingers were curled and tensed. She would happily have strangled Vounn, but now she also wanted to know what Tariic wanted with her. She forced her hands to relax and reached instead for the pitcher of warm water the maid had brought.

"Don't think this is over," she told Vounn.

"Don't worry," said the lady seneschal.

A short time later, they were walking down one of the corridors that led from the inner halls of Sentinel Tower to its middle zone. Ashi's face and hair were still damp, and the motion of their swift passage was cool on her skin.

"This is what I expect will happen," Vounn said as they walked. "Tariic will thank us for coming and apologize for requesting a meeting at such an early hour and outside of the usual agenda. I'll accept, of course. We'll exchange the usual pleasantries, then Tariic will get to the reason for the meeting: a further apology for last night. It was one of his people who actually started the chain of events, so it's on him to make amends."

Vounn sounded exceptionally pleased with herself. "He gave us words last night, so if he wants to make a greater gesture today, he'll need to raise the stakes. We'll be in an excellent position to put more of what we want in front of him. A better price per head for Darguul mercenaries. More elite fighters, I think—a few units of tiger cavalry would find high demand. Tariic might even agree to put us in touch with the Silent Clans—"

Ashi felt as though she wasn't even there. "The what?" she said, forcing her way into Vounn's conversation with herself.

The lady seneschal looked back at her as if the question had emerged from a block of particularly dense stone. "Goblin clans with lineages extending back into antiquity. There are two of them—the *shaarat'khesh,* the Silent Blades, and the *taarka'khesh,* the Silent Wolves. They're scouts and shadow fighters, bred to stealth. Haruuc is on good terms with them, but they don't align themselves with any faction in Darguun and will work for any clan willing to hire them. They have a lot in common with Deneith, actually. We could broker their services to Khorvaire at large."

"They sound like assassins," said Ashi.

"Remember your lessons," Vounn said, her mouth tightening. "House Deneith doesn't hire out assassins. The Silent Clans are scouts and shadow fighters."

Ashi lifted one eyebrow. "Ah." she said. "Scouts and shadow fighters. So what do you expect I'll be doing in this meeting with Tariic?"

"I expect that you will be standing still and speaking only when spoken to. Even better, you'll speak only when I give you leave to speak. We have Tariic in a corner. I don't want to give him any excuse to slip out."

Ashi raised her other eyebrow. "When you put an animal in a corner, it gets angry and dangerous."

"That's why once Tariic has made his offer, I'll give him this as a token of good faith."

Vounn unfolded one hand from the long, loose sleeve that had covered it and held up the gold and iron reliquary of Duural Rhuvet. Both of Ashi's eyebrows went up together. *"Rond betch!* Do you—"

"Language, Ashi!"

Ashi bit into her words, then said through her teeth, "Do you know what that is, Vounn?"

"No," the older woman admitted, "but does it matter? Clearly it's something the Darguuls want. Thief and merchant both take your money, but a merchant gives you change and invites you to come back."

They approached a door with House guards standing to each side, and Vounn slipped the reliquary back into her sleeve. "Remember," she said, "speak when spoken to, and behave yourself." She looked Ashi up and down. "Do this right and you might be forgiven—after all, if it wasn't for your foolishness, we might not have this opportunity."

"I'm so pleased I could help."

One of the guards opened the door. Vounn and Ashi stepped through, and the door closed behind them.

The room on the other side was plain by the standards of House Deneith: dark-paneled walls with only a few trophies hung on them, a simple fireplace with only a few pieces of silver plate positioned on the mantle, and an ordinary heavy table with only a light pattern of fine Eldeen carvings twining up the legs. Four chairs had been drawn up to the table. In one of them sat Tariic. In the other, to Ashi's surprise, sat Ekhaas. The *duur'kala* caught her eye, gave the slightest of nods, then looked away.

There were no guards—Deneith or Darguul—in the room. Tariic rose like a gentleman and held out one of the chairs for Vounn. "Thank you for agreeing to meet with me on such short notice, Lady Vounn," he said as she seated herself. "I'm sorry for taking up your time outside the schedule of our official visit. I hope you're well this morning."

Vounn's expression was gracious, but Ashi knew that on the inside she wore an expression as smug as a well-fed cat. "The schedule of an official visit seldom survives intact after the first meeting," she said. "Please call me Vounn, Tariic. There's no need for titles here. We're not on parade."

The hobgoblin smiled and returned to the other side of the table. "As you say." He turned his smile on Ashi as she took the last chair. "Ashi," he said by way of greeting.

It was only a single word, just her name, but there was something in the way that Tariic said it, something in the way his expressive ears stood up as he spoke, that roused Ashi's instincts. She might have felt the same way during a hunt if a lone bird had flown up from a stand of still reeds or if sudden silence had fallen over stretch of marshland. Her skin prickling, she glanced at

Ekhaas and found her friend watching her out of the corner of her eye. Ashi sat back in her chair. "Tariic," she said, but he had already turned back to Vounn.

"I'd like to apologize again for Ekhaas's actions last night. Attempting to steal from your memorial is inexcusable, but as they say, a stone can hide a treasure." Tariic put his hands flat on the table. "After last night, Vounn, I find I have a respect for you that might otherwise have come only after days of meetings. You act with a particular honor that is rare among humans."

Ashi saw some of the unease that she felt register in Vounn's eyes. This didn't, she realized, sound like the humble apology the lady seneschal had predicted. Vounn's voice, however, remained steady and unconcerned. "Thank you, Tariic. I'm flattered."

He shook his head. "It's not flattery, only the truth. And because of it, there is something I want to discuss with you now that I wouldn't otherwise have raised until the end of my time here." He reached inside the doublet he wore and produced a small, tightly wound scroll that had been sealed with black wax. "By the wish of my uncle, Lhesh Haruuc Shaarat'kor, I invite you to attend his court as a permanent ambassador of House Deneith. My soldiers and I are to be your escort to Rhukaan Draal."

Ashi started in surprise at the offer. Vounn, for a long moment, sat very still and very silent. Anyone else might have missed it, but Ashi knew there was turmoil behind that frozen mask. Vounn had worked long and hard to bring the Darguuls into negotiations with Deneith, and now Haruuc was inviting her to his court as an ambassador. It was everything Vounn could have dreamed of, a chance to advance both her status with House Deneith and the cause of Deneith with the Darguuls.

And, Ashi realized abruptly, it was everything she could have hoped for as well. Surely Vounn wouldn't take her to Darguul. She'd be free of her mentor! But Vounn's silence stretched out until Ashi couldn't stand it anymore. She leaned toward her and whispered "Vounn . . ."

The lady seneschal's eyes flickered with flame. "Sit back, Ashi," she ordered under her breath, then looked at Tariic. "There's already a representative of Deneith in Darguun," she said as clearly and confidently as if she were discussing the purchase of a horse. "Viceroy Redek d'Deneith."

"Redek is based at the Gathering Stone fortress two days ride outside Rhukaan Draal," said Tariic. "Deneith's outpost in the crown city is little more than a recruiting center. Haruuc wishes to draw the ties between Deneith and Darguun closer. He wants an ambassador from his greatest ally to be part of his court—a councilor and not just a trader in mercenaries." He held out the scroll.

Vounn considered the spooled paper but didn't accept it. Instead, she asked, "Why? And why now? The representatives of dragonmarked houses aren't usually granted ambassador status—that's a title for the representatives of other nations."

Tariic flicked his ears and shrugged. "Call it something else if your prefer. These are my uncle's words, though: Darguun has done well by House Deneith. Even when we turned on them, Deneith was the first to make peace with us and the first to support Darguun as a new nation. They are a true friend, and their voice deserves to be heard." He gestured with the scroll. "I believe that's repeated on here."

"It doesn't answer the question of why now," said Vounn. "I've been dealing with your uncle's court for years, Tariic. This is the first hint that I've heard of a wish to give Deneith a bigger voice, and it comes strangely on the heels of the very sudden and unexpected decision to send you here." She sat forward. "True friends deserve to know everything that's going on. What's really going through Haruuc's mind?"

Tariic bared his teeth at her blunt confrontation. His ears bent back and his grip on the sealed scroll shifted. If it had been a weapon, Ashi would have said he was ready to strike with it. She tensed, ready to defend herself and—reluctantly—Vounn. Her mentor, however, didn't flinch. She just kept her eyes on Tariic, and after a moment, his snarling lips stretched back into a hard grin. "You'll do well in Rhukaan Draal, Vounn."

"I haven't agreed to go yet," she told him. "Why does Haruuc really want an ambassador from Deneith at his court?"

"He's getting old," Tariic said simply. He set the scroll down on the table and sat back in his chair. "He was a young warrior when he led the uprising that created Darguun, but that was thirty years ago. He's not going to be on the throne forever and he knows it. He's going to have to name a successor soon, and when he does, he wants to be sure that Deneith's relationship with his successor is as strong as it is with him. Darguun needs Deneith. Our trade with other nations is still developing—practically the only thing we export is mercenaries."

"And why me?" asked Vounn. "Redek is already in Darguun, and as you say, he's a fine trader in mercenaries."

Tariic's dark skin darkened even further. "You cut hard, Vounn. *Ban,* Redek is a good businessman, but he's hardly known outside of Darguun. Haruuc wants you because people—*powerful* people—across Khorvaire know your name. The friendship of Deneith has given Darguun legitimacy. If you know and can speak for Haruuc's chosen successor, it will give him legitimacy in the eyes of the rulers of Khorvaire as well." He bent his head. "Haruuc wants Deneith's public support. Does that answer your questions?"

Vounn sat silent for a long moment, then she bent her head in return. "Admirably." Her face was still neutral, but Ashi could read the triumph in her movements as she reached out and took the scroll from the table. Ashi's heart rose as well and she fought to keep the joy she felt inside as Vounn continued. "The matter will need to go before the patriarch for his blessing, but surely—"

Ekhaas, who had sat silent through the entire conversation, cleared her throat. "There is one other thing."

Vounn stopped and looked at her, but Tariic was the one who added an explanation. "Haruuc would very much like for you to bring Ashi along. He has heard of your training of her and would like to meet the bearer of the Siberys Mark of Sentinel."

Ashi's joy sputtered like a candle's flame, then leaped even higher. The idea of being out from under Vounn's thumb was one thing, but the possibility of traveling again, of leaving Karrlakton to see Darguun and meet Lhesh Haruuc was something else. She looked to Vounn—

—just as her mentor slowly shook her head. "I'm sorry. That isn't possible. Ashi can't be allowed to leave Sentinel Tower until her training is complete."

"Vounn!"

The word burst from her in a cry of fury and anguish, but Vounn didn't even acknowledge it. Ekhaas and Tariic both looked at her sharply, however, before Tariic turned back to Vounn. "I understand Ashi's value to your House. I can assure you that she'll be safe. I guarantee it. My uncle will guarantee it."

"I don't doubt it," Vounn said. "But the fact is that Ashi can't be trusted to go. You saw how she acted last night."

Ekhaas's ears rose. "I know how she acted last night. I also know how she acted before she came to House Deneith. You've tried to make a lady out of a savage, Vounn d'Deneith, but you've only made a girl out of a woman."

Vounn looked at her again, her eyes hard. "Who are you?" she demanded.

"Ekhaas!" said Tariic sharply. Ekhaas didn't sit back, but she closed her mouth and said nothing more.

Understanding grew in Vounn's eyes, however. "The hobgoblin from Ashi's adventures," she said. "I should have realized. Did Haruuc send you as a companion for Ashi?"

"Ekhaas's role in my delegation is my concern alone." Tariic spoke with steel in his voice. "You know how exceptional this invitation is, Vounn. Haruuc wouldn't withdraw it. He can't withdraw it without being shamed. He wouldn't, however, look kindly on having a simple request denied. Is that how you want your tenure in his court to begin?" His voice softened. "She doesn't have to stay. Haruuc only wants to meet her. A time of change is coming for Darguun, Vounn. Don't you want to have an honored place at the center of that change?"

Once again, Vounn was still and silent. This time, Ashi didn't say anything. Neither did Tariic or Ekhaas. After a time, Vounn lifted her head and looked Tariic in the eye.

"I'm pleased to accept Lhesh Haruuc's invitation to join his court," she said coolly, "provided that Baron Breven d'Deneith grants me permission to go. The patriarch will also need to give his permission for Ashi d'Deneith to accompany me." Vounn rose, then paused. "In exchange for the favor that Lhesh Haruuc has shown me, I present a token of my esteem for him."

She set the reliquary on the table. Ashi thought Ekhaas's eyes might roll right out of her head. Vounn, however, didn't stop to appreciate the triumph of her gesture. She turned and marched to the door. "Ashi!"

Her heart racing with excitement, Ashi flashed Ekhaas a quick smile and went after her mentor.

"Vounn," she murmured as they swept past the guards and along the hall back to the inner zone of Sentinel Tower, "thank you."

"Tell *no one* what happened in that room," said Vounn without looking at her. "Don't thank me again. And don't go against me before we go or I'll find a way to leave you here if it means crippling you."

"Yes, Vounn." Ashi bent her head so that the lady seneschal wouldn't see her smile. Now she understood why Ekhaas had urged her to apologize to Vounn at the watch station the night before.

Then she almost stumbled over her feet as she realized something else from her conversation with the *duur'kala.* She froze in the corridor, thinking it through.

"Ashi!" snapped Vounn from ahead.

"Coming," Ashi said and hurried to catch up. Her mind was still working though. Ekhaas hadn't known until last night that Vounn was her mentor—she hadn't known that Ashi was in Karrlakton at all. If she hadn't known, how had Haruuc? Or did he know?

Ekhaas and Tariic had just lied to them.

CHAPTER SEVEN

The official meetings between the delegation from Darguun and House Deneith carried on for another week. While Ekhaas watched for Ashi, she didn't see her again. Vounn was, of course, at every meeting, from the most mundane to the purely ceremonial. Ekhaas suspected that she was deliberately keeping Ashi in seclusion, maybe as a way of venting her frustration at being forced into bringing her charge to Haruuc's court. The lady seneschal's frustration showed at the meeting tables too. Every draft agreement that came before her was negotiated as if it were the Treaty of Thronehold or as if Vounn were not about to depart for a position where she would have Haruuc's ear and the ability to influence any dispute that might arise. Tariic said nothing about it, however, so neither could Ekhaas, stuck at the back of any gathering of delegates as she was. Officially nothing more than a representative of the interests of the Kech Volaar in Tariic's delegation, her lips were sealed and her hands tied.

Of Haruuc's invitation to Vounn, nothing more was said. For all that Vounn revealed, the small scroll might never have been delivered. Ekhaas felt like she might chew a hole in her table as she waited through meeting after meeting. On the next to last day before they were due to leave Karrlakton, Tariic, Vounn, and Baron Breven d'Deneith, patriarch of the house, emerged from a private discussion to make the grand announcement that Vounn would become Deneith's envoy to the court of Lhesh Haruuc Shaarat'kor. The excitement that swept Sentinel Tower was astounding. Within an hour, the Darguuls of Tariic's party went from being looked upon with suspicion to being greeted as allies. Ekhaas overheard more than one conversation declaring Vounn would be remembered as the new Jannes d'Deneith, responsible for bringing even greater wealth and influence to the House.

There was no word of whether Ashi would be joining Vounn, though. As soon as she had a chance, Ekhaas slipped up behind Tariic as he mingled at a reception. She didn't even need to ask the question—as soon as she caught Tariic's eye, he nodded and mouthed, "She's coming," before turning away to chat with some Karrn junior underminister of harvests. Ekhaas felt as if a yoke had been lifted from her shoulders.

Or at least as if one yoke had been lifted. Others still weighed her down, and they'd still be there through another week.

The Darguuls departed Karrlakton on the twenty-second day of the month of Lharvion with as much spectacle and ceremony as when they had arrived. They formed up in a courtyard near one of Sentinel Tower's wide gates, and Ekhaas finally caught a glimpse of Ashi. Her friend, shrouded again in her ever-present scarf, stood quietly behind Tariic and Vounn. After a pretty speech by Breven d'Deneith, the trio climbed into an open carriage. To the cheers of House Deneith, their procession—led by House guards from Sentinel Tower marching alongside a unit of the Karrlakton watch—paraded out into the city and through the streets toward the ship that waited in the harbor. As they went, increasing numbers of people came out to stare at the goblins, hobgoblins, and bugbears with their flashing armor and thunderous war music. The tigers of the cavalry probably would have drawn even more awestruck excitement from the crowd, but they had already been taken down to the ship, along with any baggage, during the quiet of the night. At some point the crowd of city-dwellers began cheering Tariic as well, and he waved at them from his carriage. They likely, Ekhaas suspected, had no idea whom they were cheering for, but they cheered anyway.

At the harbor, more officials of Deneith and even some of Karrlakton waited to make more farewell speeches. Tariic and Vounn stood to accept them while soldiers and councilors shifted with poorly disguised impatience. Eventually, however, they were all on board the ship and lines were being cast off. The ship's captain, a half-elf of House Lyrandar, called hands to stations, then gripped the ship's wheel. From where she stood on the deck, Ekhaas saw a look of concentration cross his face as he invoked the dragonmark of his house. The morning air stirred in response and the sails of the ship filled. They began to move, and Karrlakton fell away behind them.

The first part of their journey lay west along the long arm of Scion's Sound that formed the border between Karrnath and what had once been Cyre but was now only the Mournland, blasted and cursed in the final days of the Last War. The captain kept his ship as close to the Karrnathi coast as possible without grounding her, but the arm of the sound was narrow and the unmoving bank of dead gray mist that cloaked the Mournland loomed over them. From time to time, weird cries and howls echoed out of the mist, provoking answering snarls from the tigers caged below deck. More substantial and threatening things had been known to emerge from the mists, and every Darguul soldier on the ship stood at the rail, eyes on the mist, ears raised, hands on weapons.

Ekhaas stood with them, all the tales of the Mournland that she'd ever heard running through her mind. When a quiet footfall came on the deck behind her, she barely noticed it. When Ashi whispered her name, she all but jumped. *"Khaavolaar!"*

"Sorry," said Ashi. "Can I join you?"

She'd changed, Ekhaas noted, out of the formal robes she'd worn in the carriage and into clothes like those she'd worn the night they'd encountered each other at the memorial. Her scarf was loosened to show her face, and her sword was on her hip. She was ready to fight if necessary.

"Does Vounn know you're up here?" Ekhaas asked her.

"She's in her cabin," said Ashi. It didn't really answer the question, but Ekhaas suspected it was as close to "no" as Ashi was willing to go. She made room for Ashi at the rail, and for a time they watched in silence as the mist glided past.

Eventually Ashi spoke. "You lied," she said. "Haruuc hasn't asked to see me."

They were the words Ekhaas had been expecting—and dreading—for the last week. She'd known Ashi would figure out the flaw in their plan sooner or later. Her ears folded back and she said, "He was curious about you when he heard my story of Dah'mir and the Master of Silence. He did say he'd like to meet the bearer of a Siberys Mark."

"That's not the same thing."

"Have you told Vounn?"

Ashi turned and looked at her. "If I'd told Vounn, do you think I'd be here? She hasn't let me out of the inner halls of Sentinel Tower for the last week, though, or I would have asked you about it before this. What's going on?"

Ekhaas didn't want to lie to her friend, but she couldn't tell her the truth. Not yet. Fortunately, Vounn's stubbornness had given her time to work out what she could say. "Do you want to go to Darguun?"

"Blood in your mouth, yes! You know I was going mad stuck in Sentinel Tower." Her eyes narrowed. "You didn't do this just to give me a chance to get out, did you? You couldn't have—you had Tariic working with you." She paused for a moment as she thought, then added, "You're not just here as a representative of your clan."

Ekhaas cursed silently. Ashi could be uncommonly perceptive sometimes. She stuck with what she had planned to tell her, though. "Ashi, finding you in Karrlakton was an opportunity that Tariic and I couldn't let pass. Having you here is important, or we wouldn't have used Haruuc's name to make sure it happened. We'll explain soon, though. By the Blood of Six Kings, you have my word on it."

Ashi grimaced. "How soon?"

"Soon. That's all I can say."

Breath hissed between Ashi's teeth. "I trust you, Ekhaas. I don't like not knowing what's happening, but I trust you. I am really going to Darguun, aren't I?"

"You're really going to Darguun," Ekhaas said with a smile. "And you will really meet Haruuc, too. We may have lied to get you there, but I promise that he'll be happy to see you."

"Good." Ashi started to turn away, then looked back. "Is his invitation for Vounn to join his court real or is it a lie, too?"

"It's real."

Ashi grimaced again. "Too bad."

The arm of the sound opened up late the following afternoon, and they sailed beyond sight of the gray mist of the Mournland. The mood on the ship lightened immediately, at least for the soldiers and crew. Ekhaas found herself exchanging glances with Tariic almost every time they passed each other. The time when they would have to reveal the whole truth of their visit to Sentinel Tower was approaching.

On the fourth day out from Karrlakton, they made harbor at Flamekeep in the nation of Thrane and the first leg of their journey was over. Officials wearing tabards with the silver crest of flame and sword boarded the ship to inspect their credentials. The ship's captain and crew, Vounn, and Ashi were left largely alone while the officials focused their attention on the Darguuls. They'd had the same experience on their initial voyage to Karrlakton. Ekhaas held her tongue with difficulty, but she could see that even Tariic had little patience for the Thranes' probing questions.

Eventually the officials ran out of reason to delay them, but there was one final indignity they could inflict. A squad of soldiers was summoned, and the delegation that had been cheered in Karrlakton was escorted under guard, packs on their shoulders and caged tigers on hand-drawn wagons, through the streets of Flamekeep to their destination at the lightning rail station.

Ekhaas's ears quivered with fury as she marched. "Incredible," she snarled at Ashi, walking beside her. "Once we ruled an empire that spanned this continent, and now we have to fight to be recognized as a nation by these . . . these . . ."

"Chaat'oor?" Ashi offered.

"Chaat'oor!" Ekhaas said.

To one side of the street, a stick-thin merchant raised her voice as if offering her opinions as much to the Darguuls as to the other Thranes around her. "Darguun? A nation of goblins? What filth! Flame forgive me, but you can't civilize the uncivilized—Treaty of Thronehold be damned!"

A murmur of anger rose from the Darguuls who had heard and understood the comment. Ekhaas bared her teeth. "Uncivilized?" she said, her voice rising. *"Maabet,* the vaults of the Kech Volaar hold records and artifacts of a civilization that was old when your ancestors were splashing around in boats trying to get here!"

Ashi took Ekhaas's arm, urging her onward. "You're going to start a brawl. You know not every human thinks of goblins that way, Ekhaas."

It was all Ekhaas could do not to shake her friend's hand off. "Really? Did you ever wonder where that word or where the names you call our races come from? Before humans came to Khorvaire, we called ourselves *dar*—the people. Hobgoblins were *ghaal'dar,* the mighty people. Bugbears—what kind of name is that?—were *guul'dar,* the strong people. Goblins were *golin'dar,* the quick people." Her ears bent down. "And they were the ones that humans met first. Your people mistook the name of our smallest race for the name of our entire people, and they didn't even get that right. Now many of us use your names for our three races instead of our own. Even I do it!"

She gave a bitter little laugh. The rant and the admission left her feeling drained. Ashi patted her shoulder awkwardly. "You know," she said as they turned a corner and the lightning rail station came into sight, "if I'm going to be in Darguun, I should learn to speak more of your language. *Ghaal'dar, guul'dar, golin'dar* . . . does 'Darguun' mean something in Goblin?"

"The land of the people."

"Does Darguul mean the same thing as *guul'dar* then?"

Ekhaas laughed again, but this time with genuine humor, and stood straight. "No. It just means someone from Darguun."

"Ah," said Ashi.

The *duur'kala* smiled. "And do you remember back in the watch station, when you said *shaat'aar* instead of *chaat'oor?"*

Ashi nodded.

"A *shaat'aar* is a kind of sweet bun with honey cream in the middle. They're different."

Above her scarf, Ashi's eyes lit up with a smile. "I'll say." She jerked her head back in the direction of the arrogant merchant. "I'll bet she hasn't had honey cream in her middle in a long time."

Ekhaas's laugh was so loud it brought the Thrane guards' heads—and Tariic's and Vounn's—around. Ekhaas, still chuckling, just waved at them.

Fortunately, the members of House Orien who were the staff and crew of the lightning rail system found a customer's money more important than their race. As soon as the soldiers of Thrane had delivered their charges, the station master saw to it that Tariic, Vounn, Ashi, and the other important members of the delegation were settled in the station's private lounge while water and food were brought for the common soldiers. Tariic had rented three private lightning rail carts on the northward journey and left them at the station for the return trip. While these were brought back around to wait for the next coach running south, the station master apologized profusely for their rude treatment at the hands of the port officials, insisting that House Orien would lodge a complaint.

They were enjoying a lunch of spicy Thrane cuisine when the shriek of a whistle signaled the arrival of a lightning rail coach. Flamekeep was the terminus of the line; the coach would reverse direction for the journey back south. Not long after the scream of the whistle, the coach came into the station, sliding grandly past the windows of the lounge. The distinctive humped shape of the crew cart was first, fins along its side still cracking with the power of the bound elemental that drove the rail. Passenger carts with eager faces pressed to the window and sealed cargo carts followed, the whole gradually slowing until it came to a stop with a last crackling sigh of dissipating energy. Within moments, the station was filled with passengers disembarking and porters rushing to unload cargo.

The station master appeared again. "We'll connect your carts as soon as the train is unloaded. The coach departs again at the seventh bell this evening, but you'll be able to board your carts whenever you wish."

There seemed to be a consensus among the delegation that they would prefer to wait several hours on board the cart rather than go back into the city. Ekhaas was certainly in agreement. Besides which, the carts—or at least the cart that Tariic had hired for himself and the other senior members of the delegation—were remarkably comfortable. When the time did finally come to board, she heard Ashi gasp as she climbed up into the cart.

"By Kol Korran's golden bath, this is amazing!"

"Stop staring, Ashi," said Vounn, pushing past. "You look like a peasant in a cathedral."

Ashi didn't stop staring, and Ekhaas couldn't blame her. The interior of the cart was as luxurious as a fine House Ghallanda inn, with thick carpets, soft couches, and cabinets of books and good wine. "Didn't you travel to Karrlakton on the lightning rail?" Ekhaas asked.

"Not like this," said Ashi.

"We travel as representatives of Darguun," Tariic said. "The lords of any other nation would travel in the same way. To accept less would only confirm everything people like that merchant say about us."

Other passengers on the southbound coach appeared over the course of the afternoon, settling into the passenger carts or waiting in the terminal until the coach was ready to depart. Together with Ashi, Ekhaas wandered the platform, peering into the other coaches and resolutely ignoring the hostile glares that many of the Thrane passengers directed at her. The Darguul soldiers had been settled into the two other private carts hired by Tariic. They traveled in far more modest conditions than the senior members of the delegation, especially the cavalry riders who shared a cart with their tiger mounts and the delegation's baggage. The great tigers dozed in their cages. Ashi studied them with a healthy respect, going right up to the bars before stepping back.

"I wouldn't want to face one of those in the middle of a battle," she said. She looked around. "There's a lot of room still in this cart. Couldn't Tariic have hired one less?"

"The tigers need space," Ekhaas lied. "No one wants to sleep too near a cage." So close and still not able to tell Ashi the truth! She gestured. "We should go back to our cart. It's almost time for the coach to depart."

Precisely at the seventh bell in the evening, the elemental bound to the crew cart snapped and crackled into activity. Leaning out the window of their cart, Ekhaas and Ashi saw the ring of lightning that was the manifestation of the elemental's power spitting and hissing around the crew cart. A shudder ran through the entire coach. On the platform, the station agent blew a last piercing whistle to signal that all passengers were aboard. The crew answered with a shriek from the coach's whistle. As smooth as milk poured from a pitcher, the carts of the coach began to move, sparks of lightning arcing between their undersides and the conductor stones laid out in a straight path below. They moved slowly at first, and the evening lights of Flamekeep crept by, but as the coach left the city behind, it gathered speed until they were fairly flying through the falling night.

They would take it, Ekhaas knew, all the way to Sterngate near the border of Breland and Zilargo, the homeland of the gnomes, before transferring to horses for the final journey to Rhukaan Draal—the lightning rail would carry them four times the distance of that final leg in only a quarter of the time.

But there would be, she knew as well, one interruption to their journey.

The first stop on the line south of Flamekeep was the city of Sigilstar, and when they arrived there in the middle of the next morning, Tariic summoned a station agent. "Have our carts disconnected from the coach," he said. "We'll stay overnight and take the morning coach tomorrow."

The station agent nodded and left. Vounn—and most of the senior Darguuls—looked at Tariic with puzzled expressions. The lady seneschal of Deneith, however, gave voice to their curiosity. "Why the delay?"

"We're waiting for someone," Tariic said. His gaze took in all of them. "Stay close to the carts. Someone pass that order to soldiers, too. No one is to go wandering off."

The Darguul carts were pulled out of the coach and towed by a small work cart off down a side line in the lightning rail yard. The day was hot, and the motionless carts rapidly grew warm in the sun. The distractions offered by the cart, well-stocked though it was, faded quickly and the members of the delegation were reduced to sitting around fanning themselves. Like the tigers in their cages, Ashi fell into a languid doze. Tariic and Vounn retreated to the private compartments that their rank afforded them. Ekhaas wished she could do the same, but the best she could manage was to sit in a sliver of the meager shade outside the cart and hope for a wind. Some of the Darguuls begged her for a tale from her store as a *duur'kala* to pass the time, and she put in a half-hearted effort. Inspired by the reliquary in her pack, she gave them a story of Duural Rhuvet and his battles against the nomadic halfling tribes that had harried the edges of the Dhakaani Empire as it faded into the lean centuries of the Desperate Times. Her enthusiasm grew in the telling of the tale, though, and when the story was over, she gave her audience another, then another, eating up the day. The soldiers lifted their ears to listen as well, and she told more tales, this time of the heroes of Dhakaan at its height—Kamvuul Norek, the slayer of illithids; Moorn Basha, who sang an island out of the sea; and Duulan Kuun, the first of the name Kuun and the hero who founded a line of heroes.

Night had fallen when she folded her hands and spoke the traditional words that finished the legends of Dhakaan, *"Raat shan gath'kal dor."* The story stops but never ends.

Her audience of soldiers and councilors—the entire Darguul delegation, in fact—sat in silence for a moment longer, then rose in twos and threes and began to drift away, back to their places in the carts. Ekhaas let out her breath and allowed herself a smile. Enraptured silence was one of the greatest tributes a *duur'kala* could hope for.

"I can see why my uncle seeks an alliance with the Kech Volaar," said a voice from above her. Ekhaas twisted around to find

Tariic leaning out of the open window of his compartment. "That was stirring."

Ekhaas's ears flicked. "We both know your uncle wants more than tales from the Kech Volaar."

"True, but I wouldn't underestimate the power of a good story, either." He nodded across the yard in which the carts had been left. Ekhaas turned and looked. In the direction he'd indicated stood three grubby goblins, wavering back and forth as if uncertain whether to approach. They weren't Darguuls. Ekhaas guessed that they must have been inhabitants of Sigilstar, probably employed at the lightning rail station in some menial job. She glanced over her shoulder to say something more to Tariic, but he had already left the window. She looked back to the three goblins and beckoned to them.

They came forward like nervous supplicants. The boldest of them dropped down to his knees in front of her, gesturing for the other two, maybe his sons, to do the same. "Thank you," he said to her. "It's been a long time since I heard anything so exciting." He spoke Goblin with a distinctly human accent. "We can't pay you for what we heard, but we want you to have these."

He held out a dirty cloth on which were piled three greasy bundles. Ekhaas's nose twitched at the smell of food. The bundles were likely the goblins' dinners. "You don't have to do that," she said. "I don't need to be paid."

The bold goblin looked at her, then at the bundles. He didn't lower the cloth. "They say you should always pay what something's worth. My Tunee, most people say she makes the best goblin food in Sigilstar. I think these might make a start at paying for your stories."

"Won't you be hungry tonight?"

"Your stories filled us up, *chib,*" said one of the other two, his big ears perking up.

Ekhaas smiled and took the bundles but returned the cloth. "I'll remember your kindness," she said.

The three goblins grinned as if one of the heroes from her stories had just come to life and thanked them. They stood up, dusted off their britches, and scampered back toward the lightning rail station, all the time grinning like fools. Ekhaas shook her head as she watched them go, then turned back to the cart.

Ashi crouched by the door, watching her. Ekhaas gave her a mock scowl and switched back to the human tongue. "I'm getting tired of people coming up behind me!"

"Sorry," said Ashi. "I was just waiting for you to finish. Those must have been some stories. I wish I could have followed them all."

"We need to start on your Goblin lessons then. Why don't we begin with food?" Ekhaas passed one of the greasy bundles to her.

They climbed up onto the roof of the cart, the better to catch the evening breeze. Four moons had risen above the horizon, casting enough light for Ashi to see what she was eating. Ekhaas, of course, could see the contents of the bundles with no difficulty, and as they were unwrapped, she taught Ashi the names for the food within and for the words associated with eating. The goblin had been right: His wife did make good food. The bundles contained chewy sausages pickled with bitter herbs, big steamed dumplings of starchy *noon* mash, eggs boiled in broth, and—to Ekhaas's surprise and Ashi's delight—tiny but sweet *shaat'aar.* They ate them all, sharing the third bundle between them, then sat and watched as a fifth moon, pale yellow Nymm, rose low in the southeast and began to climb up against the bright haze of the Ring of Siberys.

"The thing that you can't tell me about," Ashi said into the silence. "It's happening tonight, isn't it? That's why we've stopped here."

"It's supposed to happen tonight. We hope it happens tonight."

"And you still can't tell me anything more?"

Ekhaas shook her head. "No, not yet. But soon, I promise."

Out by the wall that surrounded the lightning rail yard, something moved. It was too far away for even Ekhaas to see clearly, but there was, for an instant, a brief eclipsing of the lights from the city over the top of the wall. Just a flicker. It might have been nothing at all. Ekhaas's breath caught in her throat, though, and she paused, watching.

"Ekhaas?" asked Ashi softly. She was alert and tense, staring after Ekhaas into the darkness. Her hand was on her sword. "Is something wrong?"

The flicker came again—and kept coming. One after another, dark bodies swarmed over the wall, caught briefly by the dim light before dropping again into shadow. Ashi whispered a curse and started to rise. Ekhaas grabbed her arm and held her down.

"Don't move," she said.

Ashi froze and sank back down into a crouch. Ekhaas crept to the edge of the cart and peered into the yard. Everything was as motionless and quiet as before, the silence broken by murmurs from the soldiers as they played some game and by crews laboring around the station. Beyond about twenty paces, she could see nothing more than Ashi, but the colorless nightvision of her people cut through the closer shadows. She watched and waited for the first hint of movement. The moment stretched out . . .

Then they were there, not just at the edge of her vision, but slipping out from behind another stationary lightning rail cart parked in the yard, so close that even Ashi could see them. Ekhaas heard her draw a sharp breath. She came close to gasping as well, and she had been expecting this.

A dozen black-clad goblins flowed through the moonlight like rats or ferrets.

"Who are they?" Ashi whispered.

"Shaarat'khesh and *taarka'khesh,"* said Ekhaas. "Goblins of the Silent Clans."

"The assassins?"

"When they need to be."

Sentries posted outside the delegation's carts looked studiously away. The goblins went to the third cart, the one that carried the tigers and that, as Ashi had observed, seemed so empty. One of them tapped a soft rhythm on the cargo door. A moment later, the door slid open and the goblins of the Silent Clans vanished into the cart. The door closed and they might never have been there at all, except for one goblin who remained outside—and looked up at Ekhaas and Ashi with glittering eyes in a dark stained face. They'd been seen. The goblin pointed at Ashi, his eyebrows and ears lifting in an unspoken question. Ekhaas nodded. The goblin turned back to the cart from behind which he and the others had emerged. He beckoned.

Another figure stepped into the moonlight, a shifter with a pack over one shoulder and the heavy shape of a hobgoblin sword at his side. Ashi started. "Geth?" she said, then "Geth!"

Before Ekhaas could say anything or even move, Ashi was on her feet and clambering down to the ground. Below, Geth stared, then ran to meet her. Ekhaas closed her eyes for a moment and let out a sigh of relief before climbing down the ladder as well. Inside the cart, the rest of the delegation was stirring in curiosity at the commotion outside. Ekhaas heard Tariic telling them to be calm and to remain in the cart.

He emerged just as she reached the ground. "So he's here," he said. "They found him."

"Did you doubt it?" Ekhaas asked.

"I sometimes doubted that they'd bring him in alive."

Ekhaas couldn't say anything to that. The same fear had nagged at her. She turned away and went to her friends, grateful that death hadn't been a necessity.

Ashi was talking more than Geth was, spilling her reasons for being in Sigilstar with a delegation of Darguuls and asking after him seemingly in the same breath. "What are you doing here? Where have you been? Where are Singe and Dandra?"

"Bear and Boar!" said Geth. "One question at a time! I wasn't expecting to find you here either." He pulled himself away from Ashi and gestured to the black-clad goblin who still stood by the lightning rail cart. "This is Chetiin. He's an elder of the *taarka'khesh.* Him and his people found me in Lathleer in Aundair. We almost fought until Chetiin explained why they'd come looking for me."

Chetiin bent his head to Ashi. He didn't say anything, but his eyes lingered on the lines of the dragonmark that patterned her face. She bent her head in return, but Ekhaas saw her self-consciously tug her scarf into place as she looked back to Geth. "What were you doing in Aundair? How did they find you?"

Ekhaas raised her voice. "I told them where to look," she said. Both shifter and human turned to her. She held her ears proudly stiff and reminded herself she'd done nothing wrong. "It's good to see you again, Geth."

Ashi and Geth both spoke at the same time, Geth greeting her with the same respect, Ashi staring and spitting out, "You? You knew he was coming? *Khyberit gentis,* why didn't you tell me?"

"I couldn't tell you," said Ekhaas. "I—"

"She had orders not to say anything about it," said Tariic as he joined them. "Not to you, not to anyone. What is happening is larger than your friendship. Chetiin, *ta muut.*"

"Cho, chib," said Chetiin. His voice was thick and strained like a scar. He spoke in the human language, following Ekhaas and Tariic's example. "It was a small task. Ekhaas *duur'kala's* magic guided us to the right area, and the *taarka'khesh* among my band were able to locate him easily enough. He travels quietly for someone not of the Silent Clans."

"High praise from you," Tariic said. He looked to the shifter. "Geth, I'm Tariic of Rhukaan Taash, nephew and emissary of Lhesh Haruuc Shaarat'kor."

"I know," said Geth. "Chetiin told me who you are."

"What else has Chetiin told you?"

Geth scratched the thick stubble on his chin. "Enough to persuade me to follow him and meet you. That Haruuc needed me"—his hand dropped to the ancient sword at his side—"and Wrath. That Ekhaas was involved, too, which is really why I came. He didn't say anything about Ashi."

"He didn't know about her," Ekhaas told him. "None of us did. Ashi wasn't part of our plans initially."

He gave her a long look. "I think it's time I heard more about these plans. Chetiin got me this far on your name, Ekhaas, but I didn't agree to go any farther until I know more. I'm not sure I like people making plans around me without asking first."

"I want to know what's going on, too," agreed Ashi.

"So," said Vounn, "would I."

The lady seneschal stood behind them, wrapped in a shawl against the night air. Her face, as ever, was expressionless, but her voice was firm.

Tariic scowled. "Didn't I tell you to wait in the cart?"

"You told your people to wait in the cart. Your authority doesn't extend to me." Her eyes narrowed. "Nor does it extend to my charge, yet it seems she's become part of something. Please, enlighten me."

"Who is this?" growled Geth.

"Geth, may I introduce Lady Seneschal Vounn d'Deneith, envoy of House Deneith to Lhesh Haruuc," said Tariic tightly. "Lady Vounn, Geth."

"She's my mentor," added Ashi.

Geth looked Vounn up and down and grunted.

Vounn's lips pressed together. "Another figure from Ashi's past," she said.

Color rushed into Ashi's face. "He's my friend!"

"And mine," said Ekhaas.

"He may be the one person," said Tariic, his ears twitching, "who can prevent the collapse of Darguun when Haruuc dies."

CHAPTER EIGHT

For a heartbeat, all Geth—and Ashi and Vounn as well, it seemed—could do was stare at Haruuc's nephew, then his voice came back and he blurted out, "I may be *what?*"

Ashi looked like she had words ready to burst out of her as well, but Vounn silenced her with a sharp hiss before looking to Tariic. "Explain this," she said. Her voice could have frozen a river.

Tariic gestured for them to move farther away from the lightning rail carts, and they followed him, Chetiin joining their group. When they were out into the yard and safely away from being overheard, Tariic folded his arms across his chest and said, "There is a succession crisis in Darguun."

"You said Haruuc hadn't chosen his successor yet," said Vounn.

"He hasn't—or if he has, he hasn't revealed it to anyone. That hasn't stopped rumors, though, and there are a number of people and groups trying to position themselves for power." His ears pressed back. "My uncle has indicated to me—and to a few others—that *who* takes power after him may not be as important as *how.*"

Ekhaas took over, and Geth heard her slip into the tones of a performing *duur'kala.* "The history of our people teaches us that we ourselves are the greatest threat to a stable nation. Before Jhazaal Dhakaan united the six kings and laid the foundations of the empire, we fought among ourselves. When the empire fell and the Desperate Times came, clan fought against clan once more. After millennia, Haruuc has united some of the clans again—enough of them that Darguun stands among the other nations of Khorvaire. But not all of the clans have pledged themselves to Haruuc. Some of the lowland Ghaal'dar clans still stand apart. Many of the Marguul clans of the highlands are restless. The clans under the mountains who have preserved the traditions of Dhakaan largely stand apart, though Haruuc draws closer to an alliance with the Kech Volaar."

She spread her hands. "Even many of those clans who have followed Haruuc as lhesh do so only because of his strength and the force of his personality. Haruuc grows old and knows he grows old. What will happen when his power passes to another? Will the clans accept his successor, or will they fight to put one of their own on the throne? Will the alliances Haruuc has forged stand, or will Darguun pass as Dhakaan passed, collapsing into the chaos of clan war?" Her hands squeezed closed as if strangling hope. "Haruuc wants to avoid that future. He wants his legacy to his people to survive. He wants Darguun to prosper."

Geth found himself caught up in her words and imagining the collapse of a nation. It wasn't difficult—the Last War had plunged all of Khorvaire into conflict for a hundred years as rival heirs fought for the throne of the ancient kingdom of Galifar. Darguun was only one nation and a young one, but he could understand the threat it faced. Still . . .

"Tiger's blood, how am I supposed to stop a war?"

"You don't have to stop a war, only help Haruuc support his successor," said Tariic. He unfolded one hand and gestured to Vounn. "House Deneith is doing much the same thing. Their good relationship with a successor will keep wealth flowing to Darguun while their support will give legitimacy to his reign in the eyes of the Five Nations."

"Deneith is a dragonmarked house. I'm just one person!"

Tariic nodded. "And Haruuc has a task that just one person—the bearer of Wrath—can accomplish."

Caution stirred inside Geth. "What kind of task?" he asked, but Tariic shook his head.

"I can't tell you," he said. "Partly because I know that Haruuc wants to tell you himself. Partly because"—he shrugged—"partly because I only know the beginning of it. No one knows what will happen after that."

"Geth," said Ekhaas, "I told you once that Wrath is the sword of heroes. What Haruuc will ask of you is the task of a hero, but you won't have to do it alone. I'll be with you. And so will others."

"Me," said Chetiin. Geth looked down at the goblin. His dark stained face was serious.

"And me!" said Ashi. Everyone looked at her. Her eyes were shining and there was a wide, enthusiastic grin across her face. Her hand dropped to her sword and she squeezed the hilt. *"Rond betch,* you're not doing anything without me!"

"What?" Vounn's voice cracked like a whip. "Ashi, you're not doing anything!" She stepped forward, high spots of color appearing in her cheeks, and faced Tariic. "Was this your 'plan' for her?"

Tariic bared his teeth at the confrontation. "No!" he said. He looked sharply at Ashi. "Our only plan was for her to act as a cover for Geth because they already knew each other."

Ashi's grin faded slightly, but the color in Vounn's cheeks only grew more intense. "A cover?" she asked.

"There's already unrest in Darguun," Tariic answered. "As Ekhaas said, not every clan fully accepted Haruuc's rule. Some of them are already stirring up trouble again, and some of the groups that want to succeed Haruuc aren't much better. Haruuc wants Geth brought into Darguun quietly so they don't take his need for him as a sign of weakness. That's why he called on the Silent Clans to find and fetch him while we carried on to Karrlakton and met with you. If he agrees to come, Geth will return to Darguun with us in the guise of Ashi's bodyguard. None of Haruuc's rivals will suspect anything."

"You couldn't have known that Ashi would be permitted to come."

"In which case Geth would have posed as your bodyguard."

The ice returned to Vounn's voice. "It almost seems," she said, "as if Deneith is merely a convenience for you in this. No wonder your journey to Sentinel Tower was so abrupt."

Geth could see the unspoken curse that flickered behind Tariic's eyes before the hobgoblin answered. "Vounn, Haruuc just saw that the timing was right to fight two battles with one army. Deneith and you are important for all the reasons I've already said."

"Indeed," said Vounn, her eyes flashing, "and it seems for our ability to act as a cover as well. As I've already said to you, true friends deserve to know everything that's going on. Is there anything else you wish to tell me?"

Tariic spoke through clenched teeth. "There's nothing else I can tell you except that we'll be meeting someone else at our last lightning rail stop in Sterngate. Don't worry. He's traveling openly and has nothing to do with you."

"Then we'll say nothing more about this until we reach Rhukaan Draal and I can raise the issue with Haruuc. He appears to be the one holding your reins. Good evening, Tariic. Ashi, come with me." She turned and marched to the lightning rail cart. After a few paces, she looked back over her shoulder. "Ashi!"

Ashi's face was split between a fierce anger and a frightened obedience. "Vounn, I want to stay. My friends—"

"Ashi," Vounn said quietly, "it's not too late to send you back to Karrlakton—and at this moment I am willing to suffer Haruuc's displeasure by doing so. Come with me or you'll be waiting for the next northbound coach."

The color drained from Ashi's face. Geth couldn't have said whether it was because of anger or out of fear at being left behind. With a last longing glance at him and Ekhaas, Ashi went stalking off after Vounn.

"Maabet!" said Tariic under his breath. "That one's going to be trouble."

"A dragon like that deserves her own lair," Chetiin told Geth. "You can sleep in the cart with the Silent Clans during the journey to Sterngate if you prefer."

Geth blinked. "I haven't said I'm going."

"Aren't you?"

Geth looked at Tariic and Ekhaas, both of them with their eyes now turned to him. He grimaced. "Grandfather Rat," he said, "this hero thing is ridiculous." He pointed after Ashi and Vounn. "I'm doing this for Ashi," he said.

Ekhaas smiled.

Tariic nodded in satisfaction. "I don't ask why," he said. "That you're doing it is enough for me. Go to sleep—we join the south-bound coach in the morning."

Chetiin nudged him toward the cart into which the other *shaarat'khesh* and *taarka'khesh* had disappeared. "Settle in," he said. "Mind the tigers."

Before they left the next morning, Geth sent a message by House Orien courier from the lightning rail station, directed to Singe and Dandra in Fairhaven and letting them know that he wouldn't be meeting them as planned but was instead going to Darguun with Ekhaas and Ashi. Ekhaas couldn't tell him how long Haruuc's mysterious task might take—not because she wasn't permitted to tell him but simply because she didn't know. Geth had written, *Will send word—watch for news of riots in Rhukaan Draal.*

"That will put a twist in Singe's britches," he'd told the *duur'kala.*

The journey from Sigilstar to Sterngate took only two days, including stops at cities and towns along the way for the transfer of passengers and cargo—two days to whisk them across the remainder of Thrane and along nearly a third of the length of the kingdom of Breland before cutting directly across the country to its southern border. The miracle of the lightning rail never ceased to amaze Geth. Two days to cross half the width of the continent. It barely seemed like enough time for him to catch up with Ekhaas and Ashi, to hear about Ekhaas's rise within the Kech Volaar and Ashi's dire experiences under Vounn's mentoring. For him to tell them about his first encounter with Chetiin and the other *shaarat'khesh.*

"They came after me down a dark street and backed me up against a wall," he told the two women as the countryside sped past outside the windows of the cart. "Chetiin pulled out his dagger, and I thought I was in for a hard fight—until he stepped up and laid the dagger on the ground. He looked at me like I was a recruit on muster, then said in Goblin, 'Ekhaas of the Word

Bearers tells me that, with that sword in your hand, you can understand our speech. By her name, will you listen to what I have come to tell you?' "

He managed a passable imitation of Chetiin's scarred voice that brought a faint smile from Ekhaas.

Ashi sat forward. "What happened?"

"You could have knocked me down with a Sharn sweet roll. But Chetiin didn't go for his dagger again, and he had mentioned your name, so I said I'd listen. Have you noticed he always gets right to the point? He said Lhesh Haruuc needed the bearer of Wrath and asked me to come to Sigilstar with him and his people to meet Ekhaas and Tariic."

"And you just went with him?"

Geth glowered at her. "I'm not stupid. He knew details from our time in the Shadow Marches that only Ekhaas could know, and he had a scroll with a message from Haruuc. He got my interest." The shifter shrugged. "Besides, it was only a trip to Sigilstar. There was no hurry for me to get back to Dandra and Singe—and I wasn't feeling welcome in Lathleer. It turned out that Chetiin had more of his people shadowing the locals who'd been looking for me. They distracted them, we got out of town with no problem, and joined up with the *taarka'khesh* who were waiting for us. After that, we just traveled across country."

He shook his head in amazement. "I thought I could get a long way in a night, but *shaarat'khesh* and *taarka'khesh* can really move. We ran into a border patrol as we crossed from Aundair to Thrane, but I don't think they even saw us. I don't think anybody spotted us on the entire journey."

"The Silent Clans know their craft," said Ekhaas. "They've lived apart since ancient times, and they keep their secrets. Anyone can hire them with absolute confidence, but they teach their ways to no one. Haruuc paid a lot to have them fetch you."

"Maybe not that much." Geth looked around, then dropped his voice. "Chetiin and I spent time talking while we traveled. He wouldn't tell me anything about why Haruuc wants to see me, but he's interesting—I like him. Did you know his first contract was with Haruuc when Darguun was founded? They're old friends."

Ekhaas nodded. "I'm not surprised. The Silent Clans are reliable, but I know Haruuc wouldn't have trusted just anyone to find you."

The sun was only a handspan above the horizon when their coach pulled into the lightning rail station at Sterngate. Geth swung out of the cart and down to the platform to look out at a scene that reminded him more of his time as a mercenary during the Last War than it did of any of the other stations they'd stopped at.

Sterngate itself was a bulky fortress nestled into the foothills of the Seawall Mountains with only a scattering of buildings—the lightning rail station among them—outside it. Steep earth embankments and wide ditches made it impossible to approach the stopped coach from anywhere other than through the station. Geth could see similar arrangements of embankments and stone walls restricting access to the other buildings and even to the trade road that ran past the station and directly into the fortress.

"There's more like this on the other side of Sterngate," said Chetiin. Geth had stopped trying to keep track of the goblin. The goblin elder's sparse hair was gray as cobwebs, and yet he still moved like a shadow.

"What's it for?"

Chetiin gave him a rare smile. "To stop Darguuls from getting into Breland unannounced. Sterngate guards the western end of the Marguul Pass."

With most southbound passengers on board for the gnome nation of Zilargo, there were few passengers boarding the coach to continue on from Sterngate. Even fewer were disembarking—the delegation of Darguuls were the only ones to come off the coach. As cargo was shifted, a squad of Brelish soldiers came marching out from the fortress to meet them. A lieutenant in a crisp uniform spoke with Tariic and checked papers. Geth was in no way surprised to discover that, aside from Chetiin, there was no sign at all of the goblins of the Silent Clans. It was as if they had simply vanished.

"How good is Sterngate at keeping Darguuls from getting into Breland?" he whispered to Chetiin.

"Good enough," said Chetiin without seeming to move his lips. "Less good when it comes to the Silent Clans."

Diplomatic status of the delegation confirmed, the soldiers marched back to the fortress. The delegation was left alone on the platform save for laboring porters and a single gnome who sat on a bench reading a small book bound in yellow silk. As the soldiers marched away, he glanced after them, then closed the book, hopped down from the bench, and sauntered over to look up at the Darguuls. Geth watched him. Startling blue eyes peered out of a long, sun-browned face made even longer by a shock of pale hair above and a curling patch of beard below. The gnome wore clothes that were dusty from travel and sturdy boots that had seen hard use.

"Tariic of Rhukaan Taash?" he asked. His voice carried the accent of Zilargo and was surprisingly rich coming from a body that was no larger than a goblin's.

Tariic looked down at him and gave the gnome a deep nod of respect. "Master Davandi," he said, then gestured for Geth, Ekhaas, and the others to join him. He presented them all by name, then introduced the gnome. "This is Midian Mit Davandi of the Library of Korranberg."

"The last person to join us," said Vounn with a cool glance at Tariic. "And tell me, what is his role in your mysterious plans?"

Midian raised a thin eyebrow, and his lips curved. "I make the tea."

Geth couldn't hold back a smile. Vounn saw it and turned her nose up at him. He ignored her.

"Midian is a researcher for the library," Tariic said in answer to Vounn's question. "He's an expert in the history of the Empire of Dhakaan. And I'm certain you'll be pleased to know that he's not a guest of Haruuc, but an employee—Midian is being paid for his services."

"That tells me very little about what he's doing here."

Tariic's ears lay back. "You shouldn't concern yourself with every matter of Haruuc's court, Vounn," he said. "Not all of them affect House Deneith. If my uncle wishes to tell you more, I'm certain he will."

Vounn said nothing more, but her jaw tightened. Midian, however, leaned over, nudged the lady seneschal's leg with his elbow, and gave her a conspiratorial wink. "Haruuc wants to know how the Dhakaani made tea," he said in a mock-whisper.

This time, Geth wasn't the only one who smiled. Ashi and Tariic laughed. Chetiin's mouth twitched. Even Vounn's face relaxed slightly at the gnome's humor, and a smile of triumph at having cracked her icy shell put a wide grin on Midian's face. He turned back to Tariic. "My pack is at the inn with your horses. I'm ready to go when you are."

"You found our horses?" Tariic asked.

Midian shrugged. "Sterngate is a fortress. There aren't that many places for visitors, especially Darguuls, to stable their mounts."

Of the group that had gathered around Midian, only one had betrayed no humor at the gnome's joking manner. When Tariic had announced Midian's area of research, Ekhaas's eyes had widened and her ears had flicked sharply. As the rest of the delegation finished unloading all of their gear from the lightning rail coach and prepared for the short walk to the fortress, Geth moved close to Ekhaas and asked, "What's wrong?"

Ekhaas shook her head. "Nothing you need to worry about."

"It doesn't look that way." He followed her eyes. Her gaze was on Midian. "You don't like him. You didn't know he was coming?"

"No, I didn't. And I don't know if I like him or not yet, but he shouldn't be here. I can't believe Haruuc hired him." She shouldered her pack and turned away. Puzzled, Geth let her go.

The moment everything—including the two caged tigers—was unloaded, the whistle screamed from the crew cart of the lightning rail and the coach began to move, continuing its journey. The delegation made its way from the platform, through the station, and onto the road beyond. At the wide gate where the trade road entered Sterngate, the lieutenant who had checked their papers waited with a pair of soldiers. They fell in behind the delegation, not so much as an escort, Geth guessed, as to be certain no Darguuls stayed behind or strayed from the road.

It would have been difficult to do either. The road was virtually a tunnel within the fortress, walled in and roofed over. When the tunnel finally did open up, it was onto a wide courtyard with only four exits: the trade road behind, the trade road ahead, a heavily guarded gate leading into the fortress proper, and, incongruously, a large inn bearing the House Ghallanda seal built as a separate structure within the courtyard.

"The captain of Sterngate doesn't like visitors getting into the fortress," said Chetiin. "Anyone who needs to stay the night here stays at the inn."

"I don't imagine House Ghallanda makes a profit here," Ashi said.

Close to her, Midian spoke up. "You'd be surprised. Sterngate and Marguul Pass are the easiest way to reach Rhukaan Draal and most of central Darguun. I've stayed at the Sterngate Inn myself, and House Orien caravans come this way frequently. Ghallanda has a captive market here. They put good money into Sterngate. You wouldn't see that kind of attention at an end of the trail inn."

He pointed as a beautiful young human woman dressed in a barmaid's dress came out to tend the flowers that grew in window boxes outside the inn. Her hands moved dexterously among the flowers, though she glanced so frequently over her shoulders at the Darguuls that she might as well have been staring openly. It made Geth's neck itch. Midian excused himself and went into the inn, returning a few moments later with a pack that included two large and heavy books strapped to it. He winked at the young woman on his way in and out, and she blushed both times.

Tariic sent several soldiers to the long stables behind the inn. They came back leading eight lively, bright-eyed horses. "Magebred for swiftness and endurance," said Tariic, and for the first time Geth saw Vounn give a nod of approval.

"Magebred horses and a first class lightning rail cart," she said. "You have an appreciation for the finer things, Tariic."

"For the things that can make life better," said Tariic, his ears standing proudly. "My uncle brought Darguun into the world. I want to bring the world into Darguun." He ran a hand along the neck of one of the horses, then raised his voice and spoke to the rest of the delegation. "We separate into two groups beyond Sterngate. Vounn, Ashi, Geth, and Ekhaas will ride with me to Rhukaan Draal. Take light packs: the rest of your gear and baggage will follow. Thuun, Aruget, Krakuul"—He pointed at three of the elite among his soldiers—"you'll ride with us as well. The rest of you take rooms at the inn. We'll have mounts and wagons sent to you from Matshuc Zaal. Fess, we need a horse for Ashi, so you'll travel with the others."

"Mazo," said the final soldier. The rest of the delegation and the remaining soldiers broke up and moved toward the inn. The barmaid saw them coming and hastened inside, presumably to warn the innkeeper of the business headed their way. The three soldiers Tariic had singled out chose horses and began to lash their gear across the animals' rumps. From their packs, they pulled banners—the scarlet blade of Lhesh Haruuc Shaarat'kor over a spiked crown—that they fixed to short poles on harnesses mounted across their backs.

Tariic looked to Chetiin and Midian. "I'm sorry," he said, "I have no smaller mounts. You'll have to ride with someone else."

"Don't worry about me," said Midian. "I brought my own horse." He reached into his pack and removed a silver horseshoe. Flinging it to the ground, he spoke a word. The horseshoe bounced once, then again, then a third time in perfect rhythm, and suddenly a white pony was cantering in a circle around them. It slowed and walked up to Midian, nuzzling him.

"Convenient," Tariic said. "I didn't realize you were a spellcaster."

"No more than any other gnome," Midian answered modestly. "I just carry a few trinkets to make traveling easier."

When they were all ready to move out, Chetiin leaped easily up behind Geth, balancing with no more difficulty than if he'd been sitting in a chair. Geth's horse didn't even seem aware of the extra rider. As they set off down the tunnel that was the trade road heading east out of Sterngate, it seemed to Geth that even at a leisurely walk they were moving almost as quickly as a normal unburdened horse might go at a trot. It was tempting to give the horse its head and see how fast it could really run.

"What about the tigers?" Ashi called, her voice echoing in the tunnel. "Couldn't your cavalry riders have come with us?"

Tariic shook his head. "The other party will need them as guards. There are bandits on the road to Rhukaan Draal and a slow moving caravan makes a tempting target."

"Even one riding under Haruuc's banner?"

"Even one riding under Haruuc's banner. They'll be less likely to come after a small group on horseback and riding fast." His face took on a more grim expression. "Especially one that's well-armed. After we're through Marguul Pass, we'll ride in armor."

They emerged from the tunnel and onto the open trade road into sunlight so bright that Geth had to shade his eyes. When he'd blinked away the brightness, he let out a low whistle of amazement.

The Seawall Mountains rose above them. Without the bulk of Sterngate obscuring the view, Geth had a sudden feeling that the massive peaks might fall down from the sky to crush him. Adding to that sense of oppressive height was the barrenness of the slopes close to Sterngate. For perhaps two hundred paces or more from the fortress's walls, the ground had been swept clear of trees and bushes. In their place was a labyrinth of ditches and embankments that made the earthworks protecting the lightning rail station look like the diggings of a child. The only easy path was along the road.

"All to keep Darguuls out of Breland?" Geth asked Chetiin over his shoulder.

"Cyre wasn't the only nation to lose territory in the creation of Darguun," said the goblin. "By that point in the war, Breland had been in possession of Marguul Pass and lands east of the Seawall for more than twenty years. Haruuc's uprising left the Brelish frightened—and their defeat at the Battle of Marguul Pass in 970 frightened them even more. They're still scared."

"Do they need to be?"

"That depends on how successful you are."

Geth grimaced.

Some time around mid-day they left the defenses of Sterngate behind and entered Marguul Pass itself. Steep slopes and ravines surrounded the constantly climbing road—hostile terrain to try to ride, let alone march, through. Side tracks that looked like they had been worn into the rock and thin soil over centuries wandered off from the road to vanish into the rugged landscape. Occasionally, the side paths seemed to split off from the road, trace around the far side of a hill or outcropping, then return to the main road. In more than one spot, cobbles displaced by time poked out through the dirt of these looping paths like broken teeth. With Chetiin dozing behind him, Geth stared at the strange side paths each time they appeared, trying to figure out why they were there.

Eventually, Ekhaas caught him staring and supplied an answer. "Marguul Pass has been one of the major routes through these mountains since the earliest days of my people," she said. "When House Orien built the trade roads, they followed older roads laid down by the Empire of Dhakaan. The side loops mark the places where humans went through when Dhakaani went around."

"Some of these side paths look like roads of their own," said Ashi. "They don't come back."

"They are roads. Dhakaani lived in the mountains as well as in the lowlands. Often they lived beneath the mountains too. Some of the people who still live in the mountains use the old roads when they come this way. Look there." She pointed along one of the paths that wound into the brush on a hillside. "That leads to the remains of a cliff-town that was once Kaal, where nobles of the empire went to bathe in healing springs."

Geth shaded his eyes and peered into the distance. Far away, he thought he could see what looked like worn blocks carved out of the living rock of an exposed rock face. "Grandmother Wolf," he said. "Is that it?"

Ekhaas nodded, but, riding behind them, Midian coughed discreetly. "It's not Kaal," he said.

Ekhaas's face darkened and her ears rose. "It is Kaal," she said. "The Kech Volaar have records of it. One of the emperors of

Dhakaan even maintained a palace there. There's a famous song written by one of his wives about the view from the baths in the cliff-side."

"Maybe he kept a palace at a place called Kaal, but that's not it." The gnome kept his voice polite. "I don't know about this song, but in my experience, descriptions of historic views are notoriously vague. Whatever view your song describes could probably match dozens of places in these mountains. Those ruins are old, no question, but they were built after the fall of the empire as a warlord's stronghold. The design confirms it. The 'baths' there are cisterns built to hold water, nothing more."

Ekhaas's mouth opened and closed several times, but no sound came out. Kicking her heels into her horse's side, she rode forward, away from the gnome. Ashi looked at Geth, then rode after her. Geth looked at Midian. "How do you know that this place isn't Kaal?" he asked.

"A research team from the Library of Korranberg studied the place before the outbreak of the Last War," Midian said with a shrug. "They wrote a classic paper. Very famous. Your Ekhaas shouldn't be so sensitive. Kech Volaar legends and songs are interesting starting points, but they don't always represent the facts."

Geth could guess now why Ekhaas hadn't been pleased to have Midian join their party. He felt a growl rising inside him but held it back. "I've seen things out of legend," he said. "Legends have saved my life."

"I don't doubt it," Midian said. He pointed at the sword hanging at Geth's side. "If I'm not mistaken, you're wearing a legend. But the Empire of Dhakaan rose fifteen thousand years ago from even older goblin kingdoms. It fell more than five thousand years ago. The legends to which modern Dhakaani clans like the Kech Volaar cling have been repeated and venerated for millennia. They're not *always* accurate." He winked at Geth conspiratorially. "That's why I'm here—to give another perspective on the legends."

"Wait, you know something about Haruuc's task?" Geth asked.

Midian smiled, white teeth flashing in his tanned face. "No more than you do, I suspect, but it involves Dhakaani history and that's what's important to me. By Aureon's blue quill, whatever happens, it's going to make a fine paper!" He looked ahead to where Ekhaas, accompanied by Ashi, was glowering back at him and sighed, then urged his pony into a trot. "We can talk more later, Geth," he called back, "but I think I'd better go try to make peace with her, or we'll have an unpleasant journey. *Duur'kala* don't often have a good opinion of Korranberg researchers to begin with."

"I wonder why," Geth said under his breath.

Chetiin's voice drifted up from behind him. "The ancient hobgoblins who first encountered gnomes in the jungles between the Seawall Mountains and the Howling Peaks thought they were somehow related to giant rats."

"Did they really?"

"That's what the legends say," Chetiin said dryly, "but they're not *always* accurate."

CHAPTER NINE

They reached the crest of the pass at dusk. The red light of the setting sun fell full on a massive keep that blocked the pass from side to side. The closer they drew to the keep, however, the less certain Geth was that it really was just a keep. The nearest side of the fortress was largely a blank wall with a reinforced ramp leading up to a single gate wide enough for three wagons to drive through at the same time. The road ended at the wall of the keep, though unlike at Sterngate, it didn't run directly to the keep's gate—ramp and gate were strangely misaligned, off-center with the road by a good ten paces. Parapets topped the wall, but behind them were a cluster of towers that rose so high it seemed as if they'd been built on top of the keep. Even odder were the buttresses filling the narrow gaps between the keep and the natural walls of the pass. Geth was no engineer, but it looked as if they were an afterthought, as if the entire keep had been dropped into the pass and efforts made afterward to make it fit the space.

Hobgoblins and bugbears guarded the ramp, gate, and parapets. Geth could hear them calling to each other as the mounted party approached and they recognized Haruuc's banner. When their party was about fifty paces from the great wall, Aruget, Krakuul, and Thuun dismounted. Facing the keep, they gave a kind of salute by thumping their chests with a fist. Tariic saluted as well, though he remained mounted.

The guards at the foot of the ramp returned the salute. Tariic led the way forward once again, riding up to a hobgoblin wearing polished armor painted with a silhouette of what Geth assumed were jagged teeth, then realized were actually mountains.

Geth leaned over to Ekhaas. "What is this place?"

"Matshuc Zaal," she said. "The Stolen Fortress. Once it belonged to Breland as Veldarren, the largest of the mobile fortresses built during the Last War. They tried to bring it against Haruuc in 970 in the Battle of Marguul Pass. It was a disaster for them. Haruuc's general trapped Veldarren in the pass and brought it down. Darguun's triumph here forced Breland to sue for peace. It's a tradition for Darguul soldiers to honor the dead of the battle whenever they approach. Matshuc Zaal will never move again, but now it marks the border of Darguun."

They spent their first night in Darguun within the walls of Matshuc Zaal. Geth could truthfully say it was unlike any other fortress he'd ever been in. There were frequent reminders of Matshuc Zaal's first life as Veldarren—splashes of Brelish blue paint, human-styled carvings, and a layout familiar to anyone with military experience—but it was all dominated by thirty years of occupation by Darguuls. Most of the carvings and decorations that might have appealed to a human sensibility had been hacked away at some point in the past and replaced, where decoration was called for, with garish fixtures of brass and banners depicting clan symbols. What Geth might have expected to be crew quarters, and probably had been intended as such, was instead the mess hall, with the open space of the mess hall turned into, from the sounds he heard as they passed, a training space.

A strange smell hung in the air, the odor of different races eating unfamiliar foods, and the entire fortress seemed strangely quiet. The mercenary company he'd served with during the Last War hadn't been unruly, but there had been a friendly camaraderie when they'd been off duty. During the time that he'd spent more recently among an orc horde in the Shadow Marches, he'd gotten used to boisterous nights of drinking and fighting, bonding with the other warriors. Matshuc Zaal, on the other hand, was pervaded by a sense of goblin discipline so strong it left him speaking in hushed tones and fighting back an urge to polish something.

The fortress was also dark. Not merely night dark, which wouldn't have presented him with a problem, but as dark as a cave or a vault. The Darguuls had no difficulty, of course—goblin sight was different from a shifter's nightvision—but only a few paces in from the big gates, Geth found himself as blind as Ashi or Vounn. Fortunately Midian had a small everbright lantern in his capacious pack, and that provided enough light for them to make their way without needing to be led.

There was a third distinct difference. As they were escorted through the fortress to their quarters for the night, Geth caught glimpses of huddled goblins or stick-thin hobgoblins, even a couple of scaly kobolds. Compared to the uniformed garrison of Matshuc Zaal, these creatures were dressed in tatters and rags. When Geth and his companions reached their quarters, another of the goblins was lighting a fire in the hearth. When they entered, she glanced up and actually cringed as if trying to make herself even smaller. She finished her work and all but fled out the door. Geth stared after her. Not even the menial goblins in the cities were so timid.

"Slaves," said Vounn with disgust in her voice. Ever since her praise of Tariic's horses at Sterngate, Geth had noticed that she'd been playing on her charm. The comment was the first hint of disapproval she'd expressed since the morning.

"Our people have kept slaves since before Dhakaan, Vounn," said Tariic. His ears dropped apologetically. "It's a difficult tradition to suppress, but since Haruuc embraced the worship of Dol Dorn and the Sovereign Host, progress has been made. He has freed his personal slaves and forbids others to bring slaves into his fortress. Warlords and clan leaders who seek his favor are following his example."

"It holds you back, Tariic," Vounn said. "If Darguun wants to be truly accepted as a civilized nation, then Haruuc—or his successor—needs to eliminate it."

Tariic spread his hands. "You wash the bather, Vounn. I freed my slaves the day my uncle freed his."

"The Dhakaani owned slaves?" Geth asked Ekhaas.

The *duur'kala* nodded. "Not all the people of the empire were heroes. The modern Dhakaani clans still keep slaves. Before I left Darguun I thought little of it, but the time I spent in the larger world has convinced me that the traditions of Dhakaan are wrong in that at least. Our people change slowly, though. Haruuc's position has not added to his popularity."

When slaves brought them dinner later, Vounn insisted that they eat a portion of the food as well. When they left, she had one of Tariic's soldiers accompany them back to the kitchens with a harsh message that she'd been the one to feed them and that anyone who objected should come to her. No one came.

Pipes and drums signaling the change of a duty shift in the fortress roused their party before dawn, and they rode out of Matshuc Zaal's eastern gate in thin but welcome light. They spent the second day of their journey in the descent of the pass and camped below the mountains that night. A well-used fire ring showed where many other groups had camped on the site.

"I'm surprised House Ghallanda hasn't set up an inn here," said Ashi.

"They did," said one of the soldiers—Aruget, Geth thought. The hobgoblin pointed to the far side of the road. "You can still see the foundation over there."

"What happened to it?" Geth asked.

The hobgoblin smiled. "Darguun."

When they rose the next morning, they armed themselves as Tariic had suggested, putting their strength on display for any bandits that might otherwise be tempted to test them. Tariic and his soldiers donned armor of chain mail and linked plates, spiked at the joints. Ekhaas wore leather armor set with dark studs of steel. Midian produced a stiff leather vest. Neither Ashi nor Chetiin wore armor—they both fought fast and light, Geth knew, relying on skill and the steel of their weapons to protect them. Vounn didn't don armor either, but just sat and watched the others with a smile of mild amusement.

For himself, Geth reached into his pack and pulled out a bundle wrapped in soft oiled leather. The bundle had taken up most of the space in the pack, and without its bulk the pack sagged like a discarded boot. He traveled light, but the bundle contained one of his most prized possessions. Setting it on a rock, he folded back the leather.

The plates of black magewrought steel that formed his great gauntlet gleamed dully in the morning light. Geth checked over each plate and every strap and buckle, then drew the gauntlet on. Interlocking strips of metal bulged around his upper arm, running all the way up to the plates of the wide, heavy shoulder guard. Flat spikes lined the ridge of his forearm and protruded from his knuckles, and three low, hooked blades rose from the back of his hand. Geth tightened the straps that held the gauntlet in place, then curled his fingers into a fist. The black steel whispered like a sword drawn from a scabbard.

The Darguuls had stopped to watch him. *"Paatcha,"* Tariic said approvingly.

Aruget grunted. "Nice armor," he said in his thick accent. "Where's the rest of it?"

Geth bent and straightened his arm, testing the fit. "I don't need more," he said in a low growl. The gauntlet had cost him a full year of his wages and bonuses as a mercenary, paid to an artificer in the now-dead city of Metrol. It had been worth every last silver sovereign.

The company must have made, he guessed, an impressive sight as they rode, sunlight flashing on armor, the banners worn by the soldiers snapping. The trade road was flat and straight as it emerged from the foothills, and they let Tariic's magebred horses run. The speed that the animals' walking gait had hinted at was no false promise. Under a cloudless sky so bright that its blue seemed almost white, the horses raced along the road, necks outstretched and hooves drumming like music, as if running were all they had been born to do.

Away from the mountains, the land became as flat as the road, broken only by the occasional gentle hill and by streambeds that were cracked and dry with the beginning of late summer. They passed ruins frequently, not Dhakaani but human, the skeletons of farms and hamlets destroyed by Haruuc's armies thirty years before. Fields and orchards ran wild, offering a bountiful but neglected harvest. "Where are your people?" Geth asked Chetiin. "I thought I'd see more of them."

"Not here. Most live away from the mountains where rain falls more frequently and life is easier."

His voice was strangely muffled and Geth glanced over his shoulder to look at him. Chetiin was facing backward, looking back the way they had come. "What is it?" Geth asked.

The *shaarat'khesh* elder turned to face him again. "We're being followed."

The road behind them was empty except for the thinning dust of their own passage. The Seawall Mountains receded in the distance, but Geth thought he could see all the way back to the pass. No one was on the road. "Where? And if we are being followed, how are they keeping up with us?"

Chetiin shook his head. "I don't know where, but I can feel it." His ears twitched. "And maybe they won't keep up, but I'll talk to Tariic anyway. We should set a double guard tonight."

Tariic listened when Chetiin told him of his concerns, and that night they made camp with the road on one side of them and the steep gullies of a dry forking streambed on two others. They drew straws for watches, Vounn and Ashi excluded because of their inability to see in the dark. Geth drew second watch opposite Aruget. When he climbed from his bedroll, shaken awake by Midian as the gnome retired from his turn on watch, Aruget pointed him roughly to the side of the camp that faced southeast. He had already claimed the northwest side of the camp. Geth shrugged, adjusted his great gauntlet, and went where he was told. The view from either side of the camp was equally empty under the combined lights of the risen moons.

In fact, Geth had no objection to sitting watch on his own. He appreciated being alone for the first time that day. As Midian and the soldier Krakuul, who had drawn first watch, found their bedrolls and their breathing faded into the same easy rhythm as those already asleep, Geth touched the collar of rune-etched black stones he wore around his neck and looked up at the hazy brightness of the Ring of Siberys.

It was the fourth day of Barrakas. Exactly one year ago, the Bonetree hunters and their monstrous dolgrim allies had attacked Bull Hollow, the little hamlet on the remote edge of the Eldeen Reaches that had become his haven after the Last War. They had been pursuing Dandra, and they'd destroyed much of Bull Hollow in their attempt to draw her out. In the process, they had killed Adolan, the hamlet's defender and Geth's friend.

Geth squeezed the stones of the collar. With his last breath, Adolan had told him to take it. The collar was a relic of the sect of druids, the Gatekeepers, to which Adolan had belonged. Through his adventures in the months that followed, the ancient magic of the collar had given him protection and guidance, turning icy cold whenever he'd been threatened by the sanity-twisting forces behind the tainted dragon Dah'mir's power.

Now it was no cooler than the night air, but it seemed to Geth that the stones were very, very heavy. He sighed and let them go. The collar fell back against his neck.

There was a rustling behind him, and he looked over his shoulder to see Ashi silhouetted against the dim glow of the banked campfire. "Can I join you?" she asked softly.

He patted the ground beside him, and she sat. "A year ago," she said.

Get looked back up at the Ring of Siberys, at the stars and the moons. "You remembered." She'd been among the hunters who had attacked Bull Hollow.

"How could I forget? I'm sorry, Geth."

"You're a friend now, Ashi. You turned your back on the Bonetree clan. There's nothing to apologize for. Anyway, you've said sorry before." He watched the sky for a little longer, then asked, "The hunter who killed Adolan—really big, fought with an axe—what was his name?"

Ashi looked at him sideways. "You killed him."

"I know." The memory of that kill, of driving his sword—not Wrath then, but a plain sword from his days as a mercenary—up through the hunter's belly and into his chest, would stay with him for a long, long time. "I still want to know his name."

"He was Hand-wit," said Ashi. "He wasn't smart, but he had a steady hand for tattooing and piercing." She tapped the rings in her lip. "He did this for me."

"Ah," said Geth.

Ashi was silent for a moment, then added, "It will be a year tomorrow since Medala killed my father for failing to capture Dandra at Bull Hollow. She burned his mind out while he was talking to her."

"I know," Geth said. "I'm sorry."

"Thank you. Do you ever think about going back to Bull Hollow?"

He thought about it, then leaned back. "There's nothing for me there but questions. Maybe I'm some kind of hero out here, but I don't want to be a hero there—" His words were cut off by a bellow from the other side of the camp.

"Toh!" Beware!

A wet thump ended the cry, but Geth and Ashi were already on their feet. "Aruget!" shouted Geth, drawing Wrath from its scabbard. "Up! Everyone up!"

The sleeping forms by the fire thrashed and rolled from their blankets to grab for weapons, but dark figures were already rushing in on the camp. With screams of *"Itaa!"*—Wrath in hand, Geth heard "Attack!"—hobgoblins dressed in ragged clothing and armor came bursting out of the dry gully on his side of the camp.

"Grandfather Rat!" he snarled. The streambeds they'd chosen for protection of their campsite had become a path to lead their attackers closer. They still had to claw their way up the steep sides of the gullies, but that wouldn't slow them much. Some of the hobgoblins were already helping to hoist others higher, and even more attackers were sprinting down the streambed, any attempt at stealth abandoned.

Geth jumped forward and swung Wrath at the first hobgoblin out of the gully. The heavy blade of the sword bit deep into his neck, nearly severing his head, before he even had a chance to rise up from his knees. The blow had nothing honorable about it, but Geth wasn't an honorable fighter. He kicked the body before it could collapse, and it toppled back into the gully, knocking down two more climbers.

But attackers were swarming up the bank everywhere. Another crawling hobgoblin stabbed at his calf with a dagger. Ashi's sword darted out, piercing the hobgoblin's arm, then flicking high to slash across his face. He cried out and rolled away.

His thrashing almost brought Ashi down as well. She stepped back and nearly fell a second time as her foot caught on a root. "Ashi, get back to the fire!" Geth ordered. "Fight where you can see!" He swung Wrath again.

"I can see just fine!" Ashi protested.

Geth swept her feet out from under her and snapped his right arm up into the space where her shoulders had been. A hobgoblin's sword crashed into his great gauntlet and went skittering along the black steel. Geth twisted, sweeping the sword aside and hacking upward with Wrath in the same motion. The twilight purple blade cut through leather armor and into the flesh beneath. The hobgoblin fell back. Ashi pushed herself to her feet and sprinted back to the fire without another word.

The others in their party were all up and fighting now, but their attackers were coming in from multiple directions and outnumbered them easily. Vounn was the only one not fighting, but she crouched by the fire, stirring it up into a blaze that threw light and shadows into the night as Ashi fought back anyone who tried to approach. Tariic and the soldiers Thuun and Krakuul stood shoulder to shoulder in tight formation. There was no sign of Aruget. Ekhaas fought on her own, beating back blows from an attacker wielding a heavy spiked mace. Chetiin leaped from shadow to shadow, striking low with one of the curved daggers he wore on his wrists and leaving squirming, wailing enemies in his wake. Geth glimpsed Midian standing still, a polished metal baton in his left hand, as a hobgoblin advanced on him—then the gnome snapped his wrist and a long, slim head swung out of the baton's shaft, locking in place and transforming the baton into a deadly little pick. Midian spun, and the point of the pick punched into the meat of his attacker's leg. The hobgoblin dropped to his knees. A second blow put a neat hole in his skull.

More attackers were coming over the sides of the gully near Geth. Three hobgoblins came at him at once, advancing in a wedge like Tariic and his soldiers, and Geth began to regret sending Ashi away. He spun to one side as the wedge came at him and swung Wrath in a raking arc. The nearest hobgoblin deflected the blow with a shield, but Geth followed it up by throwing his entire weight against the shield. The hobgoblin staggered back under the unexpected tactic, and the wedge collapsed. Geth put his opponent down with a punch that left the imprints of knuckle spikes on his temple, then rolled to his feet. The remaining two hobgoblins of the wedge had recovered and had been joined by two more.

Four to one with more enemies climbing up. Geth cursed and shouted, "I need help!"

From the corner of his eye, he saw Ekhaas finish her attacker with a long slash across his chest, then turn to him. "Stand back!" she called, then drew a deep breath and sang.

The songs with which the *duur'kala* invoked her magic were wild and powerful, sometimes even primal, as if they echoed the legendary music of the world's creation. The brief snatch of song that she sang now had a thick but flowing quality to it, like soap or half-melted butter. Geth jumped away—and saw the ground under the advancing hobgoblins' feet shimmer, then turn greasy and slick.

His attackers' legs shot out from under them, and they fell like children on an icy pond. The dark stain of the spell spread out behind them, too, dipping down over the edge of the gully. More hobgoblins yelled as they slid down the suddenly slippery slope.

"Paaldaask!" shouted someone—*Spellcaster!*—and the nearest attackers turned their attention on Ekhaas. Her ears folded back, and she sang another spell. The air around her folded, and abruptly five identical versions of the *duur'kala* stood on the defensive. Geth knew this magic. It was only an illusion, and it wouldn't fool their enemies for long. He moved to help her but a hand wrapped around his ankle and he slammed hard to the ground.

One of the hobgoblins caught by Ekhaas's spell had managed to reach out and grab him. Geth kicked at her but she rolled aside and pulled herself up his leg, slithering out of the magical mess.

Then Chetiin was there, appearing out of the shadows and leaping onto the hobgoblin's back. He grabbed her hair in one hand, pulled her head back, and slit her throat. Her grip on Geth spasmed once, then relaxed. He pulled away from her and from the blood that flooded out of her body. Chetiin, however, jumped from her to one of the other thrashing hobgoblins, plunged his dagger into him, then leaped to the next and to the next, killing them all in moments without ever touching the slippery ground. He jumped clear of the magic again and looked at Geth, still sitting in the dirt. "Ekhaas?" he reminded the shifter before disappearing into the shadows once more.

Geth twisted to his feet, caught another charging hobgoblin with a slash between the ribs, and looked to the *duur'kala*. Her illusory duplicates were gone, and she was bleeding from a wound to her left shoulder. But she had Ashi and Midian fighting beside her now, and they were beating back the attackers. Ashi's scarf had come loose, and Geth could see the fierce joy of battle on her dragonmarked and blood-spattered face. Midian's expression was more grim and focused, but he fought surprisingly well for a researcher. Geth spun around, taking in their situation. The campsite was washed in blood. The bodies of their attackers were everywhere and almost seemed to outnumber those still standing. A few hobgoblins still faced the wedge of Tariic and his soldiers, a few more were being forced back toward the edge of the gully by Ekhaas, Ashi, and Midian. Another pair closed tentatively on Geth.

He could hear sounds of retreat in the gully. The hobgoblins, large as their numbers were, had picked a target too tough for them. He turned to the two hobgoblins still facing him and pointed Wrath at them. *"Skiir,"* he growled at them. *Run.*

For a moment it looked like they might have considered it, then the gaze of one of them, a lean whip of a hobgoblin with one scarred ear, moved past Geth. The shifter glanced over his shoulder, following it.

Vounn stood alone and undefended at the fire.

In the heartbeat that he was distracted, the hobgoblin with the scarred ear moved, thrusting his hapless companion at Geth and surging toward Vounn with his sword raised. The startled hobgoblin who had been pushed at Geth flailed wildly with his weapon. Geth bashed him with his gauntlet and felt bone crunch, but he was an instant too late. The hobgoblin with the scarred ear ran past him. No one else was any closer to Vounn. Through Wrath, Geth heard and understood the words the hobgoblin screamed out as he charged: "You die here, Deneith!"

Vounn's eyes narrowed, and the dragonmark that peeked out from her sleeve on the inside of her right wrist seemed to flash in the firelight. The air rippled around the lady seneschal just as the hobgoblin's sword fell—and the blade skimmed aside, deflected by the power of the Mark of Sentinel. Left off-balance by the failed blow, the hobgoblin stumbled. Vounn parted a fold of her robes, and with a motion that had the swift certainty of years of practice, pulled a long thin stiletto from a hidden sheath. One precise blow drove the needle-like blade into the soft point at the back of his neck and up into his skull. The hobgoblin jerked, then dropped forward, sliding off the stiletto.

Vounn saw Geth's expression of amazement and answered it with a thin smile. "I am a daughter of Deneith," she said. "I can defend myself."

The last of the hobgoblins fighting Tariic cried out and fled down into the gully to join their retreating fellows. The final two attackers who had been facing Ekhaas and the others tried to do the same, but they didn't make it. Midian hooked the legs of one with the blade of his pick, then swung the weapon to deadly effect as the hobgoblin fell. The other made it to the brink of the gully before staggering back with his hands over a gash in his belly. Chetiin appeared, curved dagger dripping with blood. Ekhaas grimaced and ended her opponent's agony with a swift blow of her sword.

Ashi was the first to speak into the silence that followed. "You can fight," she said to Midian appreciatively.

The gnome shrugged. "I do my field work in Darguun. I have to fight."

"If these are the bandits you warned us about, Tariic, they're more bold than you thought," said Vounn.

But Tariic looked around and shook his head. "I don't think they were bandits," he said. "They fought too well. Those fought in formation." He pointed at the three who had attacked Geth in a wedge. "Chetiin, follow the survivors. See if you can learn anything. Krakuul, Thuun—look for Aruget."

"Mazo," said Chetiin. He bent and cleaned his dagger on the clothes of a corpse before putting it away. Geth stepped up beside him.

"I'm coming with you."

Chetiin glanced at Tariic, who nodded. *"Ban,"* said the goblin.

The first thing they found, though, was Aruget. The hobgoblin soldier lay along the gully at the end of a trail of blood, almost under a collapsed sand bank. Blood covered his scalp and he lay very still, but Chetiin felt his neck and nodded. "Still alive," he said. "Lucky." He whistled to signal Thuun and Krakuul, then led Geth on along the streambed.

They didn't come across any survivors, though they did find the bodies of two hobgoblins who had succumbed to wounds suffered during the fight. The others had gotten away. Along the streambed, carefully out of sight of the road, they discovered how: the dung of horses, still fresh, and a multitude of hoofprints leading up out of the streambed and into the night. There was one more body, too, but the only wound this one had suffered was a knife in the back.

"The leader, I think," said Chetiin. "Killed because he took his people into a bad fight." He began feeling through the corpse's clothes and grunted. "Tariic was right. They were no bandits. This one was too well fed."

Geth inspected the hoofprints left by the horses and, interspersed among them, the prints of hobgoblin boots. If it had been daylight they should have brought Ashi—she was an expert tracker. He'd learned some skills himself, though, and the story told in the dusty ground wasn't hard to read. "They rode in after dark," he said, "then waited until deep night to approach. There were a lot of horses—the survivors must have taken all of them or let them loose to try to confuse pursuit."

But the soft sound of shifting hooves drew him up the slope of the well-churned bank. One horse still stood there, grazing on a patch of dry grass, and there was a bundle still lashed behind its saddle. The horse shifted nervously as he approached, probably smelling the blood on him, but it stood still long enough for him to free the bundle before galloping away. Chetiin joined him, and Geth shook the bundle open. Clothes fell out. Good clothes, far better than the pretend bandits had been wearing. Chetiin reached out and plucked one item from the pile, a banner like the ones Aruget and the other soldiers wore as they rode.

This banner was yellow and marked with the crest of what looked like a snarling dog. Chetiin's ears rose. "Gan'duur," he said. "Eaters of Sorrow."

"Another clan?" Geth guessed.

"A clan that has chafed under Haruuc's rule. Tariic will be interested in this."

Geth's eyes narrowed. "The hobgoblin that attacked Vounn knew she was Deneith."

"I heard him," said Chetiin. "They knew who we are—or at least who she is. If something happened to Vounn, Haruuc would be shamed and weakened in the eyes of the clans. The Gan'duur would gain strength."

"They knew we were coming. Do you think they were the ones following us today, somewhere off the road?"

Chetiin shook his head and pointed to the wide path of hoofprints that led away from the streambed. Geth looked at it again, frowned, then looked again and finally recognized what the goblin had seen.

Only one swathe of hoofprints cut across the landscape. Their attackers had come from and fled into the east.

Their party had ridden out of the west.

"They didn't follow us," Chetiin said, "but they knew where to find us."

CHAPTER TEN

They rode hard for the next three days, pushing to reach the Deneith stronghold at the Gathering Stone. Ashi was glad for the speed and endurance of Tariic's magebred horses and doubly glad of the riding lessons Vounn had made her take—before she'd gone to House Deneith, she'd ridden only rarely and always at a much slower pace. Tariic had taken news of Geth and Chetiin's discoveries with bared teeth and flattened ears. Vounn and he had agreed: they needed to complete their journey as quickly as possible. If someone wanted to stop them, they had the measure of the party's strength now. Another attack wouldn't be so easily defeated.

The thought that there might not be another attack was almost depressing to Ashi. The sharply pitched battle, the smell of blood, and the very real threat of death had roused a spirit in her that had been crushed for too long. She even felt a pang of dread as they reached the Gathering Stone. The place was little more than a tall stone marker set at a crossroads, a seething camp of goblin—*dar,* she reminded herself—mercenaries and would-be mercenaries, and a squat, ugly stronghold. It was no Sentinel Tower, but it was still an enclave of Deneith.

Word of Vounn's appointment to Haruuc's court had reached the stronghold. Shortly after they rode inside, almost before there had been time to dismount, Viceroy Redek d'Deneith appeared with words of welcome on his lips and a fear for his position in his eyes. Vounn took one look at him and asked to speak with him in private. Ashi tried to slip away with Geth, Ekhaas, and the others, but Vounn caught her first and dragged her into the conversation with Redek. Once they were shut up in Redek's office, though, the only words she had for Ashi were an invitation to remove her scarf—they were back among members of their House, after all.

Redek couldn't keep his eyes off the Siberys Mark, awed by the legendary power sitting in a corner of his office. He nodded to everything Vounn said, and by the time they left the room he seemed content to accept that he would continue the mundane task of brokering the services of Darguul mercenaries while Vounn handled the larger tasks of dealing with the powers of the nation. Ashi wondered why Vounn hadn't just ordered her to strip. Had Redek seen the full extent of her dragonmark, he probably would have handed the entire stronghold over to Vounn's command if she'd asked.

When they left the Gathering Stone, it was in the company of two full squads of hobgoblin, goblin, and bugbear mercenaries. With such protection, speed was no longer important, and they took their time. They couldn't have ridden quickly anyway. So close to Rhukaan Draal, the way was busier. Merchants and travelers, all heavily armed, shared the road. They passed a House Orien caravan bound along the road back to Breland. The mercenaries who guarded it were hired from House Deneith, but even so they watched the party and their Darguul guards with suspicion until they were well past.

They reached Rhukaan Draal near sunset the next day. The road rose into a fine wide bridge that leaped across the dark water of a deep, fast flowing river. "The Ghaal River," said Ekhaas. "Ships can come in all the way from the coast, but this is as far as they go. The cataract stops them here." She pointed upstream to a boiling cascade of white water.

The city that sprawled on the southern bank of the river revealed itself as the bridge reached the apex of its gentle arc and fell again. Ashi's first impression of Rhukaan Draal was that a bricklayer and a stone mason had collided, spilling the goods of their respective trades across the landscape. The city was a riot of buildings in a range of styles. The remains of human architecture still stood, and it was possible to see the bones of the Cyran town that Rhukaan Draal had been before Haruuc took it for his capital. The flesh that cloaked those bones, however, was rough and new. Ramshackle structures had been thrown up between and against the old human buildings in a style that Ashi was already beginning to think of as distinctly Darguul. The *dar* seemed to use whatever materials were at hand—wood, mortar, bricks, rough stone, worked stone, even chunk of masonry fallen from older buildings—to erect buildings that were as attractive as a rubbish heap but, to her Deneith-trained eye, looked durable and formidably defensive.

Most of the buildings, old or new, that leaned in upon the narrow, unpaved streets were no more than three stories tall. A few were taller, but nothing approached a single tower that soared up in the center of the city. At first Ashi thought that the red of the tower came from the light of the setting sun, but then she realized it was the stones of the structure themselves that gave it a bloody tint. The Khaar Mbar'ost, the Red House—Haruuc's fortress. Unlike the other new buildings of the city, it seemed solidly constructed and even attractive in a vaguely sinister way.

Ashi looked around for someone to ask about this, but neither Ekhaas nor Chetiin nor even Tariic was nearby. Aruget, blow to his head mended by Ekhaas's magic, rode close, and he answered her question before she'd even asked it. "Lhesh Haruuc wanted something special," he said. "He had it built by craftsmen of House Cannith."

It was getting easier to understand his thick accent than when she had first encountered him in Sentinel Tower, maybe because of the lessons in Goblin that Ekhaas had been giving her. Ashi tried some of her Goblin out on him. *"Ataa so?"* she asked, pointing in the direction of a milling throng.

All of Rhukaan Draal's twisting, dusty streets were packed with a range of races nearly as diverse as she'd seen on visits to the cosmopolitan city of Sharn or the monster-dominated Droaamish port of Vralkek, but in that direction the crowd seemed to grow thicker and even more diverse. Among the goblins, hobgoblins, and bugbears, she could see humans, elves, dwarves, shifters, even a few slight halflings and towering warforged. They all had an air of suspicion about them, as if everyone was trying to keep an eye on everyone else while also keeping one hand near their weapon. A little farther into the crowd, it appeared that stalls had been set up. Those who stood within the stalls looked the most suspicious of all.

"Khaari Batuuvk," said Aruget. "The Bloody Market. Anything is for sale there." He gave her a slow look. "You should stay away. *Mo'tohiish."*

Very dangerous. Ashi nodded, but she kept one eye on the market as they rode. It didn't look any more dangerous to her than other places she'd been—in Vralkek, she'd stared down an ogre intent on picking a fight—but then again, it seemed that every second street corner in Rhukaan Draal carried a surprise that shifted her hand a little closer to her sword. On one corner, three goblin children industriously stripped a bugbear that, on first glance, she took to be sleeping, but on looking again she realized was dead. On another corner, a grubby dwarf stood beside a cart displaying a rack of the skinned and dripping carcasses of some animal Ashi couldn't identify, in spite of her years as a hunter. The dwarf saw her staring and grinned, displaying brilliantly white teeth. On a third corner, a dull-eyed human so thin and ragged Ashi wasn't sure if it was a man or a women danced in shuffling circles as goblins and hobgoblins passed by without a second glance.

"The crown city of Darguun," said Midian, riding his magical pony up beside her. "Magnificent sight, isn't it?"

"I didn't realize there would be so many races," Ashi said.

"The laws are simple here, and nobody asks too many questions. There are people in Rhukaan Draal who couldn't show their faces in the Five Nations without being arrested. In its own way, it's even more open than Sharn. Nobody here is really interested in who you are or what you've done."

Ashi could see that the gnome was right. She was staring far more than anyone else in the streets. The inhabitants of Rhukaan Draal hardly seemed to look twice at what was going on around them or even at the procession of mercenaries surrounding the party that rode under Haruuc's personal banner. They were just another part of the bustle in the streets—only the strength of their numbers earned them space on the road.

She remembered how Aruget had responded in a similar way to her when they'd faced each other at Sentinel Tower, reacting to her, not to her position. On impulse, she reached up and pulled off the scarf that had covered her head and face, exposing the pattern of her dragonmark. Midian raised his eyebrows, but there was absolutely no reaction from anyone on the street. They were under the shadow of Haruuc's fortress and riding across a wide stone plaza to towering gates before even Vounn noticed. "Ashi!" she snapped. "Put your scarf back on!"

"No," said Ashi. "I don't need to. No one here cares. I don't think they even recognize a Siberys Mark." She shook out her hair, delighting in the simple freedom.

"They will inside Khaar Mbar'ost."

"What if they do?" Ashi asked her mentor. "They'll know who I am soon enough anyway. How many humans are there at Haruuc's court?"

Vounn's lips pressed together, and she looked to Tariic. He shrugged. *"Ban,"* he said. "She's right." Vounn's mouth turned into a thin white line. Ashi felt a small glow of triumph. Geth gave her a smile, Ekhaas a flick of her ears and a wink.

Then the Deneith mercenaries were falling back and their party was riding alone across the last stretch of the plaza. Massive bugbear guards, each holding a halberd as big as a flagpole and wearing red cords fastened with bronze pins in the shape of Haruuc's sword and crown crest around their upper arms, stood straight and tall as they approached the gates of Khaar Mbar'ost. The company rode through into a hall as big as a courtyard. The unfettered noise of Rhukaan Draal vanished behind them, replaced by the controlled echoes of a fortress. From the wall opposite, an enormous relief sculpture of a hobgoblin warrior glared down at the gate, as if challenging anyone who dared to enter. Everbright lanterns ringed the hall, but its ceiling still vanished into shadow somewhere above the great sculpture's head. Tariic reined in his horse and looked back at them.

"Welcome to the court of Lhesh Haruuc Shaarat'kor," he said.

A hobgoblin wearing the red corded armband of Khaar Mbar'ost led them deeper into the fortress, to a chamber where Tariic said they would be able to leave their packs for transfer to the quarters that awaited them. Basins of warm water and small pots of soft soap that smelled of herbs were brought so they could refresh themselves. A screen made of fine fabric that Ashi suspected had been imported from Karrnath was set up for them to change behind should they wish to do so. Most of their baggage had been left with the rest of the delegation in Sterngate and would arrive with them, but Ashi was disappointed to discover that Vounn had somehow managed to transport complete sets of formal clothing in her traveling pack.

To her astonishment, however, the clothing Vounn produced for her wasn't the gown that she would have expected, but clean trousers, a shirt, and a jacket reminiscent of a parade uniform. The lady seneschal seemed to take pleasure in her surprise. "Did you think a party gown would impress Haruuc's court?" she asked Ashi. "I may have one if you prefer."

"No," Ashi said quickly. "This will be fine." She snatched the outfit before Vounn could take it back and retreated behind the screen.

Vounn nodded when she came out. "Polish your boots," she said, then took her turn behind the screen.

Midian changed into a clean shirt and a brightly colored vest taken from his pack. Tariic, Aruget, Thuun, and Krakuul gave their armor a rapid polishing. Chetiin and Ekhaas did nothing except brush the dust from their clothes. Geth, Ashi suspected, would have done nothing at all except that Tariic produced the blue tabard of a House Deneith guard.

The shifter growled at him. "Where did you get that?"

"From a guard in Sentinel Tower. If you're going to be Ashi's bodyguard, you should look the part." Tariic held out the tabard. "Put it on and be sure to walk behind Ashi."

Scowling, Geth pulled the tabard over his head and stuffed the fabric roughly through his sword belt—unlike in human courts, weapons were not only permitted here, but expected. He managed to catch and tear the tabard several times with the hooks on the back of his gauntlet, leading to a round of cursing that ended only when Vounn stepped out from behind the screen.

Ashi stared in surprise. Vounn wore a dress that was as simply cut as any Ashi had ever seen, and yet somehow it flattered her. The dominant fabric was a blue-gray silk, plain in color and with only the barest hint of a pattern yet of fine quality and excellent weight. The overall effect was one of understated wealth, of power and influence hinted at but not quite revealed. Tariic slapped a hand against his chest in applause. Vounn acknowledged him with a nod and a shallow curtsy.

Tariic dismissed the hobgoblin servant and led them himself to a large antechamber in which a number of goblins and hobgoblins waited, talking quietly together in small groups. At one end of the antechamber, a broad flight of steps rose to another hall. Ashi couldn't see past the stairs, but she could hear voices speaking in Goblin. Tariic spoke to a goblin with a red cord armband who darted up the stairs and into the next hall. Tariic turned back to them. "The assembly of warlords is meeting. Haruuc will summon us when there's a pause in the discussion."

He looked nervous for the first time Ashi could remember. "Is there anything we can do?" she asked.

"Wait." His ears twitched. "Vounn, sit with me. I'll tell you who some of the warlords are that are here."

The hobgoblin and the lady seneschal went to a nearby bench. Midian shrugged, went to another bench, produced the little yellow book he'd been reading when they arrived in Sterngate, and began reading again. Chetiin nudged Geth. "There's someone I want to find before we go in," he said. "I'll be back." He walked away toward the end of the hall.

In the next hall, a voice rose loud. Ekhaas's ears twitched toward it, and her eyes narrowed. Ashi strained to follow the voice, but most of the speech was words she didn't know yet. "What are they saying?" she asked.

"Try this," said Geth. He took her hand and placed it just below his on the hilt of his sword so they were both holding the weapon.

Instantly, she understood the words as if she'd been speaking Goblin all her life. ". . . hold us back!" ranted the speaker. "Our clans are willing! Our warriors are waiting! There are riches to be had over the Seawalls. A swift descent from Matshuc Zaal would put Sterngate in our hands. I have reports from a scout who says that he's worked out a path through the human defenses."

"Has he followed the path?" asked another voice. This one was calmer and deeper, speaking in measured, thoughtful tones. "Has he walked up to the walls of Sterngate?"

"He waits only for confirmation of our interest in his plan before he makes the attempt!"

"In other words, he hasn't and he wisely isn't going to throw his life away for no reason," said the deeper voice. "Daavn, Sterngate's deadliest defenses are the ones that can't be seen from a distance."

The first voice paused for a moment, then changed tactics. "A strike around the northern end of the Seawalls then," said Daavn. "With Skullreave as our staging base, we're three days' march from the colony the Brelish king is allowing to call itself New Cyre. You know their defenses are weak."

"Their defenses are weak because they're poor," shouted a third voice. "Sit down, Daavn."

"Respect the order of assembly," said a fourth voice wearily, as if the speaker had repeated the words too many times.

"Daavn, we will not attack Breland," said the deep voice, almost as weary. "We are bound by the Treaty of Thronehold. Yield the pole and sit down if you have nothing new to say."

A murmuring of other voices agreed with him.

Daavn was silent for a moment, then said, "Valenar."

The murmuring voices ended instantly, and Daavn went on more boldly. "The ancient enemies of our people have taken up residence across Kraken Bay. When the Valenar elves claimed their territory, they even did it on the basis of blood spilled fighting against our ancestors. They claim a victory they didn't earn. We should take ships and teach them what it means to fight hobgoblins!"

This time the murmurs that rose were excited and voices called out support to Daavn—but they all ended as the deep voice shouted. "There will be no attacks outside our borders! Valenar is also a Thronehold nation!"

"My clan cries out for war!"

"If the Marhaan want war, Daavn," said the deep voice, "look for it in the Mournland. Push back the mists and seek all the riches you wish."

Daavn had no answer, and there were no more murmurs. The deep voice grunted and said, "Lower the banner of the Marhaan. Their warlord has finished, and Aguus of the Bound Cat clan wishes to speak."

Ashi released the hilt of Geth's sword and the voices became incomprehensible once more. "Incredible. That deep voice, was that—?"

"Haruuc," said Ekhaas. "You see what he fights against."

"I didn't realize that Darguun shared a border with the Mournland," Geth said.

Ekhaas's ears twitched irritably. "Few people do, but in fact Darguun—"

"—has the longest land border with the Mournland of any nation," said a new voice, completing her thought.

All three of them turned to face the speaker, a hobgoblin in armor that had been painted with Haruuc's scarlet blade and spiked crown. By the unlined orange-red skin of his face, Ashi guessed he was relatively young, maybe a few years younger than Tariic and a few years older than her, but his hair was already a dark gray that made him seem older. Ashi thought she saw a cloud of annoyance pass through Ekhaas's eyes, but then it was gone. She would have been annoyed as well, except that the speaker stood with Chetiin and the goblin's face creased slightly as he said, "This one who speaks before he thinks is Dagii of Mur Talaan. He's the best fighter in Haruuc's personal guard, and a friend."

Dagii's eyes—shadow gray like his hair—skipped past Ekhaas, drifted along Ashi, and lingered on Geth. The shifter bared his teeth. "Like what you see, *roo?*"

"No," said Dagii bluntly, "but I don't have much choice, do I?"

Ashi actually saw Geth's eyes go wide as Dagii called his bluff, then narrow as his temper flared. Chetiin moved between them before anything could happen. "Geth, did I say Dagii is a friend? Dagii, Geth is a friend too.

Dagii hadn't moved at all. *"Ban,"* he said. "He carries Aram, but what does he know about Darguun?"

"Grandfather Rat!" Geth cursed. "Does everybody know about my sword?" He glared at Ekhaas.

The *duur'kala* shook her head, and when she answered, she didn't sound happy. "Not everyone—he just happens to be one who does."

"And why's that?"

There was no missing the look that the three goblins exchanged. Ashi's eyebrows rose, and Geth cursed again. "I really want to know what Haruuc has in store for me."

"You won't have to wait long now," said Tariic. He, Vounn, and Midian had risen from their benches. "I think we're about to go before him."

Ashi followed their gaze. Another hobgoblin was coming down the stairs from the next hall, and Ashi was quite sure he was the oldest hobgoblin she'd ever seen. His hair and thick beard were gray as ash and his skin was faded orange. He carried a heavy sword on his belt but wore no armor, though to Ashi's eye the bronze disks that decorated his long mantle and the bronze bands that circled his forearms looked heavy enough to block blows. He was also fat, with the body of a powerful man who had long since subsided into inactivity. He came down the stairs almost sideways, but his strides across the chamber to meet them were sure.

He struck his chest with a fist as he approached. *"Mo'saa*, Tariic. It's good to have you back. And *saa'atcha,* Lady Vounn." He greeted Vounn with another salute. Like Dagii, his eyes slid over Ekhaas and Ashi but paused on Midian as if confused, and lingered with fascination on Geth.

"Munta of Gantii Vus, also known as Munta the Gray," said Vounn. She returned his salute in the goblin manner, earning an approving smile from him. "It is an honor."

"Is he ready for us, Munta?" Tariic asked.

"Any moment," confirmed the old hobgoblin. "You'll want to be on the stairs."

Tariic moved like a miser afraid to miss the offer of free gold. The rest of them hurried after him, leaving Dagii behind.

Ekhaas and Tariic had drilled all of them on what would happen. Compared to the reception ceremony for the Darguuls at Sentinel Tower, Vounn's official greeting in Khaar Mbar'ost would be a simple affair, but it was bound by goblin tradition and had to happen in a very particular way. The three soldiers would enter first as an honor guard, followed by Tariic, walking on the left, escorting Vounn on the right. Ashi would follow directly behind Vounn, her head down to indicate that she was subordinate to Vounn, while Geth followed her, his head up to show that he was her watchful guard. Midian would follow Tariic, his head down as well. Ekhaas and Chetiin would come last, heads up and well back from Tariic and Vounn to show that they stood on their own. Ashi had the strong feeling that neither Chetiin nor Midian really wanted a formal presentation to Haruuc, but they had no choice. Tradition dictated that *all* members of a party arriving at a warlord's court be presented together.

They were only just assembled when a thin hobgoblin woman appeared at the top of the stairs and called out, *"Tariic gaate Rhukaan Taash bozhuumo!"*

Tariic, son of Rhukaan Taash, is summoned! The words still sounded strange to Ashi, but only Goblin would be spoken during the formal greeting, and Ekhaas had made certain that she would understand everything that happened. When their party began moving up the stairs, Ashi was ready.

With her head bowed, she could see nothing of the hall at the top of the stairs. She had a sense of a large space, of the presence of a small crowd of people attempting to be silent, of softly crackling fires, of the harsh odor of some strange blend of incense. All she could see was the stone of the floor underfoot, and that was still rough-edged, relatively new and not yet worn down by the centuries and the passing of countless feet. There were shadows—the room was dimly lit but not dark—and off to each side she could see ranks of heavy hobgoblin boots. Ahead of her, Vounn walked with calm assurance, as if out for a stroll. Behind her, Geth was swearing softly in amazement.

She clenched her teeth and kept her head down for a good fifteen paces, but then she could stand it no longer. She lifted her head for a swift and surreptitious look around—only to find that she couldn't lower her eyes again.

The throne room of Lhesh Haruuc was as big as she'd imagined it, made larger by the deep shadows that spread up the walls to the ceiling and gathered between the pools of light shed by widely spaced everbright lanterns. Tall statues of hobgoblin warriors stood against the wall, the lanterns at their feet emphasizing the fierce faces that snarled down at those below. Between the statues hung banners with the crests of the clans of Darguun. There were easily two dozen or more of them—some large, most smaller—and for each banner there was a warlord.

They stood in front of benches, heavily carved with images of battle, that had been placed at an angle to the front of the hall. Hobgoblins, some bugbears, a very few goblins, all of them dressed in robes and polished armor, all of them watching the party pacing the length of the throne room. Ekhaas had said that some of them were only warlords by formality, that many were really just clan chiefs given a place in Haruuc's assembly by tradition. When the assembly wasn't in session, they would return to territories often as small as a single crude holding.

Clan chief or mighty warlord, it made little difference. Ashi felt as though she bore the weight of each dark-eyed gaze, and it was almost enough to make her lower her head again. Almost, but not quite. The throne rose up ahead of her.

Benches, banners, and statues all seemed designed to focus attention on the dais at the end of the hall. Tall windows rose behind the dais, framing it with night's dark skies and gently swirling draperies. On the dais stood a blocky throne, and on the throne sat Lhesh Haruuc Shaarat'kor.

Ashi's first thought was that she wouldn't want to face him on the battlefield. Haruuc was powerfully built. He had big hands and wide shoulders, and his armor carried vicious spikes. A heavy hobgoblin sword, its blade stained red, leaned against one arm of the throne as if ready for use—the infamous *shaarat'kor* that had carved out a nation. Haruuc's face was strong, the sharp lower teeth that pushed over his upper lip and a thin beard giving him an expression of perpetual ferocity. He wore a spiked crown on his brow that looked like it might have been fashioned from broken swords. His eyes were bright and intense, and when they settled briefly on her, Ashi felt for a moment as if she were the focus of all Haruuc's interest.

"Who comes to the court of Lhesh Haruuc?" he asked in the same deep voice she had listened to from the antechamber. Without Geth's sword translating his speech in her mind, she heard his words in Goblin and felt the power he put behind even such a simple, ritual phrase.

"Tariic of Rhukaan Taash, son of Haluun, nephew to Haruuc, comes," said Tariic. "He comes with guards and a scholar who serve him. He returns from Karrlakton in Karrnath with a guest to the court."

"Vounn of Deneith, daughter of Sigor, comes," said Vounn in turn, her Goblin flawless. "She comes at the invitation of Lhesh Haruuc as the envoy of Deneith. She comes with Ashi of Deneith, daughter of Ner, and a guard who serves her."

"Ekhaas of Kech Volaar, daughter of the dirge, comes."

"Chetiin of the Silent Blades comes," said Chetiin, the last to speak. "He comes alone but bears the peace of the Silent Clans."

The thin hobgoblin who had summoned them into the throne room stepped onto a corner of the dais. "Do you who come owe allegiance to Lhesh Haruuc Shaarat'kor?"

Tariic and the three guards spoke in unison. "We owe allegiance to Lhesh Haruuc Shaarat'kor."

"Do you who come without allegiance pledge friendship to Lhesh Haruuc Shaarat'kor as guests to host in ancient bond?"

"We pledge friendship to Lhesh Haruuc Shaarat'kor," said Ashi along with the others.

The thin hobgoblin turned to Haruuc. "Lhesh, do you accept as host these guests who come?"

"I accept them." He held up his right hand, taking all of them in with a sweeping gesture. "You are all welcome in my court," he said—then added, "and throughout the land of the people as if you were beneath my roof."

The words weren't part of the ceremony and it took a moment for Ashi to work out what Haruuc had said. Even as she puzzled it out, though, mutters were passing through the assembly of warlords and the thin hobgoblin's ears were twitching in agitation. It wasn't the only surprise Haruuc had for them, though. Rising from his throne, he stepped down from the dais, stood before Vounn, and smiled broadly at her. "*Saa'atcha,* Vounn d'Deneith. *Ke chidar esaa roo, mo'esaa te.*"

Ashi didn't understand his words, but she watched in amazement as the high warlord of Darguun wrapped his arms around Vounn and hugged her.

CHAPTER ELEVEN

Honored greetings, Vounn d'Deneith. As your people greet friends, I welcome you."

Ekhaas stared as Haruuc pulled Vounn into a rough embrace. Among the goblin races, hugs were reserved for immediate family—and even then, only in private. Humans were far more casual about such close contact, and she'd grown accustomed to seeing human friends put their arms around each other. For Haruuc to do so with Vounn before the assembly of warlords was both more than the situation called for and spectacularly awkward. However well-intended the gesture might have been, the embrace would have been out of place even in a human court. Haruuc was lhesh, though, and it wasn't the first time he'd unexpectedly adopted a new custom.

Still, Ekhaas found somewhere else to look as Vounn stiffened in surprise, and she was fairly certain that all of the warlords would be having some kind of similar and silent reaction. Tariic abruptly saw great interest in his boots. The thin hobgoblin—a mistress of rituals named Razu if she remembered correctly—went pale and actually turned away, most likely hoping that the custom wasn't one the court was expected to follow.

If Ekhaas been any farther away from Haruuc and Vounn, though, she would have completely missed the words that the lhesh whispered, in the human tongue, into the lady seneschal's ear. "Complain about the mercenaries from the Pin Galaac clan. Say they pick fights."

She fought down her shock and glanced back just in time to see Vounn nod very slightly. Haruuc stepped back from her, his ears folding. "I trust I haven't offended you, Lady Vounn," he said, speaking out loud and in Goblin once more. "It has been too long since our great friends in House Deneith have sent someone of such prestige to us."

Vounn smiled graciously. "Your welcome is accepted in the spirit in which it was offered, lhesh." She touched a fist to her chest. "Honored greetings."

Haruuc matched her smile. "I hope your time as envoy to my court will be enjoyable and profitable for both Deneith and Darguun," he said, returning to his throne. "Tell me, do our fine warriors continue to please the lords of Deneith?" He looked out upon the assembled warlords as he spoke, including them in his pride and in his jovial mood.

"They please us and those who take their contracts," said Vounn. She paused for a moment, then added, "although I have heard complaints about mercenaries from the Pin Galaac clan causing trouble."

From the corner of her eye, Ekhaas saw one of the warlords flinch. His ears rose, and he turned to glare at another warlord. Ekhaas assumed that the first man was the chief of the Pin Galaac. She recognized the second from the broken hammer crest he wore on his armor—Daavn of the Marhaan. Confusion spread across his face and he tried to say something to the chief of the Pin Galaac, but the other warlord just turned away.

"Cause for concern," said Haruuc, all of his attention on Vounn. "We will discuss it, but not tonight." He picked up the red sword from the side of the throne, turned back to face the warlords, and slid the sword into its scabbard. "The assembly of the warlords is ended," he said formally. "Think on what we have spoken of."

"Mazo, lhesh," answered the warlords. Fists struck chests in a unified salute, but Haruuc was already walking to a door at one side of the dais. He paused and spoke a few words to Razu, then left.

Beside Ekhaas, Chetiin's eyes lit with a smile that he kept from his face. "What is it?" she asked him.

"Haruuc sows dissent," he said. "Pin Galaac depends on its mercenaries to bring wealth to the clan, but it trains them with Marhaan. Haruuc has put a knife between two allies with that trick."

Some of the warlords—the chief of Pin Galaac among them—looked like they were trying to get in close enough to exchange a few words with the new envoy of House Deneith, but Razu beat them to it. "Lhesh Haruuc wishes to speak with you privately," she said. "Come with me."

Razu led them through another door from the hall, this one below the dais, into a smaller audience chamber, then into a corridor beyond. Unlike ancient strongholds, such as Deneith's Sentinel Tower, which had grown over centuries, Khaar Mbar'ost had been built all at once by House Cannith. The passages and rooms followed an orderly plan, but Razu led them quickly along so many hallways and up so many stairs that when they stopped, Ekhaas had only the most general idea of where they were. Razu exchanged words with two hobgoblins standing guard before an unassuming door. She gestured for Aruget, Thuun, and Krakuul to remain outside, then opened the door and escorted the others through.

Haruuc was waiting for them in a chair by a window that opened onto the night. They were high in the fortress, but the sounds of Rhukaan Draal still drifted up to them. Haruuc had set aside his sword and some pieces of his armor. He looked tired and surprisingly old—he looked his age, Ekhaas realized.

Tiredness vanished as he rose, though. *"Ta muut*, Razu. *Va,"* he said. Razu nodded and left the room, closing the door behind her. Haruuc went directly to Vounn and took her hands in a gesture of greeting that, while still distinctly human, would have been far less scandalous in court. "Lady Vounn," he said, speaking in her language, "I apologize for dragging you into our intrigues from the first moment of your arrival, but you've rendered me aid. I'm grateful."

"Words from a friend are a gift given freely," said Vounn. "But

I understand this isn't the only time you intend to involve House Deneith in your politics."

Her words were light but direct. Haruuc's ears bent forward. "Never intentionally. As I recall, the Korth Edicts forbid the dragonmarked houses from engaging in the dirty game of politics. Your presence in my court is based entirely on the importance of our trade with Deneith."

Vounn smiled and nodded.

Haruuc smiled back and released Vounn's hands. "I see that you have already spoken with Tariic about the reason I wanted to bring you here."

"I've said nothing you didn't want me to say, Uncle," Tariic said quickly. Haruuc waved his hand dismissively.

"Don't be concerned, Tariic. You've done well. I'm pleased." He looked over the rest of the group standing beside the door. *"Saa,* Ekhaas *duur'kala,"* he said. *"Mo'saa*, Chetiin, old friend. I'm pleased with you both as well."

Unlike the others who had greeted them, however, Haruuc examined Ashi and Midian. Tariic turned to introduce them. "Uncle, this is—"

"—my charge, Ashi d'Deneith," said Vounn. She gave a little gesture, and Ashi stepped forward and bowed deeply to the lhesh. Ekhaas found herself holding her breath. If Haruuc questioned Ashi's presence, their lie to Vounn in Sentinel Tower would be uncovered.

But all that Haruuc revealed was pleasure. "Ashi d'Deneith, bearer of the Siberys Mark of Sentinel. *Saa'atcha!* We must speak at another time."

Ekhaas let her breath out and caught a glimpse of similar relief on Ashi's face. If Haruuc suspected something—and she was certain the canny warlord did—he said nothing. Ashi's decision to remove her scarf had been a blessing. Haruuc must have recognized the mark, remembered Ekhaas's tale of the Shadow Marches, and guessed who Ashi was. Tariic looked relieved, too. He turned to introduce Midian.

And a curious thought stirred in Ekhaas's mind. She knew why Haruuc hadn't expected Ashi's presence. Why didn't he recognize Midian when the gnome was there at his request?

Both her curiosity and Tariic's introduction were cut short as the door opened again and four more hobgoblins entered. Two of them were Munta the Gray and Dagii. The third was an older hobgoblin she didn't recognize. The fourth, however, she knew well.

Senen Dhakaan, ambassador of the Kech Volaar to the court of Haruuc, pointed a finger at Midian and, in a voice that rang with the trained tones of the senior *duur'kala* that she was, said, "What is he doing here?"

She spoke in Goblin, but Ekhaas was certain that everyone understood her tone. Senen's eyes fell on her, demanding an answer, and Ekhaas said, "Haruuc hired him, *chib.*"

Haruuc's ears rose. Senen turned on him. "You risk your alliance with our clan, Haruuc," she said, her voice seething. "This gnome is Midian Mit Davandi. He's known to the Kech Volaar and among the worst of the thieves and grave robbers who hide behind the mantle of the Library of Korranberg. He's no better than a *chaat'oor!*"

Midian's eyes and expression showed that he'd followed her accusations. "Now wait—" he said in the same language, but Haruuc cut him off.

"Be silent!" the lhesh growled. He stood tall and years seemed to drop from his scowling face. "Senen Dhakaan, control your anger! You forget your place. I wouldn't jeopardize our alliance. I didn't hire him!"

"I did," said Tariic. All of them stared at him—Senen in anger, Haruuc in amazement, Midian in utter surprise. Tariic's face flushed with guilt. "I hired him in your name, Uncle. We need more than legends. We need history, and Midian was recommended to me as the Library of Korranberg's best field researcher."

"Best thief!" said Senen.

"I am not a thief!" Midian snapped.

"Silence!" Haruuc's glare swept between his nephew, the gnome, and the Kech Volaar ambassador. "Tariic, how much does your researcher know?"

"As much as anyone else," Tariic answered. Haruuc's eyes narrowed and he twitched a finger to indicate Vounn and Ashi. Tariic nodded. "They know, but Ashi is Geth's friend and Vounn forced—"

Haruuc bared his teeth. "We will speak of it later." He looked at Vounn. "You know more than you were meant to, Lady Vounn. I trust you will be discreet." He turned back to Midian. "And you know *far* more than you should."

"Kill him," Senen said. "The leaders of Kech Volaar will thank you."

Midian's sun-browned face turned a sickly shade of gray. Haruuc glanced at Munta and the hobgoblin Ekhaas didn't recognize. The unknown hobgoblin's hands fell to twin fighting axes that hung from his belt. "It would be simplest to kill him," he said.

Munta shook his head. "He may be useful, Haruuc. If the Kech Volaar hate him, he must be good." Senen whirled to glare at the fat old warlord, but Munta met her gaze without flinching. "Your leaders have already agreed to what must happen, Senen. Accepting extra help makes no difference."

"Does it matter what I think?"

Everyone looked to Geth. The shifter spoke in the human tongue, but he stood with his hand on Aram, which meant that he had followed every word of the conversation. He faced Haruuc and Senen boldly, his jaw set firmly.

"I've been brought halfway across Khorvaire to perform a task I'm told is necessary for the survival of Darguun. I still don't know what that task is—I haven't even been acknowledged. But I do know that Midian can fight, and if this task of yours is as dangerous as I think it might be, I want good fighters beside me." He pointed at Midian. "He lives. Or I take Wrath and leave Darguun."

An icy chill plunged into Ekhaas's gut. Senen's face flushed with new anger. "You wouldn't—"

"I think he would," said Haruuc, and the room went quiet. Haruuc looked down at Geth—he was a good two handspans taller than the shifter—and Geth raised his chin to look back up at him. After a long moment, Haruuc bent his head.

"Shii marhu polto huuntad ka ruuska atchot," he said in Goblin, then spoke in the human language as Geth had. "Even an emperor must think twice when looking a tiger in the eye. You will rarely hear me say this, Geth, but you are right and I apologize. You've

waited too long to hear what needs to be said. You and Munta have persuaded me. Midian will live." Senen made a noise of objection, but Haruuc silenced her with a gesture before turning to Midian. "What you do for me, you do in secret. Your library will not hear of it."

Midian's features twisted in a kind of agony. "Surely a paper of some kind?" he said. "Maybe with some details altered? I could show it to you before I submitted it to the library."

"Your life or your silence," Haruuc said with a heavy finality, and Ekhaas saw Midian's throat bob as he swallowed.

"No papers," he agreed.

It was enough for Haruuc. He put his back to the gnome and returned his attention to Geth. "Of the welcomes I've made tonight, this is the one that I have anticipated the most. And I regret that it has been delayed. I would welcome you before my court, but I think you understand that I can't. Still, know that you have my highest respect." He put his fist to his chest and held it there. *"Saa'atcha,* Geth, bearer of Aram and hope of Darguun!"

"Saa'atcha," repeated Munta, Dagii, the unknown hobgoblin, and even—after a sharp glance from Haruuc—Senen.

The self-assurance that Geth had displayed in defending Midian seemed to evaporate before the formal greeting. Or rather, Ekhaas suspected, before the prospect of being the hope of Darguun. "Uhh . . . twice tak," Geth said, then thumped his gauntleted fist against his own chest. *"Saa'atcha,* lhesh."

Haruuc smiled. "I prefer your bluntness, Geth. You may use my name." He swept his arm around the room. "Within these walls, you may all use my name. Like thieves in a den, tonight we conspire to manipulate a nation."

There were chairs in the room, and Haruuc indicated that they should sit. Wine had been left, and the lhesh poured it for them all as he made the final necessary introductions. Midian flinched at Senen Dhakaan's name, either because, Ekhaas guessed, he knew her by reputation or because he recognized the prestige that the grant of the Dhakaan name—an homage to the great empire—carried among the Kech Volaar and the other modern Dhakaani clans.

The unknown hobgoblin was Vanii of the Ja'aram. "The last of my *shava,*" said Haruuc.

"Shava?" asked Ashi.

"A sword brother," Haruuc told her. "Someone who is trusted to fight beside you in battle, to defend you, to take charge of your affairs and deliver news of your death if you die in battle. It is an ancient and highly honored tradition." He sat down in his chair by the window. "Many warriors never trust anyone enough to have a *shava*. I was fortunate enough to have three." He tilted his cup, letting a little wine fall to the floor. "To your father, Tariic—and yours, Dagii," he said. "We owe tonight to his words."

He drank deeply. The rest of them followed his example and Ekhaas found that the wine was excellent, deliciously tart after so long drinking wine made in the human fashion.

Haruuc lowered his cup. "Geth," he said, "show us Aram."

The shifter stood and drew the sword. The light in the room shimmered on the purple byeshk metal of the blade. Ekhaas felt the same thrill that she had felt when she'd first seen Geth draw it, before she'd even recognized the weapon's name and history. It was the same thrill—or chill—that every descendant of the Dhakaani Empire should feel on seeing a true *lhesh shaarat,* a sword forged for warlords and heroes. A human might not have seen anything more than an ancient hobgoblin sword, somewhat heavier than most yet still perfectly balanced, still free from nicks and scratches in spite of its age. But to a goblin, to one of the *dar,* the sword spoke of the power of the warrior that dared to wield it.

"Ah," sighed Haruuc, leaning closer. Munta, Vanii, Tariic, Dagii—all of them shifted in awe at the sight of Aram. Senen tried to retain her aloof and angry manner, but Ekhaas saw her ears stand and her face shine with excitement. Ekhaas understood her reaction. She'd experienced it herself at first. For one of the Kech Volaar, keepers of the history of Dhakaan, possession of such an artifact was beyond a dream. Under any other circumstances, the leaders of the Kech Volaar would have sent agents—like Ekhaas—to seize the sword and whisk it away into the safety of the great vaults of secrets beneath Volaar Draal. But Aram wasn't any other sword, and she found her voice rising out of her.

"Behold Aram," she said, her voice ringing. "Forged by Taruuzh *dashoor* in the age of Dhakaan and given to Duulan, first of the name Kuun. The sword of heroes that will not suffer the grasp of a coward, held by the warrior who carried it in triumph from the ghostly fortress of Jhegesh Dol!"

Aram had accepted Geth's touch. The shifter had earned the right to carry the blade. The Kech Volaar would not have taken it from him.

"Behold Aram," Senen repeated like a soft echo.

"It's true," said Haruuc. "Everything you said about it, Ekhaas. If I had any doubts . . ." He sat back and looked around the room. When he spoke, his voice was hard once more.

"You all know that Darguun will face a crisis of succession when I die." For a moment it looked as if Vanii might interrupt with some protest at this reminder of the lhesh's mortality, but Haruuc held up his hand. "My death, like all our deaths, is inevitable. I don't look forward to it, but I must plan for the day it comes. I must choose a successor and, for the sake of Darguun, I must do all I can to ensure that my successor's reign does not see an end to what I built. Darguun is my legacy to our people, a nation that is our own. I want it to prosper. But I ask myself—why will our people follow my successor? Many warlords follow me because I am Haruuc. Will they transfer their loyalty to the one who comes after me?"

Haruuc curled his hands and rapped his knuckles together pensively as he continued. "If I'd listened long ago, I would have realized that the answer had already been given to me by Fenic of Mur Talaan. After the battle to capture the town that has become Rhukaan Draal—one of the most hard-fought battles of my life—he told me that the town had not stood by its lord, but that it had stood by the history embodied in the symbol of a feathery helmet. Only recently have those words come back to me. The lhesh of Darguun also needs a symbol of our people's history, something to tie the present to the glorious past."

Geth started and bared his teeth. His grip on the sword shifted and tightened. "You want Wrath?" he snarled.

The lhesh laughed. "I already have a sword!" he said, patting the weapon that rested nearby. "It will go to my successor as a symbol of his connection to me, but its history extends no farther than a weaponsmith's shop in the town of Rheklor. The symbol I seek must be older." His gaze stayed on Geth. "The inspiration for the symbol I wish to pass on to my successor came from your rediscovery of Aram. Knowing that I needed a connection to Dhakaan, I sought a closer tie with the keepers of history, the Kech Volaar. For thirty years, I have tried to make alliances with the Dhakaani clans, but I was rejected. The Kech Volaar, the Kech Shaarat, and the other *kech* saw no value in aligning themselves with an upstart warlord who had drifted from the pure traditions of the empire."

"Until you came to the Kech Volaar with a true appreciation for the power of history," interrupted Senen. "Don't portray us as isolationists hoarding knowledge as a dragon hoards gold. We have kept the history of Dhakaan until it was time to bring it forth. That time is now."

"As you say," Haruuc said. "We found common ground. The Kech Volaar would benefit from the resources of Darguun. Darguun would benefit from your stories and the inspiration of the Empire of Dhakaan."

"And you thought you would benefit from access to our vaults and the artifacts of Dhakaan."

Haruuc's ears flinched. "The candor of the Kech Volaar is famous," he said to Senen, then to the rest of them, "To put it bluntly, yes. I was disappointed, though. There are many wonders in the vaults of Volaar Draal, but none were exactly what I needed. Still, the potential for an alliance grew steadily. Then one day, a *duur'kala* returned from the west with stories of a tainted dragon and of a shifter who had recovered the blade Aram."

Ekhaas felt her face grow warm, and Haruuc nodded to her as he continued. "The *duur'kala* was Ekhaas, of course, and the shifter was Geth. At that time, I only knew Aram as a distant legend, but the Kech Volaar assured me that there was more to the story and that Aram might be the key to gaining what I needed." He looked to Senen.

"Taruuzh, who forged Aram," the ambassador said, "was the greatest of the Dhakaani *dashoor,* wizard-smiths whose secrets modern artificers haven't duplicated. He was the creator of many marvels, the three greatest of which were the binding stones that defeated an army of monsters during the ancient Daelkyr War, the grieving tree that we still use in a different form today, and the sword Aram. But our histories record that when Taruuzh forged Aram, he didn't forge it on its own."

Senen's voice rose into the cadence of a storyteller. *"Raat shi anaa*—the story continues. It is said that Taruuzh found inspiration in all things. It particularly pleased him to work in the mines, where he could handle the raw material of his creations, and he was so working in the mines of Suthar Draal when he found a vein of byeshk so pure that he named it *Khaar Vanon,* the Blood of Dusk. Taruuzh spent a year beneath the ground in the mine, extracting all of the ore from Khaar Vanon with his own hands. And while he worked, he saw the shape of new creations within the vein's twists and turns. At the end of the year, he returned with the ore to his stronghold at Taruuzh Kraat, where he spent another half a year smelting it, again with his own hands, refining his ideas as he refined the metal. Then, when the byeshk had been formed into ingots, he retreated from his apprentices and went into seclusion."

"When he reappeared, he bore with him three great creations forged from the byeshk of Khaar Vanon. First and greatest of these was Aram, the Sword of Heroes, which he gave to his friend Duulan Kuun, and the deeds which Duulan and his descendants performed with Aram are legend. Aram represented the inspiration that heroes provided for the people."

"Second was *Muut,* or Duty, the Shield of Nobles, which represented both the fealty that the lords and ladies of Dhakaan owed to the emperor and the protection that was their responsibility to the people. Muut was given into the care of the nobles of Dhakaan."

"Third was *Guulen*—Strength, to all appearances a simple rod of byeshk carved with symbols that had been old when the first *daashor* took up a hammer and the first *duur'kala* sang. But Taruuzh gave Guulen to the emperor with the words, 'In this are the glories of the people. Bear them in mind and the people will always know their king.' And Guulen, the Rod of Kings, became part of the imperial regalia and the emperor held it whenever he sat on his throne."

Senen bowed her head. *"Raat shan gath'kal dor.* The story stops but never ends." She looked up and her voice dropped into normal tones. "Over the centuries of the empire, the three treasures of Khaar Vanon were lost, as is the way with such things. The fate of Aram was well-known, lost by Rakari Kuun in Jhegesh Dol when he killed the daelkyr lord of that place. Muut was shattered and forgotten as Dhakaan slid toward the Desperate Times. Guulen remained the longest, but eventually it too was lost, vanishing along with *Marhu* Dabrak Riis, the Shaking Emperor, when he went out into the world to face his fears."

She fell silent. The room went quiet along with her until Geth lifted his eyes from Aram and said, "It sounds like this rod is what you need."

"It is," said Haruuc somberly. "Except that even after thousands of years of searching, no one has been able to find it."

"But you think I might be able to because I carry Wrath," Geth said. "That's the task you want me to perform."

Haruuc nodded without speaking.

"Because Aram and Guulen were both forged from the same vein of byeshk, they should still carry an affinity," said Senen. "The *duur'kala* of Kech Volaar have studied the ancient songs of our ancestors. Aram is only just stirring after its slumbers. We believe we can wake it to its full power again and that it will lead you to Guulen if the rod still exists."

Geth looked at the sword again. "Tiger, Wolf, and Rat," he said.

"Will you do it, Geth?" Haruuc asked. "I doubt that it will be easy, but you'll have whomever you choose at your side. Chetiin and Ekhaas will go with you—so will Dagii, and there's no better fighter in my service. I'll offer you gold or whatever reward you name, and you'll have the gratitude of a king, which is no small thing."

The shifter met Haruuc's gaze. "There are a lot of people in Khorvaire who don't like Darguun. They'd like to see Darguun fall apart into a bunch of squabbling clans again. They're afraid you're just waiting for another chance to come over the Seawall Mountains and attack."

"All of the human kings and queens watch each other because they're afraid of the same thing," Haruuc said. "When will Breland invade Thrane or Aundair attack Karrnath? Those people who don't like Darguun don't see it the way I do. United, Darguuls can find pride again and climb back to the heights of culture we once knew, but if Darguun falls, the chances that my people will attack are even greater. Ekhaas has told me you're a veteran of the Last War. You know the chaos of country fighting country, clan fighting clan." The lhesh sat forward. "Give my nation the chance to win its place in Khorvaire."

Geth was silent, and Ekhaas felt as if a hundred needles were being pushed into her scalp and back—then the shifter took a deep breath and nodded.

"I'll do it," he said.

CHAPTER TWELVE

The date for the ritual that would wake Wrath was set for three nights later when, Senen said, the moons would be at their brightest. At first Geth had felt a strange kind of elation. After his decision, everyone who had been in the room with Haruuc was slapping his shoulders and congratulating him. He had felt like . . . to be honest, he'd felt like a hero.

That elation had worn off like a night at the tavern. He'd awakened the next morning and just lain in bed, staring up at the ceiling of the chamber he'd been escorted to and wondering exactly what he'd gotten himself into. The feeling reminded him of a time during the war when he'd agreed to go with other members of his mercenary company to have a piercing done. Specifically, it reminded him of a moment in the piercing artist's shop when he'd looked up and seen the artist, needles and rings on a tray, working his way through the line of mercenaries. Too late to back out, too much time for second guessing.

He passed most of the next three days flipping back and forth between elation and second guessing. Plans were being made for the journey in the hope that the Kech Volaar's ritual would work and that Geth would, through Wrath, be able to sense the way to the rod, but he had little involvement in them. Chetiin, Ekhaas, and Dagii were handling the details. Geth wasn't sure about Dagii. He was willing to accept Haruuc's claim that he was the best fighter in his service and Chetiin's assurances that he was a good man, but the hobgoblin seemed strangely stiff and formal around him.

Midian, on the other hand, seemed to have adopted Geth as his best friend, and the gnome was always close, especially when Senen was around. He was no more obtrusive than Chetiin—though perhaps a little more talkative—and Geth caught him more than once observing everything that was going on around Khaar Mbar'ost with a great deal of interest. He would, of course, be going on the quest for the rod as well. Geth hoped that he and Ekhaas would get along. It seemed that Midian was going out of his way not to antagonize the *duur'kala,* but that might have been because he was still under Senen's watchful eye.

The majority of the shifter's time over the three days, however, was spent keeping up the illusion of his cover as Ashi's bodyguard. Ashi's time, meanwhile, was spent trailing Vounn as the lady seneschal settled into her duties as House Deneith's envoy to the court of Lhesh Haruuc. It seemed to Geth that she attended endless rounds of meetings with warlords—both Daavn of the Marhaan and Tugun of the Pin Galaac among them—and various independent mercenary captains, talking about very little. He might actually have enjoyed it if she'd been talking military operations with the warlords and captains, but if they discussed anything beyond the weather, the lay of the land, and the state of affairs in Khorvaire, it was usually issues of supply and personnel. Geth pitied Aruget, Thuun, and Krakuul. The three hobgoblins who had accompanied them from Sterngate had been assigned by Haruuc to act as Vounn's personal guards after hearing Tariic and Chetiin's reports on the attack by the rebellious Gan'duur clan. The three guards were around Vounn constantly. At least Geth had the chance to accompany Ashi on those rare occasions she left Vounn to do something on her own.

Which were unfortunately rare. Vounn kept her close—neither she nor Ashi had forgotten the pledge Ashi had made back in Sigilstar to accompany Geth on whatever task Haruuc set for him. Only Vounn's stern discipline had kept the two of them from breaking into an argument about it in front of Haruuc that first night. They'd argued about it many times in private, though. Geth's chamber was close to Vounn's, and he could hear their shouting. Now that Haruuc had met her, Vounn was ready to send Ashi back to Sentinel Tower as soon as Geth had departed on his quest and there was no need to provide a reason for his presence. Ashi had argued that if she were part of the party setting out on the quest, her presence would continue to disguise Geth's as he would be the bodyguard to a lady of Deneith riding out explore Darguun. Vounn had pointed out that no one simply "rode out to explore Darguun." Ashi had said she was going whether Vounn wanted her to or not because there was nothing Vounn could do to stop her.

Geth had put a pillow over his head and tried to sleep.

On the afternoon of the third day, though, he and Ashi did find some time to themselves. Vounn, under the watchful eyes of her three guards, had gone out into Rhukaan Draal to inspect an independent mercenary company and assess whether it was fit to accept into House Deneith's service—technically something she should have left to Redek at the Gathering Stone, but which Geth suspected she would be doing on a regular basis anyway—and Ashi had been left behind as a kind of punishment. Geth, through Chetiin, had found an empty training yard and brought Ashi out for some sparring. He'd been told not to draw Wrath within Haruuc's fortress for fear of revealing the weapon to anyone, so he had to make do with a mundane sword. After wielding Wrath, it was like swinging a steel bar, but the challenge felt good.

Ashi, of course, used her grandfather's honor blade, and the flashing of the bright blade in the sun added punctuation to her complaints about Vounn.

"—to the dressmaker's!" she said as she lunged at Geth. "Do you know I have fifteen dresses coming in the baggage from Sterngate? She made me bring them all!"

Each word was a slash. Geth blocked them all with his gauntlet. "That does sound like a bit much, but you are supposed to be representing Deneith in a foreign court. You're supposed to look like a lady." He whirled to bring his sword around in a backhand circle.

Ashi ducked under the swing. "I don't want to look like a lady!" She popped up again and planted her foot against his backside, shoving him into a stumble, then following up with chopping blow. Geth got his arm up, and her sword went skidding along the black steel. She sprang away before he could counterattack. "She made me learn about fashion, Geth! I know the difference between Fairhaven sleeves and Sharn shoulders. I can recognize the three main styles of lace from Zilargo. I know that green is popular in Korth this year and that I should never wear yellow."

Geth got back to his feet and stood crouched, waiting for her next attack. "Why's that?" he asked.

"It makes me look sallow!" Ashi charged, feinted left, and struck right. He was ready for her and caught her sword between the serrated teeth on the back of his weapon. For a moment the two swords were locked together. Ashi clenched her jaw as she pulled, trying to free her blade. At just the right moment, Geth twisted his sword, releasing hers. She took an involuntary step backward, he hooked her leg with his foot, and a moment later she was glowering at him from the dirt.

"Again!" she spat, standing up.

"Vounn's going to be back soon," he said.

"I don't care. All that matters to her is the honor of Deneith."

She charged again, and once again Geth locked her sword with his. This time she resisted the urge to pull away and instead pushed toward him. Geth twisted away from her and let her sprawl forward. As she picked herself up for a second time, he stepped back, lowered his sword to take a rest, and asked, "Have you tried not fighting her all the time?"

"What's that supposed to mean?"

"If what Vounn cares about is the honor of Deneith, try finding an argument that agrees with that point of view instead of challenging it."

Ashi stared at him. "Are you on her side?"

"Boar's snout, no!" Geth bared his teeth. "I'm trying to find a way to make sure you can come with me."

The words were spoiled by a loud grumbling from his stomach. Ashi raised an eyebrow. "Hungry?"

"Instead of breakfast this morning, I got a visit from Senen telling me not to eat today. I'm supposed to fast before the ritual tonight." He gave Ashi a long look. "Think about trying a different argument with Vounn?" he asked.

She scowled at him but nodded.

No shouting came from Vounn's chamber that evening. Geth, lying on his bed and resting in preparation for the ritual that was to come, took that as a good sign. He was considering going to look for Ashi—if only to distract himself from the hollow in his belly—when there was a knock at the door. The sound came from too low down to be human or hobgoblin, and Geth opened the door to find Midian. "So it seems there will be six of us on the quest," the gnome said, strolling in under Geth's arm.

"Six?" Geth raised his eyebrows.

"I passed Ashi and Vounn on their way to see Haruuc and make it official, but it looks like Ashi will be coming with us."

Geth couldn't hold back a grin. "Do you know why?"

"Vounn said something about upholding the special relationship between Deneith and Darguun. If you ask me, she's decided to send Ashi along to get in even better favor with Haruuc." Midian cocked his head. "Why do you ask?"

"No reason," Geth said with a shrug. It sounded like Ashi had taken his advice. "It will be good to have her along. She knows wilderness travel, and she's a good fighter."

"About that—well, not so much about Ashi as about me." The gnome hopped up into a chair. Given that it had been built for the comfort of hobgoblins and humans, it was as if Geth had decided to sit on top of a table. Apparently used to such inconveniences, Midian kicked his feet and looked at Geth. "I haven't thanked you for standing up for me in front of Senen and Haruuc. I know that took some nerve. Twice tak, as they say in the Eldeen Reaches."

Geth took a seat on his bed. "It wasn't nerve, really. I was just getting a little angry at being ignored, and sometimes I don't know when to shut up."

Midian snorted. "It was pretty eloquent for not knowing when to shut up."

"I saw you take down at least two hobgoblins when the Gan'duur attacked us. I'd call that good fighting."

"I've had to learn some tricks. You might have noticed that Darguuls can be a bit protective of their ruins. Generally, I find it's much easier to run. Not"—he added quickly—"that I'd run if friends were in trouble."

"You better not!" Geth gave a mocking growl.

The gnome laughed, then asked, "Speaking of the Gan'duur, have you heard yet how they knew to come west and ambush us?"

In fact, he had. Haruuc had just heard that morning and had passed the news to Vounn, who had announced it in Ashi's presence. "There was a traitor among the officers at Matshuc Zaal, someone with sympathies to the Gan'duur. The Darguuls use falcons to carry messages—he sent one to the Gan'duur telling them we'd be riding to the Gathering Stone. All the ambushers had to do was ride west until they found us."

Midian cursed. "Let's hope your sword doesn't lead us into Gan'duur territory, then." He slid from the chair. "Thank you again, Geth. A gnome remembers kindness."

He shook the shifter's hand. Geth saw him out. Once the door was closed, he turned around and surveyed the chamber. The hair on the back of his neck and on his forearms had lifted while he'd been talking to Midian. They hadn't been alone in the room, but at least the unseen presence seemed familiar. "Chetiin?" he said.

The *sharaat'khesh* elder slipped out from behind a cabinet that Geth could have sworn had been flush against the wall. "I spent too much time riding with you," he said in his scarred voice.

"How did you get in here?"

"With Midian."

"No, you didn't," Geth said. Chetiin's ears just twitched slightly. Geth shook his head and sighed. "Was there something you wanted?"

"To wish you luck in the ritual. If it succeeds, preparations are ready and we'll ride out in three days."

"Why wait so long?"

"It was Senen's suggestion. She thinks you may need time to recover after the ritual."

Geth grimaced. "That doesn't sound promising," he said. "You'll be able to use the time, though—you'll need to arrange supplies for an extra person. Ashi's probably going to come."

Chetiin's face creased in a smile. "So I heard—but that's no problem. I assumed that she'd eventually get her way and planned accordingly. We'll still be ready to go. Tariic is lending us some of his magebred horses for the journey."

"Will you need to ride with me again?"

"I have arranged for my own mount this time." the goblin said. His smile disappeared, though. "The news of a traitor in Matshuc Zaal is disturbing. I heard it from Haruuc this morning."

"A traitor could let enemies pass through Matshuc Zaal," said Geth.

Chetiin shook his head. "The Gan'duur oppose Haruuc, but they have no more desire to see the forces of Breland enter Darguun than anyone else. It's disturbing to know that the Gan'duur found a sympathizer in such a sensitive position. Their strength is increasing. For Haruuc's sake, I hope our mission is a swift one." He went to the door, then turned back to look at Geth. "I'm pleased that you've chosen to work with Haruuc, Geth."

"I thought the Silent Clans were officially neutral."

"We are. I'm pleased because I like you." Chetiin's expression was sober. "You should know that the bearer of Aram isn't as important to Haruuc's cause as the sword itself. If you hadn't agreed to help us—here, in Sigilstar, or in Lathleer—I would have had to kill you and take Aram. I'm glad I didn't have to do that."

A chill brought Geth's hair up again, but before he could say anything, there was another knock on the door. Chetiin stepped to one side of the door and motioned for Geth to open it. The shifter did. It was Senen and Ekhaas, both dressed in black robes. Senen held out a fold of white fabric to him.

"It is time," she said.

Geth glanced down and was somehow not surprised to find that Chetiin was gone. He took the white fabric from Senen. It turned out to be a simple linen robe with a loose belt. "Undress and put it on," Senen told him. "You must wear nothing else."

She and Ekhaas turned their backs. Geth shrugged and followed her instructions. As he undressed, he asked as casually as he could, "Ekhaas, what would have happened if I hadn't agreed to go to Sigilstar with Chetiin?"

"I would have gone to Lathleer or wherever you were and tried to talk you into coming myself."

The answer was direct and honest, but Geth couldn't help but wondering if it came too easily. He pushed away the cold feeling that welled up inside him and pulled the robe over his head, tying the belt around his waist.

"Ready," he said.

Senen turned and looked him over, then pointed at his throat. "Nothing else."

Geth reached up and his fingers touched the collar of black stones. "No," he said. "I keep this."

"Anything you wear could affect the ritual," Senen insisted. "Take it off." She stepped forward as if she'd pull it off him herself.

"Senen," Ekhaas said quickly, "it won't interfere. It's an orc Gatekeeper artifact, and Gatekeeper magic only makes Aram more powerful. I've seen it."

Senen looked at Ekhaas, her ears folded down, then she moved back. "Are you certain?" she asked. "Nothing can go wrong."

Ekhaas glanced at Geth, then nodded.

Senen pursed her lips and for a moment reminded Geth very strongly of Vounn. *"Ban,"* she said. "Bring Aram in its scabbard and come with us."

They led him up, climbing higher and higher in the tower. Geth's stomach gurgled unhappily, and the exertion of climbing made his head feel a little bit light. Senen nodded approvingly. "It is as it should be," she said.

Geth held back a curse.

The final climb was up a tightly wound spiral staircase down which flowed the smell of night air. The stone steps were cold under Geth's feet. When they stepped up from the staircase, they were on the very roof of Khaar Mbar'ost, a small space that was perhaps fifteen paces from side to side and surrounded entirely by open air. Geth didn't need to go near the edge to know how high above the ground they were. The sounds of the city that were clearly audible from lower windows were only a dull murmur, obscured by the constant whisper of a breeze. The sun was just settling below the horizon, and the sky that surrounded them was a fiery canopy, purple like Wrath in the east and overhead, blue, then pink, then red and orange to the west. The moons had not yet risen, no stars were visible, and the Ring of Siberys was a pale smear in the south.

Another person waited on the roof, another hobgoblin woman in a black robe like those Ekhaas and Senen wore. The third woman was old, though—so old and seemingly frail that when she moved to meet them it was like watching an injured bat crawl across a rock. Her eyes were sharp, however, and she looked him over carefully, asking the same questions about the stone collar—in Goblin this time—that Senen had. Ekhaas gave her the same answer, but at least the old woman grunted and nodded with more conviction than Senen had, then turned to Geth.

"I am Aaspar," she said. "This is the first part of the ritual that will wake Aram." She gestured around them with a gnarled hand. "Tonight you will hold vigil beneath the moons and think on the history of the sword that you hold in your hand."

"I don't know its history," said Geth.

The old woman looked at him blankly and Ekhaas murmured in her ear, translating his words for her. Aaspar clicked her tongue. "You know the history. Ekhaas tells me she has told you stories of the name of Kuun. They are the same."

Geth blinked. He remembered—vaguely—stories Ekhaas had told him to pass the nights during a desperate race across the Shadow Marches. "I . . . I might not always have been listening," he said.

Ekhaas scowled at him as she translated, and Aaspar laughed.

"Think on them. You'll remember more than you believe. Now go to the circle and kneel. Leave Aram's scabbard outside it before you enter."

There was a circle drawn on the rooftop in charcoal. Geth walked to it, drew Wrath, set aside the scabbard, and stepped into the circle, kneeling on the stone of the roof. Aaspar swooped down after him, more like a bat than ever, and with a quick motion filled in a small portion of the circle that had been missing.

"When we are gone, you may move about the roof," she said, "but you must remain awake and you must hold onto Aram through the night. Don't release it. Do you understand?" He nodded and she clicked her tongue again. "We will return at dawn."

She stepped back to form a line with Ekhaas and Senen. "Face the sun," she told Geth, and he shifted around so that the red light was in his eyes. The movement put the three women at his back. His shoulders prickled, knowing they were back there but not knowing what they were doing.

Then they started to sing.

Geth recognized Ekhaas's voice in the song, like burning cedar. He could pick out another voice, too, higher and more clear. Soaring over both voices, though, was a sound that barely seemed as if it could come from the throat of a living creature. It had a depth like the sea and a luminous beauty like a hundred beeswax candles glowing in the dark. It pulled at his heart and seemed to reach into the base of his skull to push against his mind. He felt it in his head, in his chest, in his belly, in his groin. It brought a dozen emotions washing over him at once, so many that he couldn't react to them all but could only kneel and stare out into the gathering night.

It was Aaspar's voice, and all he could think was that if this was what her song sounded like, how had the songs of the great *duur'kala* of ancient Dhakaan sounded?

Slowly, he became aware that the chorus of the three *duur'kala* was changing and growing both deeper and fainter. At the same time, the charcoal outline of the circle within which he knelt seemed to be shifting and spreading across the rooftop. Soon the stones for a sword length around him were black, then two sword lengths. The circle was growing like the shadows of the setting sun.

The sun.

He looked up and realized that the sun had almost entirely vanished below the horizon, sinking just as the *duur'kala*'s song had. He could almost imagine that the three women weren't just singing along with the sun's setting but that they were actually singing it down. Time seemed to slow as he watched the disappearing sun and listened to the fading song.

CHAPTER THIRTEEN

Geth blinked.

The night was silent—and complete. The sun had set, and even the last red smudge was gone from the horizon. The *duur'kala*'s song had ended. Still kneeling, he twisted to look behind him. The rooftop was empty. It was also completely black. The charcoal of the circle had crept over every stone, leaving only its interior, where he knelt, clear.

In the east, the first two moons of the night were rising, the pale gray twins of Therendor, big and bulky, and Barrakas, a third its size but twice as bright. Geth stood and stepped out of the clean circle with a caution that struck him as ridiculous. Aaspar had said he could move about the roof after they'd left. He made certain he kept a tight hold on Wrath, though.

His knees were already stiff and protesting the time spent kneeling on the bare stone. He could feel the cool of the night creeping through the thin linen robe, and his hunger was a constant nagging. The night wouldn't be pleasant, but that was the point of vigils, wasn't it? At least he was allowed to move. He jumped and stretched, easing some of the pain and warming his body a little, then went to peer over the edge of the tower.

He immediately wished he hadn't. The view down onto the moonlit sprawl of the city, the Ghaal River and its first cataract flashing in the distance, seized the light-headed feeling he'd had climbing the stairs of Khaar Mbar'ost and set it spinning. Geth stepped back from the edge and crouched until the spinning stopped. He considered trying it again, to see if he could get used to the view, but decided against it. There was enough to see by looking out and up at the unfettered view of the sky. He sat down as comfortably as he could with the stones of the roof chilling his backside, held Wrath to him, and looked up into the night.

Think on the history of the sword that you hold.

Geth tried to remember what he could of the stories Ekhaas had once told him of the Dhakaani family named Kuun whose history had been tied to the sword. It was easier to think of the story that Senen had told only a few nights before, of Taruuzh and the forging of Wrath from the byeshk of Khaar Vanon. He wondered about the Rod of Kings and the Shield of Nobles. What had the shield been like? Did the rod still exist? He tried to envision Taruuzh laboring over his creations. He'd seen Taruuzh after a fashion. He'd been to the ruins of Taruuzh Kraat and seen the massive sculpture of the *dashoor* that stood there. In the ancient caves beneath Taruuzh Kraat, he'd seen the wizard-smith's effigy atop his tomb and faced his ghost through a storm of unnatural cold . . .

He blinked again and jerked his head upright before he could fall asleep. "Grandfather Rat's naked tail," he muttered. The night seemed colder than it should. It would be far too easy to nod off. He got back up onto his knees, kneeling once more. It took effort to stay upright. That would, he hoped, make it easier to stay awake as well. He bent his thoughts back to Wrath, forcing himself past Taruuzh.

Taruuzh had given the sword to Duulan Kuun, the first to carry it, but the name that had always stuck in Geth's mind was Rakari Kuun, who had been the last to carry it. He'd always felt an affinity for the hobgoblin hero who had destroyed a terrible evil but in the process lost his birthright. Geth had walked where Rakari had walked and had fought the evil—or a phantom of the evil—that Rakari had fought. Sometimes he still woke to nightmares of Jhegesh Dol, the Place of Cuts. In his dreams he could hear the sound of knives and bone saws and the screams of tortured orcs, goblins, and hobgoblins. He could see their mutilated ghosts and the horrible spectacle of their amputated limbs given a terrible, vengeful life of their own. He imagined what it must have been like for Rakari Kuun to enter Jhegesh Dol when it wasn't an ethereal remnant of the past but a real place, full of pain and horror. He imagined the hero's fear at facing the lavender-eyed monster that had been the lord of Jhegesh Dol, one of the alien daelkyr, his fingers replaced with living blades as long as swords, as sharp as axes, so sharp they cut light itself . . .

And in Geth's mind, for what seemed like an instant, he was Rakari Kuun, plunging Wrath into the lord of Jhegesh Dol, forced to flee as all the blades of Jhegesh Dol fell like a steel rain.

Heart racing, Geth's eyes opened wide, and he was back on the roof of Khaar Mbar'ost. Time had passed—the twin moons had risen higher and another moon was reaching over the horizon—but he was certain that he had not fallen asleep. The memories that had played in his head had simply belonged to someone else.

He lifted Wrath into the air and stared at the sword. Did it shine a little brighter? Was there a depth to the twilight metal that hadn't been there before?

He groped for another story, the tale of Mazaan Kuun and the Hundred Elves. What had Ekhaas said of Mazaan Kuun? That he'd been a great strategist in the days when the Empire of Dhakaan had clashed with elves from the island-continent of Aerenal who had attempted to create a colony on the mainland. Mazaan had stood alone on the plains against a hundred elves, each wearing the spirit of an ancestor like a mask . . .

And he was Mazaan Kuun, luring the elves into a river-washed canyon where the stones split into a maze and where smoking fires turned friends into enemies. Wrath rose and fell only fifty times, but in the end, all of the hundred elves were dead. Half had been killed by their own kind in the frenzy of battle.

The moons had moved even more when he saw them again. Time had passed as he remembered the story. No, as he had *lived* the story. There had been details in the memories that Ekhaas had never conveyed in her story. The sound of horses, the sight of one hundred massed elf riders he might have imagined, but he couldn't have imagined the unfamiliar smell of the smoke with which Mazaan had filled the canyon.

"You," he said to Wrath. "Tiger and Wolf, you're doing this."

He tried to remember one of Ekhaas's stories of Duulan Kuun and found that he all but plunged into it. Duulan fought a roaring giant, taller than a hill, by climbing up the monster's back and thrusting Wrath—newly forged—into its ear. He leaped clear of the dying creature and swept up the woman, a princess of the beautiful city of Paluur Draal, who would become his wife.

Moons barely flickered before his eyes as the next story came over him. Duulan turning the tide of a battle against cackling gnoll tribes. And the next story, Duulan grieving over the grave of his wife, then riding into the Eternal Forest in pursuit of the dark fey creature that had killed her.

The stories came without interruption. Duulan's twin sons, Nasaar and Vanon, who wielded Wrath in turn, and all the great deeds they did with it. Mekiis, the youngest of Duulan's great-grandchildren, who took up the sword when she was a child and killed the assassin who would have killed her, who later became a *duur'kala* and the wife of an emperor. Biish, who was her nephew and became an outlaw as one dynasty of emperors fell and another began.

Geth was aware of the flow of time, of moons that seemed to rush and stutter across the sky. He was aware of the pain in his joints and the cold in his muscles. He had vague hints that he sometimes stood and staggered about the roof, trying to warm himself, but there was always the flow of stories. Some of them, like the ribald adventures of Jhezon "One-Eye" Kuun, he was certain Ekhaas had never told him, but they played out in his mind all the same.

He thought he laughed. He was certain he shouted in rage and in excitement. When Wrath once again plunged into the heart of the lavender-eyed lord of Jhegesh Dol and was abandoned by Rakari Kuun, when everything went dark as if there were no more stories and no more heroes, he cried.

But then the darkness lifted and a new story began. The story of a strange new creature not of the name of Kuun, not hobgoblin at all and almost as much beast as man, but still a hero who carried Wrath out of Jhegesh Dol and into a new age . . .

He heard music.

Geth opened his eyes to see Ekhaas, Senen, and Aaspar singing. This time, though, they stood with their backs to him, facing the rising sun as they sang the day into existence. Their song of dawn was as exquisitely beautiful as the song of dusk, ascending into something powerful but still ethereal.

Wrath was still in his hands, still raised before him. His arms ached and trembled with the effort of holding the sword, but they held firm. Beneath his fingers, Wrath seemed to pulse and surge in a way that it never had before. He felt a bond to the sword and to all those of the name of Kuun who had carried it in the distant past. With Wrath in his grasp, he felt like he could do anything.

His spirit might have been flying with the *duur'kala*'s song, but his legs weren't taking him anywhere. They were numb. When he looked down, he saw that he was kneeling exactly where he had started within the charcoal circle, once more shrunk back to only a line on the stones of the roof.

The song of the *duur'kala* peaked as the lower curve of the sun cleared the horizon and morning came to Rhukaan Draal. The three singers turned to face Geth. Ekhaas and Senen continued to sing, but Aaspar looked at him and spoke.

"Stand," she said, the word like music. Even her speech was song—how had he not heard that before?

Geth stood, rising awkwardly. His legs felt like wood at first, then they felt like they were on fire as sensation returned to them in a rush of tingling agony. He twisted and almost fell, catching himself at the last moment—but not before his gaze had turned away, just for a moment, from the *duur'kala*.

Smoke rose to the north. Great black clouds of it, twisting high up into the air to be pushed into leaning pillars by the morning breeze. There were other people on the roof, too. Chetiin, Midian, Dagii, Ashi. Munta the Gray. Tariic. Vanii. Haruuc.

The lhesh wore armor, heavy and spiked, with a helmet to take the place of his crown. Tariic and Vanii wore armor as well. Munta wore a grave expression.

"Don't speak!" Aaspar said sharply. "Look at me!"

Geth turned back to her, the motion bringing new pain into his legs. Aaspar lifted her hand and Geth, instinctively, raised Wrath to match her. The old woman drew breath and began to sing again, her voice blending back into Senen's and Ekhaas's.

The song had changed. It was deep and dark, like a cave that had never seen daylight. There was a longing in it, a reminder of . . . Home? Friends? Family? Geth found himself thinking of a village in the northern Eldeen Reaches that he hadn't thought of in years and of a man and a woman who had died long before. But he caught only the edge of the song. Aaspar was singing to Wrath.

He felt the sword's response, and new images passed through his vision. Taruuzh with miner's pick in hand, breaking rocks to expose the dark ore vein of Khaar Vanon. Taruuzh with a hammer before a forge. The song altered slightly and the image shifted to focus on a rod of byeshk, as long as Geth's forearm and as thick as his wrist, that shone in the forge light as Taruuzh polished its rune-carved surface. A tremor passed through Wrath.

"Now," said Aaspar, "turn and point the way!"

The voices of the *duur'kala* rose once more, then fell away, but the surging pulse in Wrath remained. With the certainty of a compass needle, Geth turned and pointed the sword south-southwest.

"There." His voice was cracked and raw. "The rod is there."

Aaspar clicked her tongue in satisfaction, then broke the charcoal circle with a brush of her foot. For a moment, the roof remained silent as if everyone watching Geth were afraid to say anything, then a look of annoyance crossed Aaspar's face. "It's over," she said, turning away. "It worked."

Voices broke out all around him with expressions of excitement and thanks. Ekhaas and Ashi were the first ones to reach him. As if the touch of their hands had severed ropes holding him up, Geth drooped back into their arms. Exhaustion, pain, and hunger washed over him. Senen held Wrath's scabbard, and with her help, Geth guided the sword back into it. His fingers cramped, and he had to will them to open and release the sword's hilt. The magic of the song was still in the sword—he knew that he could touch Wrath and he would feel the distant presence of the rod once more.

"I saw the stories of Kuun," he croaked.

"I knew you would," Ekhaas said. "I knew you were listening."

"No, it was Wrath—Wrath remembers," he said, but his dry throat seized and the words just came out as a rasp. Chetiin held out a cup of water. Geth took it with shaking hands and drank eagerly. Before he could try to repeat himself, though, Haruuc stepped in front of him.

"You know where the rod is? Do you know far?"

Geth shook his head. "I can feel a direction, but that's all. It could be in Rhukaan Draal or it could be across the Thunder Sea in Xen'drik."

Haruuc's ears dipped but he nodded. "It is as much as I should have hoped for. Thank you, Geth." He put a hand on Geth's shoulder. "I would have given you a week to rest after this, but we don't have that time. You have a day at most—you must leave tomorrow morning."

"What? Why?" Geth asked, then remembered what he had glimpsed and twisted around against the hands that supported him to look at the smoke billowing into the northern sky. "What is that? What's burning?"

"The fields on the far side of the Ghaal," growled Haruuc. "The Gan'duur struck last night. They're burning crops."

"Grandfather Rat."

"*Cho.* They're getting too bold. I want you away in case they try to come south of the river." The lhesh stepped back and put a fist to his chest. "Swift travel and great glory, Geth."

He turned and left the rooftop with Tariic, Vanii, and Munta following him. Tariic turned and met Geth's eyes, saluting him as his uncle had before going down the stairs. Dagii moved to face Geth. "I could have everything ready as early as tonight," he said.

The tales he had seen in the night throbbed in Geth's head. The heroes of Kuun wouldn't have waited. Neither would he. Geth drew a deep breath, braced himself, and stood. A wave of dizziness came over him, but he fought it back and took Wrath when Senen offered the sword to him.

"Do it," he told Dagii. "We ride at dusk."

CHAPTER FOURTEEN

Their first night out of Rhukaan Draal was the most difficult, at least for Geth. Although he'd broken his fast with a tremendous meal and slept through most of the day, the effects of his vigil on the roof of Khaar Mbar'ost lingered in his bones. He swayed in the saddle and kept falling asleep as they rode. More than once he wondered if maybe they should have waited until the morning, but he knew that the stories of the past wouldn't have let him. They churned inside him, demanding action. The entire party—Ekhaas and Ashi, Dagii, Chetiin, and Midian—felt the urgency to be on the road, though. Haruuc hadn't returned to Khaar Mbar'ost by nightfall, but reports of events beyond the Ghaal River had: the Gan'duur's descent on the fields had been swift and thorough. A significant portion of the crops, summer-dry and almost ready for harvest, had burned, and the Gan'duur raiding parties were still roaming the countryside, causing more havoc.

When they stopped near dawn, Geth all but tumbled out of his saddle. Dagii let none of them sleep for long, however. By midafternoon, they were riding again. It became their pattern to ride through the afternoon and evening and late into the night, sleeping through the dawn and morning hours. As Chetiin explained to Geth, in a land where most of the population was as comfortable at night as during the day, dawn was the least active time and the safest period to rest.

Geth missed riding with the goblin behind him, but Chetiin had, as he'd said, acquired a mount of his own, one that was almost as silent as he was. While the rest of the party clopped along on Tariic's magebred horses—or in Midian's case on his magical pony—Chetiin rode a great black wolf that padded beside them like a shadow. There was a disturbing, malevolent sharpness in the animal's eyes, and when Ashi commented that first night that she felt like the wolf was watching them all, the snarl that came from its muzzle sounded eerily like speech.

"She is watching you," Chetiin said, "and she'd prefer if you didn't call her 'the wolf.' Her name is Marrow. She's a worg." He scratched behind his mount's ears. "Her pack has an ancient alliance with the *taarka'khesh*. She's agreed to travel with me as a favor."

"How can she run with the horses?" Geth asked. "I'd have thought they'd be terrified."

Chetiin produced a vial of slightly milky liquid. "A *taarka'khesh* preparation. She smells like a horse." Marrow growled and Chetiin added, "Not that she's happy about it."

Like the landscape between Matshuc Zaal and the Gathering Stone, the ruins of human habitation marked the country that they rode through south of Rhukaan Draal. It lacked, however, the feeling of emptiness and desolation. The fields and orchards that had run wild alongside the trade road had been tamed, though in many places it wasn't farmers working the soil, but slaves. Through the long afternoons, the distant crack of overseers' whips was as common as birdsong. In Matshuc Zaal, the slaves had been goblins, hobgoblins, and kobolds, but Geth was shocked to see humans, dwarves, and shifters in the fields as well. Ekhaas looked ashamed when he asked her about it. "Captives taken during the war or in raids," she said "If Haruuc were riding this way, you wouldn't see them. The overseers would hide them until he passed."

"He must know they're there," growled Geth. "Why doesn't he free them?"

"Haruuc holds a sword by the blade," said Ekhaas. "Promises of plunder—including slaves—were one of Haruuc's first tools in uniting the clans. Now he's paying for that. Warlords like

Daavn of the Marhaan are hungry for more wealth and he can't give it to them. He has to balance his desire to show a civilized face to the Five Nations with a need to keep appeased the clans that support him."

"If he ordered them to free their slaves, they'd turn against him faster than the Gan'duur have," said Midian.

Ekhaas scowled but nodded at the gnome's blunt assessment.

They traveled more slowly than they had along the trade road. They still followed roads, but the byways were old and not well-maintained. It was only a little better than riding across open country. At least they didn't always need to camp rough. On several nights, Dagii led them to the stronghold of one or another clan. Sometimes the strongholds were large and sometimes they were small, but they always welcomed Dagii and the rest of the party with grace and honor. The first few times they found shelter in a clan stronghold, Geth assumed their welcome came because they traveled under Haruuc's banner, but then one night he happened to let his hand rest on Wrath as Dagii and the local warlord exchanged greetings.

"We come with peace in our hearts and our blades in their sheaths," Dagii said in a phrase that sounded like ritual. "We ride on behalf of Lhesh Haruuc, who asks you to take us in as your guests for a night."

The warlord, a powerfully built hobgoblin wearing the crest of a sundered shield, laughed at the ritual. "The lhesh might ask, but I'll take you in because you are the one at my gate, Dagii. Welcome, brother!"

"Brother?" Geth asked Chetiin.

"It's an old courtesy between friendly clan chiefs." When surprise passed across Geth's face, Chetiin's ears twitched up. "You didn't realize? Dagii is chief of the Mur Talaan."

"I didn't know that. I thought he was just a member of the clan, the way Tariic's a member of the Rhukaan Taash." Geth stared at Dagii's back as he followed the local warlord into his stronghold. "What does his clan do while he's serving Haruuc?"

"The Mur Talaan is a very small clan. It was never big and war made it smaller. I wouldn't ask him about it—it's a private matter to him. What's left of the clan gets along well enough without his interference."

"Where is Mur Talaan's territory?"

"Rhukaan Draal."

Geth looked at the goblin in amazement. Chetiin shrugged. "The Cyran town that Haruuc conquered to build Rhukaan Draal was at the edge of Mur Talaan territory. Fenic, Dagii's father and the first of Haruuc's *shava,* ceded it to Haruuc as a place that would be neutral to all the clans of Darguun. Over time, the rest of their territory was lost, but the land beneath Rhukaan Draal still technically belongs to the Mur Talaan, even if the lhesh controls the city. It brings them—and Dagii—a great deal of honor, although very little else."

"If a human clan owned all the land under a city the size of Rhukaan Draal, they'd be as wealthy as a dragonmarked house."

Chetiin's ears twitched again. "Can you imagine trying to collect rents or taxes in Rhukaan Draal?"

"I guess not." Geth glanced again at Dagii, still talking with the local warlord, and tried to imagine the warrior who wore Haruuc's crest as a warlord in his own right. Maybe the responsibilities of a clan chief were the reason he seemed so stiff.

As they traveled farther from Rhukaan Draal, roads became paths and the strongholds of warlords became increasingly far apart. Territories were larger and some areas were simply unclaimed by any warlord. Bandits roamed these areas—and local strongmen who were simply bandits settled down and gone to seed. When they camped under the moons, they posted watches; when they stayed under a roof, it was less Dagii's invocation of Haruuc's name that earned them hospitality than Ekhaas's promise of stories told with the skill of a *duur'kala.*

Several times a day, Geth drew Wrath and held it out before him to be certain they were still on course, still heading south-southwest. On the tenth night of their journey, the same night that the last path ended at the long burned remains of a farmstead, they reached the eastern foothills of the Seawall Mountains. The hills were far more rugged in the south than they had been in the north at the Marguul Pass—and for the first time they discovered the weakness in Wrath's ability to point to the distant Rod of Kings.

"Grandfather Rat's naked tail." Geth stared along the length of Wrath as if closer inspection might somehow change the fact that the twilight blade pointed straight at the sheer rock face of a long escarpment.

"It points directly to the rod, doesn't it?" said Ashi. "No matter what's in the way. *Rond betch.*"

"We'll find a way up or around," Dagii said grimly. He turned his horse to the south and urged it onward.

It was Marrow who eventually found a way up the escarpment, sniffing out a narrow trail apparently used by wild game to reach a pool at the escarpment's base. The worg was able to bound up the trail with little difficulty, but the rest of them—with the exception of Midian, who simply dismissed his pony and tucked the silver horseshoe back into his pack—had to dismount and lead their horses up. By the time they reached the brow of the escarpment, dawn was breaking.

The ground above the escarpment was no less rugged than that below. When Geth held up Wrath again, the sword pointed to a hill that was only a little less steep than the escarpment. If they'd been able to travel as the sword pointed, the even harsher slopes of the gray mountains were only a day's ride away.

Dagii's ears folded back. "We travel by daylight from now on," he said. "We need to be able to see what's coming so we can avoid it."

The rest of them replied with grunts and groans of exhaustion, although Midian added, "At least we know the rod is in the mountains."

"How do you see that?" Geth asked.

"The sword points up. If the rod was somewhere beyond the mountains, it wouldn't. We're going to be climbing."

Geth groaned again.

Vounn told herself that she had done what she could. More than she should have, perhaps. When, after days of shouting about her desire to leave Rhukaan Draal, Ashi had come to her with a simple and reasonable argument—that allowing the bearer of the Siberys Mark of Sentinel to aid in the search for the Rod of Kings would certainly bring influence to Deneith, not just with Haruuc but with his successors—Vounn had almost been too overwhelmed to resist agreeing on the spot.

She had resisted, of course. Very little got the better of her. She'd turned the issue over in her mind, considering it from all sides. She had a strong suspicion that Ashi didn't really believe in what she was saying and that, to her, it was just another attempt to get Vounn to let her follow her friends. Her charge was, though, correct for a change. Her participation in the quest would reflect very well on Deneith. The look of surprise on Ashi's face when Vounn had finally agreed was almost amusing.

She had changed her mind as she watched Ashi ride out of Khaar Mbar'ost, but it had been too late then. Ashi was gone like a bird from the nest. Most of the time she could accept that. Vounn just hoped that she would never have to explain the loss of the Siberys Mark to the patriarch of House Deneith.

And while she waited for Ashi's return, there were other duties that Breven d'Deneith expected of her.

The warlords of Haruuc's court were more than eager to become acquainted with the envoy of House Deneith, but there was one clan that defied all of her efforts. Senen Dhakaan of the Kech Volaar refused to meet with her, in spite of the secret knowledge that they shared. Formal requests were rebuffed. Casual approaches were ignored. The warriors of the Dhakaani clans were famous for their skill at fighting in formation, but Deneith had never found enough influence with the proud, independent clans to hire their warriors as mercenaries. If Vounn could bring the warriors of the Kech Volaar into Deneith's legions, it would be a triumph.

From what Vounn could see, though, the Word Bearers might

have deigned to ally themselves with Haruuc, but their attitude toward Deneith had changed no more than a mountain in a day.

So she went to Haruuc.

Aruget followed her, of course. Vounn would have preferred to have a Deneith mercenary guarding her, but she'd accepted Haruuc's offer of hobgoblin guards gracefully. At least they knew the lhesh's fortress and the city, and Aruget, at least, had proved that he understood when to keep his mouth closed and obey orders.

She found Haruuc alone, brooding over a great map laid out on a table in a room with more maps hung on the walls. Vounn paused a respectable distance away from the table and dropped into a curtsy. "Lhesh," she said.

He raised his head and looked at her with weary eyes. "Lady Vounn."

"Am I disturbing you?"

"You're a welcome change from the disturbances of the Gan'duur." He forced energy into his face and beckoned her closer. "Look at this. Tell me what you see."

Vounn looked down at the map. Bright colors stood out on a faded background—the basic map had been created many years ago and updated several times. It showed Rhukaan Draal, its outskirts drawn and redrawn as the city expanded, and the surrounding area. The Ghaal River with its cataracts and the road leading north to the Gathering Stone were easy to recognize. The map also marked hills, streams, ravines, farmholds, and lanes. Simple wooden markers painted red, black, or white had been placed atop it, mostly to the north of the city. The black markers lay in scattered patterns atop farmholds, the red in a sweeping arc, the white in widely scattered clusters.

She pressed her lips together as she considered the patterns, then said, "I'm a diplomat, not a strategist, lhesh, but I would say this shows the Gan'duur attacks."

"The attacks, my response, and sightings of Gan'duur raiders." Haruuc swept his hand through the air above the map. "They move quickly, staying ahead of my men. They strike, split up, and move on. And this concerns me—" He pointed to the northeast and southwest extremes of the activity represented on the map, to white markers that stood off on their own with neither red nor black markers around them. "We received word by messenger falcons this morning of these positions. No attacks, just riders. They displayed no banners, so we can only assume they're Gan'duur, but it seemed they were riding here—and here." His fingers moved to indicate the river west and east of Rhukaan Draal. "An old Cyran bridge across the upper river. A ferry crossing on the lower."

"They mean to cross the Ghaal."

"Cho," said Haruuc. "Boats have been dispatched downstream and riders upstream. Perhaps we can catch them, but it may be too late." He fell back into a chair and pressed his knuckles together. "The patterns of clan warfare. You see now what I hope to forestall. *Maabet.* I thought my people were past this."

"A philosopher of Karrnath once wrote 'A farmer may sow wheat, but nature had the field before him,' " Vounn said.

Haruuc looked at her over his fists. "Falko Gergus in *The Battle Called Life."*

"You know it."

" 'If you want fine wool, better to befriend the shepherd than the wolf,' " the lhesh quoted back to her with a thin smile. "Gergus's metaphors have never found favor among goblins, but his principles are sound." He lowered his hands and sat up. "But I doubt that you came here either to discuss military philosophy or to hear my complaints. What do you want, Vounn?"

She bent her head. "I would be grateful if you could arrange a meeting between Senen Dhakaan and I. There are things I would like to discuss with her."

"But that she doesn't seem interested in discussing with you."

Vounn nodded.

Haruuc grunted. "I know that feeling too well. The Dhakaani clans could teach stubborn to the sea." He rose. "Let's go talk to Senen together."

"Now?" asked Vounn in surprise.

" 'The smith who knows his iron doesn't let it cool on the anvil,' " said Haruuc, quoting once more from Falko Gergus.

"You've obviously waited too long on Senen already, and I've spent too much time looking at field positions that are out of date." He motioned for Aruget, standing at the back of the room. "Run to Senen's quarters and see if she is there."

"Mazo." Aruget left. He was back quickly. "She is in the hall of honor, lhesh."

"I might have guessed," Haruuc said. "Wait at the Deneith quarters, Aruget. Lady Vounn is safe with me." He held out his arm and Vounn took it.

The hall of honor ran the full length of one of Khaar Mbar'ost's upper floors. Vounn knew the hall—it served much the same function that gardens did in other royal palaces, giving courtiers and councilors a place to stroll and converse. To be honest, however, she could never have pictured goblins, hobgoblins, and bugbears wandering among potted plants and flower beds. The long hall seemed much more appropriate, with statues of famous heroes lining its walls and intricate windows of stained glass capping the distant ends. The windows showed scenes of famous battles, but the colorful panels could also pivot to allow a flow of air.

As she and Haruuc mounted the stairs to the hall, a voice drifted down from above. Vounn's eyebrows rose. The murmur of speech typically filled the hall, sometimes punctuated by an exclamation or a curse, but always mingled. Now there was only one voice, a storyteller's voice, chanting a tale of ancient heroism with all the zeal of a enthusiastic priest delivering a sermon to the faithful. She glanced at Haruuc.

He gave her a faint smile and his ears flicked. "That would be Senen," he said. "The tales of the empire are a religion to the Dhakaani clans. I let her speak when she wishes. Her stories are good."

They emerged into the hall. Some distance away, before one of the great stained glass windows, Senen stood in front of an audience that would have only sparsely filled the hall had it been spread out. Packed into one end of the hall, though, it made for an appreciable crowd. Curiously, it was one of the most diverse groups Vounn had ever seen in Khaar Mbar'ost: Warlords and councilors formed the core of the audience, but ordinary warriors and servants stood at the fringes as well.

Standing right next to Senen was Tariic, listening closely to the *duur'kala*'s story. Or at least appearing to listen closely. Vounn had seen junior members of House Deneith watching plays and performances with just such a slightly-too-rapt expression, attending events for the sake of being seen to attend events, conspicuously demonstrating an appreciation for cultural forms because it was expected of them. She smiled and looked to Haruuc, but the lhesh's eyes were already on his nephew.

"He takes up the sword without testing the weight," he said softly.

"Lhesh?" asked Vounn.

Haruuc's ears flicked again, almost regretfully Vounn thought. He drew her to one side, almost into the shadow of one of the statues in the hall. No one had noticed the appearance of the lhesh—all of their attention was on Senen. "In many ways," Haruuc said, "Tariic takes after his father, my brother Haluun. Stories, even the stories of a *duur'kala*, never really caught Haluun's interest. Tariic is the same, but he makes a show of interest so that others see it."

"Many people do the same thing, lhesh," Vounn said. "They do what is expected of them."

Haruuc looked down at her. "That is a difference in our ideas of honor, Vounn. To do what is expected, to do your duty and do it well—yes, that is a part of honor. That is *muut,* something you do for yourself. But it is no one's duty to appreciate a story. Appreciating a story, to be seen to appreciate a story, is a sign of personal sophistication. When others see it, they may think of you as having honor, but it is *atcha,* honor achieved through deeds."

"Is that wrong?"

"No." Haruuc shook his head. "There is *atcha* in more than fighting, and many people seek out its lower forms. Honor begets honor. But for some . . ." He spread his hands. "Tariic understands *muut,* but he is drawn to *atcha.*"

"*Atcha* shouldn't be forced," said Vounn, trying to grasp what Haruuc's meaning. *Muut* and *atcha* weren't new concepts to her, but no one had tried before to explain them in quite the same terms.

"It is more complicated than that, but you begin to understand," Haruuc said. His ears sagged slightly, then twitched and rose again. "But I insult Tariic. He is a good man, and the lure of *atcha* is hard to resist. Without ambition, there would be no Darguun. Come—Senen is finishing her story. We will talk with her."

In front of the window, Senen pronounced the formulaic ending to hobgoblin stories—*Raat shan gath'kal dor*—and her audience broke out in applause. As the applause died down and the audience drifted apart, Haruuc escorted Vounn forward.

Bowing heads made a wave as the lhesh was finally seen and recognized. Tariic, offering his personal appreciation to Senen, turned with a start. "Uncle!"

Senen's response was more composed. She bent her head. *"Saa'atcha, lhesh."* She glanced at Vounn and her eyes went flat.

Haruuc seemed to take no notice. *"Saa,* Senen Dhakaan. Nephew." He nodded to Senen. "An excellent story. *Ta muut."*

The ambassador of the Kech Volaar twitched her ears in acknowledgment. "I will leave you to speak with Tariic," she said.

"Actually, Senen, we came looking for you," Haruuc said in a tone that was both casual and commanding. "Lady Vounn expressed an interest in speaking with you. I would like to think that two of my greatest allies—the Kech Volaar and House Deneith—might come to be friends."

Senen's ears pulled back and she bared her teeth. "Lhesh, she wants to hire us and nothing more."

Vounn made a swift decision—if the *duur'kala* could be blunt, so could she. "I do want to hire you," she said. "The military discipline of the Dhakaani clans is legendary. Deneith and the Kech Volaar would both find profit in selling your service."

Surprise and perhaps outrage at such honesty flickered in Senen's face, silencing her for a moment. Vounn stepped into the breach she had made. "But I've come to see that renowned discipline before that can happen, Deneith needs to know the Kech Volaar. How can we understand your people without understanding your traditions?" She bent her head to Senen. "Will you tell me your stories, Senen Dhakaan? Will you let me visit Volaar

Draal and show me the glories of the Empire of Dhakaan that the Kech Volaar keep alive?"

"Volaar Draal is not open for casual visitors," Senen said slowly, as if trying to find refuge in the words. "Especially *chaat'oor.*"

Quick as thought, Vounn turned the rejection around on her. "Then you must visit House Deneith in Karrlakton to see our memorials and understand our traditions." She raised her head. "The Mark of Sentinel was the first of the dragonmarks to manifest in humans, and long before Deneith was a House, we were proud warlords. Our history isn't so old as yours, but it is good. I offer you the chance to learn our story."

"And a generous offer it is, Senen," said Haruuc. "An invitation to the seat of power of a dragonmarked house is not extended lightly." His mouth was curved in a barely suppressed smile, and Vounn knew he had followed her strategy: the exchange of stories, irresistible to a *duur'kala,* between two groups with a common interest in the accomplishments of a martial past.

She could tell from Senen's expression that she understood as well that there was no graceful way to decline the offer entirely. The Kech Volaar ambassador's ears quivered, then bent. "I cannot accept on my own, and certainly I cannot leave my post in Rhukaan Draal, but I will relay your invitation to the leaders of my clan," she said.

"What about your stories?" Vounn asked her. "Surely you don't need to consult with the leaders of your clan before you share stories."

Interest flashed in Senen's eyes. "You are clever, Vounn d'Deneith. Call on me again and perhaps I will have a story to tell you." She nodded to Haruuc and walked away.

"Nicely done, Vounn," said Tariic quietly, watching Senen go. "*Paatcha!* I couldn't have done better."

Vounn thought she saw regret flit again across Haruuc's face but she couldn't be sure—one moment he was looking at his nephew, the next at a goblin messenger wearing the red-cord armband of Khaar Mbar'ost and hurrying along the hall of honor. The goblin clutched a loosely rolled scroll that he passed to Haruuc as if eager to be rid of it. Haruuc's face darkened as he scanned the message.

"The Gan'duur have crossed the Ghaal at the eastern ferry," he said. "They attacked wagons on their way to market in Rhukaan Draal this morning." He glanced at the messenger. "Tell Munta and Vanii I'm on my way." The goblin nodded and dashed away. Haruuc looked to Vounn. "Iron should not cool on the anvil, nor should it be left in the forge. I appreciate the distraction you offer me."

Vounn bent her head. "You helped me, lhesh. *Ta muut.*"

Haruuc turned to go. Tariic sprang to his side. "Wait," he said. "I'll come with you."

Vounn thought she saw Haruuc's shoulders stiffen before he nodded to his nephew.

CHAPTER FIFTEEN

Following Wrath through the mountains was like fighting a battle from sunrise to sunset. In a time years ago—a time that felt like another life—Geth had fought just such a battle along the border between Cyre and Karrnath. In the end, he hadn't been able to tell whether any ground had been gained, only that he would have laid down among the corpses on the battlefield if it meant a chance to rest.

He and the others felt the same way at the end of every day now. Their pace slowed even more as they crept up toward, then climbed among, the Seawalls. Distances they should have covered in a few hours took an entire day as they went around canyons and sought out gentler inclines to follow. The weather turned colder as they pushed higher. Occasionally, they saw signs of habitation, of the rare goblins who lived in the mountains, but they made no effort to seek shelter with them. As Chetiin pointed out, if someone chose to live in the wilderness, they probably wanted to be left alone.

One night Midian pulled out a map and some shiny brass instruments. He made observations of several stars, worked out calculations in chalk, traced a line across his map, and cursed. "Sage's shadow! We're traveling on a line with Paluur Draal and Korranberg."

"What's Paluur Draal?" asked Ashi.

"It was a shining jewel of the Empire of Dhakaan," said Ekhaas. "A great city, now ruined, overrun in the past by gnomes and kobolds—

even humans tried to live there for a time. The rod couldn't be there, though. The ruins have been thoroughly explored."

"Don't be sure of that," Midian said, stowing his instruments back into his pack. "The last time I was there, the expedition I was with found evidence that the roots of the city extended deeper than anyone expec—" He caught Ekhaas's glare and quickly changed the subject. "The point is that Paluur Draal is quite close to Korranberg. We could have ridden back to Sterngate, caught the lightning rail into Zilargo, and been there already."

"What if the rod has already been found?" Chetiin asked. "You said we're also on a line with Korranberg. What if the rod rests in your famous library?"

Midian flushed. "Now see here! If the library held a Dhakaani artifact as significant as the Rod of Kings, I'd know about it!"

"I notice you don't say that the library would give it back," said Ekhaas.

"Maybe no one has asked for it!" Midian screwed up his face. "Not that we have it. I mean that if we did have it and Haruuc sent someone to explain why it was important that it be returned to Darguun, I'm sure the library would repatriate it immediately. Trust me, no nation wants to see Darguun remain peaceful more than Zilargo."

"All those gnomes helpless before the threat of invading Darguul slavers?" asked Chetiin dryly.

"Exactly!" said Midian. "It's in Zilargo's best interest to support a stable leadership in Darguun."

Chetiin scratched Marrow's head. "You don't have to worry," he said. "I understand Zils make terrible slaves."

Midian's mouth opened, but no sound came out and his face turned an even deeper shade of red.

Geth sighed and put an end to it. "The rod can't be in the library. Korranberg's below the mountains and we"—he drew Wrath and held it out so that everyone could see the angle of the pointing blade—"are still going up."

They caught a bit of luck the next day. During their time in the mountains, they'd passed a number of ancient ruins, some Dhakaani, some dating from the Desperate Times after the fall of the empire—Ekhaas and Midian generally agreed, surprisingly, on what belonged to which period. Most of the ruins had consisted of a wall or two, sometimes even less, emerging from the undergrowth or perched high on a bit of bare rock, but that day they rounded the shoulder of a hill to find themselves on a stretch of Dhakaani road.

The stone surface was washed with drifting soil, broken by weather and by the roots of trees that were themselves centuries old. It coiled across the landscape, running roughly northwest to southeast along the line of the mountains in that area. Both behind and ahead, it seemed to appear in stretches, then vanish among the trees before reappearing once more along the curve of a distant ridge.

Geth could guess at what they were all thinking: the curving road might take them out of their way, but it was still a road, and following it was easier than breaking their own trail. He lifted Wrath. The sword pointed in the same general direction as the road. "Grandfather Rat smiles for a change," he said.

Even when the ancient road was under the canopy of trees that had grown up through it, they made good time. "Where do you think it goes?" Dagii asked as they paused to take some food.

"We're not likely to follow it to the end," Geth pointed out.

"No, but the Dhakaani must have. No one builds a road to nowhere."

"We're approaching the headwaters of the Torlaac River," Ekhaas said. She pointed to a distinctive cleft peak far in the distance. "I think that's the back of Giim Astraa. There are extensive ruins there."

Midian's eyebrows rose and he took a sudden interest in the hazy peak, but Ekhaas didn't seem to notice.

Dagii nodded and said, "I think you're right. Well done."

Ekhaas flicked her ears casually in response, but Geth could see the expression of self-satisfaction she tried to hide.

His prediction that they wouldn't see the end of the road seemed accurate, though. When they started on the road again, he checked their direction. Wrath didn't point anywhere near Giim Astraa, but rather along the road and directly to the massive bulk of a much closer mountain. The road curved wide around the mountain's flank. He grimaced. "It was nice while it lasted."

"Follow the road around," Ashi suggested. "It might curve back again."

It didn't. As they came around the mountain, a stray sunbeam, the last light of the day, fell on the road ahead. The way was remarkably clear, the road a pale ribbon—one that snaked off in the direction of Giim Astraa and away from where they needed to go. There was no chance it would curve back.

"Rat," cursed Geth.

"We'll make camp here for the night," said Dagii. "We can carry on in the morning."

"Aye," Geth said. Out of habit, he drew Wrath and held it out to get a new sense of their bearings.

His gut twisted. The sword no longer pointed south-southwest, but northeast toward the mountain they had just come around. "Look," he said, then louder, "Look!"

Everyone turned to him and froze. Ekhaas's ears rose sharply. "It's here. Guulen is on this mountain."

Excitement ran high in the camp that night. They ate a dinner of sour sausages and starchy dumplings in silence, each of them wrapped up in his or her thoughts. Ekhaas stared into the fire. Midian dug out his little silk-bound book and seemed to read it, though Geth noticed he was very slow in turning the pages. Dagii set himself to inspecting his armor. Chetiin examined the edge of his curved dagger, honing it with a worn sharpening stone: Geth realized for the first time that, though the goblin wore a pair of daggers sheathed to his forearms, he only drew and used the one on his left arm. He would have asked Chetiin about it, but it seemed somehow wrong to break the silence of the camp.

When his time came to sit watch, he stood and stared up at the mountain overhead. In his hand, Wrath throbbed as if in anticipation. Geth's heart beat in the same time and he wondered if this was how the heroes of the name of Kuun had felt as they drew close to the ends of their adventures. "Grandmother Wolf," he murmured, squeezing Wrath's hilt, "the *duur'kala* are going to need to come up with some new stories for us!"

They were all up with the sun and ready to attack the mountain. It was still a daunting chunk of landscape to search. Broadleaf trees hugged the lower slopes, giving way to the thick dark green of pines and firs higher up. The peak, shining in the morning sun, was a cap of bare rock dotted with thin patches of grass like hair on the head of a bald man. Dagii rode a little farther along the old road to get a different view and came galloping back to them. "There's a saddle just around the mountain and about halfway to the peak," he said. "We should be able to reach it. Using Aram there should eliminate the need to search at least half the mountain."

It was frustrating to leave the road again and re-enter the green world of the forest. The trees seemed particularly thick on the mountain. Within paces of leaving the road, they had lost site of it. It took a long while before the ground started rising, and they had to stop and wait at least twice while Chetiin climbed a tree to check their position. The second time he came down, he said, "I see the saddle," and led them off at an angle to the way they'd been heading.

The ground began a sharp ascent shortly afterward. By midmorning it was too steep to ride the horses, and they had to dismount. Even Chetiin got off Marrow and let the worg pad about on her own. The speed of Tariic's magebred horses had ceased to be a benefit days before. Geth was glad that they had also been bred for endurance.

"Should we leave them behind?" he asked Dagii after a particularly difficult stretch that left them all sweating. "We could go faster on our own without them."

"I'd rather haul them up the slope than risk something happening to them. We'll still need to get out of the mountains and back to Rhukaan Draal." The warrior was covered with dirt and leaf mould from slipping face first to the ground during the climb, but he still managed to keep his stiff manner. Maybe he was even more stiff, as if trying to hold onto his dignity. Geth felt the distinctly unheroic urge to push him down again, just to see if he could get him to laugh.

He didn't have a chance to act on the urge. Marrow, who had been wandering ahead, came loping back. Her black fur stood on end, adding bulk to her neck and shoulders, and she was growling. She trotted to Chetiin and said something in the snarling language of worgs. Chetiin stiffened, and his ears flicked.

"What is it?" Dagii asked, and suddenly his stiffness didn't seem so out of place.

"Bugbears. Marrow caught their scent. They're not close, but we're in their territory."

"That's not good, I guess," said Ashi.

Dagii shook his head. "The Marguul tribes of the mountains have resisted swearing allegiance to Haruuc," he said. "A few Marguul tribes are loyal, but others only acknowledge their oaths when it's convenient to them. Tribes in the high mountains often don't even bother to pretend."

"And these are the high mountains."

"Oh, yes."

Chetiin listened to a few more yips and growls from Marrow. "There's a hunters' trail a short way ahead."

"We need scouts," Dagii said. "Chetiin, Geth, Ashi—follow Marrow and see what we're dealing with. We'll wait here."

"Mazo," said Chetiin. Geth shrugged out of his pack, Ashi did the same, and the three of them slid into the forest after Marrow.

The trail was only about thirty paces away. If they'd kept going, they would have blundered right into it. The four of them crouched in the brush a short way off the trail and watched for a short while. When there was no movement, they crept closer. Geth gestured, and Ashi stepped out into the open while Geth and Chetiin remained behind, hands on weapons. Ashi walked a few paces up and down the trail, then rejoined them.

"I don't know what bugbear footprints look like, but a lot of big creatures on two feet use this trail frequently," she said, and pointed first south, then north. "They walk that way with light loads and return heavily laden. There's drops of old blood. Most likely hunters returning to a camp or a village with prey."

"Camp or village?" asked Chetiin.

"Given how often the trail is used, I'd say smaller than a village, but more permanent than a camp."

Geth cursed and drew Wrath. The blade pointed across the trail but at an angle that followed it up the mountain. "It doesn't look like they're in our way."

"There's no telling where this trail ends," said Chetiin. His big eyes narrowed. "Bugbears are more nocturnal than other goblin races. We should take advantage of that to have a look around."

Geth cursed again. He kept Wrath out as they made their way cautiously up the trail with Marrow shadowing them from the cover of the trees. The trail followed a relatively gentle slope up the mountainside. If nothing else, it was easier than walking with the horses. When the slope became even more gentle and the trees began to thin out, Geth guessed that they had almost reached the top of the saddle. A little farther on and Marrow whined gently in warning. "She smells the camp," said Chetiin.

"I smell the camp," Geth whispered as a gentle breeze from above brought a stink of rotten meat and dung.

A ridge rose from the woods on the left side of the track. Geth nudged Chetiin and pointed to it. The goblin nodded. A short time later, the two of them and Ashi were stretched out on top of the ridge in the afternoon sun and looking down on the bugbear camp.

Ashi was right. It was more permanent than what Geth would normally call a "camp" but it was also so disgustingly dirty he couldn't call it anything else. Half a dozen large huts dotted the camp, as well as a longhouse that had been built against the steep fir-covered slope leading to the mountain's peak. Geth suspected that the longhouse concealed the entrance to a cave in the mountainside. The whole camp was surrounded by what could loosely be called a yard of patchy grass and worn soil. Animal carcasses—deer, boar, mountain lions, wolves—hung from rough frames between the huts, and a big firepit lay at their center. Pots of something dark and steaming were dug into the ashes at the edge of the pit. Pine pitch to be used as a weapon, Geth guessed. Nasty stuff that would stick as it burned. Thick stakes sharpened, smeared with more pitch, and set into the ground at an angle made a crude barrier around the camp. Three bugbears dressed in rags of leather lounged sleepily near the opening in the barrier that was the closest thing there was to a gate.

Geth couldn't see what the camp harbored that was worth protecting, but he could see why the bugbears would want to protect a claim on their territory. The saddle of the mountain opened onto something of a miracle, a snug little vale sheltered on the north by another ridge sweeping down from the mountain peak. The ridge blocked the north wind, hid the vale from anyone traveling south along the ruined road, and trapped the sun's warmth. What was more, the southern saddle they'd climbed wasn't the only approach to the vale. A second trail led from the camp down another gentle slope to the west. From atop the ridge, Geth could look down both the southern and western saddles and see broad, level plateaus among the surrounding mountains. Judging from the carcasses strung up around the camp, hunting was very good.

A third way led down from the vale as well. Between the ridge on which they lay and the western saddle, the land plunged into a deep valley. The way down into the valley wasn't gentle. There was no trail and it didn't look like the bugbears went that way often or at all. There was a patch of worn dirt at the edge of an especially steep bit of the valley wall, and the bushes below seemed broken, as if things were frequently thrown down into the valley. Maybe the valley served as the bugbears' waste dump—though from the condition of the camp, Geth would have guessed they otherwise lived happily among their own filth.

Wrath left no doubt of which way they needed to go. The blade pointed unerringly into the valley.

Geth peered over the edge of the ridge. The valley wall below was so steep as to be almost sheer, and spiked with stunted trees that poked out of the crumbling rock. Climbing down that way wasn't an option. If they wanted to get into the valley, they'd have to go past the camp.

"Any ideas?" Ashi whispered to Chetiin.

"Yes," said the goblin. "Ekhaas."

CHAPTER SIXTEEN

She began singing before the camp came into sight over the last rise of the trail. The song was an ancient one, gentle and soothing, a song for lingering afternoons, composed in a time when the emperor of Dhakaan was the sun and the long night of the empire's fall was something not even imagined. She took her time, walking up the trail in time to the song. When she reached the crest of the rise and stepped into the vale, the bugbears guarding the crude camp had already turned eyes and ears in her direction.

Her first sight of the camp brought a silent curse of disgust. It really was as foul as Geth had described. How far, Ekhaas thought, the *dar* have fallen!

The disgust never reached her voice or her face. She kept walking with a measured pace, still focused on the bugbears and singing to them as if each one were an emperor. None of them moved as she approached. They just stared at her, caught in the beauty of her song.

Ekhaas had found the music when she was thirteen, though sometimes she felt as if the music had found her. The *duur'kala* had taken her for training in her eleventh year, recognizing a quick mind and a zeal for the great history of Dhakaan. Not all of the children chosen for training with the mothers of the dirge found the music, but Ekhaas learned later that there had been very high expectations of her talent almost from the first. On the day that those expectations had been fulfilled, she had been singing a lament of the Haata Dynasty for one of the mothers when something had begun to resonate within her. She'd lost herself in the music, the words of the lament fading into the pure sorrow beneath. The performance had left the mother with tears in her eyes and Ekhaas forever tuned like the strings of a *kiirin* to the music of the ages. In her waking moments she could feel it in her bones; when she slept, she thought she heard it in her dreams.

After years of training, drawing it up to fill her songs and stories with power was as natural as the simple act of singing.

She stopped when she was close enough to the camp that the smell of pine pitch that bubbled in the firepit almost covered the fetid reek of rot. Bugbears had the most famously sensitive noses of all the goblin races, and she wondered how the tribe could stand their own stench. The guards still stared at her, unspeaking, big ears cupped in relaxation. There were no sounds from the other crude buildings of the camp—if the other members of the camp heard her song in their sleep, they would only drift farther into their dreams. Ekhaas focused on the largest of the three guards and wove a suggestion into her song.

"Rest," she said. *"This is a daydream. You see nothing."*

The guard's eyelids drifted down until they were half closed and a contented smile spread across his face.

Ekhaas looked to the next guard and pointed at the peak that rose behind the camp. *"Listen to the bird that sings on the mountain. Isn't it beautiful? You see nothing."*

The second guard turned to look up at the mountain's slopes, scanning them with rapt attention for a bird that didn't exist. Ekhaas fought back a smile and sang to the last guard, *"The sun is warm and your friends are watching for danger. Sleep and see nothing."*

The final guard's head sagged down so quickly he must already have been half asleep before her song had caught him. Still singing to the bugbears, Ekhaas raised her hand in a signal.

She heard the quiet rush of feet as the others left the cover of the trail to slip past the camp and down into the valley. There were no hoofbeats—they'd left the horses in the forest, blindfolded to keep them calm, guarded by Marrow to keep them safe. Ekhaas winced at the speed with which the others moved in spite of her warnings. The trance brought on by the song was fragile—any hint of a threat, even fast movement, could break it—but it was also more subtle than the focused power of a spell. It seemed an eternity until she heard the soft birdcall that indicated all of the others were out of sight once more. Ekhaas risked a glance over her shoulder to be sure she was going in the right direction, then backed away from the camp. None of the guards showed any sign of breaking free of her suggestions, but she still kept singing.

Her heels found the steep slope of the valley, and hands reached up to help her keep her balance. Ekhaas took a few more paces backward before crouching below the valley's rim. The camp and the guards disappeared from sight. On her left, Geth nodded. Ekhaas let her song fade. Quiet descended on the afternoon once more. She, Geth, and Dagii on her other side waited, listening.

A loud snore broke the silence. It was followed by a curse and a reprimand for sleeping on duty. There were a few grumbles of discontent, a muttered comment about snoring loud enough to scare birds on the mountain, then the guards were silent again. Geth grinned at her before creeping down the slope. Dagii touched her hand lightly, and she glanced at him.

For a moment she stared directly into his shadow gray eyes, then he lowered his gaze and dipped his ears in recognition. She gave him a brief nod in return before hurrying after Geth as quickly as the slick grass that covered the slope would permit.

Ashi, Chetiin, and Midian were waiting just a little farther down, close enough to come charging to their aid if the guards had woken from the song with any suspicion that intruders had come past them. No one said anything, though, until they were all well down the slope and out of sight of the camp, then everyone clustered around her to murmur congratulations. Ekhaas accepted their praise with nods, but reserved a sharp glance for Chetiin. "How did you know I was able to do that?" she asked him.

His ears twitched. "There's an old saying among the Silent Clans: Know your friends as you know your enemies. I've heard stories of *duur'kala* singing their way across battlefields."

"Do you believe all the stories you hear?"

"I heard that!" said Midian. The gnome gave Ekhaas a crooked smile. "I knew the *duur'kala* had to have a bit of sense when it came to stories."

"I know a story about a gnome, a *duur'kala,* and a dull knife that I'd believe," Ekhaas said. Through their journeys she'd found Midian to be a better companion than she had expected when he'd joined them at Sterngate, but the researcher could still grate on her.

Dagii put an end to the conversation. "Enough. Let's get out of the open. If one of those guards happens to look into the valley, we could still be seen."

The steep grassy slope that led into the valley gave way to thick bushes where the valley floor grew level and broad. Bushes quickly turned into trees. Ashi, looking far more like the hunter Ekhaas had first encountered nearly a year before than the scion of Deneith she'd found in Karrlakton, led the way. The bushes were dense and thorny, difficult and painful to squeeze past. Ashi slipped through easily, Chetiin and Midian with only a little less difficulty. Ekhaas, Dagii, and Geth had to pick their way carefully, always trying to be quiet. They weren't far enough away from the bugbear camp that thrashing about in the bushes wouldn't attract the attention of the guards. At least Dagii had armor to protect him from the thorns. Ekhaas wished she could sing the plants aside.

The bushes continued under the first ranks of trees at the forest's edge, where light from above was still plentiful. The farther they went, however, the taller the trees became and the denser the canopy that their branches formed. When the brambles finally fell away, the gloom under the trees was deep enough that Ekhaas was grateful for the sensitive eyesight of her people.

"These trees are old," said Midian. He touched the trunk of one that was easily half again as wide as he was tall.

"I doubt anyone has ever come cutting timber here," Dagii answered him.

"Not even the bugbears? Doesn't that seem odd?"

"There are easier slopes to the south and west and plenty of timber above their camp, too," Ekhaas said. "They don't need to come down here."

Geth bared his teeth. "You really think that's all it is?"

Ekhaas shook her head. The song of ages had sunk back to a dull beat in her gut. Geth growled and drew Aram. The sword pointed along the valley floor and down. Without saying anything, he returned Aram to its sheath. His hand, however, didn't leave the weapon's hilt. Ekhaas found her hand on her sword as well.

The trees became even older, shaggy with moss and fungi. Smaller trees were mixed among them, starved of sunlight and the soil's richness by towering siblings. They found a place where one of the giants had come crashing down, allowing for new growth. Sunlight raked across the canopy, drifting down in a white-gold haze over the great fallen corpse that rotted slowly among bushes, ferns, and saplings left spindly by the opportunity for sudden growth. It came to Ekhaas that for all the forest in the valley was alive, passing under its deep green roof and between its great pillars felt more like walking through some ancient tomb.

"The sun is going down," said Ashi. "It's going to be dark as Khyber here when that happens."

Dagii looked to Geth.

The shifter shook his head. "We're close. I can feel it."

Midian spoke for all of them. "I'd rather keep going in the dark than spend a night sitting still in this place."

"Ban," said Dagii. "We go on."

Soon enough, the darkness under the trees was so complete that Ashi could see nothing. Ekhaas and Chetiin led the way now. Geth and Midian, their nightvision reduced but better than blindness, followed. Ashi walked with one hand on Geth's shoulder, her face tense with the mingled expression of concentration and uncertainty that all humans adopted when forced to struggle in the dark.

Midian had his everbright lantern at the ready. The rest of them had left their packs with the horses, but Midian had insisted on bringing his store of magical trinkets. "Better burdened than naked," he'd said.

Dagii, however, had refused to allow him to open the lantern and release its light. "Better half-blind," he'd said, "than a target."

The chief of the Mur Talaan moved at the end of their party, ostensibly to keep an eye on Ashi. Ekhaas knew he was also watching behind them. Night in the valley was as quiet and still as the day had been. They all walked with their weapons drawn.

In Geth's grasp, Aram pointed sharply downward. The rod was somewhere still ahead, but also somewhere below. Underground? In a cave? Ekhaas and Chetiin watched for holes, gaps, chasms—anything that might lead beneath the ground. They had to be close to the far end of the valley, Ekhaas thought. Maybe there would be a cave entrance on the valley wall. She didn't relish the idea of scrambling across the steep slopes hunting for a cavern, but the thought of getting out of the valley was deeply appealing.

"So," whispered Midian into the silence, "Dabrak Riis, the Shaking Emperor who lost the rod. I don't think I've read about him in the histories."

"There wouldn't be much to read," said Ekhaas. "He belonged to the Riis Dynasty, the last dynasty of the empire, when the blood of the Six Kings had run thin, been reinvigorated, and run thin again. From what I learned from Senen Dhakaan, he ruled for about ten years. If he hadn't lost the Rod of Kings, the most significant thing about him would have been that he lived in fear every day of his life."

"In fear of what?"

"Everything. Closed spaces, open spaces, insects, snakes, monsters, being assassinated, strangers, friends." She gestured around them. "The dark, even though he could see in it. His fears were why he was called the Shaking Emperor, a name that shamed him. One day he left his palace with a troop of guards, declaring that he would face the source of his fears and return to rule as an emperor should. His heir, a cousin, wasted no time in declaring himself regent, and that was when the disappearance of the rod was discovered. They tried to find Dabrak but without success. It turned out that the one thing he had a talent for was eluding pursuit. Rumors of sightings of him and his guards sprang up across the empire, but he was never located. The regent became an emperor, and life carried on."

"And that's when people started hunting for the rod?" asked Geth.

"Almost," said Ekhaas. "They looked, of course, but with no

idea where Dabrak really was, there wasn't much they could do. Then fifty years after Dabrak vanished, a body was discovered floating down the Torlaac River—a body that was identified as one of Dabrak's guards, not looking a day older than when he'd ridden from the palace with the Shaking Emperor. Hunts for the rod had died down by that point, but with a solid if unexplained clue before them, hunters swarmed the entire Torlaac watershed for another century before the fervor cooled off again. The last emperors sent out expeditions every so often for generations after that, but as the empire passed into the Desperate Times, people had other things to worry about. Eventually even the rod itself was all but forgotten. *Raat shan gath'kal dor.*"

"You said we're not far from the headwaters of the Torlaac River," said Ashi. "We're only a day's travel from a Dhakaani road. Could the hunters have come this way?"

"I'd be surprised if they didn't," Ekhaas told her. "But the mountains and the forest aren't likely to have changed much. Between them and the position of the valley—and with the rod underground—it would be easy to miss something."

"Even something," asked Chetiin, pausing beside a massive old tree ahead, "like this?"

His scarred voice was tight. Ekhaas's fist clenched around her sword. She stepped up to stand beside him and instantly understood what he meant.

Beyond the tree, the valley floor dropped away into a vast pit.

The slope was at least as long and steep as that from the bugbear camp into the valley, and the bottom of the pit lay beyond the range of her sight. Trees grew up from the pit, however, and if the trees of the valley were old, the trees of the pit were truly ancient. As deep as the pit was, the trees in it reached almost to the height of the valley's canopy, their branches as thick and luxuriant as a forest in themselves. Anyone looking into the valley from above would have seen no hint of the pit save perhaps a dip in the treeline.

But once there had been people here. The canopy thinned above the slope and moonlight reached through to shine on the lichen-stained stone of a staircase that plunged into the pit. Big blocks, hollowed with age, formed the steps, with long narrow blocks making borders to each side. If the steps were worn, though, the borders were practically untouched, rounded on top and heavily carved in a style that was almost but not quite familiar. Unlike the road through the mountains, the stairs were whole and unbroken.

"Khaavolaar," she breathed. Chetiin was right. Perhaps hunters for the rod might have missed seeing the pit from above, but if they'd passed through the valley, how could they not have seen it and the stairs?

The others moved up to join them. Ashi was still almost blind, but Geth and Midian blinked at the moonlight as if they'd stepped into the sun. Geth stared down the length of the steps and slowly raised Aram. The twilight blade pointed straight along the stairs and into the pit.

Midian, however, dropped to his knees beside the carved borders. "By the quill," he said, his voice quivering. "These are pre-Dhakaani—and in such perfect condition . . ." His words trailed off into a wet moan of excitement.

"Pre-Dhakaani?" asked Ashi. She squinted into the dark in Midian's direction. "Ekhaas, what's here?"

Ekhaas described the stairs to her and explained the gnome's excitement. "Before Jhazaal Dhakaan united the Six Kings to form the empire, there were independent goblin kingdoms scattered across southern Khorvaire. The carvings on the stones are in the style of one of the kingdoms that ruled in this area. These stairs are older than the Dhakaani Empire."

"If they're that old, how come the forest hasn't swallowed them?"

"Some kind of preservation magic most likely," said Midian. "There were *dashoor* before the empire. Sage's shadow, what I wouldn't give for a better look at these carvings!" He looked up at Dagii and waved his everbright lantern hopefully.

"No," Dagii said firmly. He caught Midian's arm and pulled him to his feet. "I don't like this. If as many people hunted for the Rod of Kings as the stories say, we can't possibly be the first to find this place."

"The stories also say," Ekhaas said, "that many of those who set out to search for the rod were never seen again. Maybe the stairs have been found before. Maybe the people who found them were among the hunters who didn't return."

Geth's eyes narrowed. "How long do you think the bugbears have been camped above the valley?"

"No more than a generation," said Chetiin. "Maybe two."

"There was a place on the rim of the valley that looked like they'd been throwing garbage down. If they've been dumping garbage here for that long, shouldn't we have seen or smelled a heap when we came down?"

Ekhaas looked at the shifter. "Something's been happening to their garbage?"

"Nothing has happened to their garbage. It's all still lying around their camp."

"Sacrifices." Dagii's ears, protruding through holes in the helmet that he wore, pulled back flat. "They've been feeding something down here."

"If something has been down here for thousands of years, it doesn't need to be fed," said Midian. "On the other hand, it isn't unknown for one creature to take over another's abandoned den." The polished metal baton of his pick was in his free hand. He flicked his wrist and the narrow head flipped out to lock into place. The click it made seemed loud, but there was no echo. The forest consumed it.

"We need to know what's at the bottom of that pit," Dagii said. "Chetiin, scout it. We'll wait in the forest."

"Mazo." The goblin turned away.

"Wait," said Geth. "I'll come too."

Chetiin shook his head. "Not this time." Avoiding the stairs, he took a step down the slope and seemed to vanish into a patch of shadow.

Geth wore an expression of disappointment as Dagii led them away from the edge of the pit and under the thick canopy of the forest once more. Ekhaas moved close to him. "You wouldn't be able to see down there," she murmured. "And as stealthy as you can be sometimes, you're not one of the *shaarat'khesh*. Let Chetiin do what he came to do."

"I know," Geth said. "But I should be doing something more than pointing the way."

Ashi had her hand back on his shoulder, following his guidance. She gave a low laugh. "Don't worry, Geth. I'm sure you'll still have your chance."

Back among the trees, Geth gave Ashi over to Midian's care while he checked the straps and buckles of his great gauntlet. Dagii was crouched against the trunk of one of the valley's shaggy old trees, his eyes darting around at the night. Ekhaas sheathed her sword and crouched beside him. "What do you think is down there?" she asked.

"I don't know. My mind buckles at the possibilities. Undead. Some creature of Khyber. A dragon? All I can think of are the stories of *duur'kala.*" Dagii grimaced, exposing his teeth. "Your guess is likely better than mine. The histories of the Kech Volaar say nothing of this place?"

"The Kech Volaar see the greatest glory in the legacy of Dhakaan," Ekhaas said with a shake of her head. "Tales of the time before the union of the Six Kings are almost as scarce and unreliable as tales of the Desperate Times. Maybe some mention of ancient stairs in the wilderness exists in the archives of Volaar Draal but if it does, I've never seen it, and it has never been linked to the legend of the Rod of Kings. The stairs would have been here in the time of Dabrak Riis, though."

"Assuming they really are pre-Dhakaani."

Ekhaas's ears stood up. "You don't think they are?"

Dagii's eyes remained on the darkness of the forest. "I'm a soldier, not a *duur'kala,* Ekhaas. I can't always accept that things are what they appear to be. The stairs may be carved in a pre-Dhakaani fashion, but isn't it possible they were fashioned some time later?"

She turned to look at him. "You've been talking too much with Midian!" she said.

"Cho, but Midian is even more enamored with the age of the steps than you are," he said with a snort. "I'm looking at alternatives. Why should the steps be as old as you say?"

"You'll be doubting the existence of the rod next."

"I don't doubt the existence of the rod. The existence of Aram proves part of your story, and Aram is pointing to *something.*" He tilted his head to the side and looked at her. "I won't follow the past like a slave following his master. Haruuc is lhesh because he saw beyond the way things have always—"

Ekhaas saw his gaze slip beyond her for an instant. She saw his eyes go wide—and in the next moment, Dagii had dropped his sword and lunged at her. His arms wrapped around her and his armored torso slammed into her body, knocking her backward and along the ground.

"Toh!" he roared, and through the shower of dirt and leaf litter that accompanied their roll, Ekhaas saw the massive clawed hand that had dug into the ground where she'd been crouching.

She followed it up, past a bizarrely long arm to powerful shoulders and a hideous drooping face. Behind clumped hair, and dark eyes stared down with baleful hunger. The moment seemed to slow. The clawed hand lifted, scattering dirt as it rose, ready to strike again.

The moment of shock ended. Time resumed its frantic pace as the hand fell. Ekhaas and Dagii acted in unison this time, pushing away from each other. The claw came down between them, so close Ekhaas could smell a stink like wet and moldering canvas. "Troll!" shouted Dagii, rolling to his feet and grabbing for his sword.

It wasn't the only one. Two more of the creatures burst out of the forest as if the trees were giving birth to them. Their thick hides were as knotted and warty as mossy bark, and they were tall, easily half again as tall as Ashi or Dagii. They wailed and howled, and the night that had been so silent was suddenly loud.

But Dagii's warning had been enough. Geth met the attack of one troll with sword and gauntlet. Midian tumbled away from another, drawing it after him. Ashi, blind, put her back against a tree and sank into a defensive crouch, her head darting in the direction of every noise, trying to track the battle by sound. Dagii's sword was back in his hand—he rose just in time to meet another blow from the first troll. Claws raked across metal, and if Dagii hadn't been armored he probably would have been eviscerated. Ekhaas drew her sword and slashed at the troll, trying to drive it back. Confronted with two attackers, it paused for a moment, then pushed on with its attack. Dagii was ready for it this time, though, and slid under its wild swing.

The troll that Geth fought howled, and from the corner of her eye, Ekhaas saw it smash at the shifter with both hands. Geth leaped aside, and a look of concentration passed across his face as he called on his heritage and shifted.

His hair grew even thicker and more coarse, his skin tougher and hide-like. When he looked at the troll again, there was fury in his eye that would have given any other creature pause. The troll went after him once more, claws slashing for his belly. Geth twisted, letting the full force of the blow slide off him. The troll's claws caught in his shirt and tore the fabric apart, but Ekhaas saw only shallow scratches on Geth's skin as he answered the blow. Turning inside the troll's reach, Geth swung Aram in an arc that cut halfway through the monster's torso. He whipped the sword free and dark blood sprayed out after it—then stopped.

Like two pieces of clay pressed together, the edges of the terrible wound merged and sealed. The troll staggered for a moment, then threw itself right back at Geth.

CHAPTER SEVENTEEN

"Fire or acid!" Dagii called. "You have to burn the flesh!" He risked a glance at Ekhaas as he blocked another blow from the troll facing them. "Do you know any fire magic?"

If her ears weren't already back, they would have been. "No," she said. *"Duur'kala* can't manipulate fire."

"Maabet!" Dagii spun his sword in a deadly circle, but the troll just reached past the blur of metal. Dagii's blade put a deep nick into one arm. It took the other hand off completely. The troll hissed and jerked back. Snatching up the severed hand, it pressed it to the bleeding stump. The rush of blood stopped immediately, and an instant later the troll was wiggling its taloned fingers once more. Dagii and Ekhaas backed away from it.

"Alchemist's fire," Midian gasped. The gnome was whirling around the third troll. Watching it swat at him was like watching a dog trying to bite at a flea. Midian's pick, however, was having about as much effect as a flea's bite. No sooner had he pulled it out of the troll's flesh than the thin puncture wound was healed. It was clear he was only fighting to keep the troll busy and away from Ashi. "In my backpack. Give me some room and I can get it!"

"Open your lantern too!' said Ashi. *"Rond betch,* I need to see!"

The sound of her voice brought Midian's troll around, and Ekhaas saw its dark eyes seek out the human woman standing alone. Her gut twisted. "Midian! Be ready!" she shouted, then she drew a breath and sang the music of the ages up from her belly.

Her will shaped the song, giving it form and power beyond the pure notes that poured from her throat. The spell was simple, the only thing she could think of quickly—a dizzying barrage of emotion and raw music. The troll stumbled and clutched at its head, howling at the confusing assault.

Midian moved, racing past the howling troll to his pack where it lay abandoned on the ground, shed for the sake of mobility. "Ashi! At your feet!" he called and bowled the everbright lantern to her. As Ashi dropped to her knees and groped for the lantern, he dug into the pack and pulled out a flask wrapped in woven straw.

"Hurry!" said Ekhaas. The troll was already shaking its head and looking around as the short-lived magic faded. This time, however, its eyes fixed on her. Dim intelligence flickered in them. It knew she had used magic against it, and it knew that made her a bigger threat than the others. She raised her sword as it howled again and reached for her.

Light that seemed as brilliant as the sun flooded the forest as Ashi snapped open the lantern. The sudden flare was dazzling, and for a moment even the trolls screeched and covered their eyes. With the weird fluting cry of a Bonetree hunter, Ashi threw herself onto the troll that had been about to strike Ekhaas. Her bright blade flashed, plunged deep between its shoulders, and ripped down its back, dragged through lumpy blue-green flesh by Ashi's weight. She twisted, and the sword cut into its spine—the troll dropped like a rag doll.

"Back!" Midian snapped, and Ashi stepped away. The gnome darted in, ducking and weaving as the troll tried to drag itself around and flail at him with its claws. The horrible wound in its back was already starting to close. Midian leaped over its useless legs, pulled open the flask, and dashed the contents up the length of the troll's back.

The liquid in the flask was thick and yellowish. For an instant, Ekhaas could smell an acrid odor in the air, then hot blue flames erupted along the troll's back. Healing flesh turned black, its rapid regrowth halted. The troll let out a scream of agony and twisted around, trying to beat at the flames, but the burning liquid only clung to its hands. Midian flung the flask at the creature's head and it shattered, the remaining liquid inside engulfing the troll's scalp in a licking blue halo. The troll tried to push itself over, to smother the flames against the ground. Grimly, Ekhaas moved forward and hacked at one arm. Muscles severed, the arm folded and the troll fell back, mewling horribly as the alchemist's fire ate into its body.

The other two trolls paused, staring as if they had never seen one of their own brought down before. The hesitation was their undoing. Dagii let out a roar and spun around in a tight circle, putting all of his weight behind his sword. The blade sheared through one hip of the troll he fought, and the monster crashed down. Before it could even wail, he brought his sword down again and through its neck. Its head rolled into the darkness beyond the lantern light. Geth punched his troll in the belly with his gauntleted fist. As it folded over, he dropped into a low spinning kick that swept its legs out from under it. The troll fell back with a grunt—and Chetiin dropped out of the shadows, landing on its chest and plunging his curved dagger into its ear. The troll spasmed, then lay still. Chetiin rolled off and gestured for Geth. The shifter raised his sword and chopped off the monster's head.

"Maabet!" cursed Dagii. "Midian! More fire!" Ekhaas spun. Dagii was staring at the neck of the troll he had killed. The bloody flesh was twisting up into a knob. The creature's *head* was growing back.

Midian was pale. "There is no more fire! Sage's shadow, the stuff isn't water!"

"It wouldn't matter," Chetiin said. "There are more trolls at the bottom of the stairs. A whole nest—at least half a dozen. These three must have been guards."

Dagii's ears rose. "Trolls don't post guards."

"These do." He twisted around, back toward the stairs, and Ekhaas heard what he had: the slap of running feet on stones.

Their combat had been far from silent. Chetiin's stealthy scouting had been wasted. The rest of the nest was coming.

"Run," said Dagii.

"Where?" Geth had Aram raised. In the lantern light, his wide shifter eyes flashed with a strange excitement Ekhaas had never seen in him before. He looked like he was willing to go down fighting.

Inspiration struck Ekhaas. "The bugbears!" she said. "They had pitch ready as a weapon. They must know about the trolls."

"They're Marguul," said Dagii.

"They're more likely to help us than the trolls. Do we have another option?"

Dagii slammed his sword down through the bud of the troll's regenerating head, severing the raw flesh once more. "No. Everyone go!"

They ran, and the night filled up with the thrashing sound of their flight. Ashi carried the lantern, the light like a beacon for the pursuing trolls, but there was no other option. Sound alone would have given them away, and Ashi needed light to see where she was going. The shadows were more of a problem than the light. Brilliant illumination and the colorless clarity of goblin nightvision flashed in Ekhaas's eyes as the lantern swung. Trees and bushes blended together. She saw a half-fallen tree she thought she recognized from their trek into the valley, but she couldn't be certain.

"We need direction before we run in a circle!" she said.

"Geth, take the lead," Dagii ordered. "Go opposite to the way Aram points and keep us on a straight line."

The shifter moved forward to run ahead of them. Howls and hoots rose from behind—the trolls from the nest must have encountered their stricken guards. There was a single crash like a tree being knocked over, then abruptly nothing more from their pursuers. A faint hope rose in Ekhaas that the trolls had seen what they were capable of and turned back, but she saw how ridiculous the idea was almost as soon as it passed into her head. The valley belonged to the trolls. They knew the territory. The guard trolls had been able to slip up on them easily. The other trolls would be stalking them with the silence and speed of wolves.

"Stop!" she said. "Cover the lantern!"

"Are you insane?" Midian choked, but Ashi had already slid to a stop on the leaf strewn ground and slammed the shutter on the lantern. Colors disappeared as darkness blanketed them once more. The others stopped, too. Ekhaas's instincts screamed at her to stop and listen, to try to locate the pursuing trolls, but she didn't need to listen to know the monsters were too close. If they were going to escape the valley, they needed to put room between them and the trolls.

She focused her will and sang again, softly this time, the song bright and urgent. A short distance away, a light blossomed among the trees like a second lantern.

A whisper sent it darting through the forest on a course away from theirs. Somewhere in the darkness, something grunted in confusion. The bait had been laid, but she needed to make it more tempting. Ekhaas concentrated, altering her song, and noise sprang up to follow the phantom lantern—the crashing sound of six people running.

There was a low hoot of triumph and the faint snap of a twig as the trolls followed her illusion. Ekhaas spun back to the others. "Open the lantern and run again!"

"They'll see us!"

"As long as the illusion lasts, they'll have to chase two lanterns. Now go—and everyone stay close to me!"

Just as she had expected, the trolls spotted them almost as soon as they began to run again. They howled at each other for a moment, then Ekhaas caught the sound of something bashing through a bush. The pursuit had split into two groups, but hopefully her first trick had bought them enough time to give them an edge. She began to sing once more.

The song of ages surged, and rushed out of her to wrap around the others. They fell into pace with each other, the measure of the music sustaining them and speeding them on their way. Faster and faster they ran, until it seemed that they were running like horses. Dagii and Midian wore looks of wonder, Ashi of excitement. Chetiin's face was as unreadable as ever, but Geth, who had experienced this magic before during a grim race across the Shadow Marches, just kept his head down and ran. Ekhaas would have liked to look back and see where the trolls were, but she kept her eyes on the ground. The power of the song gave them the speed to outpace the trolls, but it would only take a snagging root or a turned stone to end her song and allow the trolls to catch up.

A howl of rage rolled out of the dark—the trolls chasing the false lantern had discovered the deception. Another howl answered them as the trolls on their trail realized their prey was pulling ahead of them. Trees crashed and bushes snapped as they abandoned silence for speed. Ekhaas raised her voice, singing her song to the night and pushing the rhythm as hard as she dared. Ashi still carried the lantern, and with her every stride, light and shadow danced. The pillars of the forest flashed by, one indistinguishable from the next. How much farther, the *duur'kala* wondered, until they were out of the forest? They'd entered slowly, carefully, and it had taken them through late afternoon and dusk.

The sounds of pursuit began to fall behind. They passed the heavy undergrowth that marked the fallen forest giant, darting into and out of the moonlight like fish striking the surface of a pond.

"Close!" Geth hissed between clenched teeth. As if they had realized the same thing, the trolls screeched and howled. New sounds came out of the darkness: thumps and cracks and crashes. The trolls were throwing things, trying to hit the fugitives as they raced away, but their hurled missiles fell far short.

The canopy started to thin out. Smaller plants appeared on the forest floor, moonlight came again in patches through the leaves, and there was once more a gentle but noticeable slope to the ground. The song almost caught in Ekhaas's throat. They were nearly out!

Then she remembered the final barrier at the forest's edge. The brambles. They wouldn't be able to run through those!

And just as she imagined the thorns tearing at her, the fall that she had feared happened—except that it wasn't her. It wasn't even Ashi stumbling by lantern light.

It was Dagii. Running just in front of her, he staggered suddenly. There was a very audible *snap,* and Dagii was down. This time the song caught in Ekhaas's throat. Between one step and the next, as she leaped high to avoid Dagii's sprawled form, the magic disappeared. The rushing trees snapped back to a normal pace. The galloping horse slowed to a walk.

Ekhaas landed badly, sliding across the ground and scraping the skin from the heel of one palm. The sting was bad, but not as frightening as the sound of the trolls still in pursuit. The others had stopped running, too, but Dagii was still down on the ground. He didn't say anything—too much the warrior to give voice to his pain—but his lips were drawn back, his teeth clenched tight, and his ears were down against his head.

She scrambled back to him, barely rising up from her hands and knees. "Dagii?"

"Ankle," he said shortly, his voice thick. "There was a hole."

Ekhaas looked to the foot he had drawn up close to himself. His boot was stiff leather and showed no sign of the injury beneath, but it was surely a sign of how hard he had fallen that the metal greave above was wretched sideways, one leather strap snapped in two.

Geth, well ahead, came trotting back to them. "What happened?"

"I think his ankle is broken."

"Grandfather Rat!" Determination crossed his face. "Chetiin, Midian—watch for those trolls! Ashi, scout forward and find the edge of the thorns. We're close." He squatted, dropped his voice, and spoke to Dagii and Ekhaas. "Can you walk, Dagii?"

"With help," Dagii said. "But I can't run. *Maabet!* You're almost out—leave me!"

"No. Ekhaas, can your magic get him back up?"

The shifter had some idea of the capability of her songs to heal. She'd used them on him before. Ekhaas looked down at Dagii's ankle, still encased in the boot, trying to guess at the damage. "I don't know how bad it is, and I don't think we have time to get the boot off to look. It would need to be set—"

Geth dropped Aram, grabbed Dagii's foot by toes and heel, and pulled hard.

Dagii roared in pain. He reached forward, lashing out, but Geth rocked back away from his punch. "It's set! Do what you can."

"Geth!" shouted Midian. "The trolls have gone quiet!"

The crashing had stopped. The trolls must have realized they weren't fleeing anymore. The monsters were stalking them again.

Ekhaas looked at Dagii. "I can heal it partially. You'll still be in pain and you might hurt yourself more by trying to run."

"Do it," Dagii said through his teeth.

She wrapped his hands around his ankle and drew on the song again. She heard Dagii gasp and knew that he'd felt the touch of healing magic, as wild and sharp as if her song had drawn on the beginnings of life itself. His eyes opened wide. His ears rose again. Ekhaas held on as long as she dared, letting the magic do its work of knitting bones and flesh together, then released him. Geth was already standing, and he helped Dagii to his feet. Dagii put his weight on the ankle and winced, then nodded. "It will do. Where are the trolls?"

"Too close," said Chetiin. He stared into the darkness, ears twitching, then pointed. "That way. They'll break if we run, and I don't think the thorns will slow them down. They'll catch us before we're through."

Geth cursed. "We need to slow them. Ekhaas, can you make another phantom lantern?"

"It wouldn't fool them again. I have an idea, though." Her throat was raw from the power that she had channeled through it—from Dagii's healing and the illusions she had cast, from the sustained song that had gained them ground on the trolls—but she had the strength for one more song. She focused her attention in the direction Chetiin had pointed and shaped her voice into bright and rippling notes.

Bright sparks of light condensed out of the air, like sunlight given form. The sparks drifted and floated, leaving a glittering dust on the undergrowth, but especially on the trolls.

The lurking monsters were caught off guard. Five of them stood confused among the sparks. They swatted at the glimmering cloud as if at insects, but the whirling lights only seemed to get thicker. Dust stuck to them, turning rubbery flesh golden. One of the trolls wailed and scrubbed at its eyes. An instant later, they were all doing it, blinded by the dust. The trolls didn't stop, though. With eyes watering and arms groping ahead of them, they kept coming.

"It won't last," said Ekhaas. Her voice was a croak. "It will buy us time, though. Come." She gestured at the lantern glow that was Ashi, waiting at the edge of the thorns.

Geth bared his teeth and his hand tightened on Aram. "It won't buy enough time. You, Dagii, and Ashi go. Chetiin, Midian, and I will see what we can do to slow them even more while they're blind. It takes them time to regrow legs and heads, right?"

Midian looked aghast at the suggestion. Ekhaas would have protested herself, but Dagii met her eyes and silenced her with a shake of his head. He looked at Geth. *"Paatcha,"* he said and thumped a fist against his chest.

"We'll be right behind you."

The shifter charged at the glittering, dust-blind trolls. Midian, face pale, went after him. Chetiin paused for a moment, though, and glanced up at Ekhaas and Dagii.

"In case he's wrong," he said, "you should know I made it past the troll nest. The stairs end at some kind of shrine."

Then he turned and followed Geth.

An old hobgoblin warrior's proverb came to Ekhaas's mind: *Chiit guulen pamuut ran.* "There is strength in honoring sacrifice." She put her back to the goblin, the shifter, the gnome, and the trolls and hurried to Ashi. Dagii must have been thinking of the same proverb because he turned with her, moving with a grim expression on his face and a limp in his step. Ashi's face was tight when they reached her. "What are Geth and the others—?"

"They're buying us time," said Ekhaas. "Go."

They plunged into the thorns, moving as fast as they could. There was no need for silence now—Ashi swapped the lantern for Dagii's sword and hacked at the brambles, clearing a path. The springy branches still leaped back and forth, leaving them all with bloody scratches on their hands and faces. The trolls were howling behind them and Geth was roaring, but Ekhaas refused to turn back and look. Abruptly, the sky was open above them, and they were out from under the trees. Only a few moments more and they were clear of the thorns altogether and racing up the grassy slope of the valley.

Flames burned on the valley rim, and big silhouettes stood against the rising disk of the orange moon Olarune. The bugbears, drawn by the howls and screams of the trolls, had emerged from their camp to stare down at the dark forest. A few of the bolder members of the tribe had crept a little way down into the valley, torches in one hand, small pots of pine pitch bound to leather slings in the other. Confusion erupted as the bugbears spotted the three of them—clearly not trolls—climbing the slope. Ekhaas shouted at them in Goblin. "Brothers! Sisters! By the blood that makes us one people, help us! The trolls are coming! In the name of ancient Dhakaan, we need your help!"

The words were barely out of her mouth when a new crashing came from the forest and, like an explosion, two trolls erupted from the thorns. The confusion of the bugbears changed to rage and fear. A deep voice rose above the chaos. "Trolls, go back! By blood and fire, we have peace! Go back!"

As if they understood the words, the trolls came up short—then reared back, roaring and thumping big hands against their chests.

The owner of the deep voice repeated his warning. "Go back!"

The trolls whooped louder. "Torches and pitch!" the voice boomed out, and along the valley rim flames leaped higher as the bugbears began to wave their torches. The bugbears who carried them swung their pitch pots in whizzing circles, the motion fanning the smoldering flames and turning the pots into screaming balls of fire. The trolls' cries faded and their flailing arms came down. It seemed that they grumbled to each other, then they backed away from the fiery display and disappeared into the thorns once more.

"Geth," said Ashi numbly. "Chetiin. Midian. Where are they?"

Ekhaas turned away from the forest and climbed higher on the slope, scanning for the source of the deep voice. She found him—a big bugbear holding a massive fork-like trident. *"Chib!"* she called. "We have friends in the forest! They need help, too!"

The bugbear chief gestured with his fork. *"Utaa!"*

One of the other bugbears moved, his arm whipping around as he hurled something. Ekhaas saw a heavy shape fly at her out of the night, then pain and darkness exploded in her head.

CHAPTER EIGHTEEN

To Baron Breven d'Deneith,

Greetings.

The week since my last report has been eventful in Darguun. The rebel Gan'duur clan continue to raid out of their stronghold in the north of the country. Their leader, a hobgoblin named Keraal, claims the problem is with the individual warriors of his clan. He says that they are restless and that, while he disciplines them at every opportunity, their spirits will not be broken.

His words are widely seen for the hollow excuses that they are, but at the same time they have a power here, where ferocity and strength are valued. The "unbroken spirit" of the Gan'duur evokes a kind of respect, as though they fight for a just cause under the rule of a tyrant. In fact, Lhesh Haruuc seems to be bound by Keraal's claims. The swiftest means to end this rebellion would be to move against the Gan'duur territories, but Haruuc cannot. The tradition of clan territories is strong, and as long as Keraal makes attempts to discipline his people, Haruuc must respect his territory.

I suspect he has another reason for not moving against the Gan'duur as well: If he brings down Keraal, the other warlords will wonder how long it will be until they, too, might be brought down. The armies of Darguun are in the main composed of the armies of the warlords. If a warlord does not agree with Haruuc's measures, he may withdraw his soldiers—an act of rebellion in itself, but one that could produce a cascade of mistrust. Haruuc's own clan, the Rhukaan Taash, and the most loyal clans, such as the Gantii Vus, would be enough to take on the Gan'duur, but I believe Haruuc sees the greater danger of placing his warlords into a position where they must choose. Better for his rule that he allow the fiction that Keraal has spun.

The Gan'duur raiders that are caught outside Gan'duur territory are another matter, of course. Haruuc has every right in goblin tradition to hunt them down, and he does so with a will that betrays his frustration at Keraal's tactics. Other warlords join him in this, wrapping themselves in a mantle of loyalty, though I suspect that a few may actually be staving off Gan'duur raids with wealth rather than arms—I note that some clans seem to be less troubled by raiders than might be expected.

The raiders continue, in the main, the pattern that they began last month with the burning of the fields north of Rhukaan Draal. They have ventured south of the city now, and there has been something of a race to bring the crops in before the raiders strike. Disturbing news arrived only a few days ago, however, that the Gan'duur have taken the next step and begun striking at granaries and storehouses. Haruuc has personally ridden out to lead warriors in a hunt for those responsible. I have no doubt that he will catch them and that they will die in unpleasant ways. Stories return to the city of new scarecrows that watch over the burned fields. The zest with which the goblin people lap up these stories is a reminder that I am in a land made foreign by more than distance.

The Gan'duur strategy has, I believe, a deeper purpose than just challenging Haruuc's warriors. The fields and granaries that they strike are those that would normally support Rhukaan Draal. I have heard rumors that the price of noon, the starchy balls that goblins eat like bread, is rising along with the price of grain. I notice that the loaves of human bread served on my table are smaller than they were when I arrived. Goblins are not a naturally agricultural people—their food stores are not as plentiful as in our nations, and hunger comes more quickly to the city than anywhere else. Food shortages in Rhukaan Draal will undermine Haruuc's power as surely as rebel warriors. He may be able to purchase grain from the stores of his warlords, but this will in turn drain their supplies as well as his treasury. Farm wagons traveling to market at Rhukaan Draal have already been attacked. If Haruuc is forced to purchase grain, I have no doubt his supply lines will become targets as well.

How can Deneith benefit from this situation?

First, I would suggest the offer of additional mercenaries to House Orien as guards for their caravans. There have been no reports of attacks on Orien caravans moving through Darguun to date, but surely we can play on their fears for our profit. Other dragonmarked houses operating in Darguun may also feel the need for greater security.

Second, I would like—with your permission—to offer Haruuc the services of a few mercenary companies from beyond Darguun. Clan politics add to the tension between warlords and among the people. I think Haruuc will quickly see the benefit of using outsiders to supplement his guards, especially if it becomes necessary to move food on a large scale. This is an ideal opportunity to begin addressing the unbalanced relationship between Deneith and Darguun.

Third, I believe we should stand ready to offer mercenaries—again from outside—to any warlords who become sufficiently enraged with the Gan'duur to move against them on their own. Haruuc may not be able to act against Gan'duur territory, but I have seen him subtly pushing other warlords in that direction. If hostilities were to open on a small scale between the Gan'duur and another clan, I expect he would turn a blind eye. The availability of our mercenaries might tip that balance, and we would earn Haruuc's favor for helping to end the Gan'duur threat.

I also strongly advise that you send out instructions that any hobgoblins with Gan'duur affiliations serving with our companies be immediately removed from sensitive positions. Clan ties are strong, and we should be ready for desertions as Gan'duur goes to the aid of their clan. If we are prepared, we may be able to avoid embarrassment in the face of our clients.

I continue to make contacts among the warlords, of course, as well as among independent companies who want to sell their services to Deneith. Interesting leads are forwarded to Redek at the Gathering Stone. Senen Dhakaan of the Kech Volaar seems to be warming to me, but I will bide my time before again raising the possibility of brokering the services of Kech Volaar warriors. Ashi

Vounn paused, lifting her pen from the paper, and considered what to write. It had been more than two weeks since Ashi had departed Rhukaan Draal, but it was too soon to be concerned. Word had trickled back, almost lost among the news of the raids, that Haruuc's questing party had been seen close to the Seawall Mountains in the southwest. From what she'd learned of the geography of that part of Darguun, there would be no further word of them until they left the mountains again—or crossed them and entered Zilargo. Another two weeks, perhaps three, and then she might worry. She reapplied pen to paper.

Ashi will remain longer than we had planned. She has taken a great interest in the history and politics of the goblin peoples. Given how rare such a thoughtful activity is for her, you'll understand that I have encouraged her to pursue it.

Wishing you health and prosperity—Vounn d'Deneith. 2 Rhaan, 999 YK.

Vounn returned the pen to its stand and sifted fine sand over the report to blot the excess ink. She stared at it as she waited for it to dry, wondering again if she had done the right thing by allowing Ashi to leave Rhukaan Draal. And crushed the moment of doubt before it could go any further. She picked up her report, shook the sand back into the shaker, then folded the paper and slid it into a thick envelope. Blue wax had melted in a tiny vessel over a candle's flame. She poured it along the envelope and pressed a seal down into the blue pool. When she lifted it, the three heads of the chimera that was the Deneith crest stared up at her.

On the other hand, she thought, the last two weeks had been more peaceful than the previous months. When she had accepted Breven's request that she act as mentor to Ashi, she hadn't expected to be chaperone to a willful savage who challenged every instruction that was given to her. Several times she had come very close to leaving Ashi at Breven's door like some overgrown foundling and inviting the patriarch to take a turn at educating her.

But giving up would have been failure, and Vounn d'Deneith did not fail herself or her House. One day Ashi would have to accept the demands that Deneith made of her. Vounn rose from her desk, tucking the report into one deep sleeve of her dress. Out of habit, she checked her stiletto in its hidden sheath. When she'd been young, she hadn't wanted to wear it. A diplomat should have no need of a weapon. Her mentor had forced her to carry the knife, and she'd been glad of it many, many times since.

Aruget was on duty outside her door when she opened it.

"We're going into Rhukaan Draal," she told him in Goblin. "I need to deliver a letter."

He didn't blink or twitch his ears, but she heard the tightness in his voice. "It will be dark soon, Lady Vounn. Can I take it for you, or can you wait until the morning?"

"I need to deliver it myself," Vounn said. "Don't worry. We're only going to the Orien compound. The letter needs to go now so it can leave with the dawn coach to Sterngate. We'll be back before sunset."

He nodded reluctantly. *"Mazo,* lady."

Their departure from the fortress wasn't as quick as she had anticipated. A group of dirty and bloodied horsemen was dismounting as she and Aruget came out into the great entrance hall of Khaar Mbar'ost. Haruuc's party had returned from their pursuit of raiders. The warlord saw her and gestured her over as he removed his helmet. "It's late to be going for a walk, Lady Vounn."

"A quick errand, lhesh." In private meetings she might call him Haruuc, but they both understood the need for formality in public. "I trust your hunting went well?"

Haruuc's ears flicked and he tossed his helmet to Vanii—his *shava* was seldom far from him. "Come with me a moment, lady."

He led her a short distance from the soldiers who had ridden with him. When they stopped, he looked her in the eye. "You went out in the city this same day last week and visited the compound of House Orien. Are you by any chance on your way there now, perhaps with a letter back to Karrlakton?"

Vounn kept her face neutral. In spite of the pressure the Gan'duur put on him, Haruuc was constantly surprising her with how much he knew of the day to day events in his court. He had probably even guessed who she was writing to. "I am."

"Could you send a message for me as well? A number of young warriors of the Atiin Noor clan wish to enter the service of House Deneith as mercenaries. The clan chief's sons are among them. I'd like to see that they find respectable positions, perhaps in the Lhazaar Principalities or the Eldeen Reaches."

She'd heard of the Atiin Noor, a wealthy clan with territory south of Rhukaan Draal. If she had been back in Karrnath, where rich families commonly used their influence to find choice positions for their children, she might have thought nothing of the request. Over the short time she'd been in Darguun, though, she'd developed the distinct impression that offspring were expected to earn their positions. Nor could assignments in Lhazaar Principalities or the Eldeen Reaches be called "choice." Both nations were very nearly as far from Darguun as it was possible to get without leaving Khorvaire entirely. Vounn raised an eyebrow. "Isn't this a matter for Viceroy Redek?" she asked.

"The warriors won't be stopping at the Gathering Stone," said Haruuc. "They'll be riding directly to Matshuc Zaal. I would appreciate if they could be met at Sterngate and escorted to their assignments." He frowned, the action emphasizing his tusks. "In fact," he added, "I think it would be best if their assignments were with humans rather than with other Darguul mercenaries."

"It sounds like they're being banished," Vounn said carefully.

Haruuc gave her a long look, then said, "The chief of Atiin Noor is an old and loyal friend. If you had a friend whose sons had made a poor decision, would you not want to spare him some grief?" He leaned a little closer. "Not all of the scarecrows in the fields of the Atiin Noor were Gan'duur."

Admiration for the "unbroken spirit" of the Gan'duur warriors was becoming something more active. Vounn nodded. "I understand. I will send the message by the swiftest means."

"Ta muut." Haruuc stood straight. "I hope that the sons of Atiin Noor will learn responsibility and honor from House Deneith."

The compound of House Orien was a busy place not far from the bridge that crossed the Ghaal River. Within its walls, the stink of Rhukaan Draal was replaced by the more familiar, if no less pungent, smells of horses and sometimes tribex, the muscular three-horned antelope creatures that were the common beasts of burden in Darguun. Most of the workers were humans, and for a moment it sounded strange, as it had on Vounn's last visit, to hear her own language again.

While Aruget waited in the compound's courtyard, Vounn went directly to the courier office and demanded pen, ink, and paper from the young attendant. The girl was well-trained—she produced what was required without hesitation and even set out an envelope and sealing wax. Vounn quickly wrote a second note to the patriarch of Deneith with Haruuc's request and her own suspicions, sealed it into the envelope, then bound both her letters together with string and sealed the knot on that as well. When she was done, she returned to the attendant. "I need to see Viceroy Pater."

The attendant looked surprised. "He is at table."

"Tell him that Vounn d'Deneith is here on business for her House."

The girl pulled on a bell cord. A servant emerged from a door at the back of the office, and she whispered to him. He vanished through the door, then reappeared more quickly than Vounn might have expected with an invitation for her to follow him.

The rooms beyond the door were as fine as any in a mansion, though the smell of horses still lingered on the air. The servant left Vounn in a comfortable parlor, and a few moments later a broad-shouldered man running to fat as he advanced into his middle years appeared, still wiping soup from his beard. A napkin protected the snowy front of his shirt and he removed it as he walked. Vounn rose to greet him. "Viceroy Pater."

"Lady Seneschal Vounn, envoy of House Deneith to Lhesh Haruuc." Pater d'Orien gave her a sour look. "Nice bit of work for Deneith that is. Cheek by jowl to the lhesh."

Vounn smiled at him. "It's wonderful to see you again as well, Lord Pater. We spoke at the feast Haruuc held shortly after I arrived."

"Aye, I remember. Do you intend to make a habit of interrupting my eating?"

"Not if I can help it. I'm here on urgent business for Deneith." She held out the bundled letters. "These need to go to Karrlakton."

Pater looked at the letters as if she'd scooped up a handful of manure from the compound's horses. "You can put them in at the courier office."

"These need special attention. They're going to Baron Breven.

They must be in Karrlakton tonight." She smiled. "And I happen to know you can get them there."

The man's eyes narrowed. "Khyber's codpiece. You know something. What's happening?"

"Nothing that you haven't guessed at," Vounn told him, shaking her head. "The urgency is a personal matter for Breven."

"Tomorrow morning, then?" Pater asked.

"Tonight."

"The service will cost you."

"Breven's secretary will pay the fee."

Pater groaned and took the bundle. "Kol Korran wills it. Baron Breven will have these tonight. Good evening, Lady Vounn. Someone will show you out." He tugged on a bell cord and started to walk away.

Vounn cleared her throat, and he looked back. "Now," she said.

"What?" he choked. She could have taken an axe to his head and he wouldn't have looked as surprised. "You go too far, Deneith! Let me finish eating at least!"

Vounn crossed her arms. "The letters go now," she said. "Did I not make it clear these are going to the patriarch of Deneith on an urgent personal matter?"

Pater's face turned red, and he looked on the verge of shoving her out the door. Vounn let him boil a moment longer, then added, "Pater, have you ever heard of Karrnathi vedbread? It's a crusty loaf baked with sharp ved cheese. It's best when it's served right out of the oven and smeared with onion butter." She paused to let the idea of the delicacy sink into Pater's angry mind. "There's a baker at a tavern hall in Sentinel Tower who people say makes the best vedbread in Karrlakton if not all of Karrnath. I happen to know that on autumn evenings, he keeps batches of vedbread coming out of his ovens continuously. If the letters go to Breven tonight, I could write you a note of introduction to the baker to be sure you had a chance to try his bread."

The struggle between rage and a love for food was obvious in Pater's features. Finally he grabbed for the bell pull again and jerked it several times. "Tars!" he called. "Bring my traveling coat and boots!" He glowered at Vounn. "You play foul. Write your note. There's pen and paper on the desk."

By the time Vounn had scribbled down a message to the noted baker of Sentinel Tower—along with a request that Pater also be served up the best Karrnathi ale and sausages available—another servant had appeared with a pair of boots and a pale coat embroidered with the crest of House Orien.

"Tell the staff and my wife that I'll be back in the morning," Pater told the servant as he pulled on boots and coat. "And show Lady Vounn out once I'm gone."

The servant nodded, then pulled out a handkerchief and wiped a spot of grease from Pater's face. The viceroy ignored him and instead gave Vounn one final glare. "You owe me, Deneith," he said. "This bread better be good."

He glanced at her note, tucked it into a large pocket along with the bundled letters, and took a step back. He closed his eyes, and a distant expression crossed his face, as if he were picturing some far away place. After a moment, his nose wrinkled in concentration as he invoked the power of House Orien's dragonmark. He took a step—and vanished.

He would already be in Karrlakton, probably stepping out of the air in some Orien waystation and sniffing the air for sausages and vedbread. The essence of diplomacy, thought Vounn, was using what people wanted to get what you needed. She felt a warm glow of satisfaction.

"This way, lady," said the servant, ushering her to a door.

She was a little surprised to discover that night had fallen while she'd been inside. Olarune was just rising, its orange disk fat and full, though the moonlight would be little help against the shadows of Rhukaan Draal. The Orien compound was lit, but the street beyond the gate was very dark. Vounn found Aruget waiting where she had left him. The hobgoblin was pacing back and forth. His ears rose when he saw her. "You've been too long," he said in his own language.

"I did what I came to do," she said. "Take me back to Khaar Mbar'ost."

He held something out to her. At first she thought it was a blanket stolen from one of Orien's horses, then she realized it was a cloak, speckled with straw and heavily patched. Her mouth turned down in disgust. Aruget bared his teeth.

"It's cleaner than it could be," he said. "I bought it from a carter. Put it on."

Vounn raised an eyebrow. "I don't need a disguise. I can defend myself."

"You haven't been in Rhukaan Draal at night." He shook out the cloak and thrust it at her. "Wear it or we stay here until morning. Lhesh Haruuc assigned me to protect you. I will not fail him."

Grimacing, she took the cloak and threw it around her shoulders. Aruget had been right—it didn't smell as bad as it could have. The hobgoblin had purchased a torch as well. He lit it from another torch beside the Orien gates and they left the compound for the shadowed streets. Vounn looked around as they walked. While the streets may have been dark, they were far from abandoned. Goblins, hobgoblins, and bugbears went about their business without light, as did a fair number of dwarves, elves, and shifters. A few humans and halflings were abroad as well, but most of them walked in the darkness rather than use torches or lanterns. Fixed light sources were few and far between, and unlike in the cities she knew best, they were open flame rather than cold fire.

"You walk too proudly," Aruget growled at her.

"Do you want me to shuffle like a slave?" Vounn asked. "I'm being escorted by one of Haruuc's soldiers. No moth-eaten cloak is going to hide that!"

"If you walk with less pride, you will go unnoticed. Right now, you are attracting attention."

Vounn knew better than to look around, but she couldn't help thinking of the Gan'duur attack on the road to the Gathering Stone. She slouched a little and shortened her stride. "Who's watching?"

"No one special," said Aruget. "Only the usual thugs and thieves. Harmless enough if they keep their distance."

His hand stayed near his sword, though.

They were almost halfway back to Haruuc's fortress when Vounn heard the noise. At first it seemed like nothing more than a murmur, but it quickly grew into the swollen rumble of a crowd. Chanting voices. Marching feet. A high, shrill voice swirled around the noise, but Vounn couldn't make out what it was saying. She wasn't the only one on the street to notice the sound, though. All around them, people were looking in the direction—ahead and to the left—of the noise. Many of them looked concerned and began to vanish into buildings or away down alleys and sidestreets.

Aruget's ears flicked and his jaw tightened.

"What is it?" Vounn asked him.

"A famine march. There have been rumors among the guards that one might be taking place."

"What's a famine march?"

He looked at her. "A response to the food shortages. A rite of the Dark Six."

Vounn's stomach knotted. In civilized lands, ordinary people might invoke the names of the Shadow, the Keeper, the Traveler, or the other sinister counterparts to the gods of the Sovereign Host in order to stave off misfortune. Outright worship of the dark gods was only for the cruel and the mad, though, and no matter how evil or deranged the worshippers, it was never conducted in public. There would have been an uprising.

But if she needed another reason to remember that Darguun, for all of Haruuc's efforts, was not yet a civilized nation, she had it. For centuries before Haruuc had forged them into a nation, the goblins had followed the Six. Popular tales of Darguun painted lurid pictures of massacres in the name of the Fury and torture in the name of the Mockery. She'd seen nothing of the sort since she'd arrived, only the rites to the Sovereign Host conducted within Khaar Mbar'ost, but apparently the faith of generations wasn't far below the surface.

Vounn swallowed and returned Aruget's gaze. "What do we do?"

"We run," said Aruget. "We don't want to be caught out in the open, but we might still be able to make it past the march and back to Khaar Mbar'ost."

Vounn lifted up the skirt of her dress. "Lead," she said.

They were hardly the only ones running on the street, but they were among the very few running *toward* the noise of the march—and they were the only ones running toward it that didn't wear expressions of beatific anticipation. The march was drawing in new participants. Vounn ran harder and cursed her age. Aruget slowed to keep pace with her. She was grateful he didn't just leave her behind.

The sound of the march grew louder, words in Goblin condensing out of the chant. *Devourer, leave us be! Let our sweetest offerings soothe your hunger! Devourer, pass us by!*

"They're on the wide street ahead," said Aruget. "We'll be past them in just—"

His words cut off. Vounn raised her eyes and looked ahead. The street they ran along was blocked on its other side. Carts had been drawn across it and figures stood across the makeshift barricade, watching in the direction of Khaar Mbar'ost. There was no easy way across.

Aruget bared his teeth. "They're trying to block Haruuc's soldiers from interfering," he said. "We need to go around them."

He grabbed her hand and pulled her around the corner onto the wide street—and into the path of the famine march.

For an instant, Vounn had a glimpse of the marchers, a mob that filled the street from side to side. Some among them carried torches, and the leaping flames cast color onto the moonlight-washed crowd. Most of the marchers were hobgoblins, but there were goblins and bugbears, kobolds and crazed humans as well. At the head of the mob was a bugbear. Riding like a child on his shoulders was a wizened old goblin woman. Above her head, she held a cluster of bloody bones with their ends sharpened to points—the symbol of the Devourer, the most primal god of the Dark Six. Hers was the shrill voice Vounn had heard earlier, and it rose again.

"Feed the Devourer! Feed his unending hunger, and we may survive!"

Then the glimpse was gone as Aruget dragged her on down the street, fleeing before the mob. The way ahead of them was completely empty, all doors closed, all windows shuttered. Vounn waited for the mob to spot them and rush forward, howling for blood, but they didn't. They just came on at the same constant, unstoppable pace, and Vounn wished that she had House Orien's abilities to step across vast distances in the blink of an eye.

"Here!" Aruget hurled the torch away and turned to one side so sharply that he wrenched her arm. Pain shot through her shoulder, but she followed his guidance and stumbled into the mouth of an alley. Stinking garbage made the footing unsteady, but the alley was narrow and she could brace herself against the walls. Aruget followed her in, pressing her back and hiding her with his body.

"We'll wait until they pass, then go back," he whispered. "They'll be heading for the Bloody Market."

"Why?"

"They'll make their sacrifice there—or try to. They may try to wreck the market too. If Haruuc is smart, he'll have soldiers assembled to meet them before they can do any damage." His ears flicked. "Hush!"

The noise of the famine march was a vibration in the air and the ground. The footfalls and chants of the mob, intertwined with the shrieks of the old goblin woman, came closer, then abruptly the march was on them. Moonlight flickered on the face of the old goblin, and Vounn saw that her eyes were filmed and pale. She must have been blind. There were dark stains running down her arms, and Vounn wondered if the blood that slicked the symbol of the Devourer was her own.

Then she was gone, and the marchers, their faces smeared with ash, were streaming past. There were children among them, looking around in confusion. A hobgoblin boy stared down the alley and his eyes met Vounn's. She glanced away and when she looked back, the boy was gone.

Almost all of the marchers carried baskets heaped with food. Aruget drew back his lips in a silent snarl and put his mouth close to her ear. "Dark Six cultists hold famine marches in times of shortage. They try to avoid a full-scale famine by sacrificing the best of their food to the Devourer in hopes that he'll leave them what scraps remain. All they do is make things worse for themselves."

Vounn felt sick at the waste—and even more sick as the ranks of the marchers thinned briefly to reveal a dozen ragged figures, bound to one another by ropes, being forced along the street. Slaves. She pressed her lips together. Aruget nodded, confirming her unspoken fears. "The Devourer hungers for meat of all kinds," he said.

"Are the shortages that bad already?"

"They don't have to be. The life of a common slave is cheap." He looked out of the alley again as the last of the bound figures passed from view. "If there truly were famine, there would be no slaves left to sacrifice."

The mass of the mob had passed, the rumble of their chant fading with them. There were only stragglers on the street now, and soon they were gone as well. Aruget eased his head out of the alley, looked up and down, then took Vounn's hand to pull her after him. She would have gone with him gladly except for the familiar voice that drifted down into the alley from above.

"They make us look like ignorant savages," said Tariic.

Vounn stopped and looked up. High up on one of the walls of the alley was the dark shape of an open window. Another voice came down, "You don't honor the Dark Six?"

Daavn of Marhaan. Vounn had thought the warlord had left Rhukaan Draal to return to his clan's territories. She tugged Aruget back into the alley and pointed up at the window. There was no need—his face was already turned up, his ears already high.

"I honor them in their place," said Tariic. "A famine march is the kind of stupidity that makes the other nations of Khorvaire look on our people as brutes."

"You sound like your uncle, trying to appease the humans as a famine march tries to appease the Devourer. Do you intend to leave Darguun eating stale *noon* and chewing dry bones?"

"Peace and war, like the Dark Six, have their place." There was a pause and Vounn imagined Tariic sipping wine. "My uncle favors me. He trusts me with the most sensitive of missions. I am the most obvious of heirs—a warrior of his blood, trained as a bridge between Darguun and the Five Nations. He believes I share his vision for our people."

"*I* believe you share his vision," Daavn said.

"I believe that now is the time to honor peace," Tariic answered. "I came to assure you that war will have its time as well. Bide your time, Daavn. When I receive what is due to me, I want the Marhaan to stand with the Rhukaan Taash in support of me."

He received a grumble as an answer.

Tariic's voice took on a sharper edge. "Do I have the friendship of the Marhaan, Daavn?"

"You're not Haruuc's heir yet, Tariic. I don't gamble on coins beneath a bowl when the bowl may never be lifted." Daavn seemed to hesitate, then said, "Give me a sign. You want the Marhaan to stand with you. Tell me something I want to know."

There was another pause, longer this time. Vounn doubted if wine was being sipped. "What?" Tariic said finally.

"I have heard that Dagii of the Mur Talaan has ridden to the southwest, along with a number of those you brought to Khaar Mbar'ost with the Deneith envoy. One of the *sharaat'khesh,* a *duur'kala* of the Kech Volaar, a gnome, a shifter, and a human bearing a Siberys dragonmark. A strange group of people. My instincts tell me that something is going on. What are they doing?"

"Why do you want to know?" asked Tariic. "The southwest is a long way from Marhaan territory."

"I ask as a warlord of Darguun—and as someone you want as your friend. Does such a group ride our nation on their own accord?"

Tariic paused again, then said, "They ride at Lhesh Haruuc's command."

"But you know why he sent them out? Does it have something to do with House Deneith?"

"I'm saying nothing more."

"When do they return?"

Tariic laughed at that question. "I can't tell you what no one knows, Daavn. Not even Haruuc is certain when they'll come back. Now you tell me—will the Marhaan stand with me? I want an answer."

Daavn answered with sincerity. "You have given me the sign I asked for. When you are heir, Tariic of Rhukaan Taash, the Marhaan will stand with you. By the honor of my clan, I swear it."

There was the sound of metal touching metal. Vounn guessed that the two men had crossed their knives, the goblin tradition for sealing an oath. "I must go," said Tariic. "The famine march will have stirred things up. I'd counted on my uncle not noticing my absence tonight from Khaar Mbar'ost, but he'll probably be looking for me."

"Tell him you were caught in the city by the march," Daavn suggested. "It's the truth."

"It is at that. Swift travel back to your territory, my friend."

"Great glory, Tariic."

Aruget touched Vounn's arm and she made out his gesture as he pointed to the street. She nodded. If they wanted to avoid encountering Tariic on the street, they needed to go. They slipped out of the alley and ran as swiftly as she could manage. The moonlight gave just enough light for her to see where she was going and that the street was still empty. There were sounds of violent confrontation in the distance. The famine marchers had encountered Haruuc's soldiers.

As they reached the street that led to Khaar Mbar'ost, Vounn glanced back. Tariic was only just emerging from the house beside the alley. They would return to the fortress ahead of him. She slowed gratefully to a brisk walk.

"What we heard tonight," said Aruget, "was not treason. Tariic did not act or plot against the lhesh."

"He didn't," Vounn agreed. She couldn't help thinking of what Haruuc had told her in Khaar Mbar'ost's hall of honor: "Tariic understands *muut,* but he is drawn to *atcha.*"

Aruget's head turned in the moonlight and he looked at her. "Still, I feel Tariic would not appreciate that we know these things. We will have this secret between us, lady?"

She thought for a moment before answering. Aruget saw secrets. She saw diplomacy—and the essence of diplomacy was using what people wanted to get what you needed. Tariic had wanted *atcha* and the future support of the Marhaan. Why had Daavn needed to know about Haruuc's quest?

Vounn pressed her lips together, then looked back at the hobgoblin. "We will, Aruget," she said. "Just between us."

CHAPTER NINETEEN

As he charged back through the trees, Geth heard Ekhaas, Ashi, and Dagii beating their way into the hedge of thorns at the edge of the forest. The dust-blind trolls heard, too, and turned their ugly heads toward the sound, screaming their frustration.

At Geth's heels, Midian said, "You're insane."

"I'm beginning to think that myself." Geth reached inside himself and shifted once more, feeling the rush of invulnerability that was his heritage flood his body. He tightened his grip on Wrath and the sword pulsed in his hand. If nothing else, he thought, he was going to die like a hero.

Then they were on the trolls. Intent on their escaping prey, the monsters didn't notice them until it was too late. Geth roared and hit the first troll in his path, trying to inflict the most damage he could, striking not to kill but to disable. Wrath sheared through its hip. The creature toppled over as its leg collapsed, but the wound was already closing. Geth didn't stop. He moved on to the next troll. A swing took off its hand. The follow-through severed its knee from behind. The troll, still blind from Ekhaas's spell, squealed and groped for the limbs as it went down. Geth kicked them out of its reach.

Midian, joined by Chetiin, was also striking for knees. The gnome's pick shattered bone, and a twist of the weapon ruined the joint. The damage was temporary, but it brought trolls low while quick work with Chetiin's curved dagger opened horrific wounds at critical points that would take longer to heal. In only moments, they had taken down four trolls. Geth turned to the last of the trolls—and was met with dark eyes clear of Ekhaas's magical dust. A wide hand lashed out.

The troll's talons gouged his shifting-toughened skin but didn't break through. If they had, Geth might have been staring at his own guts as they spilled across the ground. The blow was still powerful, though. It threw Geth off his feet and slammed him hard into the trunk of a tree. Shadows swirled across Geth's vision, but he blinked them back and pushed himself up again, Wrath ready to meet the troll's charge.

It didn't come. Hooting at the downed trolls as if in command, the creature turned and ran after Ekhaas and the others. The troll Geth had slashed across the hip rose and went with it, its lurching gait smoothing out with every stride. They disappeared into the brambles, heedless of the thorns that tore at their rubbery hides. The remaining trolls, free from the blinding magic, glared at their attackers and let loose a flurry of howls. Half-healed joints popped as they moved. Half-healed limbs clawed at them. Geth slapped aside a soft, raw hand with his gauntlet and whirled Wrath in a short arc that carved a gash in a troll's torso, then jumped away before the monster could attack again.

Chetiin and Midian ran to his side. "Two between us and the others," said Chetiin as the trolls tried to crawl toward them. "Three here."

"We can take them down again," said Geth.

Midian cursed. "Enough fighting, big man! Learn from a gnome!" He dug into a side pocket of his pack, pulled something out, and ordered, "Look away!"

Geth caught a glimpse of two tiny objects as Midian hurled them at the clustered trolls, then he quickly obeyed the gnome's orders. And was glad he had as two intense flashes of light erupted with muffled bangs and new shrieks from the trolls. Blind again, they staggered back.

"Now run," said Midian. "That way—as quiet as possible!"

He pointed not in the direction Ekhaas and the others had gone, but along the forest edge toward a tall and sturdy tree. Geth would have hesitated—the trolls were vulnerable again—but Chetiin grabbed him and pushed him toward the tree. They sprinted for it, Geth making the most noise of any of them, and even that the barest whisper. Midian ran like a rabbit and Chetiin like a shadow. The trolls were still howling, covering up any sound their quarry made. Midian flicked something else back along their trail. Geth heard a soggy splat and caught a whiff of a terrible, pungent odor. The trolls, caught in whatever Midian had thrown, moaned as if angry skunks had been thrust under their noses.

They reached the tree while the trolls were still reeling under the effects of the lights and the stink. Chetiin scrambled up it faster than Geth would have thought possible, seeming to run right up the trunk. Geth paused to give Midian a boost, then sheathed Wrath and pulled himself up. A shifter's heavy nails weren't sharp enough to be much use in a fight, but they dug into bark easily enough. In only moments, even with one hand encased in his gauntlet, he had reached the lowest branches.

"Higher!" urged Midian. The gnome was climbing with ease.

Geth growled and kept going until the leaves below all but concealed the forest floor, and moonlight came through the leaves above—moonlight and a view of the valley's grassy slope, of the torches carried by the bugbears standing above, of the three figures that broke from the thorns and raced up the slope.

Ekhaas's powerful voice echoed in the night. Without Wrath in his grasp, he couldn't understand the Goblin words she spoke, but he understood the urgency in them. Even as she called to the bugbears, though, the two trolls that had gone after them burst out of the thorns and the bugbears reacted. Torches and pitch pots whirled. One of the largest bugbears shouted something that sounded like a challenge. Confronted, the trolls backed down and retreated into the thorns. The three figures that were Ashi, Ekhaas, and Dagii began to climb again. Geth felt a rush of elation—they'd found allies!

Then the large bugbear shouted again. Another bugbear threw something, and one of the figures dropped to the ground.

"Tiger's blood!" Geth said. "What—?"

"Hush!" Chetiin perched on a branch just above him. The goblin pointed down through the masking leaves.

The trolls were prowling beneath the tree. Geth bit his tongue and held still.

It didn't seem as if the monsters had seen them climb. They stalked around the tree, roaming through the forest and growling quietly at each other. Geth raised his head and looked back to the slope of the valley. The bugbears had closed in. The two remaining figures on the slope—Ashi and Dagii, he could tell from the stances—had put their backs together, but bugbears had the advantage of numbers. His friends went down beneath the crush of their big, hairy bodies. Geth heard Ashi shouting and cursing in the language of the clans of the Shadow Marches. When the knot of bugbears opened again, the massive goblins carried two struggling forms on their shoulders, along with a third that was limp and unresisting. Under moonlight and torchlight, the bugbears streamed out of the valley and back to the camp in the vale.

Geth bared his teeth in silent rage.

On the forest floor, the growls of the trolls changed and moved away, then were joined by new voices. The two trolls driven back by the bugbears had returned. They didn't seem happy to learn that they'd been denied all of their prey. The growls grew soft. Geth, listening carefully, caught the sound of feet moving on the forest litter. The trolls had split up to search for them.

He turned to look up at Chetiin and, on another branch nearby, Midian. "What now?" he whispered.

"We could stay here until morning," Chetiin said. "The trolls didn't seem to be active during the day."

"What about Ashi, Ekhaas, and Dagii? What are the bugbears going to do to them?"

Chetiin's face was somber. "The tribes of the Marguul deal with prisoners in many different ways. They could keep or sell them as slaves. They could kill them as an offering to the Dark Six." He nodded out to the valley. "They could give them back to the trolls. I think we know what the bugbears were sacrificing to now. They must give the trolls food, and in exchange the trolls stay in the valley."

"That's not normal behavior for trolls," said Midian. "Trolls usually eat everything in sight."

"I don't think these trolls act normally at all. They show far too much discipline." His big ears twitched. "In any case, if we want to do anything about the bugbears, we need to get past the trolls first. Or wait until the morning when they're gone."

"We can't wait," said Geth. "Midian, do you have anything else useful in your pack?"

"It depends on what you consider useful. I have a few more flash pellets, but no more stench bags. No more alchemist's fire."

"Grandfather Rat." Geth shifted on the uncomfortable perch of the tree branch. "We can injure the trolls, but we can't put them down permanently."

"We can take some of the bugbears' torches and pitch when we come back in," Midian said, "but that doesn't help us now."

Geth looked at him sharply. "Wait. Come back in?"

"You're coming back into the valley, aren't you?" asked Midian. "The rod is still in here."

"Past the trolls? That's crazy."

The words sounded hollow, though. In the pit of his stomach, he knew he'd come back. He'd promised Haruuc he would follow Wrath's blade, and if the blade pointed into the valley . . .

"We'd need to avoid the trolls and maybe fight them on the way out," he said, "then again on the way back in. We don't even know what's at the bottom of that staircase."

"I do," Chetiin said.

Geth looked him in astonishment.

"I went past the troll nest before I returned. There's a rock wall at the bottom of the pit and some kind of shrine built against it." The goblin returned Geth's gaze and added slowly. "I think I have a way to stop the trolls."

"Sage's shadow!" Midian choked. "Why haven't you used it already?"

Chetiin scowled. "It's not something to be used lightly." He held out his right arm, wrist turned up to show the sheathed dagger that was strapped there, the dagger that Geth had noticed he never used. "The *shaarat'khesh* call this Witness. It is a treasure of my clan, an honor to the one chosen to carry it. It is not drawn except to kill—and the soul of what it kills is trapped forever. Those slain by it are forever dead. No magic in the world can bring them back, not the prayers of priests or the wishes of wizards."

He eased the dagger a little way out of its sheath. If Geth had thought the curved dagger the goblin wore on his left arm was a sinister piece of work, the dagger on his right brought an eerie prickle to his skin. It was a plain weapon in shape and color, dull metal forged into a tool with no other purpose than killing. The steel of the dagger, however, was etched with a single twisted rune—and set with a long blue-black crystal that resembled a slit eye peering out of the blade.

The crystal, Geth knew, was a Khyber dragonshard, valued by wizards and artificers for its affinity for magic of binding and trapping. The idea that such a shard would have been used in a weapon was somehow deeply troubling. He looked away.

Midian had turned from the dagger, too. "That's a Keeper's Fang. Why would you even have something like that?" he asked, his voice thick.

"When the *shaarat'khesh* kill, it's a matter of pride to know that the task is complete beyond any doubt." Chetiin pushed the blade back out of sight and lowered his arm. "Its power might stop a troll from healing—if it's used to strike the killing blow."

"Trapping the troll's soul," Midian said.

Chetiin frowned at him. "Do you think a troll would be less dead if we burned it to death? What about the troll you left by the steps? When we fled, it was still alive. It may never die or fully heal. Is that a kindness?"

Wolf and Tiger, thought Geth. He drew a breath and let it out before making a decision. "We'll try to sneak past the trolls first, and use the Fang only as a last resort. Are you certain it will work, Chetiin?"

"No."

"It's something, at least." He nodded toward the slope of the valley. "We'll head over to the valley wall and try to make our way out from there. The thorns seem a little less thick at the edge. If we run into any trolls, Midian and I will try to bring them down—Chetiin, you use your dagger to deliver the killing blow. If Tiger dances, we may make it out of here."

"How are we going to deal with the bugbears?" Chetiin asked.

"Let's deal with the trolls first. If we can't get out of the valley, bugbears won't matter much." Geth eased himself from tree branch to trunk and climbed down until he was close enough to the forest floor to jump. He left himself drop the rest of the way, landing with a quiet thump and sinking into a defensive crouch. He scanned the forest, then called up, "All cl—"

He caught movement out of the corner of his eye as the troll rose up from where it had crouched beside a tree stump, its rough and warty skin blending with leaves and moss. Geth started to turn, to reach for his sword, but the troll was faster. Claws raked along the shoulder of his unarmored sword arm.

His shifting had faded while they hid in the tree. The troll's claws tore into his flesh, and Geth felt hot blood drench his back. He bit down on a scream and forced himself around, abandoning the attempt to swing Wrath and instead bringing up his great gauntlet just in time to block another strike. Claws dragged along black steel, provoking a hiss of frustration from the troll. But there was bloodlust in its eyes and it raised both arms again. Geth jumped away to put his back against the tree. The troll lunged—and Midian dropped out of the shadows, his pick in hand. With his falling weight behind it, the head of the pick plunged into the troll's back. The monster staggered backward, suddenly off balance, its arms spread wide and its chest exposed.

When Chetiin followed Midian out of the tree, he had an easy target. The blue-black crystal in the dagger called Witness flashed as the blade pierced the troll's heart.

Geth couldn't have said what he expected to happen. Something sinister—some dark release of energy or a sudden cold wind, maybe. A final wail or howl from the dying troll as the dagger drank up its soul. There was nothing. The troll jerked and swayed on its feet. Chetiin jumped clear, but Midian clung to the shaft of his pick, riding the body as it fell against a tree and slid to the ground.

Its dark eyes stared blindly into the night. It didn't move again. Midian pulled his pick free. Blood oozed from the wound, but the rubbery flesh showed no signs of healing. Geth looked at Chetiin.

The goblin held up Witness. Not a spot of blood clung to the dull metal or the blue-black dragonshard.

"Put it away," said Midian with loathing in his voice.

The smell of the bugbear camp was strong from a distance. From inside, it was overwhelming, like being wrapped in meat and left in the sun.

Ashi thrashed and cursed from the moment the bugbears picked her up, but they had tied her wrists behind her back with leather thongs, and their grip on her was solid. At first, the big goblins had laughed at her and jostled her as if she were a doll. By the time they carried her past the pitch-smeared stakes of the barricade around the camp, though, their humor had faded. A bugbear with a ragged ear muttered something in accented Goblin about accidentally dropping her over the stakes if her struggles continued. It didn't slow Ashi's bucking at all, and the comment earned him a blow to the head from the bugbear with the trident. The bugbear with the ragged ear snarled and paid the blow forward with a slap at Ashi. She snapped at his hand.

She stopped struggling when they tossed her into one of the huts, and only because she hit the ground hard enough to send streaks of pain through her twisted shoulders. Her impact with the ground was followed by another hard blow as Dagii landed on top of her, the weight of his body driving the air out of her, the metal of his armor gouging her painfully. For a moment, all Ashi could do was try to draw breath. She heard a third thump, then the light of the camp's big firepit was cut off as the bugbears dropped a big piece of leather across the doorway of the hut. It took her another moment to realize what the third thump had been.

"Ekhaas!" Ashi writhed beneath Dagii, trying to get out from under him. He moved slowly, rolling over like a drunkard. She kicked him. He grunted and gave her the room to get up on her knees and shuffle to where Ekhaas lay.

The *duur'kala,* her hands tied as well, had curled up like a child. Her breathing was shallow. The hut was not well constructed, and in the firelight that fell through the many gaps in its walls, Ashi could see a massive mark across the side of Ekhaas's head. Her yellow skin was dimpled with the imprint of the hurled club that had brought her down. She'd have a big bruise when she woke up. If the bugbears gave her a chance to wake up.

Ashi sat back and cursed again, giving vent to her rage in the guttural blasphemies of Azhani.

"How is she?" asked Dagii.

Ashi twisted around to look at him. He'd struggled upright, and it looked like he'd have a few bruises across his face as well. "The blow was hard," Ashi said. "It doesn't look good, but it could be worse. If I could touch her, I might be able to tell more, but . . ." She twitched her bound hands.

Dagii, bound as she was, pushed himself over to her and examined Ekhaas carefully. "Her color is good and her ears are up," he said. "If they were down, it would be bad. She'll wake when she's ready."

"If she doesn't, I'll tear this camp apart with my teeth."

Dagii sat back and stared at her. "You fight like a wolverine."

"I come from a clan in the Shadow Marches," she told him. "Raiding between clans was common. If you don't fight, you're too weak to live."

His ears flicked in surprise. "You weren't born to Deneith? But you act so much like one of them, I thought—"

The assumption stung Ashi. She acted like any member of Deneith? "You thought wrong," she said, cutting him off. She wondered what Vounn would have said.

She looked around the hut. The light that filtered through the walls revealed bundles of stiff hides, maybe intended for trading with other bugbear tribes. There was nothing that could cut her bonds or be used as an effective weapon, even if she could get them loose. The bugbears had taken her sword and all of her knives. Dagii had been stripped of weapons, too, and Ekhaas as well.

"What are they likely to do with us?" she asked.

"Slavery. Sacrifice. They probably aren't going to kill us outright. They would have done it already."

"Ransom?"

"Not likely." He clenched his jaw and looked her in the eye. "We have to assume we're on our own."

Ashi knew what he meant. Geth, Chetiin, and Midian hadn't been captured, but that didn't mean they were still alive or in any situation to come to their rescue. In her mind, she saw again the two trolls that had come crashing out of the thorns in the valley. Geth wouldn't have let them pass without trying to stop them, but then again Ekhaas had caught five trolls in her spell. Five to three—bad odds for Geth and the others to hold back all their opponents.

Bad odds to survive.

She put steel in her heart and turned her attention to the cracks in the walls of the hut. They probably could have broken through the walls, but the shadows that moved frequently against them suggested the camp beyond was busy. They wouldn't have gotten far, especially with Ekhaas still down. Ashi crawled to the wall and squatted at one of the wider gaps, peering out.

The camp was as busy as she'd guessed. The fire in the great pit had been built up high, and torches stuck into the ground burned everywhere that she could see. Bugbear children were busy scooping pine pitch out of crude troughs made from hollowed logs, transferring it into smaller pots. Older youths were preparing the leather slings by which the burning pots could be swung and hurled. Most of the adult bugbears were standing by the barricade, watching the darkness beyond. It looked like the tribe was afraid the trolls might come back in the night.

"How many trolls did we see, Dagii?" Ashi asked. "Ten?"

"Nine," the hobgoblin said, speaking through his teeth. He was still crouched beside Ekhaas, his arms straining as if he were trying to snap the leather thongs that bound him—or maybe just stretch them enough to work a hand free. He relaxed for a moment and caught his breath. "Chetiin described a nest of them, but I don't think there could be many more. Trolls are ravenous. Even if the bugbears are throwing meat to them, I don't see how the valley could support many more."

"There are at least twenty adult bugbears out there, and they're armed with fire. Why do you think they leave the trolls in the valley? Wouldn't it be easier to burn them out instead of trying to appease them?"

"There's something strange about these trolls," said Dagii. "They're organized. They use tactics. I've never heard of trolls doing that before. It makes them more dangerous. Usually they just charge into battle and fight until their opponents are dead. You might as well ask why the trolls tolerate the bugbears living here." He strained against the thongs again.

Ashi shifted to another crack in the wall and found herself with a view of the massive bugbear with the trident, presumably the chief of the tribe. He stood close to the fire with three other large bugbears. They were speaking emphatically, but with low voices as if they didn't want other members of the tribe to hear. Every so often, one of them would gesture toward the hut from which she watched. Their fate, it seemed, was still being decided.

Then the chief turned and strode for the hut, two of the large bugbears following in his wake.

Ashi jerked away from the wall. "Dagii! The chief is coming!"

Dagii's head snapped up and he rose awkwardly to his feet, wincing has he put weight on the ankle that had been injured. "Stand!" he said. "Don't face him on your knees or he'll think you're submitting."

Just like among the Bonetree clan. If you don't fight, you're too weak to live. Ashi rose and moved to stand beside Dagii just as the hide over the doorway was torn aside and the chief entered.

He was nearly as tall as a troll and big enough that the hut seemed small as soon as he was inside. The smell of pine pitch clung to the thick hair of his body. Big ears, not nearly as mobile as those of hobgoblins, turned like scoops in their direction. A black button-nose that was comically bearlike wrinkled as if the chief was sniffing them like a dog.

He had her sword thrust into his belt. *"Khyberit gentis!"* Ashi snarled. She might have hurled herself at him if Dagii hadn't twisted to block her way.

The two bugbears who had entered with the chief stiffened and lifted their weapons, a big mace and a heavy sword. The chief growled at them. He planted the butt of his trident in the dusty earth floor of the tent and said in thunderous Goblin, "I am Makka!

This is my territory." His free hand pointed at Dagii. "You, low-lander. What is your tribe?"

Dagii stood against the roar of the bugbear's voice like a wall standing against a gale. "I am Dagii of Mur Talaan." He pointed at Ekhaas where she lay on the ground. "She is also Mur Talaan."

A blunt lie. Ashi wondered if the bugbears of the Marguul tribes had some complaint against the Kech Volaar. Makka didn't challenge Dagii, though. His black nose wrinkled again, and his mouth curved in a sneer. "This means nothing to me. I have never heard of the Mur Talaan." Ashi saw Dagii bristle at this insult to his clan, but Makka's thick finger shifted to point at her. "The human carries a dragonmark. What is her clan?"

Dagii's ears rose slightly and he looked at Ashi sharply. "I don't think he speaks your language," he said in the human tongue before she could answer Makka in Goblin. "Don't let him know you understand what he's saying. It could be an advantage. Do you want me to tell him your House?"

Ashi watched Makka and the other two bugbears carefully for any sign of reaction to what Dagii had just said. The only thing she saw was impatience. They hadn't understood him. "Yes," she said. "Say whatever you think you need to."

He nodded and turned back to Makka. "She belongs to the mighty clan Deneith," he said, speaking Goblin once more, "whose armies are so vast that Lhesh Haruuc Shaarat'kor sends his soldiers to fight for them."

The bugbear who carried a mace opened his eyes wide and murmured something to Makka that was too soft for Ashi to hear, but the chief only growled at him. "I don't care what Haruuc does—he bows to humans like a goblin!" he told Dagii. His sneer faded, though, and he looked speculatively at Ashi for moment, then pointed again, this time at Ekhaas. "We heard singing in the valley, the song of a *duur'kala*. Her?"

"No. She is only a scout. We had a *duur'kala* with us, but she and the others of our party remained in the valley to cover our escape while we sought help from you."

Makka's already tiny eyes narrowed even more. "How many others?"

"Six," Dagii lied.

The bugbear with the mace hissed at this. "Nine of them altogether! Makka, the trolls will be angry for certain!"

"If the other six haven't escaped the valley, the trolls will be well-fed, Guun." Makka glared down at Dagii and Ashi. "What were you doing in the valley?"

"We were lost. We slipped past your camp during the day while the sentries dozed. Our scouts told us there was a way through the valley."

Dagii spoke with utter conviction, but Makka wrinkled his nose. "You were lost," he said. "Where were you trying to go?"

Ashi felt a chill seep along her back. Makka's tone was dangerous. Dagii, however, continued to stand tall and confident. "At Lhesh Haruuc's orders, we are seeking a new route through the Seawall Mountains to Zilargo."

"And you thought there was a way through the valley?" Makka's voice rose to a roar. He lunged and grabbed Dagii's arm with his free hand. "Come!" he said, dragging Dagii out of the hut with no more difficulty than an adult pulling a child. Guun and the other bugbear looked confused for a moment, then prodded Ashi into motion after them.

Makka didn't take Dagii far. The hut into which they had been thrown stood near one edge of the camp. The tribe stopped its labors to stare as Makka pulled Dagii up to the barricade and twisted him around so that he looked out over the valley. Ashi was pushed up alongside him. With the firepit behind her and the moons shining bright overhead, she found she could see vague shapes and silhouettes a surprising distance into the night. Makka thrust his trident toward the valley.

"There is where you went," he said, then gave Dagii a half-turn that left him facing in the direction of the western trail down from the mountain. "There is where you could have gone. Is it hard to see? Does the way look more difficult?" He shook Dagii hard. "There is no exit from the valley! No one of any sense would think there was! Why did you go down there?"

"Treasure!" Dagii gasped, his teeth rattling. Ashi saw Guun's ears turn up, but once again Makka only growled. The shaking stopped. Dagii pointed at her. "She hired us to locate a treasure lost by Deneith during the Last War."

Ashi felt astonishment cross her face before she remembered she wasn't supposed to be able to understand what was being said. Fortunately, Makka didn't seem to notice. Teeth bared, he released Dagii and whirled on her. A massive paw of a fist cracked across her face, driving her to the ground and sending bright spots whirling before her eyes. Rage burst inside her as she stared up at the bugbear chief, her grandfather's sword in his belt, and she would have leaped at him if Guun and the other bugbear hadn't seized her shoulders and held her still.

"Treasure?" Makka said. "You entered the valley for treasure?" His angry face moved between her and Dagii. "You've stirred up the trolls, you fools! You may have doomed us all. My tribe has held this territory by keeping peace with the trolls, giving them meat to keep them quiet and driving them back when they get restless. And you went looking for treasure?" He grabbed Dagii again and sent him sprawling toward the hut. "Get them out of my sight! Tomorrow we'll give them to the trolls. That may restore the peace."

"Makka *chib,* wait," said Guun. There was a hungry look in his beady eyes. "What about this treasure? If we could get it—"

"No one goes into the valley. It's been a cursed place since the mountains were young. If there's treasure lost in the valley, it will remain lost until they are dust!"

Dagii, however, seized on Guun's curiosity and greed. "The Deneith are idiots," he said to Makka. "They went into the valley during the Last War while they were looking for Marguul to fight for them. The treasure is their pay chest, full of gold and gems. The wealth of a king! We got close to it before the trolls drove us away." He dropped his voice. "How many trolls do you believe are in the valley, *chib?* We only saw nine. With fire and pitch, your tribe would be a match for them. You could wipe them out for good and claim the treasure."

The idea sank into Makka's head and he paused, anger slipping away. Dagii had hit on something even more valuable to Makka,

Ashi realized, than the treasure. Wiping out the trolls would eliminate a drain on the resources of the tribe's territory—how much of the meat that hung on racks around the camp must have been there just to feed the trolls? The thought of a chest full of treasure probably didn't hurt either.

After a long moment, Makka snorted. "Put them back in the hut. I must think about this." He stomped away to the longhouse at the back of the camp.

Guun and the other bugbear pushed Ashi and Dagii inside the hut, then dropped the hide door as they went after Makka. Ashi nodded at Dagii once they were gone. "That was nicely done, turning Makka against the trolls."

"It may not work," Dagii said. "I think Makka may be too afraid of the valley. It may give us a chance, though."

"It may give some of us a chance," said a quiet voice from the ground.

Ashi looked down and stifled a cry of delight. Ekhaas's amber eyes were open and looking up at them. She dropped down beside her. "How long have you been awake?"

"Long enough to know that I've joined the Mur Talaan and been given the position of scout." She sat up slowly, her eyes squeezing shut as she moved.

"If they'd known you were a *duur'kala,* they would have watched you more closely or maybe just killed you right away," said Dagii. "This way we have a secret they don't know."

Ekhaas nodded, the motion bringing another brief wince to her face. "There's more than muscle and honor between your ears," she said. "The problem with the story you've told to Makka is that he doesn't need all of us to pull it off. You told him that we almost reached the treasure—that means he only needs one of us to find it again."

"Maabet," said Dagii. "I'm a soldier, not a *duur'kala*. Do you think you can come up with something?"

"We can start by telling them Ashi needs to be the one to open the chest. At least we've got time to think of something more." She looked around, her ears flicking. "Geth and the others?"

Ashi took the job of telling her that there had been no sign of their friends. Again, there was no need to speak aloud the possibility that they were dead. She could see in Ekhaas's eyes that she had considered the same thing already.

The hut grew quiet as Ekhaas thought and Ashi and Dagii rested. The bright light, moving shadows, and wary tension in the camp beyond the flimsy walls continued. There would be none of the tribe's usual activities that night—the risk of a troll attack kept them all close to the camp and alert. Ashi found herself a spot on the piled hides in the hut that was neither too hard nor too smelly. In spite of the noise of the camp outside, she even managed to fall into a light doze.

She couldn't have said exactly how long she slept, but it was Dagii's voice that roused her to semi-waking. The hobgoblin warrior spoke softly in Goblin. "Thank you for healing my ankle, Ekhaas. I've never felt anything like your magic."

"No thanks are necessary," Ekhaas answered. "We couldn't leave you."

Dagii stirred, as if he were sitting up. "Thanks *are* necessary," he said. "We got out of the valley because of you. Your songs distracted the trolls and kept us ahead of them. Without you, we wouldn't have had a chance. *Ya panozhii kita atcha.*"

I owe a debt to your honor—the most formal way of offering thanks among goblins. Ashi opened her eyes and glanced at the two hobgoblins. Ekhaas was looking at Dagii, amber eyes meeting gray. After a moment, she gave a slow and graceful nod of acceptance.

It was another moment before Ashi realized that the camp had gone still and quiet as well. She sat up sharply. "What's going on?" she whispered.

Dagii and Ekhaas looked up as if they'd forgotten she was even there. A faint flush spread across Ekhaas's face, but Dagii was the first to understand what she'd really meant. He twisted around and put an eye to one of the gaps in the wall of the hut. "They've stopped," he said. "Everyone's staring at something."

"The valley?" asked Ekhaas.

Ashi rolled off her bed of hides and found another gap to look through. The bugbears of the camp were staring into the night, just as Dagii had said, but they weren't looking toward the valley. "No," she said, "they're looking west along the trail." No, she realized, that wasn't quite right either. "They're looking into the forest."

Beside the barricades, one bugbear guard conferred with another, then went running to the longhouse. Ashi suspected he was looking for Makka. She changed gaps, keeping him in sight. Sure enough, very shortly after the guard disappeared into the longhouse, Makka emerged with Guun at his side and strode to the barricade. His trident was in hand and his black nose wrinkled as he sniffed at the air. Guun did the same thing.

"Horses," said Guun.

Makka's head turned to catch the breeze in different directions. "Many horses," he said. He turned to the nearest guard. "Get the young ones into shelter."

The guard grunted and began rounding up the bugbear children and youths, herding them in the direction of the longhouse. At the same time, the adult bugbears of the tribe all began drifting to the western side of the camp, eyes—and noses—trained on the forest. Ashi watched, too, but she could see and smell nothing.

Just like all the bugbears, though, she flinched back when a deep voice rolled out of the night, shouting in Goblin, *"Release our friends!"*

CHAPTER TWENTY

That's Midian!" said Ekhaas. She climbed to her feet and walked unsteadily to the wall. Ashi nodded without taking her eyes from the gap. It was Midian. There was no mistaking his voice, though she could pick out no sign of the gnome in the darkness. Her heart was beating faster. If Midian had made it out of the valley, there was a good chance Geth and Chetiin had too.

Dagii, however, was almost growling as he moved from crack to crack, trying to find the best view. "What is he thinking, bringing the horses here?"

"*How* did he bring the horses?" Ashi whispered back to him. "That's the wrong side of the camp! We left the horses along the south trail."

Dagii's growling stopped abruptly.

By the barricade, Guun had his head bent close to Makka, and Ashi had to strain to make out what he said. "The lowlander said they left six behind in the valley."

"The lowlander lied," said Makka. For a moment, Ashi's gut twisted, then the bugbear chief clenched a fist around his trident, and snarled, "Do you smell all those horses? Flayed god's skin, there were more than six!"

Guun looked worried. "They couldn't all have escaped the trolls. How many do you think there really are?"

Makka's lips peeled back from his teeth. "Let's find out." He raised his voice. "What will you give us for them?"

Another voice came out of the dark trees a surprising distance from where the first had. "Your lives!"

Ashi started. The second voice was unfamiliar. "Who is that?"

"Midian again," said Ekhaas. *"Khaavolaar,* I didn't know he was such a good mimic."

"We already have our lives!" Makka roared. "You would have to take them from us."

A third voice answered from yet another spot, and this time Ashi thought she caught the subtle inflections that identified Midian. "We can do that."

The gnome must have been moving quickly to cover the ground necessary to give the illusion of a hidden force, even a force of just three. Ashi wondered where Geth and Chetiin were—if they were indeed alive. Maybe it was just Midian out there.

Makka wasn't the only one responding to the challenge from the night now, though. Other bugbears had joined in, shouting and shaking their weapons at their hidden assailants. Their shouts covered up Guun and Makka as they spoke. Ashi cursed, but then Makka turned back toward the forest and shook his trident in the air. "If you think you can, come and take us!"

The shouts of the tribe rose to a deafening volume. There was no response until they fell, then Midian's own voice came out of the night again. "What challenge would that be? Bugbears are supposed to be masters of stealth and ambush, aren't they? Come meet us and prove it"—There was a flash of white among the trees, the hint of a horse's flank like a taunt, and Midian's voice took on a mocking note—*"gaa'taat."*

Ashi didn't know the word, but she could guess at it. *Gaa* was Goblin for "baby" and *taat* was an insulting term for someone of low status. Combined, the words must have been extremely insulting. Makka's thick hair bristled, and his dark eyes flashed in the firelight. He thrust his trident high above his head and roared, "Gold and flesh for every tongue! *Itaa!"*

The tribe answered with a matching roar. Bugbears surged out of the gate in the barricade, charging for the forest, leaving only a few guards to watch the camp. There was little stealth in the attack—Midian had managed to infuriate Makka and his tribe beyond any point of sense. Makka was like a battering ram at the head of the charge. Even if there had been an army hidden in the trees, Ashi didn't think they would have been able to stop the bugbear chief.

"I hope Midian knows what he's doing," Ekhaas murmured.

"I think he does," said Dagii, stepping back from the wall. "He's drawn off more than enough of the tribe for us to make a run for—"

The cracking of wood interrupted him. All three of the prisoners spun around. A chunk of the hut's wall had been broken out—just big enough for Chetiin, curved dagger in hand, to slip through. "It would be easier to run," the goblin said, "if someone cut your hands free for you."

"Rond betch!" Ashi was the first one over to Chetiin, turning so that he could slice at her bonds. "What about Geth? Where is he?"

The sound of fighting outside the hut answered her question. Ashi felt the thongs on her wrists part. "Go help him," said Chetiin.

She ran from the hut, throwing aside the hide over the doorway to emerge into the nearly empty camp. Just a few paces away, Geth fought with one of the few bugbears who had remained at the camp, a big brute wielding a massive club. The shifter darted and dodged as the club came down like a falling tree. Ashi didn't think the great gauntlet would be any defense against that weapon. One good strike and Geth would be flattened. The blows he returned seemed strangely weak, and she saw that the shoulder of his sword arm had been bandaged. New blood was already seeping through the linen strips. Clenching her jaw, Ashi threw herself in behind the bugbear, rolling against his legs. His arms flailed as he tried to keep his balance. Geth seized the opening—Wrath cut a deep, deadly gash across the bugbear's belly—then finished him with another blow across his chest.

Ashi came to her feet and gave Geth a smile. "It's good to see you."

"Same," he said, then turned to meet two more bugbears, one with an axe, the other wielding two swords. They were Ekhaas and

Dagii's swords, Ashi realized, and the big goblin was swinging both of them as easily as she might have swung one.

Cursing Makka for making off with her sword, she bent down and wrapped her hands around the shaft of the first bugbear's club. The weapon was heavy and inelegant, but it was also almost unstoppable. The bugbear with the axe came at her. Ashi spun in a circle, hauling the club into an arc that clipped the bugbear's shoulder before he could dodge away. The momentary contact was enough to spin him around. Ashi tightened her swing and raised the club higher.

As the bugbear turned back to her, she slammed the club into the side of his head. He wore a helmet, but it didn't do him much good. The metal rang like a bell as he went down, blood spraying from his nose and mouth in a red mist.

Dagii raced past her to grab one of the arms of the bugbear that Geth fought. With an angry snarl, he wrenched the limb back sharply, and Ashi heard a pop. The bugbear shouted in pain, a shout that was cut short as Geth slashed her throat. She slumped forward as Dagii released her. Geth spun, searching the camp for more attackers.

There were none. The last guard was fleeing for the forest. Geth wiped Wrath quickly and slammed the weapon into its scabbard. Ashi scooped up Ekhaas's sword and handed it to her as she emerged from the hut with Chetiin. Dagii reclaimed his own sword and wrenched the helmet off the head of the bugbear Ashi had killed. It was his helmet, she realized, now so dented it was unwearable. "Sorry," she said.

"I wouldn't have been able to use it anyway," he said, spinning it around to show her the crack that had been opened in it to fit over the bugbear's head. He hurled it away into the darkness.

"Don't just stand there," ordered Geth. "Grab as many torches and pitch pots as you can carry." He already had three steaming pots dangling by their leather straps from his gauntleted hand and another two, presumably cool, slung over his shoulder along with a strange, bloody bundle. Two unlit torches were jammed into his belt. A third, burning bright, was in his other hand.

"What?" Ashi asked. "Why?"

"For the trolls. We're going back into the valley."

"When?"

He nudged another pitch pot with his toe, touched the burning torch to the pitch within, then kicked the pot against the wall of the hut in which they had been imprisoned. The clay of the pot shattered and burning pitch spattered across the wood. "As soon as the camp is on fire." he said. "Burn it and the bugbears won't have anything to come back to."

Ashi stared, then went after him as he moved around the camp, setting fire to the huts. "Not the longhouse!" she said. "The tribe's children—"

"I know," he said. "Chetiin and I saw. We came in over the barricade on the other side while Midian had the tribe's attention. We'll leave the longhouse, but everything burns. If they've got nothing to come back to here, it will make it easier for us to get out of the valley again. Now hurry! We don't have much time."

Ashi started grabbing pitch pots. The huts roared up into columns of flame that lit the night. Shouts came from the forest as the bugbears realized that they'd been tricked and that their camp was burning. No sound came from the longhouse, and she could imagine the bugbear children huddled inside, staying silent in the hope of avoiding attention—maybe they even had another way out through the slope the house was built against. She hoped so. "How did you get the horses to the other side of the camp?"

"We didn't," said Chetiin, coming up on the other side of her with an armload of torches. "The horse you saw was Midian's pony. He had the horseshoe in his pack."

"What about the horses the bugbears smelled?"

"The *shaarat'khesh* preparation that kept our mounts calm around Marrow," he said. "If we escape, I'll have to ride well away from you on the return journey."

Ashi stared at him. "Midián couldn't have spread all that around himself."

"He had help. We brought Marrow into the plan, too. She's helping Midian keep the bugbears distracted." He looked around. "Are we done?"

All of them were laden with torches and pitch pots. The huts were burning. Even the barricade was on fire, the pine pitch that had smeared the sharpened logs set ablaze. "We're done," said

Geth. "Let's go." He headed for the gate in the barricade, the only part of the ring that wasn't burning. Chetiin jogged back toward the great firepit, flung something into it, then sprinted away. An instant later, a ball of white flame burst from the pit with a piercing whistle and streaked high into the night sky.

Somewhere in the forest, a wolf howled. It seemed to Ashi that there was a malevolent joy in the sound. The shouts of the bugbears grew louder—then one of them turned to a scream before ending abruptly.

"Marrow's reward," Chetiin said as he emerged from the flames. "Once she's finished hunting, she'll go back to keeping watch over the horses."

Ekhaas and Dagii were already over the slope and down into the valley. Geth followed. Ashi stopped outside the burning barricade, a sudden hollow in the pit of her stomach. "Makka—the chief—he still has my sword!"

Geth looked back at her, then at Chetiin. The goblin shook his head. "We can't wait, Ashi," he said. "We need to be out of sight before the bugbears come back. We can't fight all of them."

"But my sword—" She turned to Geth. "It was my grandfather's. It was Kagan's."

"I'm sorry, Ashi," said Geth. "We have to leave it. We have to go."

"Your sword or our lives," Chetiin added.

Marrow howled again, closer than she'd been before. Ashi looked over at the edge of the forest, just in time to see Midian pop out of the trees and run like fox across the fire-lit vale.

"What are you waiting for?" he shouted. "Go! Go!"

Ashi pressed her lips together and ran down into the valley.

For the third time, Ashi plunged into the thorns that ran along the forest edge. There was a path through them now, thanks partly to their hacking a passage on the way out and partly to the trolls' headlong pursuit of them. The brambles were bent and chopped, twisted and trampled, and getting through them was no longer a torturous ordeal. Ashi barely noticed. The loss of her sword, the

Sentinel Marshal honor blade that had been her first connection to House Deneith, ate at her like sorrow.

Geth kept only a single torch burning so that she could see, extinguishing the others before the light could reveal them to the bugbears. They heard the tribe return to the burning camp just as they cleared the thorns and made it into the cover of the trees. Shouts of fear and anger drifted down into the valley, followed by shrieks of joy—the children of the tribe must have emerged from the longhouse. There was also one long roar of rage. Ashi knew in her gut that it was Makka, furious at the destruction wrought in the rescue of his prisoners. His wasn't the only voice of rage to rise from the camp, though. The tribe, it seemed, was angry with their chief. She wondered if they would consider killing him with the stolen sword and leaving it and his body behind as they fled.

The dream was comforting, but unlikely.

"Sage's shadow," said Midian as they paused at the inner edge of the forest. "Did any of you happen to carry my everbright lantern out of the camp?"

"Quiet, Midian," growled Geth.

"I'm not going to be happy if those bugbears still have it. That lantern was really useful."

The shifter turned on him. "I said, quiet!"

Midian flinched and closed his mouth. Geth caught Ashi's eye as he turned away from the gnome. She gave him a grateful half-smile.

"You know, we may have fire now," said Dagii, "but I still don't like the idea of fighting through the trolls to get back to those stairs."

"We've got another deterrent." Geth pulled off the bloody bundle that he'd carried across his back and opened it. A troll's head stared at them. Dagii's ears twitched back.

"We cut off two of those before," he pointed out. "It didn't even slow the other trolls down."

"This one's different," Geth said. He pulled out a long torch, hacked the wooden shaft into a long, sharp stake, and stuck it into the stump of the troll's neck. Holding the head up like a gruesome standard, he said, "This one's dead."

"Dead?" asked Ekhaas. "Dead dead?"

"Dead and not coming back. We found a way to kill them."

"Maabet! Why don't we use it?" said Dagii.

"We will if we need to," said Chetiin. "It will be even better if we can keep the trolls from attacking us in the first place, though."

Geth—troll head in one hand, Wrath in the other—and Chetiin led the way into the dark forest. Ashi, Ekhaas, and Midian followed with smoldering pitch pots and relit torches. Under the trees, they didn't need to worry about the bugbears seeing the light, and the open flame was something else to give the trolls pause. As he had before, Dagii came at the end of their party, watching the trail behind.

Ashi carried a pitch pot in each hand, slowly swinging them back and forth in their leather slings so that the thin veil of blue fire atop each hissed and popped. Pungent, resinous smoke made a faint, swirling trail behind her. The forest felt somehow less disturbing the third time through, Ashi thought. Maybe she was getting used to the silent atmosphere. Maybe she was numbed by the loss of Kagan's sword. Maybe she was just exhausted—she would have happily camped for the remainder of the night and continued in the morning, but there was nowhere to camp. Caught between the bugbears and the trolls, their only choice was to keep going all the way back to the mysterious stairs.

Hiss, went the pots as she swung them. *Hiss, hiss, pop, hiss—*

Chetiin stopped. "Troll," he said softly.

"Where?" asked Geth.

Chetiin pointed, then pointed again. And again.

"Behind us, too," said Dagii. "Two more. Five altogether."

"Light more torches," Chetiin said. "One for each of us."

"Not me," Ashi told him. She took a careful step away from Ekhaas and Midian and began to spin the pitch pots as the bugbears had when they'd confronted the trolls on the valley's slope. The slow hiss turned into a steady rush. The pots became blurred, blue-glowing orbs. As more torches were lit and the circle of light around them grew, the blue glow seemed to fade, but the sound of the flame was still there. *Hiisssshh . . .*

The expanding illumination caught the trolls at its edge. Their lumpy, blue-green flesh seemed to meld with the mossy trees. They almost could have been trees, tall and thin and twisted, still as old wood, their dark eyes like shadowed knots. Geth turned slowly, looking at each of them in turn and making sure that they saw the head that he carried.

"Dead," he said. "This one is dead. No healing. No coming back. Do you understand?"

They gave no indication that they even heard him.

"They reacted when Makka challenged them," said Dagii. "Try Goblin."

"Let me." Ekhaas moved forward to stand beside Geth. The tallest of the trolls stood directly in front of them, and Ekhaas faced it. She stood up straight and spoke in Goblin, "Let us pass! We carry fire. We can hurt you." She let her voice drop into a whisper that matched the rush of Ashi's whirling pots. "We can kill you." She pointed at the severed head.

The tallest troll blinked and tilted its head slowly, looking first at the severed head, then at Ekhaas. Its warty, rubbery face betrayed nothing more.

"Let us pass," said Ekhaas again. "We mean you no harm. Let us pass and we will not hurt you."

Silence again, a silence that stretched out. Ekhaas didn't move but just kept looking at the troll. None of the other trolls around them moved, nor did Chetiin or Geth. Midian moved, squirming. Dagii moved, tightening his grip on sword and on torch. Ashi tried not to move, but she found herself swinging the pitch pots faster so that their hiss grew louder and more shrill.

Then the troll moved, throwing back its head and letting out a weird hooting sound. Ashi gasped in surprise and might have released both pitch pots right at it if Ekhaas hadn't thrust out a hand. "Do nothing!" she said. Her eyes were bright. "It's calling something—or someone."

They held still. A few moments later, they heard the sound of something being dragged through the forest. Two somethings, Ashi realized, as the sound drew closer. Two trolls came to the edge of the light, each of them pulling another troll. They released their burdens, then stepped back into the darkness.

The first troll must have been the one Geth's head belonged to. Its neck was cut through and the stump showed no signs of healing.

The rubbery flesh of the corpse had turned gray. There was no doubt that the troll was dead.

There was equally no doubt that the second troll was alive. It groaned and wept quietly, moaning like someone with a fever. The injuries that tortured it, however, were far worse. It was the troll they had defeated near the stairs, the one Ashi had cut open and Midian had burned. Its back was an open wound, a mess of scorched bone and flesh that was either black and charred or red and weeping.

"Rond betch," she murmured. She saw Chetiin throw a hard glance at Midian. The gnome's face was expressionless.

The tallest troll hooted again, softly this time, then growled and brought up a gangly arm. It pointed at the dead troll, then at the weeping one. It looked at Ekhaas and hooted again.

"You want us to kill it," the *duur'kala* said slowly.

The tallest troll hooted a third time. Once again it pointed from one troll to the other, but this time it followed the gesture by stepping aside for a moment. Its message was clear: Kill the injured troll and they would be allowed to pass.

"These are *not* normal trolls," said Dagii under his breath.

Ekhaas looked at Geth, who looked at Chetiin. The goblin nodded. He approached the weeping troll cautiously, drawing the dagger he kept on his right wrist. Ashi didn't get a good look at the weapon, but what she could see left her with a strange chill. She let the twirling pitch pots slow to a gentle swinging once more.

Chetiin struck with the speed of a serpent, plunging the dagger into the base of the troll's neck and up into its skull. The troll's weeping stopped. Its body stiffened for an instant, then relaxed. When Chetiin pulled the dagger out, the blade—dull gray steel set with a thin blue-black crystal—was absolutely clean. He returned the dagger to its sheath and moved back.

The tallest troll looked down at the still, silent body for a long moment, then stepped out of their way. The other trolls around them moved back into the shadows. "Go," whispered Ekhaas.

"You trust them?" asked Ashi.

"For now," Ekhaas said. "The next time we meet them, no."

They filed past the troll, so close Ashi could smell the wet canvas stink of it. Ekhaas and Geth stood where they were until the others had gone, then followed. The troll, however, gave one last hoot and pointed at the headless body.

Ekhaas frowned. "I think it wants—"

"I know what it wants," said Geth. He went back to the body and laid the severed head beside it, then returned to Ekhaas and the others, taking his place at the head of the party once more. "Let's get out of here and find those stairs," he said.

Ashi glanced back at the dead trolls before the light of the torches had completely gone. All of the living trolls had gathered around them as if mourning. It was an eerie, almost tender sight. "I wouldn't have expected that," she said to Midian.

Before they'd gone much farther, though, new sounds broke the silence of the valley. Wet tearing. Dry crunching. Popping. Chewing.

"I hate this place," said Midian.

CHAPTER TWENTY-ONE

The sound of the feasting trolls urged them to a faster pace. With the monsters behind them—for the moment at least—they abandoned caution and all but raced through the forest. It seemed to Ashi that they were back at the scene of their first battle with the troll in almost no time at all, then through the trees and standing at the top of the stairs with only a few steps more. When they'd come upon the stairs the first time, there'd been only moonlight, and all she had been able to see was the dim form of the steps. With torchlight, she got a better look and marveled at the carved gray stone, perfectly preserved in spite of its age. No one else seemed much interested in the stairs this time, though. Even Midian scarcely glanced at the carvings in the stone. The party paused at the top of the long flight.

"Go ahead," Chetiin said. "The way is clear."

Geth's first step onto the stairs was almost tentative, but he bared his teeth and his pace became bolder as he led the way down into the pit. Ashi thought she could feel the same thing he had. The stairs were ancient and imposing, but once she was walking on them, they felt like any others. Steep maybe, and subtly higher and wider than normal steps, but ordinary stairs just the same.

Then the edge of the torchlight fell on the massive trees that reached up out of the pit. Ekhaas had described them to her before, but even a *duur'kala's* description didn't do the size of them justice. The trunks were as big as small towers. The thin moonlight that had given some illumination to the upper stairs vanished behind the unseen branches. Darkness closed in, with all the eerie silence and tension of the valley focused, it seemed, on the small pool of light that crept along the stairs.

"There are trees in the Eldeen Reaches that are almost this big," Geth said, "and they didn't get that way naturally. How much farther, Chetiin?"

"Not much."

Just a little farther along, the wet canvas smell of trolls rose to meet them. On each side of the stairs, deep pockets had been gouged into the living wood of the trees and lined with an assortment of leaves and fern fronds. Chetiin gestured for them to keep going. "It's the troll nest," he said. "We're almost at the bottom."

Ashi studied the dens dug into the trees. Each looked big enough for one troll to sleep curled up inside, but there weren't just nine pockets for the nine trolls. There were dozens, some disappearing into the shadows high above. The majority, however, seemed abandoned. They had no linings, and the scarred wood had long healed into puckers of bark. Makka had described the valley as being a cursed place since the mountains were young. Ashi wondered how long trolls had been living here.

Beyond the nest was the bottom of the stairs—and the bottom of the pit. The ground leveled out among the roots of the great trees in an expanse of dense, black soil. Somewhere else, Ashi might have called it a small clearing. Here it felt like a kind of void. On its far side rose a sheer rock face. Built against the rock was the front of a simple shrine, fashioned from the same gray stone as the stairs and carved with a band of the same twisting shapes. Through a narrow doorway, the interior of the shrine extended into the rock as the trolls' dens extended into the trees.

"Aureon's blue quill," said Midian. "It's in perfect condition."

"Pre-Dhakaani?" Dagii asked.

"Pre-Dhakaani," Midian confirmed. He stepped off the stairs and walked across the bare earth to hold his torch up before the structure. Illuminated, the carvings sprang into sharp relief. Ashi thought she could see animals in the swirls. Animals, plants, maybe even figures that could have been members of the goblin races. As the others came to join him, Midian frowned and stepped closer, examining the carvings up close. "This isn't possible," he said. "The grooves and edges haven't weathered at all."

"They'd be well protected down here," Ashi pointed out. "And you said there was probably some preserving magic on the stone of the stairs. Wouldn't it have been applied to the shrine as well?"

"Preserving magic doesn't work *that* well. There was lichen on the stairs and some weathering, and I thought that was amazing." He touched a carved swirl. "These are more than fifteen thousand years old, and they might have been carved yesterday."

"It's here, though," said Geth, his voice excited. They all turned to look at him. He was standing in front of the shrine's door, his eyes bright, and he held Wrath out in front of him with both hands, as if trying to keep a grip on the sword. "The rod is here, in the shrine. If you're finished looking at carvings, let's go get it!"

"It's not going anywhere, Geth," Ekhaas said. "We'll go in when we're ready."

"Grandfather Rat, how much more ready can we be? Chetiin, Ashi, are you with me?"

Ashi—and Chetiin as well—glanced at Ekhaas before answering. The *duur'kala's* ears stood up, but after a moment, she nodded. "You're right. Let's go. Just be careful."

Chetiin went through the door first with Geth and Midian after him. Ashi would have followed, but Ekhaas caught her arm. "Has Geth seemed more impetuous than usual to you lately?" she asked quietly.

Ashi considered the question for a moment, then shook her head. "He always throws himself into a fight."

"Yes, but generally only the ones he knows he can win."

"Maybe it's the strain of our quest," said Dagii from behind them. "He has been our only guide and his task is nearly complete."

"Maybe." Ekhaas didn't sound convinced.

"Coming?" Geth's voice echoed out of the door.

Ekhaas's ears stood even taller and her eyes looked into Ashi's, then Dagii's. "Watch him," she said, "both of you."

Ashi nodded, then stepped into the shrine. A rough-walled passage extended beyond the door, no taller or wider than the door itself. She could just barely squeeze through—looking back, she saw that Dagii had to turn sideways to get in. A few paces ahead, Geth and the others were already out of the passage, the light of their torches spreading to illuminate a larger space. She hurried after them and emerged into a small chamber that was partly worked stone and partly natural rock. When all six of them were standing in the chamber, it felt nearly as crowded as the narrow passage.

And there was a stillness to it, as well. Eerie like the valley and tense like the pit, but moreso. Ashi felt a foreboding, as if the stillness had a physical form and was standing somewhere just behind her. There was something else about it as well . . . something she couldn't identify at first—or at least couldn't describe.

"Do you feel that?" she asked.

The others nodded. Silently, Geth pointed with Wrath to the wall opposite the passage. It was the most natural of the chamber's walls, split by a wide crack and untouched by tools except for a grate of iron bars that had been placed across it. Once the gate must have blocked the crack. Now it hung open.

Litter lay on the ground beyond in a jumble of strange objects: cups and knives and trinkets of all sorts, most similar in design and decoration to the carvings on the shrine and the stairs.

"Offerings," said Ekhaas quietly. "When the grate was closed, they would have been shoved through into the darkness."

"Offerings to what?" Dagii asked.

Ekhaas spread her hands. "I don't know. Whatever power is in this place."

Midian held out his torch. "They've been sorted."

Ashi looked again. The gnome was right. The jumble actually lay in several heaps, separating small objects from large, moderately valuable from worthless. There seemed to be nothing of great worth, though she had a feeling that perhaps there once had been.

A clear path led between the heaps. The back of the crack opened into another passage, a little wider than the first.

"Leave the pitch pots," said Dagii. "They'll just get in the way."

They left the clay pots in a heap, carefully extinguishing the ones they had lit, then stepped, one by one, into the crack. Ashi scanned the heaps of offerings for a weapon she could use and selected a long knife that was only a handspan away from being a short sword. Ekhaas glanced at it as she picked it up, then looked again more sharply.

"That's not pre-Dhakaani," she said. Ashi passed her the dagger and she turned it over in her hands, cursed under her breath, and held it out for Midian to see. The gnome's eyebrows rose.

"Riis Dynasty," he said. "The time of the Shaking Emperor."

No one said anything else. Ashi took the dagger back and tested the edge. Still sharp.

The new passage hadn't been worked at all. It was wide enough that Ashi didn't feel cramped, but she had to watch closely for projections from the walls and raised stones underfoot. It twisted from time to time, turning or dropping suddenly. She had the feeling that they were generally going deeper. At least there were no side passages. No way to go but forward and back.

The foreboding stillness grew with every pace. Sounds seemed muffled. Ashi fought the urge to reach back and take Ekhaas's hand, just for the reassurance of knowing that it was the *duur'kala* behind her and not someone or something else.

She was the first to notice that the torches had stopped flickering, suddenly becoming as steady as everbright lanterns. Ashi looked up at her torch and saw that the flame was still. Not merely steady, like a candle protected by a lantern, but *still,* like a piece of bright orange-yellow glass. All of the torches they carried were still.

She found the description for the stillness that had eluded her earlier. It was "stopped." It felt as if their little party moved through a world in which all other motion had ceased. She bit down on her alarm, instead lowering the stopped torch to show Ekhaas. The *duur'kala's* ears pulled back flat.

At the head of the party, Chetiin and Geth went around another twist in the passage—then were back and pressed up against the wall. The hair on Geth's arms and neck was standing up. His eyes were wide. "We're here," he said.

"What is it?" Ashi asked.

"I think you need to see for yourself." Geth took a deep breath and slowly stepped around the corner. Chetiin followed. Midian, Ashi, Ekhaas, and Dagii looked at each other, then Ashi braced herself and went after Geth.

Beyond the twist, the passage went a couple of paces more, then opened up into a cavern. The floor was reasonably level and the cavern itself was quite broad, spreading twenty paces or so in any direction from the passage. The ceiling was low, though. Ashi could have reached up and scraped it with the tip of her newly acquired knife. It made the cavern feel much smaller than it really was, crushed by the weight of the mountains above.

More disturbing than the low ceiling, however, were the symbols that spread across the rock. They were on the ceiling, the walls, and the floor—dozens of them, each an armslength across and shining with a greenish light that gave a soft glow to the entire cavern. Seen from the corner of her eye, they almost seemed to move, but looked at directly they were steady and unchanging. In a way, they resembled dragonmarks. Her stomach churning, Ashi stretched out her hand and looked from the marks on the wall to the marks on her skin. The strange light made her blue-green mark look as black as darkness, yet also weirdly bright and reflective. She let her hand fall with a shudder.

"There are seven caves in the north of the Seawall Mountains," Ekhaas said, standing beside her and staring in fascination, "that are said to look like this, save that the signs move and spell out the future for those who know how to read them."

"Do those caves have occupants?" asked Chetiin quietly. "Look here."

They turned. Partway across the chamber, a strange rock formation stuck up from the floor. Chetiin and Geth were on the other side of it, staring. Geth still held Wrath, but loosely, and the purple of the byeshk blade gleamed through the green glow. Ashi went to join them. As she drew closer, she realized the formation wasn't rock at all, but wood and cloth—a heavy chair draped with fabric. And as she passed around the chair, she realized that it wasn't empty.

A hobgoblin, or what was left of him, sat in it. The body was wizened, orange-tinged flesh wrinkled and dry like a withered pumpkin, but the hobgoblin's face was calm and his eyes closed. The cave's air—or perhaps its strange power—must have mummified him upon his death. The garments of a larger man were draped around his skeletal frame. Ashi had never seen anything quite like them in style, but the fabric was fine and dyed with rich colors of gold and red. His hair, longer than she'd ever seen a male hobgoblin wear it and held back by a wide band of gold, was still thick and dark. He hadn't been old when he died. His feet were raised on a small stool that was as heavy as the chair. His hands, covered in gloves studded with gems, rested in his lap.

They were wrapped around a purple rod of byeshk, as long as her forearm and as thick as her wrist, its polished surface carved with strange symbols.

Ekhaas drew a deep, slow breath. "The story stops but never ends," she said solemnly in Goblin. "Guulen, the Rod of Kings, is found again, and the fate of Dabrak Riis, the Shaking Emperor, is known at last."

"Taat," rasped the hobgoblin on the throne. Red-brown eyes opened to glare at Ekhaas and lips drew back from sharp, white teeth. "I am Dabrak Riis, but I shake no more! Bow before your emperor!"

Ekhaas jerked back.

Ashi heard Geth curse. She saw Chetiin and Dagii raise their weapons and step back as well. She didn't step back. With reflexes honed in the practice yards of Sentinel Tower, she snatched the long knife from her belt and lunged forward, thrusting the blade straight into the seated hobgoblin's heart. His eyes opened wide in shock—

—then he shoved her away with a strength that sent her flying into the cavern wall.

Ashi pushed herself up and stared as Dabrak Riis, Emperor of Dhakaan, tugged the knife out of his chest.

CHAPTER TWENTY-TWO

For a terrifying moment, Ashi thought he would hurl the knife at her. She rolled to her feet, ready to dodge, but the withered hobgoblin's arm didn't move. Dabrak Riis held the knife up in front of his face and studied it. Ears rose, so dried and leathery they resembled the wings of bats.

"I know this knife," he said. "It belonged to Rhazala Shaad. What have you done with her, assassin?"

Ashi hesitated, not certain how to answer. It was hard to understand the Goblin that Dabrak Riis spoke. The accent was odd and seemed strangely stilted. Was that how the goblins of the Dhakaani Empire had spoken? She threw a glance at Ekhaas, a silent appeal for instruction, but before the *duur'kala* could speak, Dabrak's eyes had moved from the knife back to her. They narrowed sharply.

"By the Lawbringer, what manner of creature are you?" he asked. "You're not *dar,* and you're not elf." He looked around at the others. *"Ghaal'dar* and *golin'dar"*—he paused to stare at Midian and his dry lips twisted in disgust—"and one of the jungle rats, dressed like a person."

The gnome looked like anger might overcome his shock at being addressed by a corpse, but Dabrak's gaze had already moved on to settle on Geth. His ears stood, and his eyes widened. "You . . . whatever you are . . . that's Aram!" he sputtered. "You carry the lost sword!"

Geth bared his teeth and lifted the twilight blade. "I found it," he said, his Goblin thick and simple compared to the emperor's. "I carry it. It led us to you."

"Another assassin? Are all of you assassins?" He swept his eyes across them all once more—then put his head back and laughed. "If you have come to kill me, you'll find it more difficult than you thought!" He dropped Ashi's knife to the floor of the cavern and plucked at his garments, pulling the cloth out tight where she had stabbed him.

The fabric was whole. There was not a tear, not even a mark. It was as if she hadn't attacked him at all. Ashi stared in amazement.

"You're Dabrak Riis?" said Midian. "You're *really* Dabrak Riis? Sage's shadow, how is that possible?"

The amusement in Dabrak's face vanished. He looked first to Ekhaas, then to Dagii. "To which of you does that creature belong? Silence it. I will not hear its screechings."

"Your pardon, Marhu Dabrak," Ekhaas said quickly. "It will not speak again." She stepped forward and dropped to her knees, gesturing for the others to do the same. It seemed like a very good idea to Ashi, and she sank down. They all did, even Midian. Dabrak sat back with satisfaction on his face. Ekhaas looked up at him and said, "We're not assassins, *marhu*. We just didn't expect to"—she hesitated, then added—"find you still alive."

At any other time, in any other place, Ashi might have laughed at the understatement. How could Dabrak still be alive? The Empire of Dhakaan had been gone from the world for more than five thousand years. Dabrak couldn't just have been sitting in the cavern all that time—could he?

He only nodded in response. "So that much time has passed," he said. "The world thinks me dead. I suspected as much."

Ekhaas looked startled. "You know that time has passed?"

"Of course I know." He gestured at the cavern around them. "I may not feel it here, but before they abandoned me, Razhala and my other guards would go out through the shrine and report on the passing of the seasons." He sighed. "They didn't have the strength to stay, though. One by one, they left me—faithful Razhala was the last. But eventually the trolls came. They have been my guards."

"The trolls are your guards?" said Dagii.

"You encountered them, didn't you, warrior?" Dabrak looked pleased. "They were wild things when they came, but I tamed them. The smallest of them entered the shrine and ventured in here. It was a challenge to work with them, but I had the power to mold them."

He lifted the Rod of Kings and it seemed to Ashi that even that simple gesture carried with it a swirl of power. For a frightening moment, it seemed that Dabrak wore authority like a cloak—then the cloak vanished as the rod settled back into his lap. "I still feel a distant connection to them," the emperor said, as if the display of power was something so casual he barely even noticed it. "I know their pack still watches over the Uura Odaarii. You must be mighty indeed to have passed them."

Ashi could tell from the faces of the others that they had felt the rod's power as well. Dagii seemed awed by it, Chetiin stunned. Midian looked gray with fear. She felt a little bit afraid herself. This was the power they would bring back to Haruuc?

Ekhaas struggled to speak again. "The Uura Odaarii, *marhu?*" she asked. "Is that this place?"

Ashi didn't recognize the words. Chetiin was closest to her, and she glanced at him. "The Womb of Eternity," he translated for her.

Dabrak's attention was all on Ashi. "You haven't heard of it. I'm not surprised. I traveled across the length and breadth of my empire just chasing down the rumors of it," he said. He sat forward, the movement making the shriveled folds of his face slip like a loose mask. "Tell me, what stories do they tell of me?"

"They say that you left your palace to face the source of your fears, vowing to return and continue your rule," said Ekhaas. "You were seen now and then across the empire—until one day you disappeared completely."

"The day I finally located the Uura Odaarii," said Dabrak. "You speak with the grace of a *duur'kala*. What is your name?"

"I am a *duur'kala*. I am Ekhaas of Kech Volaar."

"The Kech Volaar. I don't know that clan." Dabrak sat back. "If you are a *duur'kala,* Ekhaas of Kech Volaar, you understand the nature of emotion. Tell me: What is the source of all fear?"

"The unknown," Ekhaas said.

Dabrak gestured angrily, as though her word were flies he could shoo away. "Some would say that," he said, "but it's not true.

What about someone who was afraid of spiders? They are hardly unknown. He sees a spider and knows it, yet he is still afraid. What is he really afraid of?"

Chetiin answered. "He's afraid of what the spider might do."

"Well said, *golin'dar.*" Dabrak held up a finger. "He's afraid of what might happen. His fear isn't in the moment, it's in the *might.* What might a spider do, what might happen in the dark, what might happen if I venture into the water? The source of all fear is the future, and the future is inescapable. Except here."

He rose to his feet and gestured with both hands. Once again the power of the rod washed over them. Ashi thought she could feel an echo of the profound fear that had earned Dabrak the name of the Shaking Emperor. She shivered herself and pressed her hands against the cold stone of the cave floor to keep them from trembling. Dabrak noticed nothing, though thankfully he lowered the rod again.

"I first heard of the Uura Odaarii from an old *golin'dar,* a traveling midwife who came to the palace to deliver a son to my cousin," he continued. "She cast an augury during the birth, as was customary, but as she did so, she saw my terror. She was the first to recognize all the fears that plagued me as a single fear of the future. She told me the scrap of a legend, that in the time before Jhazaal Dhakaan brought together the Six Kings, there was a secret shrine in an ancient kingdom where it was said all of the future was born. People would search out the shrine and make offerings there in hopes of staving off a bleak destiny."

His eyes looked into the distance. "When I left my palace, it was to find this mysterious shrine. I consulted *duur'kala* and *dashoor.* I even ventured into the dark marshes to speak with orc druids and onto the dry plains to speak with halfling shamans. If it had been necessary, I would have crossed lines of ancient enmity and spoken with the undying elves of Aerenal. But it wasn't. I found a name, the Uura Odaarii, and the hint of a location hidden only a day's travel off one of the empire's roads. But most importantly, I discovered a clue to its true nature. When I reached the shrine and broke through it to this place, I knew that I had conquered my fear." He looked down at Ekhaas.

"What the ancient people believed to be birthplace of the future is far more than that. Within the Uura Odaarii, time has no power. The future is out there, but not in here. Within this cavern, there is only an eternal present." Dabrak Riis smiled. "Within this cavern, I have nothing to fear!"

Ashi couldn't hold her tongue. "But that's impossible. Time's passing right now."

"Time passes, but it has no effect. Can't you feel it? Can't you see it?" The emperor pointed one gloved hand at her torch. "Fire is frozen as soon as it enters. While you are here, you won't grow hungry or thirsty." He touched his chest where she had stabbed him. "Nothing changes here. If you were assassins, you couldn't kill me. However you are when you enter the Uura Odaarii, that is how you remain until you leave. The power even extends into the valley—I've always believed that's why the trees around the shrine are so huge and ancient."

"And why the stonework of the stairs and the shrine is so well preserved!" Midian burst out. "By the quill, it's incred—"

"Ekhaas of Kech Volaar, silence your slave!" snarled the emperor.

"Silence yourself!" Midian said sharply. "If nothing changes in this cavern, you can't hurt me."

Dabrak thrust out the Rod of Kings. *"Be silent!"*

Ashi felt the force of the command like a shiver in the air. Midian's mouth snapped shut with such force that agony crossed his face.

"I cannot kill you," said Dabrak, "but I can hurt you. You can still feel pain. You *will* be silent, rat, or your mistress will have to carry your quivering carcass out of here." He seated himself and glared at Ekhaas. "As you can see, I am no longer the Shaking Emperor. I am without fear. You have heard my story. Now tell me yours, *duur'kala*. If you are not assassins, why are you here? Why have you used Aram to find me?"

Ekhaas pulled her eyes away from Midian, sitting pale-faced and wide-eyed on the ground, his mouth still firmly closed. She looked to Dabrak, and Ashi could tell that she was choosing her next words carefully. "Take no offense, Marhu Dabrak. We sought what we believed to be your grave. We come charged with a quest by a great ruler who seeks to prevent a terrible division among the people." She bowed her head. "We come for Guulen, the Rod of Kings."

Emotion flared in Dabrak's eyes. His body shifted subtly and he held the rod close to him, as if Ekhaas might at any moment leap up and try to grab it away. "No," he said softly, fearfully. "You can't take it. I need it. I vowed that I would return, and I will. I've faced my fears."

Ekhaas kept her voice low and soothing. "It doesn't seem to me that you've faced your fears. You've only found a way to avoid them. Are you really ready to leave the Uura Odaarii?"

"I will be!" Dabrak looked up at her. "One day I will be. The rod is mine by right, and you won't take it. I am the emperor!"

"*Marhu,* there is no more empire."

Dabrak flinched in shock. "No more empire? By the Six Kings, what happened to it?"

"Time. Dhakaan has fallen."

"Time?" His shriveled ears flicked and stood back in disbelief. "Dhakaan, the empire of ten thousand years, fallen in only a few centuries? How can that be?"

Ashi looked to Ekhaas. So did all the others. Ashi felt her stomach tighten into a wary knot. Ekhaas paused for a moment, then faced Dabrak again. "Is that how long you think it's been since you entered the cavern? A few centuries?"

"Long enough," said Dabrak defensively. "You said the world thinks me dead."

"The world thought you dead more than five thousand years ago, *marhu*. The Empire of Dhakaan has been only memory for millennia." Ekhaas rose to her feet. "The Kech Volaar preserve its lore. A few other clans respect its traditions. Most of the *dar* remember it only as an inspiring legend."

"It's not possible." Dabrak clutched the rod even more tightly. "I've been aware of every passing moment. I would have known—"

"How many generations of trolls have there been? How long did Rhazala and your guards wait before they fled?" Ekhaas pointed at the discarded knife. "We found that among the offerings in the shrine. Rhazala must have left it behind. Everything of value had been taken."

"Lies," Dabrak whimpered. "Lies. There is no future in the Uura Odaarii. I have nothing to fear."

Geth stood and spoke, his voice taut. He didn't bother trying to speak Goblin. "Ekhaas, I've heard of something like this in the Eldeen Reaches. There are parts of the forest where a night in a fairy glade can turn into a year. What if this cavern is like that? We could come out and find we've been gone for months."

Dabrak's head came up. "What did the beast man say?" he demanded.

"He said that we've been here too long," the *duur'kala* said grimly, her ears back flat against her head. "You have, too, Dabrak."

Dry lips peeled back from sharp teeth. *"Taat!* You will address me as I deserve to be addressed!"

The rest of them rose as well. "What do we do?" Dagii asked, speaking the human tongue.

"We ask for the rod again," said Chetiin. "If he won't give it to us, we take it."

"Your dagger . . . ?" Geth asked him.

"Will work only if I can strike a killing blow, and we've seen that won't work. I think we can overpower him."

"Be careful," Ashi warned them. "He's stronger than he looks."

Dabrak followed their words with his eyes. "What are you saying?" he demanded. "What are you doing?"

Ekhaas looked at him and Ashi heard the soft persuasion of a *duur'kala* enter her voice. "Give us the rod, Dabrak. It does you no good here, but if we take it, perhaps a new Dhakaan can rise again." She stretched out her hand.

He stared at it, then looked up to her. His body began to shake, not from fear but from anger. "No," he said. "No!" He started to rise from his chair. "I am Dabrak Riis, *marhu* of Dhakaan, twenty-third lord of the Riis Dynasty—"

"Get him!" roared Geth.

But the rod lashed out. *"—and you will kneel all before me!"*

The power of the rod drove Ashi down before she could even think of resisting. It slammed against her mind with as much force as her knees slammed against the cavern floor. She saw Ekhaas, struggling against the compulsion, draw breath, perhaps to blast Dabrak with a song of magic, but the withered emperor held out the rod again. *"You are slaves,"* he snarled. *"You belong to me. You will not rise up against your master."*

Ekhaas sagged back, her lips falling slack. On Ashi's other side, Chetiin drooped with a groan. Ashi tried to fight back against the rod's power, tried to throw it off, but she could feel herself slipping under its influence. The *marhu* was her master. She couldn't rise against him.

But beyond Ekhaas, beyond Dagii, one figure was still standing firm against Dabrak's commands. Geth. For a moment, he looked confused, then he glanced at the sword in his hand and smiled. He lifted Wrath.

"Two artifacts forged from a single vein of byeshk by the hand of Taruuzh," he said in broken Goblin.

Dabrak's ears went back. "Even when the shield had been shattered and the sword lost, legends were passed from *marhu* to heir that they were the only things capable of resisting the power of the rod. It seems the legends were right."

"Give me the rod." Geth dropped into a fighting stance, Wrath's twilight blade crossed over the black steel of his great gauntlet.

"Give me the sword, beast-man." Dabrak reached into the folds of cloth that draped his chair and drew out a sword. It was a little lighter than Wrath and forged of steel instead of byeshk, but it was still a good blade. He stepped clear of the chair and those who knelt before it.

Geth followed, circling him like a wolf.

Dabrak turned to keep him in sight. "What will you do, beast-man?" he asked. "You can't kill me."

"No," Geth growled, "but I can hurt you." He lunged, byeshk ringing on steel as he spread his arms. The gauntlet rose to block Dabrak's sword while Wrath cut low. Dabrak moved with surprising speed, though, kicking back to escape the blow. The sword caught only silk, and even that was left unharmed. Geth pressed closer to try another swing, but Dabrak turned sharply and was suddenly behind him on his sword arm side.

Geth got Wrath up in time to tangle Dabrak's sword, but the sword wasn't the hobgoblin's only weapon. With the same strength that had thrown Ashi into a wall, he slammed the rod into Geth's bandaged shoulder. Geth grunted and twisted away. The shifter and the hobgoblin circled each other for a moment, then crashed together again in another flurry of blows.

The pair was evenly matched, neither finding any advantage over the other, both invulnerable in the weird timelessness of the cavern. There was something about the battle that brought a new fire to Ashi's heart, though. Every attack that Geth made, every blow that he took seemed to give her a little more strength to push back the domination of the rod. She wanted to cheer for Geth, even as the rod's power reminded her that Dabrak was her master, that she must remain kneeling as he had ordered.

No, she told herself. Geth is fighting for us—we should be fighting for him.

And a bit of what Senen Dhakaan had said of the creation of Wrath came back to her. *Aram represented the inspiration that heroes provided for the people.*

She clenched her teeth and pushed harder against the hopelessness brought down by the power of the rod.

Across the cavern, Geth raised Wrath and stepped back a pace as if searching for a weakness in his opponent's defense. Dabrak lunged—and Geth struck, swinging his blade down against the hand that held Dabrak's sword. In any other fight, Dabrak's fingers would have been cut from his hand. In the Uura Odaarii, the blow passed harmlessly through flesh.

It struck hard against the steel of the sword clutched in them, though. Dabrak's weapon was torn from his grip to fall, ringing, to the cavern floor. The ancient emperor flailed at Geth with the Rod of Kings, but his blows only rained down on the armored gauntlet. Geth tried to bring his sword back into play in the tight quarters, but Dabrak grabbed for it as if he could pull it out of the shifter's grasp. His hand closed on Wrath.

A crack like lightning split the air, and Dabrak was flung back. He slid across the floor of the cavern, smoke rising for a moment from his clothing, the rod still clutched tight in his hand. Geth swung the twilight blade around as he stalked after him. "Wrath is the Sword of Heroes," he said, showing his teeth in a savage grin. "It won't accept the touch of a coward."

Dabrak rose to a crouch, his teeth bared too. "Maybe the rod can't affect you," he said, "but I've spent a long time in the Uura Odaarii. I've learned its powers well."

He closed his eyes.

Ashi's heart seemed to clench. Uncertainty clouded Geth's face, and he leaped to the attack, swinging Wrath high.

Dabrak's eyes snapped open. No longer red-brown, they shone the same pale green as the symbols on the walls of the cavern. Smaller versions of the symbols glowed through his skin.

Geth froze in mid-leap, as still as the flame on Ashi's torch. The faintest shimmer of green flickered around him. Dabrak rose and examined the unmoving shifter. His eyes flashed and Geth came crashing to the ground. He hit the cavern floor hard and curled up into a trembling huddle, his eyes wide and frightened. Wrath clattered down beside him. Dabrak looked at the weapon, snarled, then retrieved his own sword and walked back to his chair. The symbols faded from his skin and the glow from his eyes. Their passing seemed to leave him looking even more withered than before. Geth, however, remained curled on the ground.

Ashi stared at him. He'd been defeated. But he couldn't have been—he *shouldn't* have been. Rage welled up within her and she screamed in her mind, finally finding the strength to push back the rod's power enough that she could focus her will. Dabrak's legends might have said the Sword of Heroes and the Shield of Nobles were the only things capable of resisting the rod, but she had something the ancient emperor had never seen before. Something unknown in the time of Dhakaan.

Her dragonmark burned hot on her skin, and the burst of clarity that it brought shattered the rod's hold on her mind. She stood, jaw clenched. "Release him," she said.

CHAPTER TWENTY-THREE

Dabrak stopped halfway into his chair. His ears flicked up in disbelief, and the rod darted out. "By the Six Kings, you will *kneel!*" he commanded.

A tingle crawled across Ashi's scalp as the order fell away from her. Dabrak's eyes went wide—then he squeezed them shut. The glowing symbols darted across his skin again, as if they'd transferred there from the walls. His eyes opened and flashed green.

The foreboding stillness that Ashi had felt when she'd entered the shrine swirled around her, even heavier and more terrible than before. This time, though, she knew it for what it was: a dread of what might come to pass, a dark hint of the future preying upon her mind. But it couldn't reach through the shield of her dragonmark. She shook her head, and it disappeared like a daydream.

The green drained from Dabrak's eyes. Its passing left his flesh more shriveled, but he didn't seem to notice. His gaze was on Ashi. "You defy me," he said in amazement.

She pointed at Geth again. "Release him," she repeated, then expanded her gesture to include the others, as well. "Release all of them."

A smile touched Dabrak's sagging lips. "Why should I?" he asked and sat down. "We've already established that Aram can't harm me, and you're not even armed. What are you going to do?"

He was right, she realized. He couldn't affect her with the rod or with his strange command of the power of the cavern, but at the same time, there was nothing she could do to him. She swallowed and squeezed her fists tight, trying to think of something. Her dragonmark was only defensive. The ferocity and fighting skills she'd learned among the Bonetree clan and honed in Sentinel Tower weren't going to help her. The only thing she had left to rely on . . .

Ashi almost bit her tongue at the thought that came to her, but she could see nothing else. She dragged her wits into line, forced all expression from her features, and asked in the calm voice that Vounn had taught her, "What do you want, Marhu Dabrak?"

"What do I *want?*" The withered hobgoblin glowered. "Until you came, I wanted nothing more than to be left alone. What else did I need? I was safe in the Uura Odaarii. Nothing could touch me. I wasn't afraid anymore."

"Can you go back to that now?" Ashi pointed at Ekhaas. "She was right. You vowed to confront your fears, but you didn't. You just hid from them."

"*Ban.* What if I did? If what you say is true, my vow is meaningless. Dhakaan is gone. I'm emperor of nothing but a pack of trolls!"

"If you're emperor of nothing, then you don't need the Rod of Kings," Ashi said. "If you give it to us, we'll leave you alone. You'll still have the Uura Odaarii. You'll still be safe, and you won't be afraid."

His ears flicked and his eyes narrowed. "But as you say, it's a false safety. Can I go back to that? You've also shown me that fear can come for me here." He gestured with the rod, though this time Ashi, protected by her dragonmark, felt no swirl of power from it. "When you threatened to take this, I was terrified. That's a future the Uura Odaarii can't protect me from. It's no safer in here than it was out there now."

"Then come with us," she suggested. "You must have learned something about controlling your fear from sitting here for five thousand years. The world has changed. Come see it! The Kech Volaar would probably give anything to learn about the empire from you, and I'm sure Lhesh Haruuc would welcome your experience."

"Lhesh Haruuc?" Dabrak almost sneered. "That's the name of the great ruler you follow?"

"Lhesh Haruuc Shaarat'kor," Ashi said. "Yes. He united the *dar* and carved out a new homeland for his people."

"And he claims the title of lhesh. A lhesh is a general. You think an emperor should be satisfied with giving advice to a general?" He held up the rod. "Do you think I would be content to share this? For generations of emperors, it was only a trinket. I've unlocked its powers. I've bonded with it—over five thousand years, if you're to be believed. You think your Haruuc would be able to use the rod as I have?"

"He doesn't want it for that," said Ashi. "He wouldn't use it that way. He only wants it as a symbol."

Dabrak sneered. "If he won't use it, he doesn't deserve it—I wouldn't show him how. I would as soon stay here."

Frustration surged up her throat like bile, and she had to clench her teeth to keep it inside. *"Marhu,"* she said bluntly, "I think you lost all claim to the Rod of Kings when you abandoned your empire to hide in a cave like a mole. We need it. What do you want for it?"

He gave her a level glare. "Who taught you negotiation? They should be whipped."

"We agree on that." She met his eyes. "What do you want in return for the Rod of Kings?"

Dabrak Riis leaned forward. "I want you to die. Right here in the Uura Odaarii."

Ashi started. "You want me to die? Here? But that's—"

"Impossible. Yes." He sat back. "But those are my terms. You die and I'll give you the Rod of Kings. I'll even release your friends.

She stared at him—then felt a flood of inspiration. "Done," she said. "I accept. But I'll need a sword and I'll need her." She pointed at Ekhaas a second time.

Dabrak smiled again. "Very well. She's yours." He gestured with the rod and Ekhaas sagged abruptly, then caught herself and looked at him with hatred in her eyes.

Ashi caught her arm and pulled her to her feet. "Not now," she said in the *duur'kala*'s ear. "Have you heard what I've said?"

"Yes, but—"

Ashi shook her head, cutting her off. "Don't argue. I need you to hold a rhythm for me."

Ekhaas's ears and eyebrows rose at the same time.

Ashi smiled. "You saw the sword dance at Sentinel Tower. While we were in the guard station, you clapped some of the drum rhythm from memory. Can you do that again for the whole dance? Slow opening, quick first part, slow second part, quick third part, slow end. Watch me for cues if you need to."

"I can sing the viol part if you need me to. What are you doing, Ashi?"

"What Vounn had me trained to do. Give me your sword."

Ekhaas started to draw the weapon, but Dabrak coughed like a courtier. "Not that sword," he said. He pointed across the cavern to Wrath. "That one."

Ashi looked at the twilight blade, then at Dabrak. Geth had put her hand on the sword once so that she could use its gift of understanding Goblin. That wasn't exactly the same as trying to wield the weapon. Would the sword let her use it? She could only try. Bracing herself, she went over to the sword. Geth was still huddled and trembling beside it. She tried to ignore him, dropping her torch on the ground and bending over the sword. "Wrath," she murmured. "I need to use you to help Geth and the others, and to get the rod. Please accept my touch."

She felt stupid talking to the weapon, but her first light touch on the sword's hilt was still tentative. Nothing happened. She curled her fingers around it and raised it, offering a mock salute to Dabrak. The emperor, risen from his chair to stand and watch her, looked disappointed. Ashi walked to an open part of the cavern and nodded to Ekhaas. It was time to see who had been right all those weeks ago in Sentinel Tower: Vounn, who'd said she couldn't do it, or her old instructor Baerer, who'd believed she could.

Ekhaas took a deep breath and raised her voice in a long, clear note. Ashi swept into the rigid first position of the sword dance, held it for a long moment, then dropped her blade and walked around it.

Wrath wasn't the best sword for the dance. A proper human sword would have been slimmer, with a pointed blade instead of the broad, forked tip of hobgoblin swords. At least the ancient weapon was well-balanced and surprisingly light for its size. She completed the walk-around without letting the blade waver at all.

In Sentinel Tower, the difficult step would have earned applause. Dabrak gave no reaction at all. Ashi ignored him and focused on the music. The hardest part of the dance was yet to come.

Ekhaas's hands began to clap along with the rise and fall of her voice. Ashi moved into the attack phase of the dance, lunging and stamping her way across the cavern. Baerer had made this part of the dance look light and precise. She couldn't match that precision. Instead, she threw herself into the raw energy that Baerer had said was her greatest strength.

She imagined that a sea of enemies stood between her and her goal. As they came rushing at her, she met each one, cutting her way through them. She could almost let herself go, could almost lose herself in the dance as Baerer had taught her. Her body knew what to do. She couldn't do that this time, though. She kept her focus, and when Ekhaas's song and rhythm slowed, she was ready. She entered the second part of the dance, the battle, as easily as stepping into real combat.

The unseen fight slowed along with Ekhaas's song, but in Ashi's mind it only became more intense. Each blow was deliberate, drawn out so that the audience could appreciate the sweep of the blade, the unfolding of a bent arm into an elbow strike, the long lines of her body as it extended into a kick. The battle was grace and power combined. Ashi didn't look to see Dabrak's reaction. She concentrated on the battle as if her life depended on it—which, in a way, it did.

Ekhaas's voice rose again. The slap of palm on palm became increasingly rapid. It was different from dancing to viol and drum, but that was good. It was more primal, more suited to Ashi's style of dance. Baerer had been elegant like the viol. She was unshaped, like a wild song. The battle she fought in her imagination took place on an open hill beneath the light of many moons. Wind lifted her hair, and the smell of churned soil filled her nose. Her enemies came at her faster and faster, in time with the rhythm of Ekhaas's clapping. Ashi fought them off, but her movements become tighter as they pressed at her. She backed across the battlefield in the dance's third phase, the defeat. Her enemies pursued her. She blocked their blows, feeling the impact.

The song whirled faster. Her enemies crowded in close, so close she couldn't move. Her sword rose, perhaps in an effort to parry once last attack, before a body that stood rigid once more. The dance was almost over—

Now, she told herself, and broke free of the movements Baerer had trained into her. In Deneith tradition, the sword dance ended with defeat, the warrior caught among the blades of his opponents. Ashi had to take it one step farther. In her imagination, a sword thrust up into her breast. Cold metal pierced flesh, forced ribs aside, and buried itself in her heart. Her eyes went wide. Her mouth opened slightly. Her rigid body arched backward.

And she died. Ekhaas's song rose briefly into a keen of mourning, then fell away like a fading wind.

Ashi held her pose in silence, then gulped air and straightened up. Across the cavern, Ekhaas stood still, but her eyes were shining and her ears were tall. The dance had been perfect. Ashi could feel it. She turned and looked at Dabrak. The withered hobgoblin watched her with undisguised appreciation.

"In my palace," he said, "I had twenty-five dancing slaves. I don't believe any of them ever danced like that. The performance was flawless."

Breathing hard, Ashi walked to Geth's curled form, laid Wrath beside him, and retrieved her torch. She held her hand out to the emperor. "The rod, *marhu*."

Dabrak's shriveled ears twitched. "No," he said. He gathered his robes around himself and turned back to his chair.

"No?" Ashi's voice cracked with disbelief and she stalked over to confront him. "We had a deal, Dabrak!"

"We did. We agreed that if you died here in the Uura Odaarii, I would give you the rod." He sat down. "Did you really think that a trick of dance would satisfy me? It was a pretty illusion, nothing more." His face was hard. "Take your friends—I give you their freedom as a reward for your performance—and get out." The rod flicked once, then vanished into the folds of Dabrak's robes as his hands dropped into his lap.

Around Ashi, the others fell out of their kneeling postures. Midian gasped and gingerly worked a jaw that had been clamped shut. Near Ashi's feet, Geth groaned and moved as well, rising slowly to hands and knees. Ashi kept her eyes on Dabrak, though, as if she could burn him with her anger. "You put no conditions on our agreement!" she protested. "I died!"

"You made a pretty show, but you did not die," Dabrak said harshly. "I know what death looks like, and you're not dead."

"But I can't *die* here. You said yourself, it's impossible."

The ancient emperor sat forward. "Of course, it's impossible! That's why I asked. It's not my fault you agreed." His lips curled back from his teeth. "This is the Uura Odaarii, you fool. There is no future here. There is no death. Nothing changes!"

Ashi's hand thrust out to point at him. "You've changed," she snarled without thinking.

Dabrak stared at her in surprise for a moment, then spat. "No, I haven't."

"You have!" The truth of what she had just said spread into Ashi. Her hand fell back. "You changed when you used the power of the cavern. It made you wither. If time has no effect in the Uura Odaarii, then you should look the same as you did when you entered. But you don't. You're all shriveled up."

"What are you talking about?" Dabrak thrust out his hands. "I'm not shriveled. I'm strong!"

"Maybe you are," said Chetiin. "But you're wearing gloves."

Dabrak looked at his hands as if seeing them for the first time, then grabbed at the fingers of one glove and pulled it off.

The hand that emerged was like a bundle of crooked twigs with orange skin hanging loose. Dabrak stared at it as though it didn't belong at the end of his arm. "What is this?" he croaked. The hand crept up to his face, and he gasped as it encountered the wrinkles and folds there. "This is a trick."

Midian had his arm up to his elbow in his pack. He pulled it out with a flat leather case clutched in his fingers and opened the case to reveal a polished steel shaving mirror. Jumping up onto the side of the chair, he thrust the mirror in front of Dabrak's face. "Look for yourself!"

Dabrak looked—and screamed. He slapped Midian away. The mirror spun across the cavern. Dabrak stood up, suddenly a strangely ridiculous figure in his loose, flapping clothes. "This isn't possible! Nothing changes in the Uura Odaarii. Nothing!"

"Maybe it's your future catching up with you," Geth said, rising to his feet. His voice was rough and shaky, but the hand that held Wrath was steady.

Dabrak spun around and hurled the rod at him.

Geth snatched the rod out of the air with his free hand. For a moment, he just stared at it in astonishment, then his fingers curled around it and he grinned.

"Yes, take it!" spat Dabrak. "Take what you came for and get out!" He collapsed back on his chair, his body wracked with silent convulsions that might have been sobbing.

No one needed a second invitation. "Twice tak, *marhu!*" Geth said and ran for the passage that led out of the weird cavern. Ashi followed him, pausing at the edge of the passage to make certain everyone else got out. Chetiin raced past, another torch in his hand to light the way for Geth. Midian, his pack clutched in his arms. Ekhaas and Dagii—Ashi flung herself after them, racing through the narrow twists of the passage. Her frozen torch began to hiss and flare as she ran, and she thought it was possibly the most beautiful sound she had ever heard.

It wasn't the only sound she heard though. A voice drifted suddenly out of the darkness below. "Wait! Wait, bring it back! Bring the rod back to me!" Dabrak's voice rose to a roar. "I said bring it back!"

Ashi glanced over her shoulder. The passage behind her was only dark as far as the last twist. Beyond that, a pale green glow was growing.

"Khyberit gentis," she breathed, then shouted, "Faster!"

Up and down the rises and drops of the passage. Around corners. It seemed as if the darkness ahead wouldn't end, and every time she dared to look back, the green glow was brighter. Dabrak's angry roaring was constant—then suddenly it swooped up into a shriek of triumph. Ashi looked back once more and saw the undying emperor racing up the passage. The signs of the Uura Odaarii shone bright on his skin and his eyes were green flames.

Then her feet were crunching and skidding among the offerings left at the grate in the shrine. She almost fell, but Dagii and Ekhaas reached back together and pulled her up. They burst into the little chamber of the shrine. Chetiin was trying to set fire to the pitch pots they had left there. "No time!" said Dagii and swept the goblin ahead of him into the narrow doorway of the shrine. Ekhaas plunged after them.

Ashi paused. Chetiin had managed to light some of the pitch pots. Snatching them up by their leather straps, she whirled them around once, then let them fly back into the passage and the approaching green glow. She spun as soon as the straps left her fingers and thrust herself through the shrine's narrow exit. Clay shattered, and there was a sudden whoosh of flame. Ashi felt a searing heat on her back, but then she was out and standing on the black soil at the bottom of the pit where the others were waiting for her.

No, she realized. Not waiting. Clustered together, they faced the trolls that crouched like guard dogs on the ancient stone stairs. Dabrak's voice rolled out of the shrine.

"Bring back the rod!"

Empty-handed, she turned to stare into the firelight that spilled from the shrine's door—firelight that was swiftly blotted out by an intense green glow. Shining with power, untouched by the flames of the pits, a withered figure filled the doorway. Around it, the fine carvings of the ancient shrine became dull and dusty, as if the long delayed years of its preservation were being drawn away. Green light cast sharp shadows into the bottom of the pit. The low growling of the trolls rose into frightened mewling.

Burning from within like a coal from a fire, Dabrak Riis, *marhu* of Dhakaan and twenty-third lord of the Riis Dynasty, stretched out his hand. "Give me the rod!" Time shivered at his words.

But Ashi stared at his fingers.

They were shriveling, shrinking away even as he opened them. His arm grew thin. It was a stick, then a switch, then a long, dry twig. Ashi looked up at his face and watched wrinkled skin draw tight over bone that became green ash. Dark hair sifted away. Silk crumbled. Gold flared bright, burning up as if it were paper.

And like a coal from a fire, Dabrak's power consumed its fuel. Without speaking again, the last living emperor of Dhakaan collapsed in a winking shower of green sparks that were dark before they hit the ground.

Darkness fell over the pit once more, and its silence was broken by the wailing of the trolls as they fled. Ashi and all of the others stared at the black dust that had been Dabrak as it slowly trickled from the featureless ruins that had been a perfectly preserved pre-Dhakaani shrine.

Then they turned to look at Geth. The shifter held out the Rod of Kings. "We have it," he said.

Dawn came as they climbed back up the stairs from the pit. Like the shrine, the ancient stonework had crumbled, but the same weird stillness remained in the air. The Uura Odaarii still held its power, even if some of it seemed to have been drawn back. Midian even recovered enough to moan about the loss of the astounding artifacts.

Ashi and the others were less interested in the crumbled stairs than in the trees and the forest around them. How much time had passed while they were in the green cavern? Had a night turned into a year as in Geth's story of fairy glades? It was hard to tell. The air felt different than it had in the night, but that could just have been the breaking day. The forest in the valley seemed as it had the day before, but what was there to tell one day in the forest from the next? There was no sign of the terrified trolls.

The hedge of thorns, when they reached it, still had the fresh smell of trampled plants, though. Above the slope of the valley, the remains of the bugbear camp still smoldered. Marrow was even waiting for them, still licking red blood from her black muzzle. She yipped and growled at Chetiin.

"She says the bugbears have fled into the mountains to the west. She's disappointed we came back, though. She wanted to find out what a magebred horse tastes like."

Midian let out a hiss of relief. "One night," he said. "One night was one night."

"Cho," said Ekhaas, "and I don't want to have another one like it." She gestured to the south, where they'd left the horses. "Let's

get back out to the Dhakaani road and make camp there. We'll start back to Rhukaan Draal tomorrow."

"Wait—how far have the bugbears fled?" Geth asked. He looked at Marrow. "Was Makka, the chief, still with them? Is there any chance we could catch him and get Ashi's sword back?"

Marrow snarled an answer. "Beyond this mountain," Chetiin translated. "Beyond the length of the valley before Marrow stopped following them, but they were still running. They probably won't stop until night falls again. Makka was with them when they left. Whether he is still is uncertain—the pack has turned on the leader."

"Bugbears move fast, especially in their own territory, and they'll be alert for pursuit." Dagii's ears bent down. "I doubt that we'd be able to catch them without spending days to do it. The sword is lost."

Geth's jaw tightened.

Ashi felt the loss of Kagan's honor blade all over again, but it wasn't the only thing making a knot inside her. "I know," she said. "Thank you for considering it. There's something else, though." She swallowed, not quite certain how to say what she knew in her gut needed to be said. She threw herself into it. "Should we take the rod back? Haruuc sent us to retrieve a symbol of power. We're bringing him real power. Should we put that in his hands—or anyone's hands?"

She looked around at the others and nearly bit her tongue when she saw the same concern written on their faces. "I've thought about that," said Dagii.

Chetiin and Midian nodded as well. So did Ekhaas, but more slowly. "Dabrak said that it took him centuries to unlock the powers of the rod," she said. "For generations of emperors, it was nothing more than a trinket. Dabrak is gone."

Geth held out the rod again. Unlike the other things that had been preserved by the Uura Odaarii, it had remained whole and untouched by the withdrawal of the cavern's power. Its surface did seem duller, though, not quite so bright as it had while Dabrak held it. "I think it might even be asleep," Geth said. "The way Wrath was when I found it."

"But Wrath had powers even when it was asleep."

"Speaking languages and fighting monsters."

"Have you tried to do more with it?"

"Why should I?"

Chetiin raised his hand. "That may be our solution," he said. They all turned to him and he spread his fingers. "If we keep the true power of the rod to ourselves, there's nothing to hint at what it can do. The tales preserved by the Kech Volaar said nothing. Haruuc wants his symbol. Let him have his symbol."

They looked at each other. Finally, Ashi said, "It's a dangerous plan. What if Haruuc—or his successor—does discover the rod's power?"

"Then we do what we have to," said Chetiin. "But what else can we do now? Put the rod back and return empty-handed? Haruuc trusted us with the future of Darguun."

Dagii's ears bent back. "You don't offer us an easy choice, Chetiin."

"The choice between two secrets," the goblin said, "is seldom easy."

CHAPTER TWENTY-FOUR

Haruuc had summoned the assembly of warlords back to Rhukaan Draal. When Vounn entered the gallery that overlooked the lhesh's throne room, a clan chief was speaking below. "What you ask is difficult for my clan, lhesh. The Gan'duur raids left us with just enough food to see us through the lean months. If we give you what you have requested, our stores will run out."

"They will be replenished, Ruuthic," said Haruuc. "Not just in gold, but in kind. Food will come from Breland before your storehouses are empty."

"Why not buy from Breland now?" Ruuthic asked.

"It takes time to negotiate the purchase and the shipment. The stores of Darguun are close at hand. Working together, we will overcome the weakness that the Gan'duur have inflicted on us."

There were a number of people already in the gallery. Pater d'Orien. Sindra d'Lyrandar, viceroy of House Lyrandar in Darguul, together with a trio of men wearing the jackets of ships' captains. Tariic, chatting with the Brelish ambassador. Senen of Kech Volaar and a few other representatives of clans who shared relations with Lhesh Haruuc but didn't directly follow his rule. The gallery had been built specifically so that people like them, who had no place among the assembly, might have a place to listen discreetly to those proceedings they had an interest in. Vounn nodded courteously to Sindra, Senen, Tariic, and the ambassador from Breland, but took a seat beside Pater.

"Have I missed anything?" she asked. She suspected that she already knew the answer, and Pater confirmed it.

"Not a cursed thing. A few clans like the Atiin Noor who support Haruuc without question are ready to give him everything he asks for. Nearly everyone else protests that they don't have enough to share with Rhukaan Draal." Pater gnawed on his thumbnail. "They keep coming back to repayment, the safety of their shipments, the speed *and* safety of food to come from Breland. I'd almost think some of them had been paid to ask questions." He threw an angry glance at Sindra d'Lyrandar.

Vounn suppressed a smile. Houses Lyrandar and Orien were rivals in the shipping business. Each was uniquely suited to bring freight to Rhukaan Draal—Orien overland, Lyrandar by sea. Orien had the advantage of a shorter route from the fields of Breland through Sterngate and the Marguul Pass. Lyrandar had to ship cargo down the Dagger River, all the way around the coast, and back up the Ghaal River, but the voyage was far safer. Lyrandar could have used its flying airships to guarantee both speed and safety, but the cost that would have been involved in such shipments had stopped even the staunchest of Haruuc's critics. Which was probably just as well for House Orien.

"More guards on your caravans, perhaps," she suggested. "I imagine that we could arrange a special price if it would help you win the contract."

"Your concern for our prosperity is noted," Pater said sourly.

"Deneith serves." She inclined her head, then leaned out over the edge of the balcony and looked at the warlords assembled before Haruuc's throne.

The Gan'duur raiders had been largely suppressed or driven back into their own territory for the clan chief Keraal to deal with as was his responsibility. Keraal had duly shown off the executed bodies of hobgoblins he claimed were the rogue warriors, but Vounn had her own reports of the grisly display. The corpses of the "warriors" were so scrawny and undernourished they could only have been slaves. The true warriors were probably enjoying rewards for a job well done. A little more than a month after the first wave of raids, Rhukaan Draal was feeling the effects of the devastated harvest, with the threat of even leaner times ahead. The price of food in the market was rising, and while the famine march two weeks before had been dealt with harshly—the old goblin woman who had led the mob was, Vounn had heard, imprisoned somewhere below Khaar Mbar'ost—scuffles over the food that trickled into the city weren't uncommon. Haruuc had ordered a *noon* dole distributed in the poorest parts of the city, but uncertainty and unrest were growing. And not just among the people of Rhukaan Draal. There were empty places among the benches in Haruuc's throne room. A number of warlords had found excuses not to attend the assembly.

Keraal of Gan'duur was, unsurprisingly, one of them.

But Daavn of Marhaan was not. He sat calmly among the assembly, newly returned from his clan's territory. Vounn turned and looked across the gallery at Tariic. She'd been watching him since the night of the famine march. There had been no hint of a conspiracy and nothing of substance to report back to Karrlakton. Tariic had, however, become increasingly friendly with some of the most powerful people at Haruuc's court, Darguul and non-Darguul alike. People like Breland's ambassador. If he was trying to draw up support for himself as a successor to Haruuc, he was doing a very good job of it.

Tariic looked up and met her gaze. She nodded to him again. He smiled at her, said something to the ambassador, then came across the gallery to her. As he walked, Vounn considered briefly what it might be like to deal with Tariic as lhesh. Of all the Darguuls she had met, he was perhaps the most familiar with the manners and customs of the Five Nations. He had talent and intelligence—and he was already on good terms with Deneith. She could work with him.

Pater d'Orien shook Tariic's hand, then departed in search of something to eat. Tariic seated himself with an easy smile, but Vounn was becoming more adept at reading goblin body language. Tariic's ears were slightly stiff and his right hand was held slightly away from his body. Shaking hands was not a part of hobgoblin culture, and while Tariic might have been familiar with the manners of the Five Nations, he clearly wasn't completely comfortable with all of them. Vounn kept her hands folded in her lap and instead returned Tariic's smile.

"I would have thought I'd find you with the assembly, Tariic," she said.

He bent his head. "Unfortunately, no. The rules of the assembly are clear by tradition and my uncle's decree. Only clan chiefs, warlords, and the arbiter of order and her assistants are permitted in the throne room while the assembly meets. Not even guards are permitted."

A lesser rule extended over the gallery. Vounn's guard—Thuun today—waited outside the door of the gallery along with the guards who served the other dignitaries. Vounn looked back down into the throne room and nodded toward the end. Late morning light poured through the tall windows behind Haruuc's throne. A big figure stood at the lhesh's side, hands tucked into his belt alongside twin axes. "Vanii is there."

"Haruuc's decree," Tariic said. "His *shava* are a special case. When I was young I remember seeing all three of them standing around him. It was a sight that spoke of the respect Haruuc commanded . . . commands."

Vounn raised an eyebrow. Tariic sighed and his ears dipped. "We shouldn't fool ourselves," he said quietly. He gestured out over the throne room. "Thirty—even ten—years ago, this wouldn't have happened."

"Haruuc sees it, too, Tariic," said Vounn. "That's why he sent Geth and the others."

"I hope they find what they're looking for soon," Tariic said. He looked at her sideways and his voice dropped even lower. "Speaking of which, have you heard anything from Ashi?"

She shook her head. "Haruuc or Senen would be more likely to have had communication from one of the others."

"I thought maybe Ashi would have contacted you." He sat back. "They've been gone for more than a month. I know they're not likely to be close to a House Sivis speaking station, but I would have thought there would be some word."

"Patience," Vounn said. It was the same thing she told herself every night. The fear was beginning to grow in her that she would soon have to deliver the truth of Ashi's whereabouts to Breven. She pushed the thought back and looked down into the throne room again to cover her feelings of unease.

Yet another warlord had risen to protest that he didn't have food to spare for Rhukaan Draal. Haruuc's frustration with the near-constant denials showed in his face. Abruptly, he gestured to the thin hobgoblin woman who was the arbiter of order. She nodded to an assistant and the banner of the speaker's clan dropped from the Pole of Order. Murmurs spread around the hall, and the warlord who had been speaking closed his mouth in surprise. He stood for a moment longer, then sat down.

Haruuc looked across his assembled warlords. "Some of you," he said, "'speak the truth. Your fields and storehouses were burned. I saw this with my own eyes. But I know that many of you are lying." His angry gaze lingered on the warlord who had just sat down and the man flinched. Haruuc's gaze moved on. "Is it fear that the Gan'duur will begin raiding again and you'll be left with nothing? That won't happen. Is it greed? Do you hoard now in hopes of commanding a higher price later? I promise you that won't happen either—I will not allow it."

He paused, then added, "Or perhaps you support the Gan'duur?"

The silence, both in the throne room and in the gallery where everyone was listening now, was solid and thick as a winter morning. Vounn pressed her lips together. The rebellious sons of the Atiin Noor clan were safely away thanks to Deneith and Orien, but there had been others who had spoken and acted in favor of the Gan'duur. They'd been dealt with in the same way as the raiders. None had been found to stand among the high ranks of Darguun, but if there were . . .

Haruuc spoke into the silence. "Do you hold back in the belief that you are showing that coward Keraal where your true heart lies? Do you hold back because you think it weakens me? Maybe you don't want to see your stores feed Rhukaan Draal but the thieves and bandits of Gan'duur instead. Stand then. Stand and show your true feelings!"

"Yes!" called a new voice. "Stand!" And at the back of the throne room, a hobgoblin wearing a helmet that shadowed his features rose. He stepped out into the central aisle and stood facing Haruuc. The lhesh's ears lay back flat.

"Keraal."

Beyond the open doors of the throne room, guards in the antechamber jerked and turned at the sound of the rebel warlord's name. One of them drew his sword and shouted for an attack. The helmeted hobgoblin whirled, one hand up. "Hold! No one may enter the assembly who does not belong! That is the law of Haruuc!"

The guards stopped just short of the doorway, crashing into each other as they came to a sudden halt. The one who had called the attack looked to Haruuc. The hobgoblin who stood in the aisle, however, reached up calmly and removed his helmet. Thick, dark hair spilled free, and Keraal turned a strong, hard face toward Haruuc as well. "Does the law not also say that no violence may be offered within the assembly?"

Haruuc stared at him, then dismissed the guards with a gesture. He stared at Keraal for a long moment before he said in a growl, "Law or not, it takes a brave jackal to enter the den of a tiger."

Darkness flushed Keraal's red-brown face. "You call me a jackal? You call the Gan'duur bandits? You are both jackal and bandit, Haruuc! You, who could have led us against the *chaat'oor* of the Five Nations—or at least against our ancient enemies in Valenar, but instead you sign treaties with them!"

"I call you a jackal," said Haruuc tightly, "because you come to the assembly in disguise, like a jackal that rolls in the stink of another animal to disguise its own scent."

Vounn heard Tariic suck air through his teeth at the insult. No one else moved or spoke. Keraal stood straight and glared at Haruuc. "I come in disguise because otherwise I would have been denied my place at the assembly. Your guards would have stopped me at the door, if they had not arrested me on the road." His ears rose tall. "A violation of your own law that the assembly is a place of neutrality and that none are to be harmed as they come and go."

"My guards would have done nothing of the kind!" Haruuc said.

"Wouldn't they? Can you say that I would be here now if I hadn't disguised myself?"

A neat trap, Vounn thought. Haruuc couldn't deny his own law, even when it had been turned against him. The lhesh didn't answer the warlord's question. Instead he growled, "What do you want here, Keraal?"

"To do what it is the right of every warlord to do: attend the assembly and speak my mind. Those who darkened the name of Gan'duur have been dealt with. Am I a criminal or a traitor to be denied my right?"

Once again, Haruuc didn't answer. His eyes narrowed. "You are here. Speak."

Another warlord might have bowed his head. Keraal raised his arrogantly. "It is not in the nature of our people to share land. We are conquerors and rulers. How many other clans must suffer as the Gan'duur have, our warriors driven to rebellion by inaction?"

"Warriors," said Haruuc, "must know when to fight and when to serve the people by keeping their swords sheathed."

"Warriors don't serve the people, Haruuc. You sound like a human. Warriors serve the warlord—unless you intend that all of our warriors should serve you." A soft murmur spread through the assembly, but Keraal wasn't finished. "Or perhaps you already think they do, since you sell them like slaves into the service of Deneith!"

He turned sharply and flung up a hand to point into the gallery—directly at Vounn.

She didn't move. She forced herself to remain still, to meet Keraal's blazing eyes. The warlord didn't hold his dramatic pose for long, though. Haruuc stood up from his throne. "Our warriors are not slaves, Keraal! Remember that I served Deneith, and Darguun stands today because I did. Service to Deneith brings wealth to our nation, to warriors and warlords alike!"

Keraal let his arm fall and turned to Haruuc with a smile on his face. "And wealth," he said, "to the high warlord who betrayed Deneith to create Darguun. Would you trust one who had betrayed his trust before, Haruuc?"

The lhesh stared at him, then asked, "Have you said what you came to say, Keraal?"

"Not quite," Keraal said. He bent his neck in a nod. "Gan'duur has an excess of grain this season. Enough to share with Rhukaan Draal if it is necessa—"

"Be gone, Keraal!" snapped Haruuc. Beside him, Vanii drew his axes.

Keraal pointed at the *shava*. "Remember your law, Haruuc! None are to be harmed as they come and *as they go.*" He flung the helmet he had worn to the floor, the crash of it startling, and strode from the throne room. The guards in the antechamber parted—reluctantly, it seemed to Vounn—to let him go. Vanii would have gone after him if Haruuc hadn't flung up an arm to stop him. The assembly of warlords burst into chaotic conversation.

Tariic let out a long breath. *"Maabet!"* he cursed. The watchers in the gallery were as deep in conversation as the warlords.

Vounn just looked after Keraal. "What do you think he hoped to accomplish by that?" she asked.

"I think he wanted to show just how much he could defy Haruuc," said Tariic, pulling his lips back from his teeth. "Maybe he's trying to draw Haruuc into making a mistake that will turn the other warlords against him once and for all. Keraal's a brilliant strategist—or else completely mad. Either way, he's got huge—"

His voice became just a buzz in Vounn's ears. Behind his head, through the great windows of the throne room, thick smoke was rising in columns across Rhukaan Draal.

"Fire," she said. "There's fire in the city!"

Tariic broke off and turned around to follow her gaze. The warlords ceased to argue and looked as well. Haruuc stepped around his throne to stare out the window. Vounn struggled to pick out landmarks in the cityscape and identify what was burning, but she could tell Haruuc's experienced eyes saw immediately where the smoke was coming from. He whirled to face the warlords. "The assembly is dismissed, but we are not finished. Do not depart Rhukaan Draal."

"What burns?" someone shouted.

Haruuc's face darkened. "The city houses of the Atiin Noor, the Pin Galaac, and the Haranhra." Cries came out of the crowd. All of the clans he'd named, Vounn knew, were strong supporters of

Haruuc. Then the lhesh looked to the gallery and added, "As well as the Orien compound and the Deneith enclave."

Somewhere behind her, a plate crashed to the ground and Pater d'Orien ran from the gallery with a curse. Vounn stared down at Haruuc, her eyes meeting his for a moment, then he turned, seized the red sword that leaned against the throne, and raced out of the throne room, shouting for guards and his horse. "Send messages and runners," he snapped. "Anyone suspicious near the fires is to be taken into custody—alive. Anyone armed who isn't wearing my colors is to be ordered off the streets!"

Vounn looked out at the rising smoke again. She could recognize one of the burning buildings now as Deneith's small enclave in Rhukaan Draal. It wasn't nearly as important as the Gathering Stone, but it still belonged to the House. She rose. "Tariic, I must go. Good day."

She didn't wait for his reply, but swept after Pater. Thuun was waiting outside, milling around with the other guards of those still in the gallery. She snapped her fingers at him. "We need to go into the city—the Deneith enclave is on fire. I want Aruget and Krakuul with us." After her experience the night of the famine march, she didn't go out in Rhukaan Draal without at least two of her escorts.

"I'll take you to them, lady." Thuun stepped in front of her and led the way, pushing aside anyone who found themselves in his path. Vounn made plans in her head. If the clerks at the enclave knew their jobs, their first move would be to ensure that enlistment records and contracts, more valuable to the House than gold, were saved. She would take charge of the papers first, then worry about saving the building.

The smell of food—goblin food, sharp with vinegar—hit her, and she emerged from her plans to look around. They were somewhere near the kitchens of Khaar Mbar'ost. Unlike the grand halls, these passages were cramped and dim. "Where are we going?" asked Thuun.

"Aruget and Krakuul spend their time off-duty close to the kitchens, the better to get at the richest scraps," her guard said. "Stay close, lady."

Vounn looked around. There were few hobgoblins in sight along the corridor or through the doorways they passed. There was an atmosphere of uneasy excitement. It seemed word of the fires in the city had already spread down here. "Haruuc has called an alarm," she said. "It's possible Krakuul and Aruget have already gone looking for us. Perhaps I should return to my quarters and wait for you all there."

"This would be the worst time to be alone. We're almost there. Have patience, and I'll go back with you."

She could smell a draft of fresh air. They must have been approaching a rear gate or kitchen entrance. It seemed unlike Aruget, she thought, to spend his time lounging near the kitchen. The hobgoblin was a brisk and efficient soldier. If he wanted something from the kitchen, he would have sent a runner for it. From what she knew of Krakuul, he might have gone to the kitchen on his own, but he would have stayed near there until he had what he wanted. Judging by her glimpses through the corridor, she and Thuun were already past the kitchen.

And was it strange that Thuun, the least talkative of the three guards, had just said more to her than he ever had before?

Vounn looked at her guide sharply. His broad shoulders hid his hands, but he had pulled something from his belt and was manipulating it where she couldn't see. A prickle of unease crawled up Vounn's neck. Keeping her pace steady, she narrowed her eyes and concentrated on the dragonmark that curled around the inside of her right arm. A gentle warmth passed through it and the power of the Mark of Sentinel manifested around her, an unseen barrier that brought with it a feeling of safety.

That feeling was only an illusion. The danger, Vounn felt certain, was real. Something was wrong. Between one step and the next, she turned and ran as fast as she could back the way they had come.

CHAPTER TWENTY-FIVE

Thuun didn't curse or cry out. In an instant, Vounn heard his long, heavy strides coming after her. She looked around for help, but all of the goblin servants seemed to have vanished like mice. The lady seneschal fumbled for her stiletto as she ran, but couldn't get at it. She drew breath to scream for help—and a strong arm wrapped around her and lifted her off her feet. Her unseen shield could do little against such a direct attack. A hand went over her face, holding a wet rag across her nose and mouth.

The rag reeked powerfully of distilled alcohol and something else she couldn't quite identify. It was herbal, both bitter and sweet, and it reminded her vaguely of a tea-like beverage she'd once been served at a feast thrown by the half-orcs of House Tharashk. She tried to hit Thuun with her elbows and her feet, hard defensive blows with no mercy. One backward kick came close to landing in his groin, but he twisted and took the blow on his leg instead. She heard him grunt, then he brought his mouth close to her ear.

"Struggle harder, Vounn of Deneith. You can do it."

He was no longer speaking Goblin. She threw herself into another furious struggle, but he just kept twisting and letting her blows slide off him. After a few moments, though, it seemed to Vounn that her arms and legs were strangely heavy, that her blows were sluggish, and she realized what a mistake she'd made. Struggling harder had made her breath more deeply, inhaling greater quantities of the fumes from the rag. They seemed to penetrate her mind and rob her of will. Her vision drifted; she couldn't focus on anything for more than a moment. Her body went limp in Thuun's grasp.

The hobgoblin eased her to the ground, supporting her if she were a drunkard while he tucked the rag away in a pouch at his belt. She caught a glimpse of a small brown bottle. "What have you done to me?" she tried to ask him, but the words came out slurred.

He must have guessed at what she was saying. "Essence of *gaeth'ad,*" he said. "Created by bounty hunters from the *gaeth'ad* tea of the Shadow Marches. Normally you'd have to drink it, but mixing it with strong alcohol gives the fumes some effect and allows for an easier delivery."

She was certain of the tea scent now. "Tharashk," she managed to say with some clarity.

Thuun chuckled. "No, just freelance."

Some servants were peeking back out into the corridor again. Thuun waved them away. "Too much to drink," he said in Goblin. "Taking her for fresh air." With a professional ease, he steered her stumbling body along the corridor and, after a few moments, into a small courtyard. Servants and even guards bustled about, many of them staring at a column of smoke that could be seen through a tall gate. No one paid much attention to the soldier with the human woman under his arm.

No one except two more soldiers who came to help, one with a cloak over his arm. Some part of Vounn knew they weren't really soldiers. They wore the red corded armbands of Khaar Mbar'ost, but their armor was rough and unpolished, the hair tucked under their helmets lank and greasy.

"Help," she called, hoping someone might hear her. No one did. The word was a croak. The cloak was whirled about her, leaving her with only a narrow gap in the hood to peer through. The three hobgoblins walked her out the gate without anyone challenging them.

At first the streets of Rhukaan Draal seemed quiet, but the farther they went, the more the sounds of chaos filled the air.

Vounn could see little through her narrow field of vision, and her drug-addled senses seemed to make everything worse. People were running back and forth. A few were screaming. She caught snatches of rumors: that the storehouses of the city were burning, that there were riots over a new supply of food, that Lhesh Haruuc had imposed martial law in the streets. She could smell smoke, heavy and choking. She mostly saw running legs and darting figures. They started to turn down one street but pulled back—Vounn saw fighting ahead. They went another way. The hobgoblins' pace, set by the traitorous Thuun, was fast. Vounn stumbled helplessly. She shook her head, trying to throw off the hood. She managed to get it half off. Thuun grabbed it and pulled it back down, but not before she'd gotten a look at him.

He was no longer Thuun. He wore Thuun's armor, and she would have sworn that his hands had never left his arms, but he was not Thuun. Instead of the familiar face of the guard Haruuc had assigned to her, she saw a stranger, some anonymous hobgoblin who could have gone unnoticed in any crowd.

"Changeling," she said thickly. This had never been Thuun, but one of the secretive, deceiving race of shapechangers.

Thuun—she couldn't think of him by any other name—didn't give her a response.

"Patrol," said one of the others. Vounn thought he might actually be a hobgoblin.

"This way," said Thuun. He dragged Vounn around a corner and into another street.

And stopped. Vounn raised her head and saw a mounted patrol just in front of them. "You there!" called a voice in Goblin. "You wear my uniform. What are you doing?"

My uniform? Vounn focused her wits and peered at the patrol. Soldiers in armor painted with the red blade and spiked crown surrounded a number of other figures. One of the most prominent was a big hobgoblin with twin axes in his belt. Another wore a spiked crown on his head. Vanii and Haruuc, she realized. They'd stumbled on the lhesh himself. She tried to push her voice out of her throat. To throw off the hood. Anything to get his attention.

But Thuun was already saluting. "Lhesh, we have a prisoner we're escorting to Khaar Mbar'ost."

"You've lost your way," said Vanii. He pointed very nearly back the way they had come. "Khaar Mbar'ost is that way."

Thuun nodded. "We were forced back by fighting."

"Leave your prisoner with the first patrol you see and get back to your posts," ordered Haruuc. He turned his horse. Thuun saluted again and pulled Vounn in the direction Vanii had pointed.

She doubted they would follow that path for long. Thuun was taking her somewhere, and she couldn't let the opportunity for escape pass her by.

Vounn dragged all of her energy together and stomped hard on the shin of the hobgoblin who held her opposite Thuun. He cursed and hopped in pain. The moment that his grip weakened, she let herself drop.

It was far from dignified but it worked. She slipped out of the hobgoblin's grasp and went down to her knees in the filthy street. Thuun's hand tightened immediately, holding her firmly. She had what she needed, though. One hand free, she clawed at the cloak, ripping back the hood. "Haruuc!" she gasped.

She saw the lhesh's head turn, then Thuun had her hood up again. Had Haruuc seen her? The other false guards grabbed her. She resisted and kicked, not at them, but backward out from under the edge of the cloak. The enveloping fabric rode up, exposing not the clothes of someone seized on the streets, but the fine dress and shoes of a courtier.

"Halt!" Haruuc's voice was thunder. Vounn heard the whinny of horses turned hard, then a curse from Thuun. His hands released her. She spun as the other guards, not as quick to react, continued to grab for her. Her hood slipped back and she saw Haruuc riding straight for her.

The lhesh stood in his stirrups, as powerful a warrior as she had ever seen. The deep yellow of his skin was like dark gold against the steel of his armor. The spikes of his crown and those set into the joints of his armor flashed as if he were surrounded by blades, but only one blade really stood out—the *shaarat'kor,* the famous scarlet blade, was a streak of blood on the air as

Haruuc drew it. The hobgoblins grappling her saw him as well. They screamed and dropped her, fleeing after Thuun. Vounn fell, unable to catch herself, unable to take her eyes from Haruuc's charge.

This was what the troops of Breland and Cyre had seen thirty years ago. A king among the goblins. An unstoppable force. A warrior clad in gold and steel and blood. Her breath caught in her throat. If she had been standing against him, she didn't think she could have raised a weapon to save her life.

His horse passed so close she felt the drumming of its hooves in the ground and caught its smell on the wind of its passage. She twisted around, captivated. The first hobgoblin hadn't gotten far. The *shaarat'kor* cut the air. Blood sprayed out, spattering her like warm rain. The hobgoblin's body toppled back, motion arrested by the force of Haruuc's blow. A section of his head landed on the ground just in front of her.

The second hobgoblin threw himself at the door of a house. The wood splintered under the impact but held. He pulled back to try again. Before he could, something hissed above Vounn's head. The hobgoblin jerked back, then slid down the doorframe with one of Vanii's axes splitting his breastbone.

Then there was just Thuun, running hard and weaving from side to side as he sought an escape. Haruuc galloped after him. He didn't raise his sword again, but just ran him down. Thuun shrieked as the horse's bulk knocked him to the street and the animal's hooves hammered his body. He curled into a ball and stayed that way as Haruuc wheeled his horses around. Thuun screamed again, but Haruuc reined in his mount and slid from the saddle. Thuun's scream faded away and he looked up to find the lhesh standing over him, red sword dripping blood onto the ground. Thuun whimpered.

Vanii dismounted beside Vounn and helped her stand. "Have you been harmed?"

The fumes of the rag still made her head spin a little, but they were easing. "No," she said, then called out to Haruuc. "He kidnapped me in Khaar Mbar'ost by pretending to be Thuun. He's a changeling."

Haruuc's ears went back. "Show me your true face, *gaa'ma,*" he growled.

Thuun nodded and his hobgoblin features seemed to melt and flow across his face. Nose and mouth faded, becoming almost half-formed. His eyes became wide and milky, his hair white. His skin turned soft and dusky gray. His body shrank a little as well, so that Thuun's armor was loose on him. *Gaa'ma,* the Goblin term for changelings, literally meant "wax baby," Vounn knew. It suited the creature that lay still under Haruuc's sword.

The lhesh shifted the blade so the blood that ran off it fell in drops on the changeling's face. "You were hired to kidnap Lady Seneschal Vounn d'Deneith?"

The changeling nodded.

"By who?"

"A hobgoblin—he wore a mask and called himself Wuud."

"Like all the others," Vanii murmured.

Vounn glanced at him, but he said nothing else.

Haruuc's face betrayed nothing except anger and contempt. "You give away easily what you know," he said.

"I was paid to snatch the Deneith envoy, not fight the lhesh," the changeling said. "I'll tell you anything you want, but there isn't much I know."

"I didn't imagine there was. Where were you taking her?"

"A boat waiting outside of Rhukaan Draal, above the first cataract of the Ghaal. Wuud's men will take her from there."

Haruuc looked to one of the soldiers who had been with him. "You—gather a squad and investigate. Bring back anyone you find." His glance shifted to two others. "You take this *taat* back to Khaar Mbar'ost. I want him held in an isolated cell—we may need his word later."

The soldiers hastened to obey their commands. When the changeling had been seized and led away, Haruuc came over to Vounn, still standing with Vanii's support. "I apologize, Lady Vounn," he said. "Such things shouldn't happen in Khaar Mbar'ost. I can assure you that the real Thuun is no changeling."

"I'm fine," Vounn said. "I hope Thuun is too."

The stiffening of Haruuc's ears, however, suggested that he suspected the same thing she did: the real Thuun was dead, removed so that the changeling could take his place without threat of being revealed. Vounn moved on to something else. "When the changeling mentioned a masked hobgoblin, Vanii said, 'Like all the others.' What does that mean? Have there been other kidnappings?"

Haruuc gave his *shava* a disapproving look and shook his head. "No, but all those captured near the burning buildings so far have been locals, all hired by a masked hobgoblin calling himself Wuud. The fires and your kidnapping were coordinated."

"Keraal," said Vounn. The Gan'duur had tried to kidnap her once before. The disappearance of a senior member of House Deneith would be as embarrassing for Haruuc now as it would have been then.

"There's no evidence to prove it," Haruuc said. "More important, how could he have been here to hire them? We've been watching Gan'duur territory." He shook his head again. "But you should worry about these things in Khaar Mbar'ost. Go back to your chambers and rest." He gestured for another guard. "Escort Lady Vounn. Let her ride your horse if she needs."

"Thank you, but no," Vounn said. "I need to get to the Deneith enclave."

"We've been past it," Haruuc told her. "It suffered less damage than the other targets we've seen. Your clerks know their duty—there were crates full of records being carried away from the flames. I offered them the shelter of Khaar Mbar'ost."

Vounn nodded. "Thank you, lhesh."

"Thank me by returning to Khaar Mbar'ost until the city is quiet again." He held the soldier's mount for her and she nodded her thanks again.

As she urged the animal around to face Haruuc's fortress, a messenger on a wild-eyed horse came clattering along the street. "Lhesh!" he called. "There's been an arrest—a group entering the city by the south who refused to surrender their arms. They claim they have come to see you."

Haruuc stiffened and met Vounn's eyes for a moment, then looked back to the messenger. "Two hobgoblins, a goblin, a gnome, a shifter, and a human?"

The messenger looked startled, then frightened. "They shouldn't be arrested?"

"Did they have any message for me?" Haruuc demanded.

The messenger just looked more frightened. "They said, 'Success,' lhesh."

Vounn saw the pallor that crept under Haruuc's skin, but his face and the hand that he held on her horse were steady. "Take a message back to your commander," he told the messenger. "The travelers are to be escorted to Khaar Mbar'ost immediately!"

"Mazo," the messenger said and rode off.

Haruuc looked to Vounn and Vanii.

"Maabet, they've done it!" Vanii said. "They've returned!"

"So they have," Haruuc said—and Vounn saw the glint of a plan form in his eyes. "Vounn, I need you to take a message to Munta at Khaar Mbar'ost for me. Tell him that Geth and the others are to be given refreshments but kept away from everyone. Tell him to recall the warlords immediately and to summon all the dignitaries in Rhukaan Draal to my throne room."

"You want a full court to see the rod presented to you," said Vounn.

"Cho—that, too." Haruuc's eyes were very bright. "Tell Munta to order troops and supplies drawn up as well. Gantii Vus and Rhukaan Taash to start. I think others will join us, but I want an army ready to march north within four days."

Vounn's eyebrows rose.

Vanii's ears stiffened. "We're attacking the Gan'duur?" the *shava* asked. "But Keraal still has us trapped. The other warlords won't accept—"

"Keraal has *me* trapped," said Haruuc, "but Geth has brought something back with him that's nearly as valuable as the rod right now." He looked at Vounn. "Ride! Munta must act!"

CHAPTER TWENTY-SIX

Their return to Rhukaan Draal was not quite as triumphant as Ekhaas had imagined it might be. All the stories she knew told of heroes returning from quests to the cheers of the people and the gratitude of lords. It was peculiarly dissatisfying to have been greeted with detention, then an escort through nearly empty streets, only to be met at the gates of Khaar Mbar'ost by Munta the Gray and hustled away into hiding. Munta himself had brought them food, drink, and wash basins like a common servant. He didn't even ask to see the rod.

Then again, most heroes did not return to a city with smoke hanging over it and signs of hunger and violence in the streets. The return journey to Rhukaan Draal had been too swift for them to stop and talk to people, but it had been hard to miss the unease that gripped Darguun as they traveled back north. Burned fields and holds, rotting bodies hung up like a warning—they'd even been attacked by bandits on the road south of the city, a sure sign of trouble if thieves were willing to ambush an obviously well-armed band. Munta, as he came and went, would give them no hint of what had been happening while they were away. No one else came to see them either. Not Haruuc, not Tariic, not Senen Dhakaan, not Vounn d'Deneith.

Which was probably just as well. Ekhaas looked around the chamber—luxurious enough that it must have been meant as a waiting room for visiting dignitaries—in which Munta had hidden them. She and the others had spread themselves out in the room's chairs and couches, each of them alone in their own private space and each of them, she suspected, thinking about the secret they had sworn to keep. They'd managed to make the hurried journey back to Rhukaan Draal as if nothing were wrong, but now that they were here, the decision they'd made in the hidden valley seemed to have grown heavier.

If asked for the story of what happened in the Uura Odaarii, they would speak only of Dabrak Riis's use of the strange magic of the cavern against them. An omission wasn't really a lie. No one beyond the six of them would ever know what power the Rod of Kings truly had.

The door of the chamber opened, and Munta appeared once again. If he felt the tension in the room, he didn't let it show on his face. "It's time," he said. "We're ready."

"Ready?" Ashi asked.

Munta's ears twitched and a smile spread across his face. "Ready to welcome you like the heroes you are!" He held out a tray polished to a high gloss, so freshly cleaned that Ekhaas could smell the wax, with a piece of rich gold cloth on it. "For you to carry the rod, Geth. We want everyone to see it."

"Who's everyone?" asked Ashi again.

"Everyone," Munta said with satisfaction.

Geth came forward with a long pouch fashioned from common wool, a strip torn from a blanket if the undignified truth had to be told. He loosened the simple twist of cord that held it closed, reached inside, and slid out the Rod of Kings. Munta's eyes went wide at the sight of it. Ekhaas saw Midian and Dagii look away, though, and none of the others gazed too closely at the rod. If they'd found themselves avoiding discussion of their secret on the journey, they'd also found themselves shying away from the rod. As the first one to grasp it, Geth had been appointed the rod's keeper with unspoken assent—no one else had wanted to touch it. Ekhaas and Midian had inspected the simple shaft and examined the runes on it, but not as closely as they once might have. Geth had held the rod for them.

Laid out on the tray, though, purple byeshk against rich gold, it did have a certain majesty. A sense of excitement rose inside her. The rod wasn't just an artifact of the great empire. It was something that had been held by the hands of countless emperors. It had seen the rise and fall of dynasties. And she had helped find it. Ekhaas of Kech Volaar had helped to bring it back into the world.

"This is what's going to happen," Munta said, passing the tray to Geth, then leading them out of the chamber and into the corridor. "Haruuc wants to have a very public presentation of the rod so that everyone who matters knows how important it is. The presentation will take place in the throne room. As you enter, a *duur'kala* will tell the story of the rod. When you reach the foot of the throne, Tariic—as a representative of the people—will take the rod and give it to Haruuc, who will then speak. After that, there's no particular order of ceremonies you need to follow. Haruuc's instructions will guide you."

"You make it sound like a pageant," Midian said.

"Rule is as much spectacle as it is action." Munta stopped at a tall door. From the other side of it, Ekhaas could hear the indistinct murmurs of a great many people. "This leads into the antechamber of the throne room," Munta said. "When the drums start, the doors will open and you'll go in." He looked at them all and solemn pride filled his face. "Haruuc won't be able to say this in public, but he asked me to tell you. *Kaas panozhii kitaan atcha.*"

We owe a debt to your honor. He turned and hurried up the corridor, heading, Ekhaas assumed, to take his place in the throne room. She glanced at the others. From their expressions, they might have been walking to an execution rather than a celebration.

"It's too late not to do this, isn't it?" asked Ashi.

"Far too late," Ekhaas said.

A drum stroke sounded from beyond the door. The murmurs of the crowd died out. The drum continued, its beat throbbing on the air in a slow rhythm. "The call to advance," said Dagii. "Armies march into battle at that pace."

At the head of their small party, Geth shifted his grip on the tray and raised one hand to touch the collar of black stones around his neck.

The tall doors opened.

Representatives of all three goblin races filled the antechamber. Ekhaas recognized minor dignitaries, wealthy merchants, and officers of Haruuc's guard. Soldiers holding crossed spears as a barrier kept clear a path through the crowd and up to the wide stairs of the throne room. Faces turned to stare at them. Ekhaas saw Geth swallow, the hair on his neck and forearms rising, then he started to walk, matching his pace to the drum.

A voice rose, speaking in Goblin. *"Raat shi anaa.* In the ancient days of Dhakaan lived the great *dashoor* Taruuzh, who found inspiration in all things. It pleased him to work in the mines, where he could handle the raw material of his creations, and he was so working in the mines of Suthar Draal when he found a vein of byeshk so pure that he named it the Blood of Dusk."

It was the same story that Senen Dhakaan had told in the small chamber high in Khaar Mbar'ost, the story that had launched their quest. This time, however, it was not Senen Dhakaan who told it. Ekhaas recognized the voice that rose and fell in time with the drum, a voice like seawater and beeswax. Walking through the antechamber and up the stairs was like passing through a legend. The ears of every goblin in the crowd lifted to listen, captivated by the words of Aaspar, the elderly mother of the dirge, as she spoke of the wonders Taruuzh created from the byeshk of the Blood of Dusk. First of Aram, the Sword of Heroes. Then of Muut, the Shield of Nobles. And finally of—

"—a rod carved with symbols that had been old when the first *daashor* took up a hammer and the first *duur'kala* sang. A rod which Taruuzh gave to the emperor of Dhakaan and which he named—"

They reached the top of the steps. The throne room opened before them. The first thing Ekhaas saw was Haruuc, seated on his throne, the light that came through the tall windows striking bright rays from his armor and the spiked crown of Darguun. The second thing was Aaspar, dressed in black and standing before Haruuc.

Then the drum paused and Geth paused with it. In the silence, Aaspar flung up a thin hand, pointing along the aisle to those framed in the doorway. Her voice soared to fill the great hall. *"—Guulen, the Rod of Kings!"*

A hundred heads or more turned to follow her hand and voice. A hundred pairs of eyes or more stared at them. At the byeshk rod that Geth carried.

In that moment, the throne room of Khaar Mbar'ost seemed as timeless as the cavern of Uura Odaarii. Ekhaas was aware of the beating of her heart. It seemed that every warlord and clan chief of Darguun was in the hall, together with dignitaries wearing the crests of every nation of Khorvaire and every dragonmarked house. She saw Munta. She saw Senen Dhakaan. She saw Vounn d'Deneith. She saw Tariic standing across from Aaspar before the throne and Vanii standing in a place of honor behind it. Through the window, she could see smoke still rising in gray streamers from Rhukaan Draal, but that hint of conflict only seemed to add to the aura of the conqueror that clung to Haruuc.

The slow cadence of the drum returned, and Geth resumed his measured pace along the aisle. Aaspar's voice continued to ring from the high ceiling, so powerful it almost seemed enough to shake the banners that hung from the walls or to wake the statues that looked down from above. "For centuries upon centuries, the emperors of Dhakaan held Guulen. For centuries upon centuries, they ruled with might and wisdom—until Guulen was lost and the Empire of Dhakaan crumbled. But now the *dar* are united once more. Now . . ." Her words slowed along with the drum as their party reached the dais upon which Haruuc's throne stood. ". . . Guulen . . . *returns!*"

Her final cry echoed for a moment, then faded. For a long moment, the hall was silent—and Haruuc spoke.

"Who comes to the court of Lhesh Haruuc Shaarat'kor?"

For an instant, an awkward horror ran through Ekhaas. Munta hadn't said Haruuc would address them with the traditional challenge. She wanted to look at the old warlord, but didn't dare. She pushed her shock aside and spoke boldly.

"Ekhaas of Kech Volaar, daughter of the dirge, comes."

The others picked up her cue. Dagii's voice rose. "Dagii of Mur Talaan, son of Fenic, comes."

"Chetiin of the *shaarat'khesh* comes."

"Ashi of Deneith, daughter of Ner, comes."

"Midian Mit Davandi, son of Tivani Mit Davandi, comes."

"Geth . . ."

The shifter hesitated. Ekhaas glanced at him. So did Aaspar. So did Tariic and Vanii. Haruuc probably would have glanced at him, too, if he wasn't frozen in a stiffly formal posture. There was confusion and maybe even struggle in Geth's eyes, then they cleared. He straightened, and, in Goblin that was far more precise than his usual broken attempts at the language and burred with the ancient accent of Dhakaan, he said, "Geth, who bears the sword Aram, who carries the honor of Kuun, who killed the dragon Dah'mir, comes."

He dropped to one knee and held out the tray. "Lhesh Haruuc Shaarat'kor, we bring Guulen, the Rod of Kings."

Ekhaas saw Tariic blink in surprise at Geth's dramatic statement. He stepped forward, though, and lifted the rod from the tray. Climbing the steps of the dais, he sank down in front of Haruuc. "As Taruuzh said to his emperor," he said solemnly, "in this are the glories of the people. Bear them in mind, and the people will always know their king."

Haruuc stared at the rod for a long moment, then reached out his hand. Ekhaas found she was holding her breath and watching the lhesh closely. Would he change when he held the rod? Would he feel the power within it?

His fingers closed on the metal. Haruuc took the rod from Tariic, looked at it, then rose and held it high. "As Guulen passed from emperor to emperor in the age of Dhakaan," he said, his voice filling the hall, "so shall it pass from lhesh to lhesh in this new age. Who holds Guulen is the ruler of Darguun. Look on this symbol of the glories of the people, warlords and clan chiefs, ambassadors and envoys, and know that it is true!"

The words were well-chosen. The gesture was perfect. Caught up in the spectacle of the rod's presentation, the crowd in the throne room burst into applause, the goblins striking hands against chest, the dignitaries of other nations slapping palm against palm. From the antechamber came shouts of enthusiasm from those spectators of less dignity. Ekhaas applauded as well. Haruuc's plan had worked—he had the symbol he would pass on to his successor. She looked up at him, light from the window flowing around him, shining from crown and rod, his ears held high, his mouth wide in a smile of triumph . . .

Her applause slowed. She squeezed her eyes shut, then looked at Haruuc again. The light still shone around him, and he still looked majestic, but no more than that. The rod, she thought; it's the power of the rod. She looked around her, at Dagii on one side and Chetiin on the other. Dagii looked worried. Chetiin looked thoughtful. "Geth's sword had powers even while it was asleep," he said under the applause. "We should expect the rod will, too. An aura of majesty is a minor magic."

Ekhaas studied Haruuc. He looked out onto the throne room with bright eyes but no sign at all that he was aware of the rod's effect. He was no more commanding its power than Geth commanded Aram. She nodded slowly. Dagii did, too, but added, "Minor magics can lead to greater. We will watch him."

"Mazo," murmured Chetiin.

Haruuc relaxed and lowered the rod to look down at the party before him. Tariic stood and moved back to one side. Geth stood as well, the tray whisked away by a goblin wearing an armband of red cords. As the applause slowly died, Haruuc raised his free hand. "Darguun commends you who risked your lives to bring back Guulen. Rewards come to the heroes who deserve them." He gestured, and the goblin who had taken away Geth's tray brought it back.

This time, four daggers rested on the gold cloth. Ekhaas caught her breath. They were exquisite, combining the best work of a weapon smith and a gold smith. The bright blades were fine steel, chased with golden letters that spelled out *atcha*—honor. The grips were fantastic constructions of gold and silver woven around sparkling gems. Set into the crosspieces were jewels the size of her knuckle, different on each dagger—a ruby, an emerald, a sapphire, and a golden crystal that was a Siberys dragonshard.

"Ekhaas of Kech Volaar, Chetiin of the *shaarat'khesh,* Ashi d'Deneith, Midian Mit Davandi," said Haruuc, "you owe allegiance to other lords, but I gift you with these in thanks, and tell you that you are friends of Darguun. If ever you have need, speak and Haruuc will listen."

The goblin passed among them, offering a dagger to each. Ekhaas received the emerald dagger, Ashi the dagger with the Siberys dragonshard, Chetiin the ruby, Midian the sapphire. After the goblin retreated, Haruuc looked down again. "Geth, who bears Aram, the Sword of Heroes. Without your aid, Guulen could not have been found. What reward can I offer you? Will you take wealth? I would give you a chest full of gold."

Geth's eyebrows rose, then fell again. He shook his head. When he spoke, his Goblin was once again broken and crude. "Lhesh, no. How would I carry it?"

"Land, then?" Haruuc asked.

Geth shook his head a second time, then a third when Haruuc offered him a rank in his army. The lhesh's ears flicked twice rapidly. Although he didn't smile, Ekhaas guessed that he had expected Geth to turn down all three offers and was somehow pleased that he had.

"Geth, who bears Aram, you show your honor and prove yourself worthy of the greatest reward that any warrior can give. You owed me no allegiance, yet you sought Guulen at my request. You performed a great deed for Darguun, yet you accept neither wealth nor power. You have my trust in all things." He stood up tall and straight. "Will you be my *shava,* to call me friend and stand at my back when I have need, to call on me to stand with you when you have need?"

It was hard to tell who was more surprised: Geth, who stood in silent shock, or the Darguuls in the throne room, who broke out in low murmurs. Ekhaas found herself among them. It had been unusual for Haruuc to take three *shava*. To take a fourth—and one who was not of the goblin races at that—was unheard of. Geth turned and glanced at her as if seeking guidance. Ekhaas spread her hands helplessly. There was no advice she could give him in this. Behind Haruuc, however, Vanii smiled and nodded to Geth. The survivor of Haruuc's three *shava* approved.

Geth swallowed. "I will, lhesh," he said.

"Join me," Haruuc said, stepping away from the edge of the dais. He reached back, set the rod aside, and took up his sword from where it rested against the arm of his throne. As Geth mounted the steps of the dais, the high warlord said, "Draw your sword."

The murmurs of the crowd hushed abruptly as Aram emerged. Haruuc raised his sword, gesturing for Geth to match the gesture. The two swords, red-stained steel and twilight purple byeshk, touched. Haruuc twisted his wrist and the teeth of the swords' notched edges locked together. He reached under the joined swords and grasped Geth's hand. Ekhaas heard him murmur, "Repeat what I say," then he raised his voice.

"Before witnesses, I make this oath," he said.

"Before witnesses, I make this oath," Geth repeated.

For a moment Ekhaas was afraid that his broken Goblin might spoil Haruuc's grand gesture, but as the shifter spoke, his words once again took on the ancient accent. It had to be some power of Aram, she guessed—the sword was giving strength to his words. If Haruuc noticed anything, he didn't react, but continued the oath, with Geth echoing every phrase with faithful intensity.

"On blood and graves, I swear I will protect you and guide you, avenge you and cherish you, in life and death so long as I draw breath." Haruuc paused. "Geth, you are *shava* to me."

"Haruuc, you are *shava* to me."

The two swords fell apart and Haruuc swept Geth into a rough hug. The lhesh's embrace of Vounn before the assembly of warlords had been scandalous, but a hug between *shava* was an embrace of brothers and warriors. Vanii was the first to applaud, the beating of his hand against his chest a lonely sound for a moment in the great hall. Then Chetiin joined him and Ekhaas, Dagii, and Ashi an instant later. By the time Haruuc released Geth and showed him to a place on the other side of the throne from Vanii, very nearly the entire crowd was applauding. Ekhaas caught Geth's eye and nodded at him. The shifter replied with an uncertain smile.

Haruuc took up the Rod of Kings again and gestured, sword in one hand and rod in the other, for the crowd to be silent. "There is another reward that must be given," he said. "Dagii of Mur Talaan, stand forward."

Dagii did. There was a slight limp in his step, a permanent legacy of her hurried healing of his ankle in the valley. Haruuc held his sword out, naked blade toward the waiting warrior. "Dagii of Mur Talaan, I offer you the rank of *lhevk-rhu*. Do you accept this challenge?"

Ekhaas's ears rose, and there was a new murmur in the crowd. *Lhevk-rhu* was the third highest rank in the military structure Haruuc had created after the war. It raised Dagii above most common warlords, leaving him outranked only by a few elder warlords, like Munta the Gray, and the lhesh himself. Dagii looked up and met Haruuc's eyes.

"I accept it," he said. He reached out and wrapped his left hand around the sharpened edge of the offered sword. With a slow, steady motion, Haruuc withdrew the sword and fresh blood ran along the blade. There was new applause from scattered warlords in the crowd—applause that Haruuc stopped with a gesture.

"Dagii," he said, "your new rank comes with a responsibility. Remind me—remind all gathered here—where the territory of the Mur Talaan lies."

Dagii's ears stood high. "Lhesh, the territory of the Mur Talaan is the land beneath Rhukaan Draal."

"If the territory of a clan has been attacked, what must its warlord do?"

Confusion and suspicion narrowed Dagii's eyes, and his gaze flicked to the smoke still visible over Rhukaan Draal. "The warlord must defend his clan's territory. If the attack cannot be defended against or occurs in his absence, he must strike back against the attacker—if the lhesh, by your law, grants him permission to do so." Dagii drew himself up. "Lhesh, has the territory of the Mur Talaan been attacked?"

"Today and in your absence," Haruuc said solemnly, drawing out the words. The hall was absolutely still. "Warriors of the Gan'duur make free with your territory, *lhevk-rhu*. They threaten the peace by starving the people. Keraal of Gan'duur claims he has disciplined those responsible. As lhesh of Darguun, I must be satisfied with this."

Dagii clenched his wounded fist. Blood dripped onto the floor of the throne room. "Lhesh, my clan's honor cannot be satisfied by words. A warlord may do what a lhesh cannot. On behalf of the Mur

Talaan, I ask your permission to strike back against the Gan'duur."

The stirring among the warlords was like a wave, as if Dagii's words had burst a dam. Haruuc smiled, looking almost smug. "You have my permission."

There was motion in the corner of Ekhaas's eye as Munta the Gray rose. "Mur Talaan has few troops, lhesh. If Dagii of Mur Talaan will lead, the Gantii Vus will follow him to support his honor."

The offer came too easily to be spontaneous, but abruptly there were other warlords calling out their support. Haruuc, Vanii, and Munta were all smiling, and Ekhaas had the feeling that someone—and she suspected it was the Gan'duur—had just been outmaneuvered. Haruuc raised his voice, too. "The Rhukaan Taash will stand for the honor of the Mur Talaan as well. Let all see that the clans of the Ghaal'dar remember tradition." He raised his sword high and held the Rod of Kings close to his chest. "Let all see that Darguun is strong!"

The roar that shook the stones of the hall was deafening. The raw emotion of the crowd was like a song. Ekhaas turned around to stare, drinking in the moment of Haruuc's triumph. Very nearly every Darguul was standing, their heads thrown back, their voices raised, their hands slapping their chests. But not everyone was so joyful. Ekhaas's ears rose.

Where the representatives of the Five Nations and the dragonmarked houses sat, reaction to the prospect of a strong Darguun was distinctly more restrained.

CHAPTER TWENTY-SEVEN

Over the next several days, it seemed to Ashi that she told the story of their quest for the rod—or at least the edited story they had all agreed to—so many times she felt like a *duur'kala*. The first time, along with the others, was to an audience of Haruuc, Tariic, Munta, Vanii, and Senen in the same small room in Khaar Mbar'ost where the quest had been planned. With excitement born of the rod's presentation still echoing through the fortress, they drank in the tale, Haruuc interrupting with curses against the Marguul bugbear clans, Senen breaking in to beg details about Dabrak Riis and the Uura Odaarii. By the time the story ended with the last emperor's destruction, however, they were silent and Haruuc bent his head before them all, then in return told them everything that had happened in Rhukaan Draal during their absence.

The second time, alone, was to Vounn in her chambers that same evening. There was a knot in Ashi's belly as she passed through the door guarded by Aruget and Krakuul. If there was anything she had dreaded on the journey back to Rhukaan Draal other than the fear that the rod's true powers might be revealed, it was returning to the lady seneschal. The quest was over—she was back under Vounn's command. The sight of her in Haruuc's throne room had almost been enough to make Ashi stumble.

And yet, as she sat across from Vounn before a crackling fire and the tale poured out of her, she felt the knot loosen. She'd crossed Darguun, fought bugbears and trolls, confronted an emperor with the power of five thousand years behind him, and in the end it hadn't been her sword that had turned the tide, but the power of her dragonmark and the skills she had learned—unwillingly—from Vounn. What could she have done if she'd worked with Vounn from the beginning instead of fighting her?

Unlike the Darguuls, the lady seneschal listened to the story without interrupting at all. When Ashi finished, she remained thoughtfully silent, looking into the fire. Eventually, Ashi added, "Vounn, could I stay in Rhukaan Draal a little longer before I go back to Karrlakton?"

Vounn looked up and her lips pressed together briefly before she said, "Baron Breven is already wondering why you've taken so long to return."

Ashi's eyebrows rose. "You haven't told him what I've been doing?"

"Not yet—but I think I will now. You've done well, Ashi. You've brought a great deal of honor to Deneith." A smile crossed her face. "I'm proud of you."

The praise sent unexpected warmth through her, but also a strange sense of disappointment. "I want to stay to continue my training," she said. "I want to learn more. From you."

Surprise pulled at Vounn's smile, but Ashi saw her contain it. "There's no denying you could benefit from it," she said, "but I think we have to follow our own paths now. I still have work to do here. Deneith needs you in Karrlakton. You'll find other teachers." The older woman rose. "You'll be here for a bit longer, though. I'm not sending you back until Haruuc's soldiers have cleared the roads and engaged the Gan'duur."

"Don't you mean Dagii's soldiers?" Ashi asked.

Vounn's smile twitched again. "What do you think?" She took Ashi's arm and walked her to the door. "You should have held back your frustration and kept negotiating with Dabrak Riis. A blunt demand betrays desperation."

Ashi felt the warmth in her flare up into a little of her old anger for her mentor's arrogance. She bit it back. "I know, Vounn."

"Perhaps we can use this as a case study. We can go over it and see what you might have turned to your advantage." Vounn paused, one hand on the door handle, and turned to look at her. "I'm sorry you lost your grandfather's sword," she said.

The words and her sympathy were genuine. "Thank you, Vounn," Ashi said.

The third time Ashi told the story was in writing in a formal report, written with Midian's help, to Breven d'Deneith. The fourth time was to Viceroy Pater d'Orien, at Vounn's suggestion, as a way to persuade him to carry the report to Karrlakton. The fifth and sixth times—and all the times beyond—were to the viceroys of the other dragonmarked houses and to various ambassadors to Haruuc's court over dinners as lavish as the food shortages permitted. She had Haruuc's approval to share the tale. The lhesh might have wanted the quest for the rod kept quiet in the beginning, but now that the ancient artifact was in his possession, he wanted the story of its return widely known: it only added to the legend. At his request, she also did her best to assure the uncertain emissaries that Haruuc only sought stability for his people and peaceful prosperity for Darguun.

Midian was her frequent companion at the dinners. The gnome scholar took to the attention like a cat. Tariic was often present as well, though his second-hand version of events seemed to grow in the telling. She overheard him relating to the ambassador from Aundair how her sword had been lost when it had lodged among Makka's ribs after she'd driven it through him. Haruuc's nephew, she discovered, was also passing the tale among the warlords and clan chiefs, sometimes with Dagii and Ekhaas, sometimes not. Dagii was frequently busy preparing for the raid against the Gan'duur, while Ekhaas seemed to spend most of her time trying to correct Tariic's exaggerations of their deeds.

Ashi half-suspected that Tariic was working under Haruuc's orders to turn the quest for the rod into an epic. There was one good side to his inflated stories, at least: Any hints of the power contained with the rod itself were buried under tales of the last *marhu's* command of the cavern's magic.

Chetiin and Geth escaped the madness, Chetiin because the black-clad goblin seemed to be found only when he wanted to be, Geth because he was never far from Haruuc's side. The first evening after the presentation of the rod, when they had all gathered in the small chamber in Khaar Mbar'ost, Haruuc had told him that the relationship between *shava* didn't mean that he had to stay constantly close, that *shava* did generally lead separate lives and that he was even free to leave Darguun if he wanted. Geth had chosen to stay with Haruuc, though, and Ashi was certain it was precisely so he could avoid being constantly pestered to tell his story. Not that he seemed to have a problem with other people telling it—Ashi was equally certain he was enjoying his growing reputation as a hero. Wrath was on display almost as often as the Rod of Kings.

With the promise of action against the Gan'duur at hand, the threat of unrest eased. Darguun's warlords remained in the city, and when they met, Vounn pointed out the various members of the assembly who had claimed critical shortages of food only days before but who now had an abundance to spare. Fresh supplies for the city were promised. Haruuc even expanded the *noon* dole that he had established in celebration of this newfound prosperity—tales of the Rod of Kings were beginning to filter down to the general population of Rhukaan Draal. At Haruuc's invitation and expense, *duur'kala* and common storytellers were sent out into the streets to tell legends of the emperors of Dhakaan who had once held the rod.

With his warlords behind him, Haruuc also spoke out against the Gan'duur and other rebellious clans. Sympathizers were as much a threat, he told his court, as the Gan'duur themselves. He received thunderous applause. A bugbear was found beaten on the edge of the Bloody Market. Ashi heard one story that said he was a food vendor who had tried to raise prices to take advantage of the last days of the crisis; she heard another that said he had been an associate of the Gan'duur. A day later the story had changed again and he was declared the victim of Gan'duur sympathizers. The *duur'kala* telling tales in the street brought back rumors that certain groups were getting ready to hunt for these violent sympathizers before they could strike again. Haruuc went out into the city and walked in the market, telling people that if there were sympathizers in Rhukaan Draal, they were unlikely to make any moves. He left the market surrounded by a cheering mob that followed him all the way to the gates of Khaar Mbar'ost.

Chetiin appeared in Ashi's chamber. "The bugbear owed too much money to the wrong people," he said. "It's nothing more sinister than that."

"I used my dragonmark in the assembly today," she told him. "If Haruuc was somehow tapping the power of the rod, it would have protected me. There was nothing."

"Haruuc has always been able to whip a crowd into a frenzy. People are just excited. Having an enemy creates unity."

On 22 Rhaan, less than a week after they returned with the rod, Dagii was gone again. He rode north out of Rhukaan Draal at the head of a column of soldiers almost three hundred strong—far larger, Ashi learned, than an inexperienced leader of his rank might normally command. The force was swollen, however, by troops from half a dozen clans, sent by warlords and clan chiefs eager to see the Gan'duur brought down. Most of the troops were infantry. An elite handful were Darguul cavalry, hobgoblins mounted on tigers and goblins mounted on leopards, separated from those officers mounted on horses. They left Rhukaan Draal with as much pageantry as Tariic had displayed on entering Sentinel Tower. Pipes wailed, drums throbbed.

The column marched to battle, however, not just in parade. Ashi remembered the fanciful armor that Tariic had worn when he came before House Deneith, still functional but ornate. In contrast, Dagii wore armor scarred by fighting. It wasn't the armor that he'd worn on their journey into the mountains, but something older and heavier. The only decoration it bore was the three horns of a tribex that must have been massive in life, mounted one behind each shoulder and one in the small of his back. They rose like banner poles and would mark him out in the swirl of combat, a mobile rallying point for his men.

"It's the armor of the lord of his clan," Ekhaas said beside her as they watched the troops pass from the fire-scarred walls of the House Orien compound. "Mur Talaan means 'horned shoulders.' His father wore it before him, his father before that, and back through five generations."

Ashi glanced at the *duur'kala*. Before Dagii had ridden to the head of the column, she'd seen her approach and pass a small casket up to him. A casket that flashed in the afternoon sun like gold and iron. "Was that the reliquary of Duural Rhuvet you gave him?" she asked. "The one you took from the tower in Karrlakton?"

Ekhaas's ears bent. "I admire Dagii, but he will need inspiration if he's to win this battle," she said stiffly.

"I would have thought it had already vanished into the vaults of Volaar Draal."

"I haven't had a chance to present it to Senen Dhakaan yet. We left so soon after we arrived from Karrlakton, and we've been so busy since we returned."

Ekhaas's voice remained level, but a flush crept into her face. Ashi raised an eyebrow. Ekhaas scowled and turned away. Holding back a laugh, Ashi looked along the street below to where Haruuc waited on horseback at the foot of the bridge across the Ghaal River, his two *shava* flanking him. Dagii stopped and thumped a fist against his chest in salute. The lhesh said something, and Dagii sat up straight for a moment, then nodded deeply and saluted again. At a glance from Haruuc, Vanii urged his horse forward to stand beside Dagii's. The two of them saluted in unison and rode on, leaving Haruuc with only Geth behind him.

Ekhaas, it seemed, had not been the only one who thought Dagii might need guidance in the battle to come.

A week after Dagii had led his soldiers away to the north, it was Ashi's turn to leave.

Messenger falcons brought word that the new *lhevk-rhu*

had engaged the Gan'duur, bottling Keraal up in his primary stronghold. Raiders who had stayed outside the walls to harry the attackers had been captured in a clever deception devised by Dagii. The roads were clear and safe. An Orien caravan, heavily guarded by Deneith mercenaries, was leaving Rhukaan Draal, and Ashi would ride with it back through Marguul Pass to Sterngate and the lightning rail.

All of her friends—except Dagii, of course—came to the House Orien compound to say good-bye to her, and even Dagii had managed to send a message with a falcon. Geth brought it and another from Haruuc expressing once more his thanks and the thanks of Darguun.

Chetiin emerged from the shadows to offer her a solemn good-bye. Midian tried to be somber as well but didn't succeed. Until a few days before, it had seemed that he might be riding out with the same caravan, but the gnome had gone to Haruuc and begged a favor. By the grace of the lhesh, he would be allowed to remain for a few more months and venture into the south of Darguun to pursue a research opportunity—provided that he shared what he found with Haruuc as well as with the Library of Korranberg.

That decision didn't please Haruuc's newest allies. The Kech Volaar had decided to formalize the alliance that had led to the discovery of the rod and had sent a message that they would swear allegiance to the lhesh. Their leaders, the *duur'kala* Tuura Dhakaan and a warlord Kurac Thaar, would travel to Rhukaan Draal. The announcement that Midian would be allowed to enter Dhakaani ruins provoked an angry outburst from Senen, but in the face of an outpouring of public enthusiasm for Haruuc and a surge in interest in the great tales and achievements of ancient Dhakaan, the Kech Volaar objections were like the sting of a mosquito. Other modern Dhakaani clans—the militaristic Kech Shaarat, the shadowy Kech Nasaar—were also making hints at allegiance, and Haruuc was listening. If the Kech Volaar wanted a position as the first of the Dhakaani clans to ally with Haruuc, they didn't dare be too loud with their objections to a single gnome scholar.

The increased activity between the lhesh and the Kech

Volaar had also kept Ekhaas busy. Senen had drafted her as an aide. She would be remaining in Rhukaan Draal, of course—unless Senen dispatched her to Volaar Draal. The ambassador seemed to regard the position as an honored reward. Ashi wasn't certain Ekhaas felt the same way about it, but the *duur'kala* held her tongue. When the time came for them to say their good-byes, she offered Ashi a hug that was almost human. She also offered her a sword, not a heavy, notched hobgoblin blade but a slim, double-edged human sword.

"Magewrought in Cyre before the end of the Last War," Ekhaas said as Ashi slid the weapon out to examine it. "Not as good as your honor blade, but still good. It's the least I can do after dragging you out of Karrlakton."

"You didn't drag me out, Ekhaas. If you hadn't let me come, I would have stowed away on your ship." Ashi gave her another hug, then turned to the last of her friends still waiting for her.

Geth smiled at her. He looked as reputable as she had ever seen him, his thick hair brushed and pulled back, his clothes clean and untorn. He didn't wear the armband of red cords—a *shava* wasn't a servant—but there was a heavy ring with the lhesh's crest on his finger. "What about you?" Ashi asked him. "How long will you be staying?"

"How do you know I won't stay?"

"Because I know you."

He laughed. "I'll stay until the fighting's over at least. All this standing around while people cheer Haruuc and talk about putting up statues in his honor is starting to bore me. There's a letter to Singe and Dandra in the post with this caravan, but I want to get back and rub it in Singe's face personally."

"You accepted Haruuc's invitation to be his *shava* so you could make Singe jealous?" said Ekhaas. There was shock in her eyes.

"No!" Geth said. "Well, maybe a bit, but what was I supposed to do? It's not the sort of offer you turn down."

"Why did you do it, then?" asked Ashi. "It wasn't exactly what I would have expected from you, either."

The shifter looked from her to Ekhaas, then dropped his voice. "It was Wrath," he said. Ekhaas's ears rose. Geth spread his hands.

"Ever since you woke it, sometimes I get the feeling that I should do certain things. Like when I charged back to stop the trolls. Wrath wants me to be a hero, and it pushes me to do things a hero would do."

Ashi raised her eyebrows and glanced at Ekhaas. Before they'd entered the shrine of the Uura Odaarii, the *duur'kala* had asked her if Geth had seemed more impetuous than usual. "Wrath takes control of you?"

"Control? No. But it . . . pushes me. Puts the right ideas in my head. During the presentation of the rod, it showed me how a hero would answer Haruuc—it even gave me the right words to say."

"I noticed that your Goblin improved suddenly," said Ekhaas.

"I don't think Wrath can give me the right words all the time." Geth's hand slipped down to grip the sword's hilt. "Only when it's important. It wants me to live up to the legacy of the heroes of the name of Kuun. To tell you the truth, I kind of like it. It's almost like having you whispering stories in my ear, Ekhaas. It's inspiring."

"Taruuzh created Aram to represent the inspiration heroes provided for the people," Ekhaas said. She frowned. "Maybe it provided inspiration to the line of Kuun as well. Just be careful, Geth."

"I'm not going to doing anything stupid." He hugged Ekhaas as well. "I'll come see you in Karrlakton."

"I'll watch for you," she said.

Tariic and Vounn were waiting, too. Haruuc's nephew bowed. "Swift travel and great glory, Ashi d'Deneith. Darguun will remember you. I only regret I never saw you perform the sword dance."

Ashi returned his bow with perfect form. "You'll have to visit House Deneith again, Tariic of Rhukaan Taash," she told him.

Tariic straightened up and looked at Vounn. "She has clearly learned from you," he said with a smile.

Vounn acknowledged the compliment with a nod, then turned to Ashi and held out her scarf. "You left this in your chamber," she said.

"I know," said Ashi. "I don't think I need it." She felt her mentor's gaze trace the pattern of the dragonmark over her face and held her head up a little higher. "I'm not going to hide anymore. Let people think what they will."

"In Rhukaan Draal or among the Five Nations maybe, but on the road to Sterngate?" Vounn asked. "You've made a reputation for yourself now, Ashi. If there are bandits on the road, you'll be a target."

"And I'll fight them. I've done it twice before. The bandits of Darguun aren't that terrifying."

She kept her voice light, trying to ease Vounn's reaction, but the expression that creased the older woman's forehead wasn't anger—it was confusion. "Twice?"

"The Gan'duur raiders on the journey from Sterngate and a pack on the way back north with the rod."

Vounn's eyes narrowed, and Ashi realized that her reports to her had focused only on retrieving the rod. They had told Haruuc, but Vounn hadn't been in the small chamber when they told their story.

"It was nothing, Vounn," she added quickly. "They were just a gang of desperate thugs along the road a couple of days south of Rhukaan Draal. We saw some locals and they said the gang had been making trouble in the area for a couple of weeks."

Vounn didn't look relieved. "Were they Gan'duur?"

"We thought of that," said Geth. "We checked their bags to see but it looks like they came from Rhukaan Draal. The locals thought they must have fled south to avoid being mistaken for Gan'duur raiders by Haruuc's men."

"But they attacked you?"

"I said they were desperate," Ashi pointed out.

"Could they have been waiting for you?"

"How could they have been? Why would they wait for me—?"

Vounn's lips pressed together. "Not just you, Ashi. All of you." She glanced at Ekhaas and Geth, Chetiin and Midian.

Chetiin's ears twitched. "It is possible," the goblin admitted. "But Ashi is right. Why would they be waiting for us? Even if they were Gan'duur, they wouldn't have known when we'd return or even if we'd come back the same way we left."

"That was why they were waiting."

"Vounn, no one outside of Haruuc's circle knew of the mission," Tariic said. "It can only have been a coincidence."

Vounn looked at Haruuc's nephew, then smiled and nodded. "You may be right. The attempted abduction has left me on edge." She stepped forward to embrace Ashi—and whisper in her ear, "By the honor of our House, be careful until you're out of Darguun."

Ashi felt unease wrap around her heart. "What's wrong, Vounn?"

"Maybe nothing. Just be cautious." She stood back again, the smile still on her face, but Ashi couldn't help noticing that she no longer stood quite as close to Tariic as she had.

Not so long ago, Ashi might have pressed her and demanded to know what she was keeping back. Part of her wanted to, but another part urged her to respect Vounn's wishes. If her teacher didn't want to say anything more, there had to be a reason. Ashi kept her mouth closed, nodded to Vounn, took one last look at her friends, then turned to mount her horse. The caravan was waiting for her. The caravan master threw a suffering look at her and raised a horn to his lips, blowing a sharp note.

"Orien caravan," he bellowed, "move ou—"

"Hold!" A goblin runner in the uniform of Haruuc's guard raced through the gates of the compound, waving his arms and gasping for breath. "Lhesh Haruuc declares the roads closed!"

The caravan master's face turned as red as the goblin's uniform, and he snatched at a scroll the runner offered to him. The noise in the compound rose at the sudden delay. The goblin, however, turned around as if searching for something more and his gaze landed on Geth. He stumbled over to him. "*Shava,* Lhesh Haruuc calls you to Khaar Mbar'ost immediately!"

Geth stiffened, and his eyes opened wide, but before he could say anything the caravan master's voice rose in another bellow. "Someone fetch the viceroy! He needs to see this. Kol Korran's golden bath—closing the roads for mourning?"

It was as if the din of the compound suddenly faded into the distance. Mourning, Ashi thought. Who died?

Ekhaas, her face suddenly gray, spoke the name that none of them wanted to hear. "Dagii."

Then the *duur'kala* was sprinting across the compound to where she and the others had left their horses. Geth would have run after her, but Vounn grabbed his arm.

"I'm going with you," she said. The shifter nodded sharply and pulled away.

Vounn looked to Ashi. "Wait here until we know what's going on."

"He was my friend, Vounn!"

Vounn's faced softened slightly. "I know, but I want you out of Darguun. If the chance comes to leave, I want you to take it."

"Why?" Ashi asked. "Vounn, what's wrong?"

But Vounn was already hurrying after Geth and Ekhaas, and Tariic along with her. In only moments all four were galloping out of the compound in a cloud of Rhukaan Draal's yellow dust.

CHAPTER TWENTY-EIGHT

Haruuc's fortress was a hub of chaos. Messengers ran in and out. Soldiers prowled the courtyard. Inside, small groups of warlords came together, split apart, and reformed as they shared rumors. Geth caught snatches of their words, wild speculations for the most part: the Gan'duur were defeated, Keraal had broken through Dagii's line and escaped, Breland was attacking the northern border, raiding parties of Valenar elves had appeared to pillage the country. Most of the warlords turned to look as Geth hurried past with Ekhaas, Vounn, and Tariic in his wake, but none tried to stop him. They respected the status of *shava* that Haruuc had bestowed on him, but they didn't fully trust him.

Some tried to hail Tariic, but Haruuc's nephew shook his head and shrugged. "We don't know anything!" he called back to them.

Just outside the antechamber of the throne room, Munta joined them, his belly rolling as he walked. "Have you been summoned?" he asked Geth.

The shifter nodded.

Munta grunted, "Did he tell you anything?"

"No, but we were at the Orien compound and he sent a message to them that the roads were closed for mourning."

Munta's ears rose. *"Maabet."* He looked at the others. Tariic just shrugged again. Ekhaas gave no reaction at all.

Vounn's eyes darted to Tariic, however, and Geth saw her lean a little toward Munta as they walked. He didn't catch what she said, but Munta gave another grunt. "It will need to wait until later, Vounn," he said softly.

A small crowd stirred in the antechamber, mostly waiting messengers, but also a few warlords and clan chiefs being kept back by guards. On the stairs up to the throne room, Razu, Haruuc's old mistress of rituals, waited with more guards. Behind her was something Geth had never seen before—a titanic slab of dark wood that filled the entrance to the throne room and extended up into the ceiling. A wall that could be raised and lowered when Haruuc wanted privacy in the throne room, he guessed. It had been carved with scenes of combat in a vast landscape. Geth thought he recognized some of the most famous battles of Darguun's birth, but there was no chance to examine the wooden wall closely. Munta mounted the steps to Razu.

"We are summoned," he said.

"Enter," the thin hobgoblin woman told him. She pointed to a pair of doors set flush into the wood. "And you, *shava*. The rest must wait outside."

"What?" Tariic said. "I need to see my uncle!"

"I know who was summoned and who was not," Razu said. "The lhesh's orders are clear. Only those he summoned are allowed to enter."

The guards around her closed their ranks. Tariic glowered but stepped back. Ekhaas caught Geth's arm. "Find out what you can," she said. Geth nodded and followed Munta up the steps and through the carved doors.

The noise of the antechamber vanished with the closing of the doors. The throne room was as still as the fortress had been chaotic. The light that filled it was cold and gray—the great windows showed a sky filled with heavy clouds, and beneath them Haruuc sat brooding on his throne, the Rod of Kings in one hand.

"Haruuc!" Munta called as they strode down the aisle. "What's going on?"

Haruuc's answer was to flick a piece of tightly curled paper, the scroll of a messenger falcon, at them. Munta caught it and scanned the lines written there. His ears rose, then sagged. He passed the scroll to Geth.

It was short but written in the dark, angular runes of Goblin. He couldn't read it. Unless . . .

He grasped Wrath's hilt and implored silently, *Show me.*

The ancient sword stirred and the runes became as clear in his mind as if someone had spoken the message aloud.

To Lhesh *Haruuc Shaarat'kor—*

The Gan'duur are broken. Keraal is my prisoner along with many of his warriors, but victory came at a price. Vanii of Ja'aram fell in the final battle.

I return to Rhukaan Draal with his body that he may be given the honors due him.

—Dagii of Mur Talaan

Relief opened inside him. The mourning wasn't for Dagii. Geth lowered the message and looked up at Haruuc. "I'm sorry."

Haruuc's ears flicked forward, and he met Geth's eyes for the first time. "A hobgoblin doesn't express sympathy for the death of a friend. A hobgoblin asks what he can do."

"Then what can I do?"

"You can stand with me, last of my *shava.*" Haruuc bared his teeth. "And you can be unoffended when I say I wish I'd sent you against the Gan'duur instead of Vanii!"

The pain in Haruuc's voice was naked. Geth bent his head. "I lost someone close to me in battle," he said. "I understand."

"Do you? It's different for *shava.*"

Geth clenched his jaw and tried to hold his temper in check. "Not so different, I think."

Munta raised his voice, interrupting quickly. "What must be done, Haruuc? We've heard that you've closed the roads, but this is a time of victory as well as mourning. How will people celebrate the triumph over the Gan'duur if they can't get into Rhukaan Draal?"

"Cho." Haruuc sat back on his throne. He stared out into the empty chamber with cold eyes. "First, we mourn, then we celebrate. For five days, no one is to travel except under my authority. No new fires are to be lit in Rhukaan Draal. At dawn and dusk, the streets

will be empty—these will be the times of mourning. Munta, I place the enforcement of these laws in your hands."

The old warlord looked startled. "Haruuc, aren't the terms harsh? That's the kind of mourning performed in a clan stronghold on the death of a warlord. You can't mean for all of Rhukaan Draal to follow those terms."

Haruuc just turned his cold eyes on him.

Munta nodded. *"Mazo,"* he said, "but it exceeds the mourning for Fenic and Haluun. Did you love your other *shava* any less?"

"Fenic and Haluun died in different times," Haruuc said. "I must be strong. I must show my power. If I could have done this for them, Munta, I would have." He leaned his head back and, after a moment's silence, added, "The people may have fire. But the punishment for failing to observe mourning at dawn and dusk is a public whipping. If the people love me as they say they do, they will mourn with me." He looked at Geth. "Your task will be to organize the games."

"Games?" Geth asked.

"Contests of strength and skill. Tales from *duur'kala*. Fights between gladiators. Razu can help you with the details. One day of games for Vanii, three days for victory over the Gan'duur. *Don't look at me like that, Munta!"* Haruuc's voice rose to a sudden roar, and Munta, who had been about to speak, closed his mouth. "It is within my right! These will be games to remember. I want them to be talked about ten—no, twenty years from now. This is my gift to the people."

"Lhesh," Munta said humbly, "they will cost money. There are still food shortages. We still need to buy grain."

"There is money enough." Haruuc pointed at Geth. "Speak with Senen Dhakaan. Ask her about the games held in the time of the empire. Make me proud, *shava."*

Geth swallowed and bent his head. "I will."

At the back of the throne room, the carved door opened again to admit a thin, nervous hobgoblin who looked more like a merchant than a warlord. Haruuc's ears went back, and he gestured for the hobgoblin to come forward. "Iizan of Ghaal Sehn, join us. The Ghaal Sehn hold the territory on the west side of the Orien trade road from the Gathering Stone to Rhukaan Draal?"

Iizan dropped down to his knees. "We do, lhesh."

"And there is a forest in your territory, not too far from the road?"

"There is, lhesh. A small one."

Haruuc nodded. "Good. Take the slaves from your fields—"

A flush sprang up in Iizan's face. "The Ghaal Sehn no longer keep slaves, Lhesh Haruuc!" he said. "We followed your example and freed them."

The lhesh stood and stepped down from his throne to stand over the kneeling hobgoblin. "I didn't ask if you have slaves, Iizan! I know that you do. I know that seven of ten warlords who swear they follow my example still keep slaves in secret!"

He seized a handful of Iizan's hair and dragged him to his feet so sharply that Iizan didn't have a chance to cry out. "I want you to take the slaves from your field and raze that forest. Take the strongest trees, strip them of leaves and small branches, and stand them along the trade road, one pair every two leagues from the Gathering Stone to the bridge over the Ghaal River. This will be done within three days, in time for the return of the soldiers from the north. You will have aid—the slaves of neighboring clans will be sent to you." He looked into Iizan's face as if searching for something, then flung the warlord away. "Do this and you will be rewarded. Do you understand, Iizan?"

"*Mazo*, lhesh," Iizan choked.

Haruuc gestured with the Rod of Kings, dismissing him, and the warlord fled. Geth stared at Haruuc as he returned to his throne. The image of a tree, bare of all but the strongest branches rose up in his imagination. He'd seen a shape like that before. From the expression on Munta's face, he knew the old warlord recognized it as well.

Ekhaas had once told him that one of the greatest creations of Taruuzh, the ancient *dashoor* who had forged the Sword of Heroes and the Rod of Kings, had been a device of execution. In the time of Dhakaan, his device had spread to every city in the empire. The secret of making them had been lost in the Desperate Times after the empire's fall, but hobgoblins of all clans, she'd said, still emulated their use in ending the lives of criminals and traitors.

Geth wet his lips and looked up at Haruuc. "Grieving trees?" he asked. His voice sounded thin in the emptiness of the throne room. "You're lining the road to Rhukaan Draal with *grieving trees?"*

"The Gan'duur must be punished." Haruuc's face was hard.

Munta actually seemed frail with worry. "Haruuc, what will the Five Nations and the dragonmarked houses say? This is too much."

"You have your instructions, Munta," Haruuc said. "So does Iizan. Dagii's instructions have been dispatched to him."

"But the Five Nations—"

"This is no concern of theirs!" Haruuc's voice rose again. "It is a matter for Darguun and Darguun alone. Our traditions are as old as our claim on this land, and both are older than the Five Nations. Go and do your duty, Munta. Let Rhukaan Draal know whom it mourns."

There was a finality in his voice that would accept no further argument. The warlord of the Gantii Vus nodded stiffly, turned, and walked back up the long length of the throne room to the carved doors. Geth was left facing Haruuc alone. After a long moment, he asked, "Can I go too?"

"No. Stay. I'm expecting one more visitor, and I want you here as witness to one of the most sacred duties of a *shava."* Haruuc gestured behind himself. "Stand at my shoulder. Where Vanii stood."

Geth stepped up onto the dais and moved behind Haruuc. The lhesh lapsed into silence. Anger and disgust whirled in Geth's mind. Organizing funerary games in memory of Vanii and to commemorate victory over a rebellion—that was something he could deal with. There was nothing he could object to except the task itself. The games even sounded like fun, but now they were irrevocably tainted by the thought of so many grieving trees and the victims they would claim.

"You know why I have to do this, don't you?" Haruuc said without turning around.

"No," Geth growled. "I don't."

"I have to show the other warlords what happens to rebels. I have to remind them of who I am—of what the lhesh is. It's ironic that in defeating the Gan'duur, I have no choice but to become the bloody tyrant they wanted me to be. Our culture is not merciful, Geth. It does not favor forgiveness. Humans have difficulty understanding that. I thought a shifter might." He paused, then added, "When your friend died in battle, what did you do?"

"I put my sword through the belly of the man who killed him," Geth said. "Blood paid for blood spilled."

"You killed him."

Geth bared his teeth. "*I* killed him. I didn't order someone else to hang him on a tree."

"Is it so different from ordering soldiers into battle? People kill and die at the command of rulers all the time," said Haruuc. "Don't think I wouldn't do it myself. When I read Dagii's message, I wanted to ride north and put a sword through Keraal—although, of course, I don't know it was Keraal who struck Vanii down. I wanted to put a sword through Dagii for letting Vanii die. I even wanted to put a sword through myself for sending him up there." He let out a slow breath. "But this isn't about Vanii, anymore. It's not even about me. It's about Darguun, just like retrieving the rod was."

He rapped the byeshk shaft on the arm of his throne, and the heavy clang echoed in the room. "That's the doom of kings, Geth. We're men and women when we take the throne, but we lose ourselves to our people. We stop being individuals and become nations. And mark my words"—he twisted around to meet Geth's eyes—"the nation of Darguun will not cry for the Gan'duur. It will dance under the grieving trees. It would dance if I hung on the tree. Darguun wants blood. The people always want blood."

"Find another way to give it to them."

Haruuc's ears lay back. "But I am Darguun," he said slowly. "I am one of the people."

The hair on Geth's arms and the back of his neck rose. He felt, for a moment, as if he was looking at Haruuc and all hobgoblins for the first time. Wide face, flat nose, mobile ears, sharp teeth—goblins were no more human than he was. Less, because his ancestors had been human once upon a time. The ancestors of the goblin races had always been goblins. But he understood what

Haruuc meant. He had felt it himself, a discomfort in the sprawling cities of humans, a predator's instinct to see crowds as either prey or threat.

But there had never been any question of giving in to those instincts. Shifters knew they were wrong. Any shifter who did give in was no better than an animal. Looking into Haruuc's eyes, he knew it would be a mistake—it had been a mistake—to assume the same of goblins. He thought of a hundred little things about Ekhaas or Chetiin or the heroes of Kuun that Wrath remembered. How they ate. How they moved. How they spoke—so many ways to express honor and hierarchy, so many ways to say, "Thank you," but no words, he realized abruptly, for, "You're welcome."

A goblin that gave in to his instincts was no animal. He was simply a goblin.

Suddenly, Geth felt like a tamed dog. He struggled to find something else to say, some other argument to put before Haruuc. "Think of the good of Darguun then," he said. "Munta was right. The other nations of Khorvaire won't like this."

"And what will they do? For the sake of Darguun, I became a sheep. Now for the sake of Darguun, I must be a wolf again—and the sheep should be wary."

The carved doors opened again. This time Razu stepped through. "Rekseen of Ja'aram comes in answer to Lhesh Haruuc Shaarat'kor's summons."

Another hobgoblin woman entered, and Razu stepped out, closing the door behind her. Rekseen of Ja'aram wore the armor of a warrior and, although many years younger than he had been, bore a strong resemblance to Vanii. As she walked down the aisle of the throne room, Haruuc spoke quietly over his shoulder. There was grief in his voice again, existing alongside the craving for blood with no hint of contradiction.

"The most sacred duty of a *shava,*" he said, "has always been to take charge of his brother's affairs when he dies and to carry news of his death. Our every tradition respects it. Vanii's death serves Darguun now, but in this at least I can serve him. The grieving trees are not your concern, Geth. You've spoken as a *shava* should. Now organize the games as I've asked—and make sure she has good seats." He rose from his throne, set down the Rod of Kings, and faced the warrior woman. "Rekseen of Ja'aram, I have news of your uncle."

The time of mourning passed. Geth spent the next five days walking with a knife in his gut. Word of the funerary games to come and of the forest that grew along the road to the Gathering Stone spread in Rhukaan Draal. Just as Haruuc had predicted, the people of Darguun greeted both with eager anticipation.

He organized the games with a kind of numb detachment. In truth, Razu did most of the work for him—Haruuc's throne room remained sealed and the lhesh in isolation, so there was little else for the mistress of ceremonies to do. Geth approved her suggestions without much thought. He wasn't sure what else there was for him to do. He felt helpless and not at all heroic, in spite of a sense of approval from Wrath. He suspected that only came because he was fulfilling his duties as a *shava*.

Ekhaas and Chetiin were no help. They came to see him the first day, and he poured his emotions out to them—at least as much as he could without offending them. Both the *duur'kala* and the *shaarat'khesh* elder offered consolation, but no condemnation for Haruuc's actions. "What did you think he would do, Geth?" Ekhaas asked. "Keraal didn't act alone. All of the Gan'duur warriors were with him. At least Haruuc's not using the rod."

"Would you have done it?" Geth asked her bluntly.

Her mouth opened and closed, but she finally said, "Tales of the Empire of Dhakaan speak of even harsher actions."

"So you would have done it."

Ekhaas's ears went back flat.

"It's the right response for the situation," Chetiin said. "I wouldn't have expected it from Haruuc, but it's what a strong ruler should have done. The warlords like it. Haruuc has greater support now than in the first years of his rule."

If the Darguul warlords liked Haruuc's actions, reaction from the representatives of the other nations of Khorvaire and the dragonmarked houses was exactly what Munta had said it would be. Razu's main distraction from helping Geth plan the games was dealing with the formal messages of disapproval that arrived at Khaar Mbar'ost from ambassadors and viceroys. Most urged mercy. House Orien threatened action if Haruuc hung his victims along the trade road. First Ashi, stuck in Rhukaan Draal while the roads were closed, and then Vounn tried to contact Geth—guessing at what they wanted, he turned them away with shame and took to avoiding them.

Midian wasn't so easy to get rid of. The gnome turned up in Geth's chamber one morning. "You've got messengers crossing Darguun lining up fighters and strong men. Get me out of here. I've got supplies ready to go. I've got guards hired and costing me money every day. I want to be on the road!"

"Wait two more days," Geth said. "You can leave then."

"With every goblin in Darguun trying to get into the city for these games of yours? No, thank you. I want to go before they come. Word about the games was spreading across the country as soon as they were announced." Midian's mouth twisted. "Just like word is spreading that Dagii reached the Gathering Stone yesterday and is traveling south along the trade road now."

A messenger falcon had come to Khaar Mbar'ost at dawn with the news that the grim march had begun. The Gan'duur were dying. Dagii's arrival in Rhukaan Draal would coincide with the end of the mourning period. Geth hung his head and closed his eyes. "Go to Munta," he said. "Tell him I said he should give you a pass out of the city."

Midian gave a sigh of relief. "Thank you, Geth."

Geth clenched his teeth. "You're welcome."

The fifth day of mourning came. The games that would commemorate Vanii's death and the defeat of the Gan'duur were ready. Spectators and participants would begin to arrive the next day and for four days after that, the fields burned by the Gan'duur south of Rhukaan Draal would become the site of a celebration that would be talked about in ten—no, twenty years. "You've done well, Geth," said Haruuc as his court gathered at dusk on the bridge over to the Ghaal River to wait for Dagii's arrival.

"Razu did well, lhesh. She knew what needed to be done." Geth looked across the crowd gathered on the crest of the bridge. The entire court had turned out—warlords, clan chiefs, and councilors. The sun's last rays struck reflections from polished armor, threads of gold, and rich jewelry. Haruuc wore ornate armor edged with the claws of great cats polished like gems. The Rod of Kings shone in his grasp, twilight metal in the twilight of the day.

Geth curled his fist inside his great gauntlet. He had dressed in his best—clean pants, a good white shirt, and a fitted leather vest purchased in Rhukaan Draal's markets—just as the other members of the court had, but by comparison he was a shadow. He felt like a shadow too. The Darguuls were filled with an excitement he didn't feel at all. He drew a breath and said, "Haruuc, I'm leaving when the games are finished."

Haruuc looked at him for a moment, then turned away to watch the road again. "It is your choice, but you judge me harshly, *shava*. I do what must be done."

Geth didn't have anything else he could say to that. He turned away.

Haruuc caught his arm. "I want you at my side when Dagii returns."

"I'll be back," Geth said tersely, pulling his arm free and slipping into the crowd. Warlords called to him. The mistrust they'd shown him only days before seemed to have vanished as if organizing the funerary games had suddenly made him worthy of attention. Geth ignored them all and pushed to the other side of the bridge.

The southern bank of the Ghaal and both sides of the way through Rhukaan Draal were filled with the ordinary folk of the city, all of them eager for a glimpse of what was to come. Haruuc and he had both been wrong about one thing: It wasn't just the goblins who wanted blood. The humans, elves, dwarves, and halflings who had found a home in Rhukaan Draal were a part of the howling crowd as well.

They were represented on the bridge, too, but Geth couldn't have called the representatives of the dragonmarked houses and the Five Nations eager for what was to come. They stood at the back of Haruuc's assembled court, dressed as well as any hobgoblin but looking far more somber. None of them wanted to be there, he guessed, but none of them wanted to be seen to have stayed away, either.

"You!" Hands grabbed him roughly and turned him around. Ashi glared at him. She was dressed as a lady of Deneith and the effect was startling. Her voice, however, was as rough as ever. "You've been hard to talk to lately, Geth!"

"Hush." Vounn appeared on Ashi's other side to draw both her and Geth back against the rail of the bridge. Ashi didn't release her grip on Geth's arms, though.

"What do you think you're doing, shutting yourself away?" she snarled at him. "I've been worried about you."

"Let me go, Ashi."

"No." Her eyes searched his. "Why have you been avoiding me?"

"You wanted me to get you out of Rhukaan Draal, didn't you?" He looked away. "I couldn't have done that. I didn't want you to ask."

Ashi slapped him. "Blood in your mouth! You got Midian out, didn't you? That wasn't why I wanted to talk to you at all! Ekhaas said you were angry at what Haruuc was doing. I wanted to know if you needed to talk about it."

"You . . ." Geth stared at her.

"Rond betch, Geth, sometimes you need a friend to talk to when you're stuck in a situation that makes you angry. I know that." She didn't look at Vounn, but Geth knew exactly what she was talking about. Vounn could probably guess as well. Her lips pressed together, but she said nothing. Ashi's eyebrows drew together. "How are you feeling now?"

"Helpless." The word slipped out before he even thought about it. He grimaced. "This is wrong, Ashi, but there's nothing I can do to stop it. Haruuc won't listen to me or to Munta. He doesn't even care what the powers outside of Darguun think."

"He knows there's not much we can do," said Vounn coolly. It earned her a glare from Ashi, but the lady seneschal ignored her. "The kings and queens of other nations can make sanctions, the dragonmarked houses can take economic action, but ultimately it's a matter internal to Darguun. And one that needed to be dealt with. If we interfere too much, we weaken Haruuc, and the unity he built in Darguun disappears."

Geth glowered at her. "And you wanted to talk to me so I'd feel better?"

Vounn's lips pressed together again. "That wasn't why I wanted to talk to you."

"Wait—Vounn?" Ashi looked from one of them to the other. "You were trying to talk to Geth too?"

"You didn't know?" Geth asked her.

"Be quiet, both of you." Vounn turned so that her back was to the crowd on the bridge and her face hidden from anyone who might be watching them. "Geth, do you remember that I tried to talk to Munta the day Haruuc closed the roads?"

He nodded but she didn't wait for a response.

"I've been trying to talk to him or to Haruuc for the last five days. They wouldn't see me. You were a third choice. Someone needs to get a message to Haruuc. I don't think Keraal was the only one plotting against him. I don't think Keraal was the one who had the fires started in Rhukaan Draal or tried to have me kidnapped."

"What?"

Vounn grabbed his hand and squeezed it tight, her fingernails digging into his flesh. "Keep your voice down! I don't have any proof. While you were away, I overheard Tariic talking to Daavn of the Marhaan. Daavn got Tariic to tell him where you'd gone. Tariic lied when he said no one outside of Haruuc's circle knew about your mission. Daavn knew you rode to the southwest on a mission for Haruuc."

"What if he did?"

"Ashi says you were attacked by desperate bandits on your return journey. What if there was no desperation in that attack? She said locals told you the bandits had come south from Rhukaan Draal a couple of weeks before. What if they'd been hired to wait along the road for your return?"

Geth frowned. "That's risky. No one could have known we'd come back that way."

"Call it a calculated risk. Based on what Tariic told Daavn, you were most likely to return to Rhukaan Draal the same way you had left." Vounn's grip tightened. "The fires in Rhukaan Draal were set by locals hired by a masked hobgoblin. The changeling who tried to kidnap me was hired in Rhukaan Draal by the same person. We assumed it was Keraal. If the bandits were hired in Rhukaan Draal, too, that changes things. It's possible Keraal might have found out about your mission for Haruuc, but Daavn definitely knew about it—and he's no friend of Haruuc's."

"It's a thin argument," Ashi said. "It's all suspicion."

"But Haruuc needs to know. Haruuc or someone who can be trusted."

"What about Tariic?" asked Geth. "If Daavn was using him for information, he should know."

Vounn shook her head. "You haven't been paying attention in court." She looked around, then nodded toward the crest of the bridge.

Tariic stood with Daavn, laughing heartily.

"Tariic's been making allies among the warlords," Vounn said. "He's expecting Haruuc to name him as his heir. Since the last assembly of warlords, Daavn has become one of his closest friends. They're not often apart." She turned back to Geth. "I don't think he'd believe me. You have to tell Haruuc. Daavn needs to be investigated."

"I—" Geth stared at her, then shook his head. "No. I can't."

"Geth!" Vounn hissed. "This is serious! If I'm right, Daavn is a threat."

"And if I tell Haruuc your suspicions, what do you think he'll do? He'll send Dagii after the Marhaan and the warriors of another clan will hang on the grieving trees."

Ashi's eyes opened wide. "Blood in your mouth! He wouldn't do that."

"Right now, I think he would."

Somewhere in the distance, a horn wailed, rising and falling in the dusk like the scream of a hunting cat. A murmur ran through the gathered warlords, and they all turned to look along the road to the north.

"That's the signal from Dagii," said Geth. "He's close. I have to go." He pulled Vounn's hand from his. "I'll tell Munta. He'll know what to do." He looked at Ashi. "If you're staying in Rhukaan Draal until after the games, we'll be able to talk on the road."

"You're leaving?"

Geth nodded, then turned and pushed his way back to where Haruuc stood, now at the front of the crowd. The lhesh barely gave him a glance as he took up his position at his shoulder.

The column of Dagii's soldiers was still just a cloud of dust on the other side of a hill in the road, but Geth could already hear the rattle of arm and treading of feet. There was another sound, too—the screaming and crying of dozens of voices. "What's that?" he asked Haruuc.

"The women and children of what was once Gan'duur," said the lhesh. "The Bloody Market will be busy tomorrow."

"You're selling them as slaves? Haruuc—"

Haruuc looked over his shoulder, his ears back against his head. "They are alive. Will you complain about that?"

Geth closed his mouth.

There was movement at the top of the hill. Not the soldiers, but a cart drawn by a pair of muscular tribex. Sound on the bridge died. Three hobgoblins crouched in the cart. Two more hobgoblins in dirty and bloodstained tunics rode on the tribex, guiding them with switches. Near the foot of the bridge, the last pair of grieving trees waited, naked as if winter had come early. Sap still oozed from the cut wood. The carters stopped their team between the two trees and swung to the ground. One took a stout ladder from the side of the cart and set it against a tree, while the other, moving with a slight limp, went to the back of the cart and hauled out one of the prisoners. It seemed as if the man was too weak to walk on his own. The carter slung him over his shoulder and mounted the ladder as the other held it steady. With a groan that was audible from the bridge, he pushed the prisoner into the branches of the tree.

His groan was met with a cheer from among the warlords, a cheer repeated as the carter produced rope and lashed the prisoner into place. On the far bank of the Ghaal, the people of the city must have realized something was happening. They began to cheer as well.

Blood stained the trunk of the grieving tree in a long, curling thread. *"Maabet,"* someone roared. "He's bleeding, he'll die too fast—don't you know your job?"

Another shout came out of the crowd. "Move, *taat!* Make way for honorable warriors!"

The carter wouldn't be hurried, though. With slow and weary movements, he fetched another prisoner and hung him in the last tree, binding him fast. This time, the prisoner looked like he might already be dead. There was a chorus of disappointment from Haruuc's court. The carter ignored them, dismissing his assistant with a salute. The second man ran back along the road to where the soldiers were now coming over the hill.

"You've still got one to hang!" It was Tariic, standing on Haruuc's other side. "Put him up and get out of the way."

The carter only took hold of the halter of one of the tribex and led his team forward onto the bridge. Geth saw Haruuc's ears flick in annoyance.

"Do your duty and get out of the way, soldier!" Haruuc called down.

The carter raised his head. "I do my duty, lhesh," he called, and Geth finally recognized the haunted face under the dirt and sweat. It was Dagii. The crowd on the bridge fell silent. In the silence, Geth heard a gasp. He looked and saw Ekhaas standing nearby with Senen Dhakaan. Her eyes were on Dagii. The cart creaked to a stop and Dagii put his fist to his chest in a salute. His hands were blistered and torn, caked with filth and blood. They hadn't gotten that way, Geth realized, from placing just two prisoners into trees.

Haruuc saw too. "How many, Dagii?" he asked in disgust.

"A pair every second league from the Gathering Stone, lhesh. Seventy-two. All of the surviving warriors of the Gan'duur."

"You give them too much dignity."

"They died as you commanded, lhesh." Dagii's weary gray eyes met Haruuc's. Geth thought he saw a rebuke there and found that he had a new respect for the young warlord. Haruuc's ears folded flat against his skull, but Dagii just stepped back and pulled the final prisoner from the cart. "Here is Keraal, who was their chief. Your prisoner, lhesh."

Keraal's face was bruised and swollen. His good eye glared at the court gathered on the bridge. "Haruuc," he croaked.

"Keraal." Haruuc's ears eased up again and he drew a deep, satisfied breath. "You told me that it is not in the nature of our people to share land, that we are conquerors and rulers. Tell me—how does it feel to be conquered?"

"You tell me." Keraal twisted his distorted features into a defiant smile. "Do you still cower on the doorstep of the humans?"

His voice rang in the silence over the bridge.

Haruuc stepped forward with the speed of a man half his age and struck Keraal hard. The defeated warlord slammed back into the side of the cart. Haruuc seized him with one hand, dragged him back to his feet, and turned to face his court.

"Lhesh Haruuc Shaarat'kor cowers before no one!" he roared. "Darguun cowers before no nation!" He threw Keraal to the ground. "Does anyone doubt it?"

No one answered. Haruuc swept the crowd gathered on the bridge with an angry gaze. "Darguun is the land of the people. The mighty people. The quick people. The strong people. The people who ruled Khorvaire before humans came." He thrust the Rod of Kings, gripped in his other hand, high against the sky. "This is the heritage of Dhakaan—a heritage that we will reclaim!"

The silence held for a heartbeat longer—then was torn away by a roar from the gathered court. Geth felt like a leaf buffeted by the wind. It was all he could do to stand upright and stare at Haruuc.

CHAPTER TWENTY-NINE

They returned to Khaar Mbar'ost surrounded by an ocean of noise. Word of Haruuc's declaration spread ahead of the procession, and the excitement that had already gripped Rhukaan Draal was doubled. People clustered at the side of the street. They hung out of windows. They clung to rooftops. The sound they made was deafening. There was no hope of talking to Haruuc. It was just too loud. Munta rode up and tried to shout at the lhesh. Tariic tried. A whole series of warlords came forward and fell back, some looking worried, many looking pleased. Whatever they said or tried to say, the cheers of the crowd killed it. Geth, riding at Haruuc's side, didn't even bother making the attempt. Haruuc just rode on, smiling and waving.

Geth felt like someone had punched him in the gut. *This is the heritage of Dhakaan—a heritage that we will reclaim!*

By the time they reached the gates of the red fortress, the cheers of the people had become a chant of war. It took a line of soldiers three deep to keep the crowd from trying to follow the court inside. The casket, borne aloft by six bugbears, that contained Vanii's body traveled within a bubble of more guards. Riots almost broke out when Keraal, back in the tribex drawn cart once more, was brought across the plaza around the fortress. It took soldiers from Dagii's column to escort him to safety—and even then, he suffered a rain of spittle from disdainful warlords before he could be whisked to safety.

In the comparative calm of Khaar Mbar'ost's courtyard, Haruuc raised his hands in an appeal for silence. The court fell quiet. "We have a fallen friend to bid farewell to," he called, "and a fallen enemy to punish. I will deal with these things before any others. But be assured"—he raised the rod—"I mean what I say!"

The court roared its approval again. At least most of the court did. There were pale faces among the clan chiefs and especially among the representatives of the powers beyond Darguun. Geth noticed that the ranks of ambassadors and dragonmarked viceroys were thin—some of them must have managed to slip away. He had no doubt that messages were already being composed. Within a day, the most powerful people of Khorvaire would know what Haruuc had said on the bridge over the Ghaal.

The lhesh acknowledged his court with another flourish of the rod, then strode out of the courtyard and along a corridor. Geth clenched his jaw and hurried after him. He wasn't the only one. Munta and Tariic were on Haruuc's heels—and with Tariic came Daavn of the Marhaan. Geth's jaw clenched a little tighter at that.

"Do you mean it, uncle?" Tariic asked as they went. "Will there be war?"

"It's a great thing, lhesh," added Daavn. "You know you have the support of the Marhaan."

Munta used his bulk to cut off the other warlord as they went around a corner. "It's madness," he said. "Haruuc, we can't go to war!"

Haruuc stopped before a door—Geth recognized it as one that led to a small chamber off the dais of the throne room—and looked back at them. His face was bright with energy and enthusiasm. "I didn't say we were going to war," he said. Tariic's ears fell. Munta's rose. Haruuc shook his head. "I didn't say we weren't, either."

"You signed the Treaty of Thronehold," Munta growled.

"If treaties were inviolable, the world would be a far different place," said Haruuc. "In any case, I haven't declared war yet."

"Yet," repeated Geth.

Haruuc frowned at him. "Keraal was right in one thing. Darguun stands on the doorstep of humans—but it's our doorstep. The Five Nations occupy our house. They need to be reminded of that." He flung open the door—and paused.

Chetiin sat on the edge of a table in the room beyond.

Haruuc glowered at the black-clad goblin. "And what do you want?"

"To add the voice of an old friend." He slipped off the table as Haruuc entered and looked up at him. "You're letting a small success turn into a big mistake, Haruuc. You've won a victory over a rebel clan. You've brought Darguun together." He pointed at the rod. "You've secured the symbol of authority that will allow your successor to hold Darguun together as well. But you're not powerful enough to take on the Five Nations. Darguun isn't powerful enough."

"Listen to him, Haruuc," said Munta. "You know it's true. You've said it yourself. Darguun has no friends in Khorvaire. If we try to attack any human nation, the others will come together against us." The old warlord squeezed one hand into a fist. "We can't fight a united force. The Treaty of Thronehold protects us as much as it limits us."

Daavn shook his head sharply. "You're wrong, old man. The Five Nations are still recovering from the war. They hate each other more than they hate us. Now is the time to strike!"

Haruuc turned to glare at him. "Why are you here, Marhaan? How did you become one of my councilors?" He looked at each of them in turn. His gaze settled on Tariic. "What do you have to say?"

"I—" Tariic hesitated, his eyes on the rod in Haruuc's grasp, then bowed his head. "I support whatever decision you make, lhesh."

"As you should," Haruuc rasped. "As you all should." He looked at them. "I am the lhesh. I created Darguun. You will follow me. Is there any question of that?" He thumped a fist against his chest.

Tariic and Daavn repeated the gesture. So did Munta, although a little more slowly—and, Geth thought, regretfully.

Chetiin did not. He stood looking up at Haruuc, and his big ears twitched. "Haruuc," he said quietly, "when we brought the rod to you, you told us that if we ever had need, you would listen. I have need. I want you to listen."

Haruuc's lips peeled back from his teeth. "Then speak," he said.

"For as long as I've know you, you've put thought before deed. Now you're letting Keraal's words goad you into action. Think before you act on your words, or you put Darguun in danger." The goblin bent his head. "That's all I can say, old friend."

"Cho," said Haruuc. "It is." He leaned over Chetiin. "Now you will listen to me, 'old friend.' Keraal's words don't goad me. They show me the way. They agree with what I see as the future of Darguun—a future as glorious as the past." His eyes narrowed. "And I should ask what the *shaarat'khesh* care for Darguun. The Silent Clans have always stood apart. They've never shown their loyalty to me."

Chetiin stiffened. "The *shaarat'khesh* owe no allegiance beyond our contracts. We never have. I am here as your friend."

"Would a friend stand against me?"

"I stand with you, Haruuc." His scarred voice strained. "I stand with you and try to make you see that you follow a path to disaster!"

Rage flooded Haruuc's face and his hand shot out. Chetiin was faster—he slid away from the lhesh. His arms crossed and suddenly he held the curved dagger he kept sheathed on his left wrist. Tariic started to draw his sword. Geth's hand snapped out and closed on his arm, forcing the weapon down again. Tariic glared at him, but Geth just shook his head.

Chetiin and Haruuc stared at each other, then Haruuc straightened. "Get out," he said. "Get out of Khaar Mbar'ost. You're no friend of mine. When I need the *shaarat'khesh,* I will hire you—or perhaps another."

For a moment, Chetiin was very still, staring at Haruuc, then he slowly straightened as well and slid his dagger back into its sheath. "You are not the Haruuc I have known for so many years. You will destroy what you have built unless you are stopped." The black-clad goblin glanced at Geth, nodded once, then put his back to Haruuc and walked out the door.

The lhesh clenched both fists around the Rod of Kings as if he could snap the wrist-thick byeshk. He turned and glared at Munta, Tariic, and Daavn. "Go wait with the rest of the court. You have places there. If you have anything more to say, I don't want to hear it."

The three hobgoblins left the room like scolded children.

Geth lifted his head as Haruuc's eyes fell on him. "What about me?" he said. "Do you want me to leave?"

"You were going to leave already, weren't you?" Haruuc eased his grip on the rod and took a slow breath. "Stay long enough to do one thing, then you may go. Leave Darguun. I'll release you from your responsibility for the games. I will not call on you as a *shava* ever again."

"What's this one thing?"

"Stand with me to honor Vanii." He looked at Geth. "For the sake of friends lost in battle, stand with me."

Geth's mouth twisted. "You're a bastard, Haruuc."

"I've been called worse. You'll do it."

"I'll do it—for Vanii," Geth said. "He has no blame in this. He deserves to be honored."

"I liked your bluntness from the moment we met, Geth. Aram chose well when it accepted you." He turned the Rod of Kings in his hands for a moment, then jerked his head at the door that led onto the dais in the throne room. "Come through. Razu will open the great door and let people in soon."

As soon as Haruuc opened the door, however, Geth could see that there had been a change in the throne room. The big, blocky throne had been shifted to one side of the dais to make way for a bench-like stone bier—for Vanii, Geth assumed—but also for something else. Standing over the bier, rising a little more than half the height of the throne room, was a tree sculpted of white stone. A thick trunk rose, narrowed, then spread and split into curved segments. The stone branches were sharp with ridges and thorny spikes that cast hard shadows in the torchlight that lit the throne room. The entire tree was cut with grooves along and across its surface. Many of the grooves were stained dark. Geth's stomach rose into his throat. He'd seen the tree's twin—the original, in fact—in the great underground hall of Taruuzh Kraat, the workshop of Taruuzh. This one was smaller than that had been, but it was still frightening to look upon.

Geth could hear the faint sound of the court waiting in the antechamber beyond the great carved doors, but for now the throne room was empty and silent. He looked to Haruuc. "That's a real grieving tree. An original Dhakaani grieving tree."

The lhesh leaned against the throne and stared up into the branches. "There are ruins in the south of Darguun that have lain undisturbed for many centuries. When I forged the alliance among the Ghaal'dar tribes that became Darguun, I traveled everywhere in search of allies—even through the Torlaac Moor and into the jungle of the Khraal. I found this in the Khraal and had it brought back into the north. It's been hidden until now. Waiting for the right time to be used." He glanced at Geth. "A secret is only a surprise once."

Geth felt sick. "Have you ever seen a true grieving tree feeding?"

"Feeding . . . I hadn't thought to call it that. But yes. One of the men I had with me when we found it accidentally activated it. I know the words." He spoke a word in something that sounded like Goblin but that Wrath didn't translate for Geth. A shiver passed through the stone branches of the tree. Haruuc spoke another word and the shivering stopped. Geth looked away and tried not to think of Keraal hung in the branches.

"Do you really want revenge for Vanii's death so badly that you want to do this to Keraal?" he asked.

"I told you," Haruuc said, "this isn't about Vanii—"

Something inside Geth snapped. "Boar's snout!" He turned back to Haruuc, his teeth bared. "If this wasn't about Vanii, you wouldn't have made Iizan's slaves move a forest in three days. You would already have planned something."

Haruuc's ears bent flat. "The Gan'duur warriors had to die. Their clan had to be destroyed."

"You could have found another way to do it! You're selling women and children into slavery. Couldn't you have sold the warriors, too?"

"I do what I must for Darguun!"

"Stop saying that!" Geth shouted at him. "It's not for Darguun! How can it be for Darguun? This . . ." He pointed at the grieving tree. "This I can see in a twisted way is good for Darguun. I can see that Keraal has to die and maybe even that he has to die painfully if that's what your tradition says is necessary. But how is going to war good for Darguun? How is risking that the other nations of Khorvaire won't destroy you utterly good for Darguun?" He walked across the dais to face Haruuc. "Chetiin and Munta were right. You're going to destroy what you've worked to build."

"I do what I must!" Haruuc thrust out the rod. "I do what a king must!"

And suddenly Geth understood. He stared at Haruuc and the rod. "Grandmother Wolf," he said. "Grandfather Rat." Slowly, he drew Wrath and held it out before him. "Aram, the Sword of Heroes. Guulen, the Rod of Kings. The sword shows me tales of the heroes who held it and pushes me to be like them." He looked into Haruuc's face. "The rod shows you the emperors."

Haruuc opened his eyes a little wider. "You too?" he asked. "Then you understand! Taruuzh said, 'In this are the glories of the people. Bear them in mind and the people will always know their king.' He wasn't speaking in a metaphor." He brought the rod close and tapped the heavy byeshk softly against his temple. "I see the wonders of Dhakaan. I want Darguun to be like that. Guulen shows me how. Guulen shows me what it truly means to be a king."

"You were already a king."

"And weren't you already a hero before you took up Aram—the sword that won't accept the grasp of a coward?" Haruuc's ears flicked. "If the sword pushes you to be like the Dhakaani heroes, you know what I feel. *Maabet,* Geth, think of it. These were Taruuzh's gifts to Dhakaan, a sword that makes heroes great and a rod that makes kings greater." He turned the rod so that the light of the torches in the throne room flashed on the dark purple surface. "The emperors of Dhakaan understood the importance of putting storytellers in the streets. They understood the bloodthirst of the people when an enemy is defeated. They understood the power of war, of the mere threat of war. Even when the empire stretched across half the continent, the emperors sought conquest! What do the heroes of the name of Kuun tell you?"

Geth could feel Wrath throbbing in his grip, could almost see its memories of the distant heroes flickering at the edge of his vision. "They tell me to be fearless," he said. "To protect my friends. To let my deeds inspire the people."

"No more? I feel a power in Guulen, Geth. I know that the emperors found more than just guidance in the rod." Haruuc smiled, as if at a secret. "I can sense it, just out of reach. I think sometimes that all I need to do is find a way to impose my will on Guulen and no command I give will ever be refused."

Geth's belly clenched. The true power of the rod was waiting to be uncovered. "Haruuc, this isn't right," he said. "You wanted the rod as a symbol of rulership."

"The ultimate symbol for something is the thing itself," said Haruuc. "I'll lead Darguun to greatness as the emperors led Dhakaan!"

"Darguun isn't Dhakaan!" Geth said. "There are no more emperors. Eberron isn't the same as it was five thousand years ago! There were no other nations to challenge Dhakaan. Its only enemies were the elves. Now the elves are only one of many nations ready to fight you. Munta said it—if you move against one, all of the others will come back against you. Look at the Valenar. They know the same thing. Darguun and Valenar might have signed the Treaty of Thronehold at the end of the Last War, but you know that every other nation is watching both of you very closely." He drew a breath through his teeth. "Dhakaan was already great when Taruuzh forged Guulen and Aram, Haruuc. The emperors who held the rod never had to fight the kind of war Darguun would."

"I haven't declared war. I don't need to declare war." Haruuc stood up straight, savagely majestic in his armor, the spiked crown flashing on his head. "You see how just the threat of war brings my warlords together?"

"You barely have a grip on some of them, Haruuc. How long will it be before one decides to make a strike in your name? Or before one of the other nations takes your threats seriously and finds a way to strike first? Breland and Zilargo are just across the mountains. And what will happen if the warlords realize your threats are just posturing? They *want* a war. The only thing that has kept Darguun at peace has been your vision of a homeland for your people."

"The warlords will obey me!"

"Keraal didn't. Look where his rebellion led." Geth lowered Wrath. "You're on the edge of destroying Darguun. What the rod is telling you might have been true in the time of Dhakaan, but it's not true now. You need to stop listening to it."

Haruuc's lips peeled back from his teeth. *"Don't you think I've tried?"* he shouted. "At first it frightened me, and I tried to block it out, then I stopped when I saw what it was trying to do for me and Darguun. But from the moment I've held it, Guulen has been in my head and I can't shut it out." He slammed the rod down onto the seat of the throne, then pointed at it. "There! I still know what the emperors knew. I still hear the call to war. I still want Keraal's blood."

Geth stared at him in shock. He could push Wrath's memories away if he wanted to—it was easy. But before he claimed it, Wrath had lain silent in the ghost fortress of Jhegesh Dol for five thousand years. The rod had remained in the grasp of Dabrak Riis, trapped in the timelessness of the Uura Odaarii. Geth swallowed. "I took the rod from Dabrak Riis. I carried it. Why didn't it speak to me?"

"Because you've already been claimed by Aram. Because the Sword of Heroes can't be held by a coward and the Rod of Kings answers only to someone with the will to rule," Haruuc said. His mouth twisted and he looked down at the rod. "The emperors knew that." His hands squeezed hard on the back of the throne. "Help me, *shava,*" he said. "Help me save Darguun again."

"How—?" Geth started to ask, but the answer burst over him before he could even finish. "Ashi! Her dragonmark may be able to block the rod's influence on you."

"For how long?"

"Long enough," Geth said. He sheathed Wrath—just as three slow knocks sounded against the great wooden door of the throne room.

Haruuc started. "Razu," he said. "It's time to end Keraal's rebellion." He let go of the throne's back and walked around it. His hand hovered over the rod, then he took it and seated himself. Geth hissed, but Haruuc shook his head. "This can't be delayed. It must be done. Nothing can save Keraal now. I would only look weak if I let him live. I know this without the rod. But hurry." The lhesh raised his voice in a powerful shout and said in Goblin, "Enter! Enter to mourn! Enter to witness judgment!"

Down at the end of the throne room, the great wooden door began to rise.

Geth jumped down from the dais and raced up the aisle. Ashi would be with the court. He could catch her as she entered and take her around to the side of the dais. She only needed to touch Haruuc and they could put an end to this—

And why do you care so much? he found himself wondering. Not so long ago, you were ready to leave and put Darguun behind you.

He ground his teeth together. Call it the influence of the sword, he thought. But Haruuc's words came back to him.

Weren't you already a hero before you took up the sword?

"Rat," he muttered as he slid to a stop beside the rising door. Shins were visible on the other side. Knees. Thighs. Waists. Geth threw a final look back at Haruuc, sitting like a statue on his throne, then ducked under the moving door.

Ekhaas watched Razu lift a massive staff from her shoulder and swing it three times against the great carved door of the throne room, then step back. There was a short pause, then Haruuc's deep voice echoed through the wood. "Enter! Enter to mourn! Enter to witness judgment!"

Razu gave a nod to some hidden assistant and the door began its slow rise up into the ceiling. Ekhaas took a breath and made herself calm. There were rumors about what judgment waited for Keraal on the other side of the door. After all that Haruuc had done already, it was hard to guess what he might do next.

Standing beside her, Senen Dhakaan spoke under her breath. "You saw Dagii. What did he say about Haruuc's announcement on the bridge?"

"Nothing," said Ekhaas. She kept her voice level and calm. It was the truth. She'd found Dagii after the procession had returned to Khaar Mbar'ost and gotten close to him under the guise of offering healing for his torn hands. As she had sung away his wounds, they'd exchanged quick words. Haruuc's announcement, to her shame, had not been what they'd discussed.

"You bound all of the Gan'duur into the grieving trees yourself?" she'd asked.

"Cho," he had whispered back—then he'd caught her gaze, haunted gray eyes to amber, and whispered what amounted to treason. "They didn't suffer long, Ashi. I opened a vein for each of them. They died on the trees, but quickly. Haruuc was wrong to order them killed that way. What happened to him?"

She shook the memory—and the image of her hands around Dagii's—from her head and looked back toward the throne room.

Just in time to see Geth duck under the partly open door. The shifter's appearance caused a small ripple among the elder warlords who stood at the front of the antechamber. Tariic and Munta both tried to speak to him, but Geth shook them off and pushed himself into the open. He stood on the edge of the steps for a moment, surveying the crowd below. His face twisted in frustration, then his eyes found her and widened. He jumped over the rail of the stairs and came across the floor of the chamber, using his great gauntlet like a shield to shove warlords and clan chiefs out of the way.

"Ekhaas!" he said as soon as he was close. "I need Ashi! Have you seen her or Vounn? Have they gone to the gallery?"

He started to turn to the passage that led up to the gallery overlooking the throne room, but Ekhaas grabbed him and spun him around. "The gallery is closed," she said. "But I saw them heading up the stairs to their chambers. They haven't come back down?"

"I couldn't see them." Geth pulled away, but she hung onto him a moment longer.

"What's happening?" she whispered in his ear.

He hesitated for a moment, then murmured back, "The rod."

She felt her ears rise and panic filled her. "Haruuc has discovered its powers?"

"Not yet. It's trying to make him a king the way Wrath makes me a hero."

"Khaavolaar! What can I do?"

"Watch him!"

Geth tore out of her grasp and charged through the crowded chamber like a bull. She stared after him until Senen asked in her ear, "What was that about?"

She twitched and turned back. "It's a private matter."

Senen's ears flicked. "Haruuc's *shava* comes rushing out of a sealed throne room looking for the bearer of a Siberys dragonmark, and it's a private matter?"

Ekhaas's teeth ground together. "Yes," she said tightly and was saved from further interrogation by a collective gasp of amazement that rose from the front ranks of the crowd. The great door was all the way up, and the way into the throne room was open. There was a moment of confusion, as if some of those in the front ranks had drawn back before entering, but then Haruuc's court was moving inexorably forward. Ekhaas was carried up the stairs—and saw the grieving tree.

"Khaavolaar!" she said again, but her expression of surprise was lost in the rolling wave of astonishment that gripped each new rank of spectators to mount the stairs. Every goblin knew what a true grieving tree was supposed to look like. Very few of them had ever seen one before. Ekhaas had, and she still found herself struck dumb by the curved and cruel branches of white stone.

The interior of the throne room was as silent as Haruuc on his throne. The only noises were the rustle of fabric and the clatter of armor as warlords and clan chiefs, ambassadors, envoys, and councilors took their places. The room was packed tight. Ekhaas was fortunate enough to find herself with a good view of Haruuc. When the court had assembled, he spoke.

"Enter the dead."

A drum beat started, and Ekhaas couldn't help but think of the drum that had followed their steps into the throne room when they'd presented Haruuc with the rod. She studied the lhesh, trying to see if she could find any clue to the truth of what Geth had said. Haruuc's fingers were white around the rod, and his face was drawn into a tightly controlled mask, but that could have been anger or grief.

There was movement in the doorway. With another rustle of cloth and metal, heads turned as Vanii's body was carried into the throne room by the same six bugbears who had carried the casket through Rhukaan Draal. It had been removed from the casket, though, and placed on a silk-draped plank. There was some preserving magic at work—Haruuc's *shava* had been dead for nearly a week, but he might have been struck down only hours before. Humans, Ekhaas knew, might have tried to make it look like he was only sleeping. Such denial was a shame. Goblin tradition honored a warrior's death. The wound that had killed Vanii was visible for all to see: a deep red rent in his chest surrounded by shattered mail and broken ribs.

At the end of the aisle, the bugbears paused before Haruuc. He rose from his throne and came down from the dais to stand over Vanii. His hand came up. He touched the open wound, then Vanii's forehead.

"Paatcha, shava," he said, then nodded to the bugbears. They took the corpse to a stone bier set beneath the grieving tree, left him there, and retired to the side of the room. Haruuc returned to the throne and looked up the aisle. Heads turned again in anticipation.

Chains clanked on the stairs in counterpoint to the slow beat of the drum, then Dagii and Keraal appeared. The warlord of the Mur Talaan had washed and donned his armor with the three tribex horns that stood tall over his head and shoulders. Ekhaas saw his ears flick at the sight of the grieving tree, but his face otherwise betrayed nothing.

Keraal's ears, however, went back flat against his head, and his eyes opened so wide the whites of them made a shocking pale ring. He had been stripped of clothes except for a loincloth. Chains bound his ankles and his wrists. Bruises and half-healed wounds showed on his body. He tried to pull back, but Dagii pushed him forward. Keraal stumbled down the aisle, his eyes fixed on the grieving tree. Dagii dragged him to a stop before the throne. Haruuc looked down on the defeated warlord. Keraal tried to stand straight, but the shackles wouldn't allow it—a length of chain between hands and feet forced him to hunch. The chains rattled as he began to shake.

Haruuc said nothing, but only gestured with the rod toward the tree. Dagii took Keraal's arm and guided him over to stand beneath the stone branches, beside Vanii's bier, then took several quick steps back. Keraal was left alone, staring up at the tree.

Haruuc whispered a word.

The grieving tree shivered—and moved. The curved segments of its branches ground together as they rotated. Haruuc whispered another word, and a thick stone limb bent down and curled around Keraal. The warlord screamed. Like a living tree caught in a storm or some weird undersea creature, the tree thrashed and whirled. Keraal was passed from branch to branch until he hung among the carved white stone. Then the ridges and thorns of the tree seemed to ripple, and Keraal shrieked again as they dug into his flesh.

The grooves cut into the branches from which he hung turned red as blood trickled through them. The grieving tree shivered again. Twitching and whimpering, Keraal hung in agony as the tree fed.

A strong person could linger on a grieving tree for days. Legends of Dhakaan told of arch-traitors and fallen heroes who had hung in a tree for a week or more.

Ekhaas saw some of the ambassadors of the other nations and some of the representatives of the dragonmarked houses—humans, elves, half-elves, a dwarf, a gnome—look away. No one of the goblin races did. Her gut twisted at Keraal's agony and her ears went back. But saliva ran in her mouth and her tongue moved, touching the points of her teeth. Her heart beat faster, taking the place of the drum that had fallen silent.

One of the warlords moaned softly. Ekhaas didn't look to see who.

Haruuc rose. He raised the Rod of Kings. "Let all witness," he said, "the end of those who stand against Darguun! Haruuc Shaarat'kor fears no one. Darguun fears no one!"

"Haruuc!" shouted a voice. "Haruuc!" Other voices took up the chant. "Haruuc! Haruuc! Haruuc! Haruuc!" The throne room shook. Haruuc raised his hands in acknowledgment.

Then another voice called, "Give us war!"

Ekhaas saw Haruuc freeze. The chant that filled the room changed. "War! *Haruuc!* War! *Haruuc!* War! War! *War!"*

A smile spread across Haruuc's face. "Darguuls!" he roared. "Was our nation not born in war? Were our *people* not born in war? From ancient days, have we not spread our power across the land?"

The knot in Ekhaas's belly grew tighter. The ambassadors of the other nations of Khorvaire were looking at each other in a peculiar frenzy. All of them seemed to have moved a little bit away from the ambassador of Breland. Another groan drifted from Keraal on the grieving tree. Haruuc looked up at him—and it seemed to Ekhaas that his smile tightened once more. When he looked back to the warlords and clan chiefs, there was nothing easy in his manner. It was almost as if he fought to get the words out of his mouth. "Our strategy must be discussed! There must be an assembly!"

But enthusiasm got the better of the crowd. "Breland!" someone cried, and the Brelish ambassador twitched.

"Zilargo!"

"Northern Breland and then into Thrane!"

"Silence!" said Haruuc. He looked out over the court. "You think small! Are you hobgoblins or halflings? Breland, Thrane . . . what challenge would they be? Ancient blood demands an ancient enemy. As it was in the age of Dhakaan, goblins shall go into battle against elves!" He thrust the Rod of Kings out before him. "Let our blades fall on Valenar!"

For a moment, there was stunned silence in the throne room, then the court burst into a wave of cheers.

"Mothers of the dirge," said Senen softly. "He's going to do it. He's going to start a war."

Ekhaas's ears rose high as she unraveled the lhesh's scheme in her head. "No," she said. "He's going to stop one."

Senen looked at her, but she just stared at Haruuc in amazement. It seemed that he glanced off to one side for an instant, off through the door that led from the dais, then smiled in triumph and raised his arms high above his head. The cheers of the crowd burst out anew.

CHAPTER THIRTY

As soon as they were back in Khaar Mbar'ost, Vounn had taken Ashi's arm, pulled her away from the crowd streaming into Haruuc's throne room, and taken her up to her chambers. "Put a pack together," she had said. "You're going to the House Orien compound. Forget the games—I want you back to Sterngate with the first Orien coach on the road. If Haruuc is talking about war, I don't want you here."

A few weeks ago, she would have argued with the lady seneschal. No more. She could see the danger as clearly as Vounn. Running back to the safety of Karrlakton felt cowardly. Staying in Darguun felt stupid. "What about you?" she'd asked.

Vounn had shaken her head. "I've lived through war. Business goes on. Deneith will need a strong voice in Darguun now more than ever."

They were almost finished packing when the door of Ashi's chamber slammed open. Ashi spun, her hand going for her sword. Vounn turned, too, harsh words on her lips. "Aruget! I told you no one—"

But Aruget and Krakuul were still standing beyond the doorway, staring at the panting shifter who pushed past them. Geth pointed at Ashi. "Haruuc needs your dragonmark," he wheezed. "Now!"

"What? Why?"

"I'll tell you on the way. Come with me!"

Ashi looked to Vounn. Her mentor pressed her lips together, then shook her head. "It's your choice."

"Ashi, if you come with me right now we might able to stop a war," said Geth.

The muscles of Ashi's jaw tightened. "Finish packing for me," she told Vounn. "House Orien won't be running any coaches yet." She looked to Geth. "Go!"

Their footsteps echoed in the empty corridors. Everyone who mattered was in the throne room or lurking in the antechamber. Servants were in their quarters. Guards were outside trying to control the celebrations of Rhukaan Draal. They went down the stairs two at a time. "Talk," said Ashi. "What's happening?"

"The rod is trying to make Haruuc into a king—an emperor. That's why he's been acting the way he has." In brief words, he described his argument with the lhesh.

When he was finished, Ashi cursed. "We were so worried about Haruuc using the powers of the rod, we didn't think about the rod using him!"

"Why should we have thought of it? Grandfather Rat, why did we worry at all? Haruuc had all the power he needed without the rod!"

A terrible scream came up the stairs. Ashi lifted her head. Geth put his head down and ran faster. He came to the bottom of the stairs and paused, looking between corridors that led right or straight ahead.

"Straight!" said Ashi.

"Right is shorter," said a voice from above.

Ashi and Geth looked up. Aruget was hurrying down the stairs after them.

"What are you doing here?" Ashi demanded.

"Orders of the lhesh. Krakuul or I are supposed to be with you or Lady Vounn at all times." The hobgoblin leaped down the final few stairs with surprising agility.

Geth grabbed him. "How much did you hear?" he asked.

Aruget's ears flicked. "Enough to know we shouldn't argue. I already know more than I should about many things." A thunderous chanting—Haruuc's name, repeated over and over—filled the air, and Aruget pointed to the right. "Decide quickly. I know a shortcut."

Geth bared his teeth, then let him go. "You better keep your mouth shut."

The chant changed—

"War! *Haruuc!* War! *Haruuc!* War! War! *War!"*

—and grew closer as Aruget led them along the corridor, then cut through rooms and halls. They emerged into another hallway just in time to hear Haruuc shout, "Darguuls! Was our nation not born in war? Were our *people* not born in war? From ancient days, have we not spread our power across the land? Our strategy must be discussed! There must be an assembly!"

"Tiger's blood," said Geth. "He's holding them off!"

"Here!" said Aruget. He swung around a corner and they were in the room off the dais of the throne room. Through the open door, Ashi could see Haruuc standing before his throne with the rod in his hands. She could see the grieving tree beyond—and Keraal as he hung on it, slowly writhing among the stone branches. She pressed her lips together and focused on Haruuc.

"I need to touch him," she said. She glanced at Geth. "You think this will work?"

"I was going to ask you that." He took a deep breath. "I'll get his attention."

From the floor of the throne room, however, came calls from warlords not willing to wait for an assembly. "Breland!"

"Zilargo!"

"Northern Breland and then into Thrane!"

Ashi saw Haruuc's chest heave and his face grow tight, but she also thought she saw something in his eyes, some flash of inspiration. *"Silence!"* he said. "You think small! Are you hobgoblins or halflings! Breland, Thrane . . . what challenge would they be? Ancient blood demands an ancient enemy."

Ashi grabbed Geth's hand. *"Khyberit gentis,* no." They were too late.

Haruuc's voice rose to a triumphant shout. "As it was in the age of Dhakaan, goblins shall go into battle against elves!" He held out a fist wrapped around the Rod of Kings. "Let our blades fall on Valenar!"

There was silence, then deafening cheers. Ashi looked at Geth.

Except that the shifter was grinning. He shook his head and said into her ear. "Of all the nations that signed the Treaty of

Thronehold, Valenar and Darguun are the least trusted. Haruuc can shake a sword at Valenar, and the elves won't find any allies. And the only ways to get to Valenar are through the Mournland or over water. Haruuc has started a war that will never happen! He's bought us time to find a way out of this!" He waved his free hand through the door at Haruuc.

The lhesh saw him and smiled—with relief, Ashi thought. Haruuc looked back to the crowd in the throne room and raised his arms high above his head. The crowd cheered again.

And the fletching of a crossbow bolt sprouted in the thin armor of his right armpit.

The grin fell from Geth's face. Haruuc's arm collapsed and he stumbled sideways. The cheering of the crowd, caught up in its excitement, continued.

"Haruuc!" Geth wrenched his hand from Ashi's and threw himself out onto the dais, but he was too slow.

From the gallery overhead, the small, black-clad form of one of the *shaarat'khesh* launched into the air. Geth caught a glimpse of a familiar, black-stained face, then a rope tied into the rafters arrested the goblin's fall. Chetiin landed on the dais with a rolling tumble and came up with two daggers in his hands.

The one in his left was curved and ugly. The one in his right, the one he had called Witness, was straight and set with a blue-black crystal, but uglier still.

Geth froze for a moment, caught in the act of drawing Wrath. Below the dais, he saw Dagii, motionless with shock was well. The cheering fell silent. The throne room seemed like a scene suspended in glass.

Haruuc bared his teeth and jumped back to put his throne between himself and the goblin. He groped for his red-stained sword, trying to draw it with his crippled arm. Chetiin slid forward like a cat stalking a mouse. Haruuc abandoned his sword and swung the Rod of Kings with his left hand. "Traitor!" he screamed.

The word broke the glass. Wrath left its scabbard. Dagii vaulted up the steps of the dais. There were shouts in the crowd.

Chetiin darted aside and rolled behind Haruuc. The lhesh tried to turn, to step on the goblin, but Chetiin's feet lashed out in a sharp kick that buckled Haruuc's knee. He fell forward onto his hands and knees. The Rod of Kings left his grip with a dull clang of metal on stone and rolled across the dais. Chetiin spun to his feet and lunged for Haruuc's neck. The hobgoblin twisted onto his back, grabbing for him. Chetiin slashed at the grasping hands. Blood spattered on the stone of the dais.

Then Geth was standing over Haruuc and Dagii was closing in on Chetiin's other side. The goblin's eyes darted between them; he spun and sprinted for the grieving tree. Dagii turned and went after him.

Geth's heart jumped. "Dagii! No!"

Too late. Chetiin dropped flat and slid across the floor into a gap under Vanii's bier. Dagii tried to pull himself back as he saw the danger, but couldn't. With a grating of stone, one of the limbs of the grieving tree bent down and snatched him up. The metal of his armor squealed under the pressure. Dagii roared as he bashed at the carved branch that held him. More branches were already reaching for him.

Geth knelt down over Haruuc. "Stop the tree!" he said. "You know the word—stop it!"

Haruuc's eyes flickered. Sweat stood out on the yellow skin of his brow. "It burns!" he gasped.

Geth cursed and pulled aside his arm. The crossbow bolt still embedded in his armpit had something black and gummy smeared along its shaft. Poison. Geth clenched his teeth and slapped the lhesh.

"Stop the tree, Haruuc!" He twisted the high warlord around so he could see Dagii struggling—and Chetiin crawling out from under the bier. Haruuc's face curled in anger. He spat a word.

The tree shuddered and stopped moving. Dagii yelled as both he and Keraal tumbled out of its branches. Chetiin's eyes narrowed. He darted at Geth and Haruuc.

Snarling, Geth released Haruuc and lunged to meet the goblin. Wrath swung low like a scythe—

—and Chetiin went high, leaping off Geth's outstretched arm and bounding over his head like a monkey. Geth twisted around to watch him tumble in the air and come down right beside Haruuc. The injured lhesh's eyes went wide. Bloody hands tried to grab at Chetiin, but the goblin twisted aside. The dull blade of the dagger named Witness plunged down and into one of the wide eyes.

Lhesh Haruuc Shaarat'kor jerked, then lay still.

Silence seized the throne room. Warlords who had been rushing to the dais stopped like statues, weapons still raised. Geth saw Ashi, who had been coming to his aid, slow and stop. Aruget, standing in the door behind her, was just staring.

Only Chetiin moved. The goblin didn't even try to pull Witness from Haruuc's body. He looked up at Geth and said in his scarred voice, "We swore we would do what we had to," then twisted away from the dead man and darted to where his rope still swayed. With sinuous swiftness, he scrambled up it and into the rafters.

Geth's voice came back to him. "Stop him!" he shouted. "Get up to the gallery! Stop him!" Someone was relaying his words back to the spectators and guards in the antechamber, but Geth had a feeling in his gut that, however fast they might be, they would still find the gallery empty and Chetiin vanished.

You will destroy what you have built unless you are stopped. The goblin's final words to Haruuc.

Geth stumbled back to Haruuc and knelt down beside him. The lhesh's remaining eye stared up blind, just like the eyes of the troll in the valley.

Ashi came and knelt on Haruuc's other side. "He said we swore we'd do what he had to."

"I think he thought Haruuc had discovered the power of the rod," Geth said. "He didn't know the rod's real danger."

The shifter looked down from the dais. On the floor of the throne room, warlords were lowering their weapons. Some were dropping to their knees in silent shock. No one spoke. Not yet. Geth saw Ekhaas and Senen, staring. He saw Munta, trembling. He saw Tariic, staring as well—until Daavn of the Marhaan leaned over and murmured in his ear. Tariic's eyes went to the throne, and Geth knew he would claim it if he could. The shifter glanced around the throne room.

Tariic and Daavn weren't the only ones whispering and looking at the throne. No tears had even been shed for Haruuc yet, and the warlords of Darguun were already appraising which of them would be the next lhesh.

The next lhesh. The next to hold the Rod of Kings.

Fear cut through Geth's shock. The danger wasn't over. He twisted around. "The rod!" he whispered to Ashi. "Where is it?"

"There!" She pointed.

It had rolled against the back of the throne. Geth thrust himself to his feet and strode over to it. The byeshk shaft lay in the throne's shadow like a thick, purple slug. The sight of it made him feel ill.

But he was the only one who could handle it. Anyone else might succumb to its power. He had to make sure that didn't happen—and Haruuc had given him the means to do it. For a while at least.

He squeezed Wrath's hilt tight. *Give me the right words,* he thought, then scooped up the rod and stood.

"Lords of Darguun," he said in Goblin, "hear me!" His accent sounded clumsy and crude even to his ears. Some of the warlords looked up at him, but not enough. He raised his voice and tried again. "Lords of Darguun, hear me—"

He felt Wrath's power move into him. His words smoothed and became clear. Syllables he didn't know formed on his tongue and slid between his lips. He tried not to think about it, tried to focus on what he wanted to say. On what he needed to say. Everyone, all of the great and powerful of Darguun, were staring up at him. He drew Wrath and held it high.

"—I am Geth, who bears Aram. I am *shava* to Lhesh Haruuc Shaarat'kor. By all traditions, it is my sacred duty to tell his heirs that he is dead. But Haruuc had no heirs, so I speak to all of Darguun. Your lhesh is dead. The father of Darguun is dead." He swallowed. "It is also my duty as *shava* to take charge of my brother's affairs. Darguun must have a new lhesh. Until you lords determine which among you will take the throne, I claim it in trust." He raised the rod up from where he had held it. "Let all bear witness! I am *shava* to Haruuc, and this is my duty!"

For a long moment, no one said anything. The throne room was utterly silent. Geth looked around. There were a lot of confused faces watching him—and a lot of angry faces as well.

Then a voice like cedar smoke rose from the throne room. "I witness it!" shouted Ekhaas. "As it was in the age of Dhakaan, I witness it!"

"I witness it!" Dagii stepped up beside Geth. The young warlord gave him an uncertain look, but his stance was strong. Geth looked to Munta. The old hobgoblin's ears flicked and stood.

"I witness it!" he said, then jerked his head at other warlords around him. Their voices rose as well.

"I witness it!" came a strong voice from the front of the room, and Geth looked down to see Tariic looking back at him. The hobgoblin gave him a short smile, then stepped onto the lowest step of the dais and faced the court that had been Haruuc's. "Let none say that we do not respect tradition. Geth who bears Aram shall hold the throne in trust until a new lhesh is chosen. It is what my uncle would have wanted."

He turned back to Geth and bent his head, meeting Geth's eyes as he straightened up. "I hope you know what you're doing," he said softly.

"I'm doing what I have to do," said Geth. Behind Tariic, a sea of heads was nodding in respect. He glanced over at Haruuc's body. Ashi was still kneeling beside it, staring up at him. Geth set his jaw grimly and brought the Rod of Kings protectively against his chest.

Raat shan gath'kal dor.

"The story stops but never ends."

— Traditional closing of hobgoblin legends.

GLOSSARY

Aram: see Wrath

Aruget: A hobgoblin warrior in the service of Haruuc, assigned first to accompany Tariic's mission to Karrlakton, then to guard Vounn and Ashi in Rhukaan Draal.

atcha: The goblin concept of personal honor, something which is earned and carefully protected. Compare with *muut*.

ban: Goblin expression of non-commital agreement, roughly equivalent to "yeah, alright" or "your funeral."

***Battle Called Life, The*:** A famous treatise written in approximately 625 YK by Karrnathi philosopher Falko Gergus. Gergus drew wisdom from everyday life to create a work still regarded as a key text of military philosophy.

Blood of Six Kings: An oath of sincerity among goblins.

Bloody Market, the: The largest market in Rhukaan Draal, the Bloody Market (*Khaari Batuuvk* in Goblin) is a chaotic mass of tents and stalls in a milling sea of bodies. Because the laws of Rhukaan Draal and Darguun are lax, nearly anything can be found for sale in the market, including slaves.

Breland: One of the original Five Nations of Galifar. Breland is a tolerant country with a keen interest in trade and commerce.

byeshk: A rare metal, hard and dense with a purple sheen.

Cazhaak Draal: An ancient Dhakaani city. Its ruins are located in the country of Droaam and are now known as the Stonelands.

chaat'oor: Goblin term for any species not native to Khorvaire, especially humans, but with the exception of elves. It is often loosely translated as "defiler."

Chetiin: A goblin and an elder of the *shaarat'khesh*. Chetiin carries two daggers sheathed on his forearms, one of which (the dagger named Witness carried on his right arm) is a dangerous "Keeper's Fang" weapon capable of capturing the soul of a slain enemy.

chib: Goblin for "boss" or "big man." Used colloquially by goblins outside of Darguun to refer to any taller humanoid, including hobgoblins, humans, and dwarves.

Chit guulen pamuut ran: A goblin expression. "There is strength in honoring a sacrifice."

cho: Goblin expression of informal agreement with or acknowledgement of a statement made, roughy equivalent to "yes" or "okay."

daashor: A goblin artificer, especially one from the time of the Empire of Dhakaan. The secret knowledge of the *daashor* has largely vanished, but at one time, they were capable of creating wonders. Most *daashor* were male.

Daavn: The hobgoblin warlord of the Marhaan clan.

Dagii: A hobgoblin warrior in service to Haruuc, but also the warlord of the small but highly honored Mur Talaan clan.

dar: Goblin for "the people. It is the ancient collective term for the hobgoblin, goblin, and bugbear races.

Darguul: A goblin inhabitant of Darguun. Non-goblins living in Darguun are not generally recognized as citizens.

Darguun: The nation of goblins, founded in 969 YK by the hobgoblin warlord Haruuc of the Rhukaan Taash clan in a swift campaign that seized territory held at the time by the human nations of Cyre and Breland. Darguun was officially recognized as a sovereign nation in the Treaty of Thronehold in 996 YK. Translated, it means "Land of the People."

Dark Six, the: Deities representing the violent and threatening aspects of the world, typically shunned in more civilized nations, but widely worshipped in Darguun. Once numbered among the Lords of the Sovereign Host, myth holds that they were cast out for their evil ways. The Six are: The Devourer (god of the ocean and destruction), The Fury (god of violence and madness), The Keeper (god of death and decay), The Mockery (god of treachery and murder), The Shadow (god of dark magic), and The Traveller (god of deception and change).

Davandi, Midian Mit: A gnome, a field researcher of the Library of Korranberg with a specialty in the history of the Empire of Dhakaan.

d'Deneith, Ashi: A former hunter of the Bonetree Clan of the Shadow Marches, Ashi turned her back on the clan after discovering her descent from House Deneith. She wields a ceremonial honor blade granted to her ancestor by House Deneith. She bears the Siberys Mark of Sentinel, a powerful dragonmark that patterns her entire body.

d'Deneith, Vounn: A dragonmarked heir of House Deneith, Vounn is a skilled diplomat with a distinguished career serving as the liaison between Deneith and its most important clients. She holds the title of Lady Seneschal, indicating her special responsibilities within the House.

Deneith, House: A dragonmarked house bearing the Mark of Sentinel. House Deneith operates services offering various forms of protection, including the mercenary companies of the Blademarks and the law enforcement services of the Sentinel Marshals.

Desperate Times, The: The dark ages of chaos after the fall of the Empire of Dhakaan. Particularly conservative members of the Dhakaani Clans might argue that the Desperate Times extend into the present, but most goblin historians agree that the Desperate Times ended with the domination of Khorvaire by humans, somewhere between 3,000 years (when the human Karrn the Conqueror established Karrnath) and 2,000 years (when Galifar I united the Five Nations in a single kingdom) before the present.

Dhakaan: An epithet claimed or given by popular acclaim among the Dhakaani clans to indicate allegiance with the ancient Empire of Dhakaan.

Dhakaani Clans: Clans of goblins, primarily hobgoblins but incorporating other goblin races, devoted to keeping alive the glories of the Empire of Dhakaan. Although they claim territory in the mountains of Darguun, they do not pledge allegiance to Lhesh Haruuc, nor do they hold any particular alliance among themselves. The Dhakaani Clans include the Kech Draguus, the Kech Nasaar, the Kech Shaarat, the Kech Uul, and the Kech Volaar.

Dhakaani Empire: see Empire of Dhakaan

d'Orien, Pater: A dragonmarked heir of House Orien, Pater is Viceroy of his House in Darguun, in charge of his House's operations in the country.

duur'kala: Among the Dhakaani Clans, particularly the Kech Volaar, *duur'kala* preserve the history and knowledge of past ages.

Their music is the most common form of magic among the clans. *Duur'kala* means "dirge singers." Because the magic manifests mostly in females, *duur'kala* are often called "daughters of the dirge" and elders are referred to as "mothers of the dirge."

Ekhaas: A hobgoblin woman and a *duur'kala* of the Kech Volaar, Ekhaas spent many years travelling southern Khorvaire before returning to Darguun with tales of her adventures with Geth and Ashi.

Empire of Dhakaan: An ancient empire ruled by hobgoblins, the Empire of Dhakaan strecthed across southern Khorvaire millenia before the arrival of humans. Dhakaan was weakened by the Daelkyr War and collapsed about six thousand years before the present.

Fenic: A hobgoblin warrior (deceased), formerly warlord of the Mur Talaan clan and one of Haruuc's three *shava*. He was the father of Dagii.

Flayed god's skin!: An oath to the Mockery

gaa'ma: Goblin pejorative term for changelings. Literally translated, it means "wax babies."

gaanu duur: "Daughter of the dirge," an alternative term for *duur'kala*.

gaa'taat: A highly insulting Goblin term suggesting that someone is less than a child.

gaeth'ad: An orcish herbal tea, most common in the Shadow Marches, that can be brewed with a variety of effects. Generally brewed and served by a *gaeth'ad* master.

Gan'duur: "Eaters of Sorrow," a rebel clan of the Ghaal'dar, originally an off-shoot of the Gantii Vus. Their banner is yellow with a crest of a snarling dog.

gath'atcha: Goblin for "without honor." In most cases used by the speaker as a means of showing contrition and offering apology, but a serious insult when said of someone else.

Gathering Stone, the: The primary stronghold of House Deneith in Darguun, located at a major crossroad two days ride from Rhukaan Draal.

Geth: A shifter veteran of the Last War, rediscovering his worth after fleeing from deeds done in the past. He wields a great gauntlet, a magewrought gauntlet that is both shield and weapon, and then ancient Dhakaani blade named Wrath.

ghaal: Goblin for "mighty" with specific connotations of prowess in battle.

Ghaal River: A mighty river in central Darguun. It is navigable from its mouth at Kraken Bay to the city of Rhukaan Draal, almost two-thirds of its length. Above Rhukaan Draal, the first of several cataracts breaks the river into dangerous stretches of white water.

ghaal'dar: The ancient name for the hobgoblin race, it means "mighty people." In the present time, Ghaal'dar is also the name of the loose confederacy of goblin clans living in the lowlands of Darguun, especially in the broad area around the Ghaal River. Notable Ghaal'dar clans include the Gan'duur ("Eaters of Sorrow"), the Gantii Vus ("Hungry Flame"), the Ja'aram ("Bright Anger"), the Mur Talaan ("Horned Shoulders"), the Rhukaan Taash ("Razor Crown"), the Marhaan, the Ghaal Sehn, and the Pin Galaac.

Giim Astra: A spectacular cleft mountain peak marking the headwaters of the Torlaac River in the Seawall Mountain range. The site of extensive Dhakaani ruins.

goblin: A term that causes much confusion as it applies both to the small-statured goblin race and to the three related races of goblins, hobgoblins, and bugbears (as well as other less well-known races).

The longstanding tradition of referring to the related races by the term "goblinoid" has been abandonned by forward-thinking scholars of Wynarn and Morgrave Universities, an attitude that is slowly spreading among the general population.

Goblin cuisine: While often unrecognized by more "civilized" races, goblins have an ancient and well-established culinary culture. Typical goblin cuisine varies by region (that of Darguul is more "pure" and exotic, that of city goblins more influenced by human cooking) and somewhat by race. Food tend to emphasize a chewy texture, and sour and bitter flavors—a preference carried over into wine and beermaking. Buns and starchy balls of *noon* are common staples and pickling is a favorite form of both preservation and seasoning. Boiling and steaming (often in flavored liquids) are the most common cooking methods. All food is relatively simple, hearty, and portable once prepared; goblin food sticks closest to this, while high class hobgoblin food can be varied and labor intensive. Bugbear food is the least finicky, often along the lines of meat on a stick or a pot over the fire. Surprisingly, goblins also have a remarkable sweet tooth and desserts such as *shaat'aar* have found popularity as street snacks in Sharn and other southern cities.

golin: Goblin for "quick." Among hobgoblins and bugbears, it refers only to speed, but goblins use it to refer to intelligence as well.

golin'dar: The ancient name for the goblin race, it means "quick people."

guul: Goblin for "strong."

guul'dar: The ancient name for the bugbear race, it means "strong people."

Haata: A dynasty of the middle Dhakaani Empire.

Haluun: A hobgoblin warrior (deceased) of the Rhukaan Taash clan, Haruuc's younger brother, and one of Haruuc's three *shava*. He was also the father of Tariic.

Haruuc: Properly Lhesh Haruuc Shaarat'kor ("High Warlord Haruuc of the Red Blade"), founder of Darguun. As a charismatic young warlord serving as a mercenary of House Deneith, Haruuc saw an opportunity to bring the goblin races out from under the shadow of humans and give them a homeland. Finding allies in other warlords of the Ghaal'dar, Haruuc hatched a plan to turn on the nations that employed Deneith's goblin mercenaries and seize power for himself. His plan culminated in a lightning swift conquest of southern Cyre (including areas claimed at the time by Breland) in the summer of 969 YK and the subsequent founding of Darguun.

Heroes of Dhakaan

House Orien: A dragonmarked house bearing the Mark of Passage. House Orien operates services related to travel, shipping and communication, including a postal service and the Lightning Rail. Orien also maintains the network of trade roads across Khorvaire.

***Itaa*!:** A Goblin war-command equivalent to "Attack!"

Je'shaarat mi paa kotanaa: A goblin expression. "A sharp sword hurts less when you fall on it."

Jhazaal Dhakaan: The greatest duur'kala of the Dhakaani age, the inspiration behind the founding of the Empire of Dhakaan and the creator of a number of artifacts now sought by modern Dhakaani clans.

Karrlakton: A city in Karrnath, ancient center of power of House Deneith. Warlords manifesting the Mark of Sentinel ruled in the area before the founding of Karrnath.

Karrnath: One of the original Five Nations of Galifar. Karrnath is a cold, grim land whose people are renowned for their martial prowess.

Kech Volaar: One of the smallest, but most influential of the Dhakaani Clans, the Kech Volaar devotes itself to gathering and preserving the history, knowledge, and artifacts of the Empire of Dhakaan. *Duur'kala* form a powerful class among them and their stronghold of Volaar Draal is known to contain deep vaults filled with the wonders of ages past.

Khaar Mbar'ost: Lhesh Haruuc's fortress in the heart of Rhukaan Draal, constructed for him by House Cannith. Its name means literally "blood-colored fortified dwelling," an allusion to the reddish stone facing used in its construction.

Khaari Batuuvk: see Bloody Market, the.

Khaavolaar!: A Goblin curse of frustration or amazement. It is a contraction of "*Khaar volaar*" or "blood of the word."

kiirin: A traditional goblin stringed instrument. Records show that it was played in the time of the Dhakaani Empire.

Krakuul: A hobgoblin warrior in the service of Haruuc, assigned first to accompany Tariic's mission to Karrlakton, then to guard Vounn and Ashi in Rhukaan Draal.

Kuun: Surname of a line of heroes of the Dhakaani Empire, first carried by the warlord Duulan, a friend of Taruuzh. His descendants included twin sons Nasaar and Vanon; Mekiis, a duur'kala and wife of an emperor; Biish, a noble outlaw; Rakari, slayer of the daelkyr lord of Jhegesh Dol; Mazaan, a legendary strategist; Jhezon, called "One-Eye," a notable scoundrel; and many others remembered in legend and history. Tales of the name of Kuun are closely tied to Aram, the legendary Sword of Heroes.

lhesh: Goblin for "high warlord." In time of the Dhakaani Empire, a lhesh was a general given command of the empire's armies for a set period of time. In modern times, Haruuc has adopted the term as the title of the ruler of Darguun.

lhesh shaarat: A class of goblin weaponry so finely-forged that they are recognized as suitable only for the greatest warriors. "*Lhesh shaarat*" means "warlord's sword," and the act of drawing one is a claim to power.

lhevk-rhu: "Skilled warlord," the third highest formal rank in Darguun's army. A *lhevk-rhu* is outranked only by a *lhevket* ("elder warlord") or the lhesh.

Library of Korranberg, the: The greatest repository of knowledge in Khorvaire and a central institution of life in Zilargo—some historians maintain that Zilargo's unique form of government and internal security were modelled on the organization of the Library.

Maabet!: An extremely ancient Goblin curse word still in use today. There is no known translation.

magebred: Any animal magically bred for enhanced characteristics (greater speed and endurance, for example), usually by House Vadalis.

Makka: Chief of a Marguul tribe living in the southern Seawall Mountains.

Marguul: The bugbear tribes that dwell in the highlands of the Seawall Mountains in the west of Darguun. Paying only lip service at best to Haruuc's authority, they live in independent, often hostile tribes.

Marrow: A worg from a pack allied with the *taarka'khesh*, but assisting Chetiin. Worgs resemble wolves the size of ponies, but are far more intelligent. They speak their own language and can understand others.

Matschuc Zaal: Once known as Veldarren, the largest of the mobile fortresses built by Breland during the Last War, it is now part of Darguun's defenses after being disabled at the choke point of Marguul Pass during the battle of the same name in 970 YK. *Matshuc Zaal* means "stolen fortress."

mazo: Goblin affirmative, stronger than "yes" and used specifically when discussing plans or acknowledging orders.

Mournland, the: A common name for the wasteland that was once Cyre, devastated by the unnatural disaster known as the Mourning. The borders of the Mournland are marked by dense banks of gray mist behind which lurk dangerous monsters and phenomena. The Mournland forms more than half of Darguun's eastern border.

Munta the Gray: The aged hobgoblin warlord of the powerful Gantii Vus clan. One of Haruuc's strongest allies.

muut: The goblin concept of ordinary honor or duty, something is gained by doing one's job properly. Compare with *atcha*.

noon: A starchy grain, most often pressed into compact balls, that is a staple of the traditional goblin diet and that still forms an important part of goblin cuisine.

***Paatcha*!:** An offer of honor through admiration, spoken as a compliment or delivered as an imperative to troops. Literally "to offer honor."

Paluur Draal: Once a city of the Dhakaani Empire, Paluur Draal now lies in ruins that have been inhabited by many races over the centuries. It is located in the southern Seawall Mountains in territory claimed by Zilargo.

Raat shan gath'kal dor: "The story stops but never ends." The traditional closing of hobgoblin legends.

Raat shi anaa: "The story continues." The traditional opening to hobgoblin legends.

Razu: An old hobgobin woman, Haruuc's mistress of rituals in Khaar Mbar'ost.

Rhukaan Draal: The capital city of Darguun (literally "Crown city"), founded by Lhesh Haruuc on the site of a former Cyran frontier town to serve as a neutral territory where all Ghaal'dar clans would be equal. Over the course of thirty years, it has grown into a rough and sprawling city with a population of approximately 80,000.

Rhukaan Taash: "Razor Crown," the largest and most powerful clan of the Ghaal'dar. Warriors of Rhukaan Taash receive a series of ritual scars across their brow as a sign of adulthood. In addition to being lhesh of Darguun, Haruuc is the warlord of Rhukaan Taash.

Riis: a dynasty of the late Dhakaani Empire.

roo: Goblin for "friendly stranger," someone unknown to the speaker but not an obvious enemy (pl. *rooz*).

saa: A casual Goblin greeting. A more formal greeting is *saa'atcha*, roughly equivalent to "It is an honor to meet you."

Seawall Mountains: Mountains forming the western and northwestern borders of Darguun, a natural barrier between Darguun and Breland.

Sentinel Tower: The primary stronghold of House Deneith, a massive keep in the city of Karrlakton. Sentinel Tower has existed for millenia, growing over the centuries. Its inner areas are ancient and access is restricted to the most senior members of the House.

shaarat'khesh: The Silent Blades. See: Silent Clans, the.

shaat'aar: A small sweet bun filled with honey cream. A common Goblin sweet.

shava: One of the most honored goblin traditions, *shava* is best translated as "sword brother," someone a warrior trusts with his life. The relationship between *shava* is exceptionally strong and carries with it significant responsibilities and expectations. Most goblin warriors never even consider taking a *shava*.

Shii marhu polto huuntad ka ruuska atchot: A goblin expression. "Even an emperor must think twice when looking a tiger in the eye."

Silent Clans, the: Although technically numbered among the Dhakaani clans, the two Silent Clans stand apart. They are formed entirely of goblins and are renowned for their stealth: the *taarka'khesh* ("silent wolves") are scouts, while the *shaarat'khesh* ("silent blades") are spies and assassins. By ancient tradition, the Silent Clans do not take sides in any conflict, instead acting as mercenaries of complete impartiality and reliability.

Six Kings, the: An allusion to the six hobgoblin warlords brought together by Jhazaal Dhakaan approximately 17,000 years before the present to found the Empire of Dhakaan.

Sovereign Host, the: A religion found across much of Khorvaire and actively promoted in Darguun by Haruuc as a civilizing influence. The Lords of the Host are Arawai (god of agriculture), Aureon (god of law and knowledge), Balinor (god of beasts and the hunt), Boldrei (god of community and hearth), Dol Arrah (god of honor and sacrifice), Dol Dorn (god of strength at arms), Kol Korran (god of trade and wealth), Olladra (god of good fortune), and Onatar (god of artifice and the forge).

ta muut: The most basic way of saying "thank you" in Goblin, *ta muut* literally means "you have honor" or more accurately "you do your duty." Spoken as acknowledgement of a deed performed correctly, it carries no connotation of debt on the part of the speaker. For comparison, see *Ya panozhii kita atcha.*

taarka'khesh: The Silent Wolves. See: Silent Clans, the.

taat: Goblin term for someone of significantly lesser status than the speaker. Derogatory and insulting.

Tariic: A hobgoblin warrior of the Rhukaan Taash clan and nephew of Haruuc. Conceived on the day that Rhukaan Draal was founded, he has a more worldly approach to culture, politics, and economy than more conservative Darguuls.

Taruuzh: A legendary Dhakaani *daashor*, creator of the original binding stones, the grieving trees, and the sword Wrath. His stronghold, Taruuzh Kraat, was located where Tzaryan Keep now stands in Droaam.

Thrane: One of the original Five Nations of Galifar. Thrane is a conservative theocracy dominated by the Church of the Silver Flame.

Thuun: A hobgoblin warrior in the service of Haruuc, assigned first to accompany Tariic's mission to Karrlakton, then to guard Vounn and Ashi in Rhukaan Draal.

To hold a sword by the blade: A goblin expression for being in a risky situation.

Toh!: A Goblin warning cry ("Beware!").

Torlaac Conquest, the: The pacification, many generations before the start of the Last War, of the area around the Torlaac River and into the Torlaac Moor by Deneith troops on behalf of Cyre, culiminating in the Battle of Starkhan.

Torlaac River: A powerful river of southern Darguun. South of the river, the land rises to become the desolate and dangerous Torlaac Moor.

Treaty of Thronehold: Signed in 996 YK, the Treaty of Thronehold marked the end of the Last War. Among its many articles, it formally recognized a number of new nations (including Darguun, Zilargo, and Valenar) and bound all signing nations in a pact of peace.

Valenar: The lands claimed by the Valenar elves as their rightful territory by virtue of ancient ties to the land dating back to conflicts with the Empire of Dhakaan. Recognized as an independent nation by the Treaty of Thronehold.

Vanii: A hobgoblin warrior of the Ja'aram clan and the last of Haruuc's three *shava*. He wields twin axes in battle.

Wrath: Properly known by its Goblin name, Aram, Wrath is the legendary Sword of Heroes. Forged from byeshk by the legendary Dhakaani dashoor Taruuzh during the Daelkyr War, it was wielded by the hobgoblin heroes of the line of Kuun before being lost in the slaying of the daelkyr lord of Jhegesh Dol. Legend says that Wrath will not bear the touch of a coward. Recently, Wrath was recovered from the ghostly fortress of Jhegesh Dol by Geth, who now carries the blade.

Ya panozhii kita atcha: The most formal form of thanks in Goblin. Translated, it means "I owe a debt to your honor." It shows a deep indebtedness on the part of the speaker and is never used casually. Compare with *ta muut*.

Zilargo: The homeland of the gnomes, Zilargo has long pursued a diplomatic policy of neutrality and conciliation. Recognized as an independent nation by the Treaty of Thronehold.

EBERRON®

From acclaimed author and award-winning game designer James Wyatt, an adventure that will shake the world of EBERRON to its core.

THE DRACONIC PROPHECIES

were old when humans first began to forge their civilization. They give meaning to the past, guidance in the present, and predict the future—a future of the world's remaking. And now, one facet of the prophecies is being set in motion, and all of it revolves around Gaven, exiled from his house, thrown into prison, and in the grips of a terrible madness.

Book One
Storm Dragon

Book Two
Dragon Forge

Book Three
Dragon War

And don't miss James Wyatt's first EBERRON novel
In the Claws of the Tiger
Janik barely survived his last expedition to the dark continent, but when he finds himself embroiled in a plot involving the lost wonders of Xen'drik, his one hope at redemption is to return and face the horrors that once almost destroyed him.

EBERRON

In the shadow of the Last War, the heroes aren't all shining knights.

PARKER DeWOLF

The Lanternlight Files

Ulther Whitsun is a fixer. When you've got a problem, if you can't find someone to take care of it, he's your man—as long as you can pay the price. If you can't, or you won't . . . gods have mercy on your soul.

Book 1

The Left Hand of Death

Ulther finds himself in possession of a strange relic. His enemies want it, he wants its owner, and the City Watch wants him locked away for good. When a job turns this dangerous, winning or losing are no longer an option. It may be all one man can do just to stay alive.

Book 2

When Night Falls

Ulther teams up with a young and ambitious chronicler to stop a revolution. But treachery may kill him, and salvation comes from unexpected places.

July 2008

Book 3

Death Comes Easy

Gangs in lower Sharn are at each other's throats. And they don't care who gets killed in the battle. But now Ulther had been hired to put an end to the violence. And he doesn't care who he steps on to do his job.

December 2008

Sword & sorcery adventure from the creator of the EBERRON® world!

KEITH BAKER

Thorn of Breland

A new war has already begun—a cold war, fought in the shadows by agents of every nation—and Thorn does all she can as a member of the King's Citadel. But her last mission has left her with gaps in her memory, and she'll have to work out what happened as she goes—after all, Breland won't protect itself.

Book 1
The Queen of Stone
November 2008

The Dreaming Dark

A band of weary war veterans have come to Sharn, hoping to find a way to live in a world that is struggling to settle into an uneasy peace. But over the years, they have made enemies in high places—and even places far from Eberron.

Book 1
The City of Towers

Book 2
The Shattered Land

Book 3
The Gates of Night

TRACY HICKMAN
PRESENTS
THE ANVIL OF TIME

With the power of the Anvil of Time, the Journeyman can travel the river of time as simply as walking upstream, visiting the ancient past of Krynn with ease.

VOLUME ONE
THE SELLSWORD
Cam Banks

Vanderjack, a mercenary with a price on his head, agrees out of desperation to retrieve a priceless treasure for a displaced noble. The treasure is deep within enemy territory, and he must survive an army of old foes, a chorus of unhappy ghosts, and the questionable assistance of a mad gnome to find it.

April 2008

VOLUME TWO
THE SURVIVORS
Dan Willis

A goodhearted dwarf is warned of an apocalyptic flood by the god Reorx, and he and his motley followers must decide whether the warning is real—and then survive the disaster that sweeps through their part of Krynn.

November 2008

JEAN RABE

THE STONETELLERS

"Jean Rabe is adept at weaving a web of deceit and lies, mixed with adventure, magic, and mystery."
—sffworld.com on *Betrayal*

Jean Rabe returns to the DRAGONLANCE® world with a tale of slavery, rebellion, and the struggle for freedom.

VOLUME ONE
THE REBELLION

After decades of service, nature has dealt the goblins a stroke of luck. Earthquakes strike the Dark Knights' camp and mines, crippling the Knights and giving the goblins their best chance to escape. But their freedom will not be easy to win.

VOLUME TWO
DEATH MARCH

The reluctant general, Direfang, leads the goblin nation on a death march to the forests of Qualinesti, there to create a homeland in defiance of the forces that seek to destroy them.

August 2008

VOLUME THREE
GOBLIN NATION

A goblin nation rises in the old forest, building fortresses and fighting to hold onto their new homeland, while the sorcerers among them search for powerful magic cradled far beneath the trees.

August 2009

FORGOTTEN REALMS®

They were built to display might.
They were built to hold secrets.
They will still stand while their builders fall.

THE CITADELS

NEVERSFALL
ED GENTRY

It was supposed to be Estagund's stronghold in monster-ridden Veldorn, an unassailable citadel to protect the southern lands . . . until the regiment holding Neversfall disappeared, leaving no hint of what took them.

OBSIDIAN RIDGE
JESS LEBOW

Looming like a storm cloud, the Obsidian Ridge appears silently and without warning over the kingdom of Erlkazar, prepared to destroy everything in its reach, unless its master gets what he wants.

THE SHIELD OF WEEPING GHOSTS
JAMES P. DAVIS

Frozen Shandaular fell to invaders over two thousand years ago, its ruins protected by the ghosts and undead that haunt the ancient citadel. But to anyone who can evade the weeping dead, the northwest tower holds a deadly secret.

SENTINELSPIRE
MARK SEHESTEDT

The ancient fortress of Sentinelspire draws strength from the portals that feed its fires and pools, as well as the assassins that call it home. Both promise great power to those dangerous enough to seize them.

Stand-alone novels that can be read in any order!